Last Chance

by

Michelle O'Leary

Sunscapes Trilogy

Last Chance

Cover Art by *Debbie Taylor*

The Wild Rose Press, Inc.
PO Box 708
Adams Basin, NY 14410-0708
Visit us at www.thewildrosepress.com

Publishing History
First Fantasy Rose Edition, 2017
Print ISBN 978-1-5092-1419-8
Digital ISBN 978-1-5092-1420-4

Sunscapes Trilogy
Published in the United States of America

"Oh Sun's blood,
the Shadow twins!" Hector moaned next to him.

Del's grungy companion now wore beads of sweat across his forehead and upper lip, eyes wide and bulging. Others reacted to the arrivals with whitened faces, worshipful eyes, and muted whispers. A new, greedier current of energy ran through the crowd, and Del watched for the two pilots with increased interest.

The new arrivals levered themselves out of the sleek slicers with liquid ease. One male and one female, they were dressed in unrelenting black. They had an air of unconscious arrogance only the rich and powerful could manage, with a hint of real danger in their fluid strides. They moved like predators coming into view of their prey, and the crowd parted before them as if they knew they were the next meal.

As they neared, Del sucked in a startled breath. The arrivals were stunningly attractive, good-looking enough to turn heads wherever they went. Blue-black hair framed refined features, hers in a severe braid between her shoulder blades, and his in short disarray over his forehead. The man's features were heavier and his skin had a dusky quality. The woman had skin like smooth cream and a lush curve to her lips.

Del was staring at her mouth when she entered the circle around Hector and the pilots. Her lips curled in a sardonic twist and he lifted his gaze, colliding with the most beautiful pair of green eyes he'd ever seen.

Praise for Michelle O'Leary

"*LAST CHANCE* is a thrill ride and a half. Back and forth we leap from the instant ignition of Del and Sin, to the deadly stalking of corporate CEOs, to the roaring exultation of space flight."

~Reviewer's Choice Reviews

~*~

"Michelle O'Leary has delivered a Sci-Fi Romance that captures love, hate and Machiavellian schemes of epic proportions. Her fluid style takes readers on an unforgettable journey that will have fans waiting impatiently for the next installment in this series."

~Fallen Angel Reviews

~*~

"Ms. O'Leary delivers a romance that seizes the elements of love and hate. Her flair for writing sends the reader on a journey that mesmerizes and enthralls while anticipating the next installments to follow. It is fast-paced action at its best…"

~The Romance Studio

Dedication

This book is dedicated to all those
with imagination enough to support me
in its creation and publication;
my family,
my dear editor,
patient readers,
and most especially my son,
for showing me worlds of wonder through his eyes.

Prologue

"Why?" Sinsudee Shay leaned back in her chair and propped her feet on the corner of the enormous desk, watching Nick with a cynical gleam in her green eyes. Her brother Manakai slouched against darkened viewers in the shadows behind her, his arms folded and expression bored. The beautiful rich, the powerful elite, deigning to watch him beg.

Their callous nonchalance stung nerves already raw from the trip through their vast headquarters to this huge, darkened room. The shadows surrounding Nick seemed ominous. He couldn't help being defensive. "Because he's my brother. He stayed in the Core for me. He deserves—"

"Not what I meant, and you know it. Why should we help? What's in this for us?"

"I'd owe you," he said through stiff lips. Owing these people would not be easy to live with.

"That's nice," she murmured with a wry twist of her mouth. "Nice, but not enough. Try again."

"You've been looking for a new pilot."

"Most pilots are easier to come by than your brother."

"Not the kind you're looking for," he challenged, setting his jaw. Let her try and deny it.

Her features lost expression and she studied him with a new glitter in her eyes, a subtle tension in her lithe form. Maybe pushing had been a mistake. "Tell me," was all she said.

He told her. It took a while. At one point, she lowered her eyes, propping her chin on one hand with a faint frown creasing her brow. When he finished, she was silent for a long moment.

Then she breathed, "Sins of our fathers," so low Nick almost didn't hear. Her brother stirred behind her in the shadows with a whisper of protest.

"Pardon?"

She raised her eyes to his again with a brittle smile. "You've asked for our help. You have it."

Chapter 1

"I see lots of pain in your future, Del. Just do the job, like a good mutt, and maybe it'll change."

Del looked up at the big man standing next to him with soul-deep contempt. This guy was proof human brutality hadn't evolved in the many millennia since people had left Earth and spread throughout the galaxy. Brax was just another drone in Quasicore's army of thugs, a small cog in the vast machine of the Core's galaxy-wide criminal organization, a petty handler tasked with keeping Del in line. Easy for Brax to threaten a guy on his knees with arms clamped behind his back in magnetic restraints, stuck in this crappy, burnt-out warehouse in the middle of nowhere with no one around to hear the torture. And no one, on-planet or off, would care if they did.

"Screw you, Brax," Del muttered.

Brax responded as he always did. The man's shovel-like face writhed in a grimace and he lifted one brawny arm, bringing it down like a sledgehammer.

Blinding pain burst through Del's skull and he went down face first. Twisting, he caught most of his weight on a shoulder but cracked his jaw on the metal floor. A spurt of fury spiraled through him, erasing common sense. He mule-kicked Brax, gratified when the man barked with a hoarse cry of pain. He'd pay for it, but when he maneuvered back to a kneeling position and caught sight of Brax doubled over, he decided it was worth it.

"Enough," said someone out of Del's range of vision, and he tensed. Brax was big, but simple and obvious. The man who walked around to crouch in front of Del was neither. He eyed Del with cold, pale blue eyes and a gentle smile. "You are out of choices, my friend. Do the job or give us what you owe."

"You want me to kill somebody. Not gonna happen, Trev."

Trevani's eyes flashed with something dangerous, but his smile didn't waver. "Squeamish, are we? Well, who'd have guessed? Then all you have to do is pull a hundred thousand credits out of your empty account and we'll part ways. Think that's gonna happen, Del?"

Del stared into the man's pale eyes with a combination of fierce hatred and black despair. Any answer he gave would put him in a world of hurt. Brax was slow, but good at following directions. Trevani loved giving directions and was very creative when it came to pain.

His smile widened. "I see we understand each other. We'll give you four days to follow through." He flicked one hand at Brax, and the big man released the restraints. Rubbing his sore arms, Del rose to his feet.

Trevani followed suit, studying him with an expression as cold as his eyes. "The job or the credit, Del. You have no other option."

Del didn't bother to answer. He turned and strode toward the exit, feeling with careful fingers at the bump behind his ear from Brax's blow.

Before he reached the door, Trevani called to him. "And, Del?"

He paused and glanced over his shoulder with weary resignation.

"I know you're thinking of skipping out on us and the job, but my heartfelt advice is this: don't run."

He ran.

****

Four days later, Del had run about as far as he could, the job unfinished and the credit only a possibility. He was in the Fringe, a ragged area of space on the edges of civilization, far away from the influence and interest of the Federated Planetary Alliance, and far away from Trevani and Brax. He knew he couldn't outrun them forever, but hoped to stay ahead of them long enough to build the credit he owed to their mutual employer, Quasicore.

In all the years he'd ruined lives in the Core's name, he estimated he'd paid back twice over what he'd owed, or more specifically what his father had owed. But somehow the ledger still had him deep in the red. He couldn't dispute the claim in a court of law, though. To the law, he was as sin-black as the beast with its claws in him.

Desperation was a sour tang in the back of his throat and a shadow at the corner of his sight, a gloom darkening his every step, his every breath. The Core haunted him, even here on the Fringe.

"Man, I know you can slice. I've seen it. But how am I s'posed to trust you?" Hector asked.

Del turned his head and stared at the little grease ball next to him. An ironic question, given the small man's reputation for backstabbing and cheating, habits that had gotten him banished from the legitimate slicing circuits, reduced to running slicer races out on the

Fringe. "When's the last time you trusted anybody? Look around, Hec. This ain't the peak of human civilization."

Hector scowled and shifted in his seat. He looked insulted, which was laughable. He stank like he hadn't sanitized in a week, and black blood spattered his chest from the krell fight in the crude pit below them. The spiked beasts were almost done. The blacker krell had cornered the reddish one, tearing at its throat. Yells and cheers from the crowd almost drowned its dying squeals.

Hector's scowl was now all for the credit he'd lost on the red. Del waited while the small man cursed and screamed insults at the shredded animal. As Hector wound down, Del interrupted, "So, am I in?"

Hector heaved a sigh and shot him a sour glance. "I got a slice goin' for tomorrow night, but nobody of your caliber."

"I don't like winning easy, but I need the credit."

"Hey, I get a cut either way, so no grind on my bones." Hec felt around in his grimy shirt for a second before pulling out a worn data crystal. "This is the spot. You lose this, show it to anybody, or let somebody follow you, they'll tear you apart like a pack of krells. You catch me?"

"Yeah, I catch you," Del muttered, taking the dirty crystal with a wince. He'd be lucky if he didn't catch some nasty germs before he made it to the slice.

"See you." Hector stood and headed for the exit, giving the dead krell a last insulting gesture as he passed the pit.

Del studied the mess in the pit with a grim kind of recognition. His life looked like this. He just hoped he didn't end up the same way; killer or victim. Clenching his fist around the crystal, he lurched to his feet and made for the exit, desperate for another choice.

The next night, Del followed the directions from the data crystal to an abandoned processing station on the border of a depleted asteroid field. At first glance, it seemed deserted. When he did a closer run in his slicer, lights gleamed deep inside one of the service hangers, and the glimmer of an atmospheric shield suggested someone was still using the place. He passed through the shield and into the hanger at a cautious pace.

Ships in a variety of sizes and shapes clustered at the far end of the hanger, and a crowd of people gathered close to a row of slicers. Del counted the racing ships as he maneuvered his own to land on the next pad in the row. Six slicers would race against him.

"Lucky number seven," he noted as he disconnected from his slicer's controls, adding up the potential winnings. At four grand a head, the total winnings would only be a portion of the amount he needed to pay his debt to the Core. But it would be a good start, if Hector didn't take too large a cut for himself.

Del levered his long body out of the slicer and worked his way toward the center of the crowd. The slicer groupies let him through without protest, a few studying his tall form with wary eyes. Del caught a glimpse of Hector in the crowd and closed on him.

"Del, where you been?" The grease ball yelled over the excited rumble of the crowd. "Been waitin' half the night."

"You found such a nice out of the way spot. Thought I'd go sightseeing first."

The little man gave him a hard grin, beady eyes narrowing like a weasel's before it bites. "This ain't no legit slicer circuit, big man. Even shootin' the Fringe, we gotta keep low."

Del inclined his head and said nothing. With a smug smirk, Hector turned toward a loose semi-circle of people. Data ports, the cybernetic neuro-implants necessary to pilot a slicer, were visible behind the right ears of several of them.

"This is Del Tower. He makes the last slicer. Got any objections or you can't ante up, now's the time to back out."

They looked Del over and several grinned. He could tell what they were thinking. His size would be a disadvantage in a race where speed was essential and the lighter the craft, the faster it would go. But they'd never seen him slice.

He eyed them in turn. Two were female, and though they both appeared capable, the bald-headed one might give him a challenge. She was a tiny thing and her gaze was rock steady. Of the four men, two were jittery; either they were new to this or high on something, which put them out of the running. The other two men weren't so easy to dismiss. They radiated confidence, one with a cocksure attitude and the other with a steady, quiet calm. The quiet one would give him the most trouble.

When no one said anything, Hector continued, "Right then, time to bleed out credit. I hold and give over to the winner, minus my cut. The track'll get downloaded to your slicers when I got the ante. It's a run through the 'roids, and it's gonna be a twist and a half. Got a problem with it?"

One of the nervous pilots grumbled but not loud enough to be a real complaint, and Hector grunted in satisfaction. Pulling a creditor from one of his grimy pockets, he held it out like a priest at communion. Del was first to stick his finger in the slot and feel the sting of the extractor taking a sample of blood from him. His DNA registered, he tapped the amount of credit to transfer, and when the creditor flashed green acceptance, he stepped back to let the others do the same.

They were down to the last two pilots when the hum of slicer engines caught Del's attention. Very powerful, very expensive slicer engines, the hum almost subliminal. The hair rose on his arms and the back of his neck, and he glanced over. Two sleek, black slicers coasted toward them, and Del fell in love. The ships made his red beauty look like a lump of used metal. Piloting one of those would be like having sex with a goddess, all smooth, profound ecstasy. Their black surface reflected the light in opalescent gleams as they settled in perfect synchronicity onto the landing pads.

"Oh Sun's blood, the Shadow twins!" Hector moaned next to him.

Del's grungy companion now wore beads of sweat across his forehead and upper lip, eyes wide and bulging. Others reacted to the arrivals with whitened faces, worshipful eyes, and muted whispers. A new, greedier current of energy ran through the crowd, and Del watched for the two pilots with increased interest.

The new arrivals levered themselves out of the sleek slicers with liquid ease. One male and one female, they were dressed in unrelenting black. They had an air of unconscious arrogance only the rich and powerful could manage, with a hint of real danger in their fluid strides. They moved like predators coming into view of their prey, and the crowd parted before them as if they knew they were the next meal.

As they neared, Del sucked in a startled breath. The arrivals were stunningly attractive, good-looking enough to turn heads wherever they went. Blue-black hair framed refined features, hers in a severe braid between her shoulder blades, and his in short disarray over his forehead. The man's features were heavier and his skin had a dusky quality. The woman had skin like smooth cream and a lush curve to her lips.

Del was staring at her mouth when she entered the circle around Hector and the pilots. Her lips curled in a sardonic twist and he lifted his gaze, colliding with the most beautiful pair of green eyes he'd ever seen.

"Sun's blood," he muttered.

"Don't do it, man. She's poison," Hector whispered as the two arrivals stopped and scanned the circle with casual propriety.

When the woman's gaze came to rest on Hector, she smiled like a shark, all sharp edges and bloodlust. "Hector, my slimy friend! You don't look happy to see me." Her voice was smooth, cool, and laced with dangerous humor. She stepped forward, her companion staying where he was, arms folded across his chest and faint amusement on his features.

Eyes bright with something like malice, she paused in front of Hector. "How's the hand?"

Del had never seen anyone quail before. Hector's shoulders hunched as he tucked his hands into his armpits in a protective gesture. Whatever had happened to Hector's hand, Del would lay odds this woman had either done the work herself or been responsible for it.

"Fine, fine," Hec rasped. "Healed up real good."

"And aren't we relieved to hear it," she drawled with biting insincerity. "You appear to be running an illegal slicer race, Hector. Can it be possible?"

"You know it is," he snarled, shooting pure hate at her from under his eyebrows.

"Well, you're in luck. As it happens, I haven't had a decent race in a long while. Can you give me a good slice this time, friend?"

Her eyes slid with narrow speculation over the group of pilots, and Del caught his breath when her gaze met his again. *Down boy,* he thought to the interested anatomy south of his waistband. *This one's way out of your league.*

"You're here to slice?" Hector asked with a hopeful note. Greed made its usual appearance in the grimy lines of his face.

She shot him a quick, hard look and he quailed again. "Yes Hector, try to keep up. Is there anyone here who can give me a good run?"

The cocky pilot stepped forward with a scowl on his face. "You expect us to slice against one of those black demons?" He pointed to the pair of powerful slicers at the end of the row.

"The skill of slicing is in the pilot, not the ship," she answered in a silky taunt, looking the man up and down. "But for those who need added incentive, I'll double the winnings if I lose."

A quick wave of whispers rushed through the crowd, and Del added winnings again with a new surge of hope.

"Nice! Very nice. There won't be any objections," Hector declared.

"I'm sure there won't," she murmured in reply but didn't take her eyes off the other pilot. He dropped his gaze, stepping back again. With a cold smile, she turned away, placing hands on hips and giving Hector an inquiring glance. "So? What do you have for me?"

"Many good slicers," he assured her like a farmer peddling his best meat stock. "I think you'll get a good run out of these."

"We'll see." She made a slow circuit around the ring of pilots, pausing before the small bald-headed woman and giving her a short bow. The expression on her face became almost respectful.

The woman flushed bright red, but returned the bow, and Del took a closer look at her. A small, blue tattoo graced the corner of her left eye, and he cursed under his breath. She was an ascetic of the Order of the Blue Sun, dedicated to mastering the balance between mind and body. They believed balance was the only way to live in harmony with the universe and ascend to the next plane of existence. With their mental and physical discipline, a Blue Sun ascetic would make a formidable slicing opponent. Del had no idea what the ascetic was doing out here in the Fringe.

Hector's black-clad tormentor had moved on, and the rest of the pilots shot each other sullen looks, appearing bitter about being inspected like a rack of meat. She paused again and pointed to one of the jittery fellows. "He goes," she announced, and a louder whisper made its rounds through the crowd.

"But he's already paid," Hector tried in a weak voice.

She waved him off. "He's rejecting his wetware."

"W-what?" the man in question yelped.

She ignored him, addressing her comments to Hector. "You can see it in his leaky eyes and the red bands around his data port. His implants are going to go critical in short order. He's a walking time bomb. I wouldn't want to be slicing next to him when the thing scrambles his brains. Would any of you?"

The other pilots shifted and muttered to each other.

She watched them with an amused smirk on her face then exchanged a hard grin with her silent companion. "Yes, kiddies, this means less credit in the pot. Never fear, I have a solution. I'll double the winnings. Again."

Quadruple the credit. Del's heart thudded a wild rhythm of hope. If he won, he'd make enough in this one race to pay back the Core.

She moved to stand in front of him, distracting from his dreams of freedom, looking him up and down with a frown. "This one's a mountain. How does he even fit in a slicer, let alone get it off the pad?"

"Del's a hit and a half, Lady Shadow," Hector interjected with a breathless note. He seemed ecstatic at the mention of quadrupling the credit. "He's your best chance for an exciting slice."

She hummed and met Del's gaze, gesturing toward the row of slicers. "Which is yours, then?"

His skin prickled with insult and irritation. Who did this woman think she was? He stepped close so she had to tip back her head to maintain eye contact. "As you said, the skill is in the pilot. Try me."

The corners of those incredible green eyes crinkled and her lips compressed as though she was trying to hide a smile. A scent wafted up from her skin, a mysterious combination of sweet and spice, and a sudden, powerful stab of lust alarmed him.

"The red X780 series, then," she said, her eyes assessing. "A good model. It's been lightened."

How did she know he'd modified his ship to take his weight? He wondered in silence, not bothering to ask; she'd only curl her luscious mouth and dismiss him.

"He'll do," she stated and turned away. "Here's how it's going to run, Hector." She snatched the creditor out of the little man's fingers, making him jump and quiver. "My brother holds and you get your cut after the winner has the take, so you won't be tempted to make off with the whole thing."

"I would never—" Hec started to protest, but she cut him off.

"You know how dangerous it would be to your health, but greed is an illness with you, my stinky friend." She slipped the creditor under his hand and raised it in front of his face, her voice lowering and laced with menace. "And some lessons need to be learned twice."

He snatched his hands behind his back with a round-eyed stare of pure terror and stumbled back from her. "N-not me, Lady! You want him to hold, he holds."

"Very prudent of you, Hector. We'd like to see the run you've laid out."

"I'll download it into—"

"Now," she barked and pulled a flat disc from her jacket the size of her palm. Pressing the center of it, she flipped it into the air. It defied gravity and paused in mid-arc, spinning so fast it seemed to disappear. Above it, a holographic stretch of the asteroid belt became visible.

Del stared at it, impressed. Holodiscs were not cheap. Hector pulled something out of his grimy clothes, but Del didn't take his eyes off the hologram. In another moment, a red line began to squiggle through the spinning rocks, marking the course of the slice Hector had devised for them. When the line terminated, Del's green-eyed temptation snorted in disgust. "You call that a run? Why don't you just have us chase each other in a big circle?"

Hector kept his mouth shut, eyes lowered.

She shook her dark head and turned toward the other pilots. "Has everyone bled credit?"

Del nodded when her eyes rested on him, gritting his teeth and trying to ignore the increase in his heart rate. While the last two pilots stepped forward to ante up, Del shifted closer to Hector. "Who is she?"

The little man gave him a look full of miserable contempt. "You don't wanna know."

"Is she Core?" Quasicore was the only entity he could think of with this kind of influence in the Fringe.

"You wanna live?" Hector hissed, gripping Del's arm with panicky force. "Don't ask those kinda questions!"

Del frowned. "What'd she do to your hand, Hec?"

"Broke it," the little man mumbled, beady eyes narrowing on her. The crediting done, she now handed the device over to her brother.

"Why?"

Hector studied Del with greasy calculation, making his skin crawl. He decided he didn't want to know. The pilots were moving toward their slicers and Del followed after them. Hector paced him, almost skipping to keep up with Del's longer stride. "She's never lost a slice, y'know."

It wasn't something Del needed to hear. He watched as the woman had a short conversation and shared a predatory grin with her brother before she moved to her slicer.

"But I got my credit on you, big man. You don't lose much, neither."

Del was on the verge of telling Hector to step off, but curiosity made him pause next to his slicer. "Why 'Shadow'?" He didn't bother asking if it was their real name.

The little man eyed him with squinty calculation again before saying, "Have a good slice," and walking away. Del wondered what the bookie was hiding and if it would be bad for his own health.

With practiced ease, Del lowered into his slicer, heart expanding with the pride and pleasure of knowing this machine was his and his alone. In all the time he'd been enslaved to Quasicore, they'd never tried to make his slicer part of the debt, maybe because he'd made credit for them with it.

Del started her up and smiled at the sweet hum of the engines, a sound more felt than heard, like a current under his skin. He settled into the cushions and slid the connector into his data port, bracing for the rush of disorienting information flooding his mind and senses.

A pilot didn't just fly a slicer; he became part of it. Del not only knew how the engines were running but could feel them, each system and part smooth and sweet. The slicer's skin became his skin and her eyes became his, an extension of himself. He welcomed it like a lover returning home.

Some pilots were unable to handle the dichotomy of being a human and a ship at the same time, or the constant flood of information from the ship's systems, the inner workings and sensor readings of the surrounding environment. It took a very cool, focused mind and a confident personality to be able to handle a slicer.

With a thought, Del lifted the slicer from her pad, sensing the others rising with him. The navigational systems drenched his mind with the specs of the course as it was downloaded into the slicer. He let it soak in until the run was as familiar to him as his skin.

Moving with the other slicers, he headed through the atmospheric shield and out of the hanger, watching how the others flew, how Lady Shadow and her black demon flew. They were beauty in motion, and he forgot to breathe as she dipped into position at the head of the course. He slid next to her, trying not to gawk like a greenie at her vessel. The others arrayed themselves around them at the starting line.

Waiting for the signal to begin the slice, Del took several deep, calming breaths, clearing his mind of clutter and settling into the cold, focused part of him that always took control in a race. He became a creature of instinct and intuition, a necessary change in a race where a second was an eternity. Taking the time to think might lose him the slice or even get him killed.

When it came, the signal was not audible but a sting on his nerves. Before his conscious mind registered it, he was on the move. Right off the line, the slice became a race of not seven slicers, but four, as three of them took too long getting their start.

Del registered the pilots with a small sliver of his mind; his Shadow beauty, the ascetic, and the quiet man dodged the first of the asteroids with him in a close bunch. The course narrowed as two massive asteroids spun together, and Del found himself squeezing in behind the black slicer, flipping his own ship on its side to slide in between the rock monsters.

Past those asteroids, the course took a ninety degree turn to the left, and a small rogue asteroid bulleted at them with suicidal intent. It wasn't big enough to smash a slicer, but it could take him out of the running if it hit right. Del twisted out of the asteroid's way, never losing his spot behind the Lady, and became aware of the ascetic dropping back a little.

On a short straight stretch, Del goosed the engines, rolling under the black slicer and trying to pull ahead of her. But her ship outmatched him for sheer power, and he couldn't manage to gain on her before the next turn, a loop like a twisted ribbon through an obstacle course of spinning asteroids.

Del didn't slow and neither did Lady Shadow, but he sensed the other two dropping back farther. It was now between him and the Lady. Belly to belly, the two of them spun, twisted, and danced through the asteroids with almost perfect synchronicity, as if they'd been practicing this course together for days. As if they were one creature, one mind.

Exaltation ran through his body in a sparkling stream, every part of him tingling with wild abandon. He ignored it as best he could. Now was not the time to get distracted, even by such a stunning flight. The finish line was drawing near and he hadn't won yet.

One more loop to go, a small straight stretch, and

then it would be over. He had a chance in the final turn around the last great asteroid. If he could cut to the inside between her and the rock, he might get the edge he needed to come out in front. As they came into the spin around the asteroid, he slid between her and it with steely determination. There wasn't enough room; he would be lucky not to scrape the ship's skin or smash on any outcroppings of rock.

But all of a sudden, there was more than enough room. The reason didn't register until after they'd cleared the asteroid and he was out in front, his slicer screaming for the finish. She was right on his tail and gaining, but he knew he'd win.

She'd moved over. She'd given him the room and opportunity to gain on her. He crossed the finish knowing she'd lost to him on purpose. Why?

Together they moved back toward the docking bay. They swung into the hanger, and Del watched the crowd go wild. This must be the high point of their groupie lives. The underdog takes out the unbeatable Queen of Shadows. The ones who'd bet on him were now rolling in credit. And none had seen.

She'd lost on purpose.

Settling his slicer onto a landing pad, he shook his head. As he opened the slicer and levered out, a hush descended on the crowd, and he glanced up. She slid out of her own ship with breathtaking grace. Wasting no time, he stepped close to her. "Why?"

She lifted her eyebrows and gave him a slow, mocking smile. Then she turned away and headed toward her brother and Hector. Over her shoulder she said, "Great slice."

The crowd became rowdy again, a roaring, many-headed animal, converging on him as he tried to follow her. Del dragged his way through the congratulations and well-wishes, struggling with them until the lady called to Hector. The crowd quieted, a thrum of anticipation rustling through them.

"Come congratulate the winner," she told the little man as she and her brother made a path back to him. The mocking smile was still on her face, which her brother mirrored. They stopped in front of him, a bubble of space forming between them and the crowd. Hector stepped into this clearing, beady eyes shining with what could have been love for Del.

"Thank you for an exciting slice, pilot," the woman said with smooth formality. Her brother stepped forward, hand outstretched. Between the tips of his first two fingers he held a credit chip, the receipt of the transfer.

"Your reward," the man murmured in a deep voice, green eyes sparkling with amusement.

Del took it, looking between them for the catch. There had to be one. The man also handed him the creditor so he could confirm the transfer. His account was now a very nice number with lots of zeros. It spelled freedom. He stared at it for an incredulous moment.

"And now for my reward," the woman said with a mischievous smile, an enticing dimple appearing next to her mouth.

Del watched her glide toward him, alarm tightening his skin at the look in her eyes. She slid the cool fingers of one hand around the back of his neck, placing the other on his ribcage as she leaned up and kissed him. The crowd roared its approval, but he stopped hearing them after the first instant of contact.

He dropped the creditor and closed his hands on her waist, his entire focus on what she was doing. Her lips were as soft and luscious as they appeared, moving with his in a playful glide and throwing every system in his body into the red. He tasted her with the tip of his tongue and was instantly starving for more. He slipped his hands to her hips to shift her closer as he deepened the kiss, tasting her again with a low groan of hunger. Her tongue teased his for a heart-stopping second before she pulled back a little, stretching up to whisper in his ear with small, tantalizing puffs of air.

A hot cloud of lust filled Del, a kind of animal hunger he couldn't remember experiencing before at the soft press of her breasts against his chest and her hips brushing his arousal. The hand on his ribcage slid down as she whispered, until her fingers slipped into his waistband, making his breath catch. He didn't register what she was saying until she called him by his real name.

"It won't be enough. It won't ever be enough, Adelmo Givliani. They'll take the credit, but they won't let you go. If you want to be free, come see me."

Then she pulled out of his grasp and spun on her heel, walking away without a backward glance. His heart thundered louder than the crowd in his ears and his head swam. Something hard bit into the skin at his waistband, and he looked down. She'd tucked a data crystal there.

Chapter 2

Sin's brother matched her stride as they moved toward the Shadow slicers. "Was that fun?" he asked with laughter running through his words in a bright stream.

"Almost forgot to give him the crystal," she admitted then gave him a smoldering glare when he began to chuckle. "Shut up, Kai."

He only laughed harder. "Could've just shaken his hand, Sinsi." When she took a half-hearted swipe at him, he dodged and held up his hands. "Now, now, Sissa, let's not get violent. Wasn't me who stuck my tongue down his—"

This time she took a real swipe at him, but he still managed to dodge, his deep laughter scraping across her nerves. "You go on ahead," she told him on reaching the slicers. "I'll take care of the rest of this."

"Oh, yeah?" He asked with a suggestive lift of one eyebrow. "How were you planning on 'taking care' of him?"

He ducked into his slicer when she lunged, shutting himself in and snickering the whole while. With a grumble, she slid into her own ship, trying to remember she loved her brother and couldn't maim him.

An hour later, she reached the rendezvous point she'd given to Del, a little café in a small way station, marking the border between Fringe space and civilization. The café was called Sun's Way and its one claim to fame was a holographic image on the walls, mimicking a strand of beach surrounded by ocean. The customers at the scattered tables could watch the course of a yellow star as it rose on one side of the café and set on the other side. The rhythmic sound of waves on sand and wind through palm trees enhanced the image.

Sin had always found it soothing and today she needed it. After she'd told the proprietor what she wanted, she settled at one of the tables, taking off her jacket and undoing the tight braid in her hair. Propping her feet on a chair next to her, she leaned back and finger-brushed the silky strands, closing her eyes against the bright sun.

The hologram was good. She could almost feel the warmth of the sun on her skin, and she wished for a pair of shorts, bare feet, and a sun top. Next vacation, she promised herself, then chuckled a bit at the irony. She didn't take vacations.

The owner interrupted her thoughts with a tall bottle of ice-cold water and a chilling tray with six old-fashioned bottleneck beers. "There ya go, love."

"Thanks, Jake," she said with a smile for the burly man.

He let her take the water bottle, and set the tray down in the middle of the table with raised eyebrows. "Expectin' company?"

"Yes, but he might be a while."

"He?" he asked with a gleam in his eye.

The eternal matchmaker, Sin thought with some amusement. "Yes."

He waited, but when she didn't add anything, he made a face at her. "Not talkin', huh?"

She shook her head with a smirk.

He sighed and turned away, saying over his shoulder, "Don't matter how long you stay. Y'know that. Yell if you need anythin' else."

She nodded and settled farther down in her seat, taking a long drink from the water bottle before resting her head on the back of the chair. She watched the sunlight dance across the restless water through half-closed eyes and thought about a kiss she should never have initiated.

She knew Del was attracted to her. She recognized the look in his eyes, but the strength of her own attraction surprised her. Some of it was physical. He had a muscular build with not a single flaw she'd been able to find and a face some would call strong and others handsome. She decided it was both. His thick, dark hair was cut short but looked so soft her fingers itched to test it, and his skin held a deep, delicious caramel color.

She was just as attracted to the steady directness in his dark eyes, his air of calm confidence, and the way he flew. She took a breath and let it out on a sigh. She'd never seen anyone slice with such smooth control. If he'd been flying a Shadow slicer instead of his lesser ship, he might have beaten her fair and square. Sorrow spiraled through her at the thought of him being rejected from the legitimate slicing circuits due to his dark association with the Core. He could have risen like a god and made history.

Brooding on the fickle twists of fate and watching the sun move across a nonexistent sky, she waited for him. The café stood empty and the sun was setting by the time he appeared at the fringe of her vision. She didn't take her gaze off the spectacular flare of colors. He entered the café and stopped several tables away.

When he didn't approach, she waved her bottle at the seat across the table from her. "Pull up a chair. Grab a beer." He didn't move. She rolled her head toward him and raised her eyebrows. "Shy?"

"Who are you?" he asked, his deep voice rough. He watched her with a mouth-drying intensity.

She rolled her head back to the sunset to cover her reaction. "Someone who wants to help you."

"Why?"

She chuckled and slanted him a quick look. "Don't worry. I'm not doing it out of the goodness of my heart. I need a pilot with your level of skill."

When he still didn't move, she sighed and straightened, turning toward him. Setting her water bottle on the table, she met his gaze with a steady regard. "Please, sit. Drink. We'll talk."

He hesitated a moment longer before coming forward and easing into the chair opposite her, his eyes never leaving hers. The strength of his gaze was almost physical; her skin warmed under it. She flicked a finger at the beer and he did a double take at the rare bottlenecks.

He lifted one and popped the top, taking a long drink. She tried not to watch the muscles in his throat move as he swallowed. When he lowered the bottle, he focused his intensity on her again. "I sat. I drank. Let's talk. Who are you?"

"My name is Sinsudee Shay. You can call me Sin," she said. "It's nice to meet you, Del. Did they take the credit?"

His dark eyes shuttered. "Did who take the credit?"

he asked in a careful voice.

She chuckled. "I like to dance as much as the next woman, but I don't think we need to. You've been indebted to Quasicore for about ten years. They've kept you on a tight leash, but you've slipped it, haven't you? Problem is, you're still wearing their collar. So when you offered to pay off the debt, what did they say?"

He hadn't moved, but his gaze turned hard and his knuckles white around the bottle. "Are you my leash?" he asked bitterly.

She shook her head. "I'm not Core. What I am is your only recourse at this point."

"If you're not Core, how did you know about me? How did you know they'd take the credit, but not let me quit?"

She now understood the intensity of his gaze was fury held in check by a thin thread. He didn't come here expecting rescue; he came looking for answers and a way to lash out.

"I knew what they would do because it's how the Core operates. I knew about you because I make it my business to know as much about Quasicore as possible. Keep your friends close and your enemies closer, as they say."

"Which are you, friend or enemy?" he growled, eyes narrowing.

She smiled and was unable to help the sad curve to it. "My brother and I own Shay Enterprises, one of the Core's competitors." The flicker in his eyes said he recognized the company name. It didn't seem to comfort him. "Right now you're weighing the evil you know against the evil you don't. But Del, I'm not evil and neither is my company. I wish we had time to let you find out on your own, but if you've contacted the Core, they'll be after you by now."

He grimaced in the light of the setting sun and broke eye contact for the first time. "I know." There was a short pause. "You made sure the ante would be enough to clear my debt then lost to me on purpose. I know you're stinkin' rich, but a hundred grand can't mean that little to you."

"I don't think I stink," she said in a light tone, but his dark eyes weren't amused. She pursed her lips and turned her head to watch the last sliver of sun disappear under the horizon. "I'm gambling you'll take this chance to free yourself instead of allowing the Core to eat you alive. The slice was the fastest way to get you to take the credit. If I'd just approached you and offered it, would you have taken it?"

He said nothing.

"In any case, I hardly had to lose on purpose. You almost had me. You slice like a dream, which is why I want you to pilot for me."

"For what?"

"Glad you asked," she responded with a small smile. "Part of Shay Enterprises is a courier service called Last Chance. While most of what we carry is done on the regular star-ways, sometimes we need a faster way and can't use normal routes. I'm sure you're aware traveling off the regular lanes can be hazardous. Hijacking occurs more often than is publicized. I'm offering you a job as a slicer pilot to make off-lane runs."

He stared at her for a long moment. "You gave away a hundred grand and are offering to go up against the Core just to get a courier pilot?"

She chuckled at his incredulous tone. "It's not as crazy as it sounds. The Core and Shay Enterprises are competitors, but in the business world we're still civil with each other. I will make it known the hundred grand came from me and I want you." The last words were out before she realized how they'd sound. Hoping the dim lighting hid the sudden flush on her cheekbones, she finished, "And they'll let you go."

He snorted in disbelief. "Just like that? No questions asked?"

"With the Core it's never no questions asked or 'just like that.'" She hardened her tone and sat back in her chair. "But it will be done."

"How am I supposed to believe you?" he asked in a voice threaded with desperation.

Sin relaxed. His tone said he wanted to accept her help and it was all she needed.

"Think of our two companies as chess players, Del. There will always be concessions between us, sacrifices if you will. To be honest, you aren't a major piece on their board. They have a million more just like you in their grasp. They'll let you go rather than risk going against my brother and me. I may have to give something as compensation, but it won't be much."

"What kind of compensation?" he wondered, rolling the bottle between his hands. The flex of his strong fingers distracted her.

"As I said, it won't be much. They may not even ask for anything, since they already have the credit you owed. It's what they would have asked for, if I'd approached them about acquiring you."

He stared down at the bottle between his hands without responding. She let the silence grow, watching the shadows deepen along his jaw and temple. "What are your terms?" he asked with harsh suspicion. For men like Del, life always held a catch.

"A place to stay, all the food you can eat, and a paycheck on the order of..." she mentioned a number and his head shot up.

"Krell dung."

She tipped her head back and laughed at the stars. "If it's not enough, I'm willing to negotiate," she teased. "Plus, you'll get a raise once a year and hazard pay for hard runs. Vacations are negotiable, but you'll get at least three weeks off a year."

"Stop," he ordered, voice rough. "My life's not a joke."

She sobered, leaning forward on her elbows. "No, it's not. The job is hard, but I take care of my people. It's also an offer I don't make often."

He was silent and still so long she got restless. Flicking a finger at the bottle he still held, she prompted, "You haven't finished."

"It's warm."

"It has friends." She hid a smile when he set the warm one aside and opened a cold bottle, only to hold it without drinking. "I'm not asking for your firstborn child, Del. What's the matter?"

"I'm thinking about hidden agendas and consequences."

She studied the shadowy planes of his face with a vague sense of unease. She hadn't expected to admire him as much as she did. "In other words, you're thinking about the catch."

"Right."

"I won't say there isn't one. The job I'm asking

you to do is dangerous, no doubt about it. Also, there's something I hesitated to mention before, but you'll hear it soon enough from the others." She paused and he tensed. He wouldn't like to hear this, but better it came from her. "You aren't the only pilot I have in my service with a dark past. I'll tell you what I've told the others. This is your last chance. You screw with me and you get shipped up river. I don't offer second chances. I offer last chances."

The hand not holding the bottle curled into a fist.

She softened her voice. "You did steal. You did cheat, extort, and hurt people or let them be hurt. I don't believe you ever committed murder…"

"I never—!" he started then cut himself off with a snarl.

"You were forced," she continued firmly. "The Core gave you no recourse and if they get you back, you'll be forced again to do much worse than you have already. At least with me and my company you can have a normal life. Or what passes for normal for a slicer pilot." She risked the small joke. His fist relaxed, though he shook his head at the same time. She tried another, just to see how he'd take it. "You know, there are people who can go whole weeks without breaking the law. Can you imagine?"

He gave a small snort. "That just ain't right."

She grinned. "So, are you ready to let me save your life?"

"Do I have a choice?"

She sympathized, but didn't relent. "There are always choices. In my opinion, this is your best choice."

"That's how it looks from where I'm sitting, too,"

he sighed.

She took a swift, triumphant breath. "I know you don't trust me, but you will."

All of a sudden, a light burst over them. Del got the brunt of it and held up a hand before his eyes with a grimace.

"Sorry!" Jake called to them from across the café. "Got busy back here and didn't see you were in the dark."

"It's all right, Jake. We had a nice, starry night. We're almost done here anyway."

"I wasn't tryin' to chase you out. Stay as long as you like. Want music?"

Still matchmaking, Sin thought with a smothered grin. "Thanks, but we're leaving soon."

"A'ight," he muttered, sounding a little put out.

Sin turned back to Del and met his dark gaze, shaken all over again by his steady intensity. She was glad the light was behind her with her face shadowed. "Do me a favor and drink some. If you leave it untouched, Jake will be insulted."

The corners of his mouth turned up. "Yes, ma'am. Whatever you say," he responded and took a long swallow.

"Now you're catching on." She rose to her feet, shrugging into her jacket. "Jake, we're off now. Thanks for the spectacular view, as usual."

"You take care a' y'self, now."

"Will do." She turned back to find Del on his feet. "Ready? You can ask questions on the way," she suggested, swinging around him to head for the exit. "As it is, we're going to have to shoot the rim to reach the Cyan star-way in time."

"Shoot the rim? You're nuts." He matched her stride as they left the café and headed down the main corridor of the station toward the docking bay.

She flashed him a challenging grin. "Don't tell me you're nervous? Don't worry, I scanned your slicer. She can handle the riptide of a black hole if we keep to the outer rim. We won't pick up as much velocity, but I think it'll be enough to get us there in time."

"Are you suicidal or just trying to get rid of me already?"

She chuckled. "Neither. Your X780 will hold together just fine." Slanting him an assessing look out of the corner of her eye, she asked, "Have you ever shot the rim before?"

He shook his head, studying her as though she were on the brink of insanity and might tip over into a crazy fit at any moment.

"I've been doing it since I was twelve. Nothing to it."

He blinked at her. "You've been slicing since you were twelve?"

"No, ten. The first time I shot the rim, I was twelve. My brother egged me into it." Then Kai had joined her so she wouldn't have to do it alone.

"Who would let a ten year old slice?"

"My father," she answered in a curt tone, turning her face away and cutting down the side corridor leading to the docking bay.

He took the hint and didn't pursue the line of questioning. "So how is this going to work? What's the plan?"

"First step is to get back to home base. Once you're safe, I'll make the call to the Core. It should be interesting," she mused, thinking of Griffin's reaction.

"I want to be in on the call," he said in a hard tone.

Sin studied his face coolly. "We'll see." She keyed open the door to the docking bay and watched Del as they stepped through. His attention swung to the Shadow slicer like a magnet. He didn't wait for her, heading with long strides toward her vessel.

When she caught up with him, he was inspecting the slicer with admiration written all over his face, running reverent hands over the sleek, black surface. She watched the slow caress of his hands over the smooth skin of her ship and had a sudden image of him doing the same to her. With a swift, indrawn breath, she shifted away and cleared her throat.

"She's beautiful," he rasped. "I don't recognize the model…wait, maybe I do. Hector called you the Shadow twins. Is this a Shadow ship?"

"Yes."

"But they're so rare. Only one company makes them and not many."

"Shay Enterprises. We also design slicers."

He shot her a quick look of surprise which changed to a frown when he touched the sides of the slicer, low near the belly. "She's heavy here, and what is this bulge?" He stopped short and stared at her, dark eyes flashing with startled dismay.

"Gun ports," she confirmed.

He straightened, expression turning unreadable as he studied her.

She gave him a faint, cool smile. "I did say the job would be dangerous."

"I thought you wanted me to quit breaking the law."

"Those aren't illegal. We have government sanction."

"How?" His brows came together and he shifted in place, staring at her like a man faced with an ominous puzzle.

"I'm not free to discuss it."

He shifted again, his eyes wary. "Hector said you broke his hand. Why?"

"He put it where it didn't belong," she answered, keeping her expression bland.

His eyes flicked over her and his features hardened; he thought Hector had put his hand on her.

She let him think it and moved past him to open her slicer. "We have to get moving. Any other questions?"

"Just one."

She turned and raised her eyebrows.

A gleam in his eyes, he planted a hand on the side of the slicer next to her shoulder, and leaned close enough for her to feel the warmth of his body. "Why the kiss?" he asked in a low rumble.

Heat built under her skin at his deep voice and the force of his gaze. She covered it with a cynical smile. "Did you want Hector's group of slice-heads knowing your real name? We both have secrets to keep, Del. The kiss was an excuse to get close enough to keep them."

"They don't know who you really are," he concluded with a twist of his mouth.

"And they didn't need to know your situation." Before he could pursue it any further, she slid into the slicer away from him. "Time to go."

He hesitated, looking down at her with indecision in his eyes, before he shook his head and stepped back.

With a silent breath of relief, she closed the slicer and started it. Her motives for the kiss hadn't been nearly so detached, but it was a secret she meant to keep.

Brushing her hair aside, she slid the connector into the port behind her ear, and took a deep breath as the Shadow possessed her. To her, it had always felt as though she became someone else when she sliced, a creature of power and certainty. As a slicer pilot, she achieved a level of clarity and control she didn't get in the rest of her life.

Raising the ship from its berth, she waited until Del's red slicer lifted off its pad. Then she contacted him. "Del, I'm sending you the course and destination."

"Got it," he answered.

Turning the Shadow, she coasted out of the bay with Del right behind her. Once outside the station, she found a speed he could match without overworking his engines and headed toward the Starkov black hole.

It wasn't visible, but its gravitational force was in clear evidence as they approached. Star systems and space debris streamed toward it in long spirals. She meant to use its massive force to slingshot around the hole, sending them with a greater velocity than their engines could create toward their destination, the Cyan solar system and star-way.

As they neared the rim, she contacted Del again. "You still with me?"

"Yeah, but it looks like I won't be for long."

An undercurrent of excitement sounded behind his sarcasm and she grinned. "Just stay close. This'll be fun."

He snorted in response, and she chuckled as she started the run on the rim. It didn't take long before the gravitational pull of the hole grabbed her Shadow. She adjusted her trajectory to skim the rim of that force. It took skill to keep the ship steady enough not to fall in, yet close enough to get the full effect of the slingshot. They shot around the hole, the pull increasing their speed until, at the pinnacle before they could be drawn into the killer vortex, they pushed their engines to maximum and broke away.

Sin's Shadow shivered at the strain of a velocity it wasn't designed to achieve on its own. Del would be experiencing much more turbulence in his lesser ship. "Still good?" she asked.

"Oh yeah," he growled in her ear and she laughed as they shot through space toward Cyan.

Chapter 3

Del was still experiencing an adrenaline high when they reached the star-way. The memory of Sin's throaty laughter didn't help. If they'd been face to face, he'd have pounced.

He took deep, calming breaths as they glided toward the station, ignoring the massive star-way ring spinning off to their portside. A dark shape, swift and close, caught his attention, and he spun his slicer into an evasive roll with a curse. Sin did the same and voiced a similar curse in his ear.

"Kai, I will strip the skin off your bones, I swear to Sun and Stars."

As it slowed and banked to match their course toward a huge cruiser ship, Del recognized the other Shadow vessel.

"Just keeping your reflexes fresh, Sissa."

"If they get any fresher, they'll bleed," she snapped and her brother chuckled. "Why are you coming in now? You should have arrived hours ago."

"I was waiting for you, of course," he answered, his tone bright with false cheer.

"Uh-huh. If an irate husband comes tearing after you, I won't do a thing to help you."

"Rosie's not married."

"What d'you know, you remembered her name. I'm so proud," she muttered, and Del smothered a laugh.

They postponed the sibling banter to confirm their passage with the cruiser and coast into its docking bay. The cruiser pilot informed them the flight would commence soon and they should hurry to their seats. Del settled his slicer next to the Shadows and disconnected, sliding out to meet the twins.

"Del, this is my brother, Manakai Shay."

Her brother held out a hand with an easy grin, and Del took it. "Good to meet you, Del."

"Likewise," he said as they shook.

"I assume I can also welcome you to the company?"

"Looks like it."

"Good." Kai gave Del's hand one last firm shake before letting go. "We could use a slicer pilot like you." Then he slanted a teasing glance at his sister. "Right, Sinsi?"

Either she didn't see the look on her brother's face or she ignored it. "That's right. Let's find our seats before they get this beast moving."

She led the way toward the entrance to the seating compartments, and Del followed with her brother. A frazzled young attendant met them at the entrance, trying to rush them forward with anxious little flaps of her hands.

The twins shared an amused glance. Manakai approached the woman with a charming smile. Slipping an arm around her waist, he led her along the hall. By the time he asked her name and complimented her on it, she looked dazzled enough to forget all sorts of things; who she was, the power of speech, and seating wayward passengers.

"Now that's talent," Del remarked.

Sin shot him a dry glance. "He's been practicing since he was six."

"I'll bet neither of you went through an ugly phase."

"You'd lose. Thirteen was not a good age." She gave a theatrical shiver and he chuckled, not believing it for a second.

As they moved along the hall, they passed the public compartments where passengers sat together in row on row of seats. The cruiser had several of these compartments, ranging from the cheapest and most uncomfortable to the most expensive and spacious seating. Del and the twins passed all of them.

Del had never seen the private compartments before, and raised his eyebrows when they reached one. "You two ride well."

"Owning a big company comes in handy for some things, like traveling without everyone's knowledge."

Del shot her a sharp look, but she slipped past him and through the door without explaining. He followed with a vague sense of foreboding.

Once inside, he stopped and stared. A full kitchen dominated one corner and a large bed filled the opposite side of the compartment. In the center of the room four plush seats faced each other in twos, with an enormous viewer against the wall displaying the outside of the ship as if they were looking out a window. Del wondered how much it cost to book this compartment.

Manakai clapped him on the shoulder as he passed. "Settle in, Del. We're on the move."

The viewer showed them pulling away from the station. Sin claimed a seat close to the viewer. Del sat next to her as Kai flopped in the seat opposite his sister with a weary sigh.

Sin leaned forward and touched the viewer, flashing her brother an arch glance. "Did Rosie wear you out?"

His slow smile was full of smug satisfaction. "In so many ways, bless her kinky, little heart," Manakai drawled.

Del chuckled. Sin frowned at him as she sat back, the viewer now showing the star-way ring. "Don't encourage him."

"Think he needs encouragement?" he retorted.

Her frown eased into wry amusement. "Good point." Then she gestured at the viewer. "We're about to make the run. Strap in, kids."

Manakai rolled his eyes. "Yes, Mom," he teased and shouldered into the straps, buckling them across his chest.

Del strapped in as well, watching their approach to the ring. The ring spun faster and faster as it built up energy drawn from the sun of this solar system. The ring's twin did the same on the opposite side of the sun, trapping the massive energy of the star between them. When it built up enough energy, it created a wormhole in space, allowing ships to travel from one part of the galaxy to another in a fraction of the time. Only the suns provided enough reliable energy to create stable wormholes; so most travelers crossed the expanses of space between solar systems by slower means. The majority of ships took the same routes from place to place for safety and convenience, creating lanes of traffic easy to govern and police. Other routes, away from frequent traffic and the watchful eye of FPA forces, were considered off-lane and dangerous.

A bright, multi-colored flash announced the ring reaching critical velocity, a wormhole forming within its circle. The hole was difficult to see, the distortion of space and time disorienting to the eye. The blur of color and light seemed to bulge away from the ring, then fade to nothing.

A deep thrumming under Del's heels announced the cruiser's engines had kicked into full power, speeding them toward the ring. Only massive ships could withstand the shock of entering and exiting a wormhole. The stress of going from normal space to warped space ripped smaller ships to pieces, so travelers, like Del and the Shays, needed large vessels for transport through them.

The shifting blur of the hole expanded on the viewer until they felt the jolt of entry. Then the viewer went black. Ships flew blind, their sensors useless away from normal space, trusting the rings to ferry them to the correct destination.

Manakai released his straps with a flick and a shrug then slouched down and lifted his feet, eyeing his sister with raised eyebrows. "Scooch."

She frowned at him, but moved over to let him prop his feet next to her. "These seats have footrests."

He waved her protest away. "They aren't long enough. Wake me when we get there." Reclining, he let out a deep sigh, closed his eyes, and appeared to fall right to sleep.

"Brothers," she grumbled.

Del snorted. "Tell me about it."

She gave him a look he couldn't interpret before unstrapping and getting to her feet. "Would you like something to eat or drink?"

"No, thanks." Over his shoulder he watched her pour something then walk back to her seat. He was having trouble not watching her, a big problem if she was his boss.

"So, Del," she began, setting her glass in the holder on the armrest, "tell me your life's story."

"I thought you knew all about me."

Her eyes flickered away from him for a moment. "I know what I've been told. I'd rather hear it from you."

He shrugged and shifted in his seat. "Not much to tell."

She gave him a wry smile, twisting his insides. He wanted to taste her again. "Let me help. You were born. Then…" She let her voice trail off, tilting her head toward him.

He looked away and fixed his gaze on the seat across from him. He didn't like talking about his past, but it would keep his mind off her mouth and every other part of her he hadn't tasted yet. "Mom died a year after she had my brother. I was six, so I don't remember her much. Dad said she died of Indigo Fever."

"She wasn't vaccinated?"

"Dad thought she got a bad batch. After she died, he raised us on the slicer circuits. He was a slice addict, gambling on them all the time. He taught us both to slice, got us racing. Made some credit off us, too, but not enough. When he died, he was into the Core for almost half a million credits." Del couldn't quite hide the bitter note in his voice. "His death didn't erase the debt. My brother and I still owed."

He fell silent, brooding on dark memories.

"So you took on your father's debt and sent your

brother away," Sin finished for him. He turned his head to meet her gaze. Her steady green eyes held respect, a quality he hadn't seen in so long, he almost didn't recognize it.

Flustered, he looked down, a frown furrowing his brow. "With our parents gone, he was my responsibility. He didn't have anybody else to take care of him."

"How long has it been since you've seen him?"

"Ten years. I found a place for him and left him there, changing my name to Del Tower so he wouldn't get burned for being my brother. He probably hates my guts, thinks I ditched him."

"I doubt it."

Her words barely registered. He remembered the last time he'd seen his brother, the pain and anger on his young face. "I told him it wouldn't take long, I'd be back when it was paid. I was young and stupid. I had no clue what the Core was like."

She didn't respond. When he looked at her, she was staring at her brother with a strange expression on her lovely face. It almost seemed like guilt and sadness, or maybe worry.

"Sorry," he said. She snapped her head around as if he'd startled her. "Didn't mean to bring you down."

Her mouth curved. "You didn't. Food for thought, though." She returned her gaze to her brother, and Del's stomach flipped at the tenderness in her smile. "You can resurrect Adelmo Givliani now. You can see your brother again."

He stared at her in wonder, speechless.

She chuckled, patting him on the arm. "You look like you need a drink." She rose and brought him a glass, orange liquid over ice.

He took a swallow and winced. It was some kind of liquor with a little juice for color. "You gettin' me drunk?"

Her lips curled in response, eyes gleaming. "Try to get some rest." She shifted out of his line of vision and moved back into the kitchen.

He downed the drink in three long swallows, shuddering at the combination of heat and cold as it hit his stomach. The heat of the liquor spread relaxation through his muscles. Setting the glass down, he reclined his seat and copied Manakai's slump, crossing his ankles on the seat across from him. The cushioned recliner was almost as comfortable as a mattress. It reminded him of the bed in the corner, and he was sliding into a fantasy about being in it with a certain green-eyed temptress when he fell asleep.

She filled his dreams. He relived the slice they'd run together in such perfect accord, his body throbbing with exaltation. Then he relived the kiss. In his dream they didn't stop at one. They were in a slicer, naked and moving, flying together, twisting and sliding and…

A touch on his shoulder prompted him to open his eyes. Sin leaned over him, so beautiful and smelling like the sweetest temptation. With the dream still clinging to him, he didn't realize he was awake. It seemed only natural to bury a hand in the dark silk of her hair, pulling her close to capture her mouth with his. She tasted better than any dream and her scent filled his senses like a drug. Reality reasserted in a hurry when she pulled away, a storm in her green eyes and a frown on her brow.

He swore under his breath. "Sorry," he rasped.

"We're here," she announced in a voice laced with ice and headed for the exit.

"Nice move, Giv," Manakai said, rising from his seat, green eyes bright with humor and mouth curled in a smirk.

Del grimaced, both for what he'd done and for a nickname he hadn't heard in a long time. Rubbing his face with rough hands to scrub off lingering disorientation, he rose to his feet and followed the twins out. They passed few people on the way to the docking bay. The Shays must have delayed leaving until most of the other passengers had disembarked.

The same young assistant who'd greeted them stood at the door to the docking bay. Her face lit when she saw Manakai. He turned on the charm again, but Sin made an impatient noise in her throat and shoved at her brother.

"Move it, Kai. We have things to do."

The woman's face fell and she wished them a mournful good day. Del offered his thanks but didn't think she heard him, her eyes glued to Sin's brother as they walked away. Del shook his head and followed them. The Shadow twins were dangerous in more ways than one.

Kai groused, "Just because your love life sucks, doesn't mean mine has to."

"Funny, I didn't think love had anything to do with your activities."

"You wound me," he drawled.

"At some point it's going to get you in trouble."

"One can only hope." He flashed a wicked grin at Del over Sin's head.

Sin rolled her eyes. "Let's go home. I hate leaving

45

the kids alone for too long."

"Kids?" Del asked. A sudden flash of Sin with a family clenched bands of tension around his chest.

"Sin's other broken birds," Kai answered with a mocking smile. "Hasn't she told you you're not the only one?"

Del clenched his jaw under the assessing gaze of the other man and didn't respond. He had a feeling his relationship with Sin's brother was going to be a rocky one.

Sin's reaction was a little less stoic. She cuffed her brother upside the head.

"Ow!" he yelled and ducked away from her, hilarity brightened his eyes and the lines of his face. "Sun's sake, Sissa."

"Don't be rude, Kai," she warned.

With a snicker Kai angled toward his slicer. Del followed Sin to hers. "Broken bird?" he asked in a low voice.

She tensed. "Kai's idea of a bad joke. Let's get going."

He caught her arm before she could slip into the Shadow. "Is broken how you see me?"

Her head rose slowly as if she were reluctant to meet his gaze. A furrow creased her brow and something like pain darkened her green eyes. "No, Del. I don't see you as broken."

In that moment, he believed her. Maybe it was just something he needed to believe, or maybe it was the look in her eyes. The hint of darkness made him ache to hold her. He could drown in those eyes.

The growl of Kai's Shadow engines broke through his reverie. Del realized he was just standing there staring at her and let her go, blood rushing through his veins. His temperature seemed to have risen a couple of degrees.

She dropped her gaze and slid into the slicer without comment. He turned to his own ship, rubbing an uneasy hand around the back of his neck. His new reality was getting more complicated by the second.

They left the cruiser together and set off away from the star-way at a fast pace. Sin downloaded course and destination to Del without speaking. For a while, silence reigned between the three of them as they sped toward their destination.

Then Manakai's Shadow flipped and slid upside down under Sin's, righting itself on her other side. Del studied the ship, but it didn't seem to be in distress. What was her brother up to? Sin's Shadow did nothing. Kai shot out in front of her and began to roll, edging closer as he did. She took an abrupt nosedive and he spun out of his roll to follow.

They were playing like young dolphins in open water. Del watched with amusement and envy as they spun, twisted, and dodged one another. He loved his slicer, but his breath caught and his mouth dried with longing while the Shadows executed even the most difficult maneuvers with lazy ease. Manakai had a flamboyant slicing style, his movements extravagant but brilliantly executed. Sin flew with a swift and simple grace, a beautiful counterpoint to her brother.

"Hey, Giv," Kai murmured in his ear and startled him out of his entrancement with the dancing Shadows.

"Here," he answered, watching them perform a series of figure eights in perfect accord.

"We're on a private frequency. Sin's not listening."

Uh-oh, Del thought and responded with a wary, "Yeah?"

"Relax, I'm not going to bang your head against a wall for wanting my sister. Just letting you know it won't work." For once, he sounded serious.

Del grimaced but wasn't surprised. "Got it. You're my bosses now."

"Not your only pitfall, Giv," the other man said, while his Shadow did a flip and he flew backward nose-to-nose with his sister. "She doesn't get involved with her projects. You can see why, can't you?"

Del ground his teeth at Manakai's callous arrogance. Sin might not consider him broken, but Kai sure did. "You speaking as her brother or her partner?" he asked through clenched teeth. A long silence followed and Del wondered if he'd just gotten himself fired. Implying Manakai was thinking of his position in the company, and not his sister's welfare, wasn't smart.

Kai's Shadow flipped over his sister's and ran straight at Del. With a muffled curse, Del dodged, but the other ship swung back alongside Sin's slicer before it reached him.

"We'll have to get you a Shadow ship, Giv," Kai said, laughter in his tone. "You can't keep up in your red thing."

Del twisted his mouth in a snarl at the other man's condescension and dismissal. Kai didn't see him as a threat on any level. He and Sin's brother were not going to be the best of friends.

Sin broke through their communication. "Put a leash on it, Kai. We're almost there, and you make them nervous when you play."

"It's good for them. Gets their blood flowing."

"And that's a good thing how?" she asked and Kai snickered.

They approached a large structure, capturing Del's attention. The size of a small moon, it orbited a gas giant, ships of all shapes and sizes swarming around it like bees on a hive.

"Your company is in there?" he asked, assuming the station was a hub of commerce.

"The whole station is Shay Enterprises, our headquarters. We have other stations, but this is our main one."

He didn't answer. He couldn't. He stared at the vast structure in amazement and misery. These two owned all of this and more besides. No wonder Kai didn't see him as a threat.

They dodged larger ships with ease and entered a massive docking bay filled with a variety of ships, including slicers. Several Shadow ships, as well as some other expensive models, dotted the bay and Del grimaced as they landed. He was in over his head and he knew it.

Levering out of his slicer, he approached the twins, who waved to a group of dockworkers and pilots. Kai said, "Still having trouble with the docking clamps and conveyers."

"We'll have to sit down with Spec and his crew."

"He'll freak out."

Sin acknowledged Del with a quick smile then shook her head at her brother. "Not if only one of us goes."

They started for the doors at one end of the bay away from the group of workers. "So which of us gets to watch him sweat?" Kai asked with a glum expression.

"He likes you better."

"No he doesn't. You just make him nervous because he fantasizes about you."

"Oh, yuck," she exclaimed with a disgusted look, and Del smothered a grin. "He does not, you pervert."

"Just because he's old enough to be your grandfather doesn't make him dead," Kai retorted as they passed into what looked like a mechanics bay.

"Well, now you have to go. I'm not…" She trailed off at the sound of loud, argumentative voices echoing through the bay.

The twins stared at each other in sudden tension then took off at a dead run. After a surprised second, Del sprinted on their heels. Rounding a corner into a double row of slicers, they neared a small group of people in a tense circle. At the center of the circle stood two men and a small woman. The woman and the taller of the men were yelling at each other at the top of their lungs.

The yelling man caught sight of the twins, turned ghost white, and bolted. The circle scattered to either side as the twins blew past after the man. Del slowed to a stop, watching Kai grab a bracing pole and fling it at the fleeing form in one smooth move. It struck the man around the knees and he went down in a tumble. He rose on all fours, but before he could get to his feet again, Sin reached him.

Del's jaw dropped when she stomped on the back of the man's neck, slamming him to the floor, and grabbed one of his arms, wrenching it straight behind him. She gave it a vicious twist, ignoring the man's yelp of pain and plucking something out of his hand.

She looked at it then down at the man under her foot with the coldest expression Del had ever seen.

"This looks like blue, Pete," she said in a conversational voice, but something in her face suggested a towering rage.

"Get off me! Ah, my shoulder!"

"Does it hurt?" she asked and gave his arm another wrench, wringing a strangled cry from him. "I'd be happy to dislocate it for you if you don't answer me."

"Yes! Yes, it's blue! My cousin must've—"

"Quiet. Lying to me is dangerous right now. You were trying to give this to Jinx, weren't you? He's a blue addict and you were going to drop him down that hole again."

"I just—"

Sin ground her foot into the back of his neck and his words broke off with an agonized gargle. She looked up at her brother, lovely face set in hard lines. "How many chances do we give people here, Kai?"

"Just one," he answered, voice as cold and hard as his sister's.

She glanced back down at the man squirming under her. "Looks like you're out of them, Pete. Systems control!"

An echoing, toneless voice answered, seeming to come from everywhere. "Sinsudee Shay."

"Connect me with Lieutenant Baker, please."

The man beneath her foot launched into desperate convulsions. "No!" he gasped, but she twisted his arm once again and he yelped, straining under her.

"Baker here." A feminine voice resounded off the bay walls.

"Lieutenant, I hear you've been searching for a

drug runner by the name of Peter Feslowski."

"We have. Do you have information for me, Ms. Shay?"

"I can do you one better. I have your man. Come get him."

Pete moaned and slumped.

"Thank you, Ms. Shay. We'll be over soon." The lieutenant didn't sound surprised. Del wondered how many of these calls she'd received from the Shays.

Sin flung the man's arm away and moved toward the group in long, hard strides. Her expression said she was ready to strip the skin off the next person to step in her way, and the others in the circle eased back from her. She stopped in the center of their circle, glaring around her with hands on hips. No one met her gaze.

"Sin," Kai said in a warning tone.

She flung a hand up at him. "I know!" she snapped and moved in front of Del.

Fascinated, he stared down into her anger-bright eyes and wondered what she'd do if he touched her.

"Welcome to Last Chance," she said with bitter emphasis. Then she strode past him, heading toward a door at the far end of the bay.

All eyes switched from her to Kai. Without a word, he turned his head and looked at the offender. Pete was rubbing his shoulder with a sullen expression, wary gaze on Manakai. Kai pointed to a spot closer to the group and snapped his fingers in uncompromising demand. Dropping his head, Pete pushed to his feet and shuffled forward.

Muscle twitching in his jaw, Kai said with ice in his voice, "You try to bolt or even take a step in any direction, and they'll have to take you to the infirmary before they lock you up. Understood?"

Pete nodded without lifting his head. Kai then turned to the rest of the people, his attention going to the other man who'd been standing in the center of the circle.

He looked young, still carrying an adolescent awkwardness, his thin face haggard and eyes sunken. "Manny, I swear I didn't take any."

The small woman who'd hollered at Pete stepped closer. "He didn't. I saw what happened and he didn't take anything."

"I know he didn't," Kai responded. "I can see it on his face. It's all right, Jinx."

The thin, young man slumped against a slicer in obvious relief and the small woman patted his arm.

They all crowded around Manakai, babbling an explanation of what had happened. Sorting through the overlapping voices, Del pieced it together. Pete had tried to sell Jinx a hit of the addictive drug blue, which Jinx was hooked on but trying to kick. The small woman had seen what was happening and interfered loudly enough to bring everyone else running, including the twins.

Manakai nodded and murmured soothing comments to each of them. Del got the disorienting impression they saw Kai as a father figure; a hard concept to grasp, considering what he'd seen so far of Kai's reckless nature. At one point, a young woman cried, "Sin was so mad!" in an aggrieved tone. The rest hushed and watched Kai with anxious expressions. He patted the young woman on the back with a gentle smile. "Bib, she wasn't mad at you. She just doesn't like being wrong about anyone."

Almost as one, their eyes turned to Pete with varying levels of hostility. He kept his head lowered and said nothing.

"You can all give her a warm welcome home when she's calmed down. In the meantime, we have someone joining our crew."

As a group, they shifted around until they faced Del. He gave them an uncomfortable nod, wishing the timing had been better. They'd just been betrayed by one of their own and would look on someone new with suspicion.

Kai seemed to sense this, approaching Del with a crooked smile. "How 'bout I introduce you later? If you go through the door over there and up three levels, you'll find our offices. Sin should be there. I'll be along as soon as they come around for our enterprising friend." His smile turned hard when he glanced over at Pete.

Del nodded and headed toward the door. Before he went through, he looked over his shoulder. The group crowded around Manakai again, like a dysfunctional family, and Del shook his head. What kind of surreal mess had he stepped into?

Chapter 4

Del left the maintenance bay, entered a service hallway, and found the lift. He keyed it to rise three levels, then stepped out into another hallway similar to the one below. Only one door stood at the end; he opened it and stepped through, stopping short at the sight before him.

Kai had said offices, but Del had never been in such grand business surroundings. The room he'd entered was huge, with a glass wall showing other offices beyond. An enormous desk presided over the space on a stepped up elevation. Behind the desk, a viewer covered the entire wall, showing a beach scene. On one side of the office, a fireplace sat flanked by overstuffed chairs. On the other side stood a full bar. A long, polished table with high backed chairs dominated the center of the room.

As the door closed behind him, Del realized he'd come into the Shay offices the back way. He shuffled in like an intruder and spotted Sin in the next office talking with a neatly dressed young man. The man nodded several times then turned to go. Sin strode toward the glass wall, which seemed to melt out of her way. Her movements were still aggressive, and she cast him a sharp glance before turning to the bar without a word.

"Uh, your brother sent me."

"Come on in. I don't stand on ceremony with my off-laners. You're free to come and go as you please, unless Kai and I are in meetings."

He took a few more steps into the room then stopped, itching all over like some Fringe degenerate crashing his way into civilization for the first time.

She walked toward him carrying two glasses, mouth quirking at his expression. "You'll get used to it. It's just for show, intimidates the competition."

He took the glass she handed him and glanced down at the liquid inside, hesitating.

"Water," she explained and moved away with fluid grace.

He cleared his throat and followed, taking a swallow of the cold water before saying, "Don't suppose you'll tell me what just happened."

She set her glass down on the bar with a click, giving him a cool look. "Kai and I gave Pete a chance to make something of his life, to make his future brighter than it was going to be. He threw it back in our faces."

"So you rolled on him."

"He rolled on himself." She pushed away from the bar, pacing across the room with fierce strides. "He knew the deal. One chance only…his last chance. He had everything he could want, but he tossed it. He couldn't give up his old life." She sent him a piercing stare. "Can you, Del?"

He settled onto a barstool, tilting his head at her. "I didn't have a life," he said with a calm he didn't quite feel. "The Core took it from me."

She turned from him, a small frown furrowing her brow, but she didn't stop pacing. Del drank his water

56

and watched her, wondering at her agitation while enjoying the smooth flex of her muscles and roll of her hips.

Silence filled the huge room, but Del didn't break it. A few minutes later, the back door slid open and Kai stepped through. Sin spun and lifted her eyebrows at her brother.

"He's gone," he responded.

Her shoulders slumped a little and she rubbed a hand across her forehead, blocking Del's view of her face.

Kai made a rude noise and strode toward her. "Cut it out, Sissa. Don't go blaming yourself for his decisions."

When he reached her, he wrapped her in his arms and she rested her head on his shoulder. Del looked away, a burn at the back of his throat. It took him a few seconds to recognize the feeling as budding jealousy. *Sun's blood, I'm in so much trouble,* he thought without even a trace of humor.

"How are the others?"

"Upset. But they'll get over it."

"I'll see them in a little while. Let's get this call to the Core over with. Del?" Sin stepped out of her brother's arms, sending Del an expectant look, and he rose to his feet.

Kai frowned at his sister. "You want him on the call?"

"He requested it," she said as she headed for the desk. "But I'm allowing it on one condition." She paused and fixed Del with a firm stare, her tone turning crisp. "I do the talking. Is that clear?"

He shrugged, crossing the room to her. "I just want

to know what's said."

"Fair enough." They stepped up to the desk together. She leaned over and tapped on a control panel. "Systems control, please connect me with Webster Griffin, visual on the viewer."

Del stared at her. *"The* Webster Griffin?" he asked in a hoarse voice. "The CEO of Quasicore?"

"Who else?" she countered with wry amusement.

The viewer flickered in its center and a regal face appeared against the beach scene. Del had never met the man but knew him on sight. Everyone did.

"Sinsudee, always a pleasure." The gray-haired gentleman greeted her in cultured tones. "What can I do for you?"

"Griff, I have a bit of a problem," she answered with an easy smile, as if she weren't talking to a man almost as powerful as the Planetary Alliance itself.

"Your problems are mine, of course. How may I assist?"

Sitting on the corner of the desk, Sin swept a hand at Del. "This man is an employee of yours. He's indebted to the Core for a fair sum of credit but wishes to end his employment with you. He is a slicer pilot of some skill, which would be useful for my off-lane courier services." She paused with a faint smile, which he returned.

"His name?"

"Del Tower."

"A moment, Sin. Let me check our records."

"Of course."

Griffin turned his head, studying something out of their range of sight. When he turned back, a slight sympathetic smile curled his thin lips but didn't warm his gray eyes. "I wish I could help you, dear, but he has acquired several penalties and fines for not performing his duties, though he has recently paid a sizable sum on his debt."

"Yes, he paid it believing he was discharging his debt to the Core. I was his source of credit."

His smile disappeared, and his cold gaze flicked to Del for the first time. Del said nothing but didn't look away, folding his arms across his chest.

Griffin's attention returned to Sin and his brow creased in an aggrieved frown. "You should have come to me first, dear. Perhaps then Mr. Tower could have avoided his penalties."

Del's stomach heaved. He knew Brax and Trev had been sent after him to exact the Core's penalties in blood.

"Circumstances beyond my control did not allow for it," Sin said in a smooth voice.

"Perhaps if he had managed to clear his account…" Griffin shook his head in solemn regret.

"Easily rectified, I'm sure you will agree."

"You would be willing to discharge this debt for him?"

"I would."

"He is fortunate to have such a generous benefactress," he said with a cynical glint in his eye.

Sin gave him a cool smile. "Just send my accountants the number. I would like a swift resolution to this, if possible."

"It's already done."

"Wonderful," she declared and rose to her feet. "Will I see you at the luncheon, Griff?"

"Certainly. It would be my great pleasure to escort

you."

"Ah, you flatter me, but sad to say, I'm saddled with my brother again."

Kai snorted at Del's elbow but said nothing.

Griffin acknowledged her brother's presence, sending him an amused look and slight nod. "I'm sure Manakai does not appreciate his enviable position."

"I'm sure," she drawled. "Thank you for taking my call, Griff."

"I'm delighted I was able to assist you. Please don't hesitate to call again."

"If I can return the favor, you know how to reach me."

He tilted his head in a dignified nod before the viewer rippled and his face disappeared.

"Pedantic old goat." Sin hissed and turned away from the desk. Kai growled wordless agreement and followed her, heading toward the bar.

"That's it?" Del asked, trailing after them.

"That's it. You are no longer Core. You're an employee of Shay Enterprises," Sin answered and stepped around the bar, pulling a couple of glasses from under it.

Kai joined her, nudging her out of the way to grab a bottle. "Saddled?"

"Well, I didn't expect him to make a pass at me over the vid," she retorted.

"He did, you said it, and now I have to go, too."

"Misery loves company, brother."

Del leaned on the bar and watched the two of them create potent drinks. They took a long swallow together.

Sin lowered hers with a sigh and rolled her

shoulders and neck. "I hate talking to him. Makes me feel dirty."

Kai was still downing his drink. When it was empty, he lowered the glass and began making himself another.

Del raised his eyebrows, looking from one to the other. Their reactions seemed extreme, considering how civil the conversation had been. "You two planning on getting sloshed?"

The twins glanced at each other and grinned. Raising their glasses, they clinked them together. "What a great idea," Sin declared. "We need dinner first, though."

At the mention of food, Del's stomach clenched with urgency. "Can't argue, I'm starving. Can you show me where I'm staying?"

"All in good time, Giv," Kai said, coming around the bar to clap him on the shoulder. "First, come have dinner and get sloshed with us. We're moody drunks if left to ourselves."

Sin snickered, rounding the other end of the bar. "Yes, come to dinner. We have a contract to discuss, and you shouldn't eat alone on your first night in a new place."

Del decided not to point out the obvious; he'd been eating alone in new places his whole life. "All right."

"Great." Kai clapped him on the shoulder again and headed toward the back door. "We cook up a mean stir fry, right, Sissa?"

"Oh, sure," she agreed with a false note then whispered to Del as they followed her brother, "But only when he's drunk."

"I heard that," Kai shot over his shoulder.

Del exchanged a grin with her, but his gaze lingered after she looked away. She'd been dangerously beautiful the first time they'd met, all cold and menacing grace, but when relaxed she took his breath away. Each smile seemed to pierce him clean through.

When he managed to take his gaze off her, he met Kai's mocking stare. "Or maybe we should put Giv to work," her brother drawled, blocking the doorway.

Del clenched his jaw.

"We don't make guests work, Kai." She paused then poked him. "Are you going to stand there all night?"

Kai moved aside, allowing his sister to pass through before stepping in behind her with a callous smirk at Del. They headed for the lift and Sin keyed it to rise several more floors.

When the doors opened, Del heaved a dismal sigh at the room before them. He hadn't had much experience with luxury in his life. On this scale it was surreal. Plush furniture and expensive decoration filled the spacious area they entered, the extravagance enough to give him a headache. Just one of the paintings gracing the walls might've paid his debt ten times over.

He hadn't noticed the twins passing him until Sin called his name, amusement in her voice. "This is our entertainment suite. Again, just for show. I live in the attached suite and Kai has his apartments on the other side of the station. As far away from me as possible." She shot her brother an arch look.

Kai blinked innocence at her. "What d'you mean?"

She snorted and led the way through a short hall ending in a doorway hidden from the ostentatious rooms. The living quarters they entered were still large, but Del breathed a silent sigh of relief. Simpler and welcoming furnishings graced the interior, built for comfort rather than intimidation. The decorations, from sculpture to painting to plant life, filled the space with an elegant, soothing serenity. The entire place carried her scent. His head spun as he took another deep breath.

"Welcome home, Sinsudee," said a melodious feminine voice reverberating out of the walls.

"Thanks, Mina."

"Will you be requiring a bath first or would you like to see your schedule?"

"Neither. I have company tonight."

"So I see. Welcome, Mr. Givliani. I am Mina, Sinsudee's house companion. Manakai, good of you to visit." The voice sounded reproachful.

Kai brushed past his sister and headed toward the open kitchen. "Don't give me crap, Mina."

"Certainly not. That would be unsanitary."

Sin rolled her eyes and gave Del a wry smile. "I keep telling him it does no good to pick a fight with an AI, but he doesn't listen. Make yourself comfortable. I'll get the contract."

She slipped into the next room and Del moved after Kai, shaking his head at the extravagance of having an artificial intelligence entity as a roommate. The expense and technical difficulty in creating artificial life forms put AIs out of reach for everyone but the elite, the well-connected, and the FPA.

In the center of the kitchen stood a long counter with stools along one side. Del sat, watching as Kai measured amounts of five different liquors into a glass with solemn care. Then he dropped a pearl of something reddish orange into the mix, and pushed the glass toward Del. The pearl dissolved in a flood of warm, swirling colors.

Kai grinned at him in challenge. "A supernova. Guaranteed to burn you clean."

"Just what I need," Del retorted.

Kai chuckled and started pulling food cubes out of a receptacle as his sister returned. She tossed a hand-sized, flat viewer on the counter next to Del. "Read it over. If you see anything you don't like, let me know. It's a standard pilot's contract, but we can tweak it." She moved to assist her brother, putting food cubes in the reconstructor.

Del picked up the contract and began to read, lifting his drink to take a cautious sip. Cautious or not, he had to pause as sudden tears sprang into his eyes. The ferocious burn of the supernova consumed his whole head before moving into his chest. He gasped as quietly as he could, but when he blinked his eyes clear, he met Kai's twinkling green gaze.

"S'good," Del croaked.

Kai's snort of amusement goaded him into taking another sip. The burn wasn't quite as bad the second time and he lifted the glass in defiant salute. Kai gave a low chuckle and turned to pull reconstructed produce from the machine, as crisp and fresh as the day it was harvested.

Del returned to reading while the siblings diced food and bickered. Del ignored them, enthralled by the contract. He'd never read a more fair and equitable arrangement. A weird sense of disorientation gripped him. He wondered if he was dreaming. He was free of the Core and he was being asked to join a company offering him every benefit without apparent gain for themselves besides his piloting services.

Del tossed the viewer down. "You can't be serious with this."

Sin lifted her eyebrows at him with a faint smile. "Found something you don't like?"

"No, that's the problem. It's a fantastic deal and it says nothing in there about paying you back for what you gave the Core."

"Paying us back isn't necessary."

"Yes it is." He held her gaze with grim intent. His new salary was more than generous; if they could be more reasonable than the Core about payments, he could clear his debt in short order. Then again, he didn't know how much extra Griffin had demanded. "Just how much do I owe you?"

She waved a hand in careless dismissal. "We can talk about it later."

"I want it in the contract," he insisted and refused to look away when she narrowed her eyes at him.

"So anxious to be indebted again, Del?"

"I don't take charity."

She grimaced, dropping her gaze. "Fine, it'll be in the contract."

"Before I sign." He shoved the viewer across the counter at her.

She pressed her lips together and frowned at him but picked up the viewer. After tapping on it for a minute, she slid it back across the counter. He scanned it and shook his head, trying not to seem dismayed at the amount there. Griffin had exacted a heavy penalty. "There's no interest or time limit on this."

She folded her arms, expression chilly. "What's your point? It's in the contract."

He stared at her for a long moment, trying to find the flaw in this paradise they were offering him. Besides lusting after his boss. "What do you want from me? What's in this for you?"

"We want an excellent slicer pilot."

"There has to be more to it."

"There isn't." Her tone was serene, but her gaze dropped and she began assisting her brother again.

He thought about calling her on the lie, but he wanted what they were offering, wanted it so much he could taste it. He took a large swallow of the supernova before placing his thumb on the scanner, sealing the deal. Neither twin seemed to notice he'd just signed his life over to them.

"Mina, can you run the schedule by us now?" Sin asked, elbowing her brother away from the sautéing meat and sprinkling some kind of aromatic spice on it.

Del's stomach rumbled in response to the enticing smells rising from the cooking dish.

"You both have a conference call with the board at seven. It is scheduled for an hour, but you've blocked it off for two."

"It always runs over," Kai responded, pulling a steaming bowl of rice from the warmer.

"You have a meeting with the accountants at nine. The dignitaries from the Yakamoro Collective have confirmed their arrival for ten."

Both twins swore and looked at each other.

"Forgot they were coming," Sin sighed.

Kai grunted. "So who gets to play with them this time?"

"I made nice last time."

"You did not."

"Did so," Sin protested, facing her brother with hands on hips.

"Fine. Hand shuffle?"

"Go," Sin answered, holding out a hand. Kai placed his hand above hers and Del glanced between them with amused disbelief. Hand shuffle was a child's game, placing hands one on top of the other while reciting a nonsense rhyme. The last hand to shuffle to the top was the winner.

"Easy peasy, Yousy Mesy,

One by one they go on top,

Watch real close it's time to stop."

Kai's hand clapped over his sister's on the last word. He grinned in triumph and she groaned in mild despair.

Del snorted a laugh and tried to muffle it by ducking his head, shaking with suppressed humor. His attempt at discretion failed.

"He's laughing at us," Kai noted.

"So he is. What'd you do?"

"Why is it always my fault?"

"You gave him the supernova before dinner."

"So it's my fault he can't hold his liquor?"

Waving a hand, Del wheezed, "Stop." Taking a few deep breaths to control his chuckles, he stared from one to the other. "You two own a company rivaling the Core, you made Hec and his slicer groupies do flips without even trying, you throw around credit like it's water. And you're playing hand shuffle to decide your schedule?"

They stared at him with blank expressions before Kai leaned close to his sister and whispered, "Does he have a point?"

"Why are you asking me?" she whispered back.

Her brother gave a careless shrug and asked Del, "Do you have a point?"

"Do you make all your business decisions this way?"

The twins looked at each other. Then Sin turned a solemn face toward him and answered, "Well, no, sometimes we arm wrestle."

Then she winked at him and began dishing out food while he swallowed more chuckles. Sun's tears, these two were going to be the death of him. He swatted at Kai when the other man reached to steal his drink from him.

"No more supernovas for you, Giv," Kai scolded with a gleam in his eyes.

The twins sat on stools beside him instead of moving the meal to the dining table, and Del appreciated the gesture. The kitchen counter made the dinner less formal, allowing him to relax. It wasn't everyday life took such a radical turn.

They were silent for a few minutes as they ate, but then Sin paused to ask, "Mina, when's our next off-lane run?"

"In three days."

"Not very long to get you ready," she mused, eyeing Del. "I wish we had more time to let you get comfortable. You have a lot to learn between now and then. Unless you'd rather sit this one out?"

"You didn't hire me to sit. Besides, you don't have to teach me how to slice."

"I know you can slice, but Shadow ships take some getting used to." She said it as if it meant nothing, then slanted him a teasing glance.

68

His heart kicked. "I get to fly a Shadow?"

"Told you we needed to get you one," Kai said, still focused on his plate.

Del sat still for a long moment. A Shadow. He was going to fly a Shadow.

"But Shadow's aren't the only thing you need to learn. Our pilots are integral in the maintenance of our slicers and other vessels. It's important for you to be aware of every aspect of your ship."

"I always maintain my own slicer," he said, but she continued as if she hadn't heard.

"You also need to learn the ins and outs of the station, or at least the parts you'll be using. Plus you need to know who to go to in case something goes wrong, which it always does—" She cut herself off with a curse and shot a glance at her brother. "Spec. We still need to talk to him about the conveyors and clamps."

"No problem. After the board meeting, you soothe the accountants and I'll corral Spec. Then while you dance with the YC, I can show Del around. Deal?"

"Deal. Mina, I want some time off in the afternoon to spend with the crew."

"You have a meeting at three with the FPA, and you've slotted your clothing designer for five."

"Right, the dress for the luncheon. Send a message to Cale asking him to move it to four. We can swing the FPA out of here in an hour."

Del finished his meal and pushed the plate away with a sigh, wondering why they needed to talk to the FPA. Then he decided it wasn't something he should be wondering. "Thanks for dinner. Sure was a mean stir fry."

They gave him identical grins and spoke at the

same time. "Our pleasure," was Sin's reply and, "Told you," was Kai's.

"Do you cook for yourselves all the time?"

"Only on special occasions," Sin answered, but the teasing glimmer in her eye told him she was playing with him again.

Unable to resist, he gave her a half-smile and asked, "What's the occasion?"

"Losing my first slice."

Del shook his head and downed the rest of his drink. He'd gotten used to the burn, but it spread a pleasant lassitude along his muscles, and he wondered if he'd be able to stand without staggering.

"Another drink, Giv?" Kai asked as he stood and gathered plates. His tone was casual, but something in it made Del send him a sharp glance. Kai grinned and lifted a challenging eyebrow.

"I'll pass," he declined in a dry tone. "Don't wanna be dog-sick with a hangover on my first day at work."

"You're no fun," Kai said, putting the plates in the sanitizer.

"Ain't there some FPA regulation against getting your employees stinkin' drunk?"

"It's flexible. Special occasions don't count," Kai responded, and Sin gave a low laugh.

It sent a shiver along Del's spine and he watched her out of the corner of his eye with rising hunger. "Special or not, I should quit while I'm ahead and get to bed. Speaking of, where is my bed?"

Kai's head snapped around. Del didn't take his gaze off Sin.

"The pilot's quarters are two levels under this one. I'll show you—"

"I'll take him," Kai broke in. "I need to let Spec know I'll be taking his time tomorrow. The pilot's quarters are on my way."

Del rose to his feet, gratified when the room didn't slide out from under him.

Sin rose with him. "Get some rest while you can, tomorrow's going to be a big day. Kai will be by to get you midmorning."

They headed for the door, Kai trailing them.

"So what do I do for the first part of the morning?"

"Sleep, relax, settle in. Decorate." She flashed him a teasing grin.

His stomach muscles tightened and he let out a slow breath. Without knowing he was going to do it, he paused and took her hand in his. "Thank you."

She raised her eyebrows and her grin turned dry, but her fingers curled into his without hesitation. "For letting you sleep in?"

"No…well okay, yeah. But mostly for everything else."

Her smile softened and her eyes took on a luminous shimmer. His throat closed with the need to taste her again. "You're welcome."

Her soft skin tantalized his fingertips and he was just about to do something stupid when Kai put a hand on his shoulder, reminding him they weren't alone. Del met Kai's amused gaze with a dazed feeling like a dreamer waking from sleep.

"Our pleasure, Giv. We'll get use out of you, though. This won't be a sun cruise, I warn you." With a pointed look, he opened the door. "Now, let go of my sister and I'll show you your new place."

His cheekbones heating, Del released her hand. Her

bland smile said such things happened to her all the time. "G'night."

"Sleep well," she answered, giving them a little salute as the door closed between them.

Without further comment, Kai led the way through the entertainment suite and into the lift. "The pilot's quarters are two up from the slicer bay, one under our offices. The level under your quarters is for the support staff, offices, and living spaces."

Del nodded and wondered when Manakai was going to give him another warning to stay away from his sister, but the other man surprised him. They rode down to the pilot's level without a word.

"I'll introduce you to the rest of the crew tomorrow," Kai said, waving Del out of the lift. "I'm sorry for not doing it before, just bad timing. You shouldn't have any trouble with them tomorrow, though. They're a good group, and Pete hasn't been here long."

They started down a long hallway with doors on either side, each spaced far apart. "Does that happen a lot?"

"One of the crew taking a dive? No, we're selective when picking our pilots."

"About that," Del started, but Kai stopped at a door and gestured at the red keypad.

"It's keyed to your DNA. My sister and I have an override, but we use it only if there's an emergency."

Del touched the pad. It flickered from red to green and the door slid open without a sound. The lights came on as they entered. Del looked around at his new home with disbelieving eyes. It was sparsely furnished, but he'd never lived in such a large space. "You sure this is all mine?"

Kai chuckled. "The few things you had in your slicer are through this door, the bedroom. You can contact supply for anything else you need. We have most of the normal stuff on the station, clothes and whatnot. For anything more exotic, we can ship it here ourselves. We don't have a courier service for nothing." Kai flashed him a grin and headed back toward the door. "I'll see you in the morning."

Del remembered what he'd been about to ask before they'd entered his new place. "Wait."

Kai half turned and lifted inquiring eyebrows, the expression a spooky mirror of his sister's.

"You said you're selective about your pilots. You also said I'm not the only one with a bad past. A while ago I watched you turn in a drug runner. Why us? Why do you pick problem people over somebody with a clean record?"

Manakai studied him with cool eyes and said with a sudden grin, "You're more fun at parties." Then he left.

Del sighed. He shouldn't have expected anything else. Alone in this new world, he swayed as a sudden wave of weariness washed over him. He'd explore his new place tomorrow. Right now all he wanted was to fall face first into bed.

Stumbling into the next room, he paused to absorb the size of his new bedroom. With a shake of his head, he made a quick stop in the large bathroom before heading to the bed, tugging his clothes off as he went. Rolling into the soft cushion, which adjusted to his body weight, he groaned with relief. Sleep tackled him without warning.

Chapter 5

Sin shifted in her seat, and Kai's foot clipped her ankle again. She sent him a quick glare, but he seemed engrossed in the droning diatribe of one of the board members. She should be paying more attention, or at least faking it, but she'd had a long night. What little sleep she'd managed had been infected with painful dreams, most about her father.

The worst dream had been Ezekiel Shay speaking to her in a casual voice about inconsequential things, a new purchase he'd made for her dead mother and a different menu at his favorite restaurant. But his hands had been covered in clotted blood, and he kept trying to touch her with them. He seemed puzzled when she drew away, but continued speaking as though he couldn't hear her horrified pleas and accusations.

These dreams were a reaction to the day before, a response to her failure with Pete and to her success with Del. Rescuing Del from the Core would bring her father to mind. "Sins of our fathers," she sighed under her breath and shifted again.

She didn't need Kai's kick to her ankle to bring her attention back to the board this time. The silence was enough for her to raise her head. All the board members were staring at her from their holographic seats. None of the members resided on the Shay station.

One older man watched her with stiff disapproval.

He'd been with them since her father was alive and still sometimes saw them as the holy terrors who used to disrupt meetings to steal their father away. "Perhaps you could do me the courtesy of paying attention while I am speaking," he lectured.

She didn't allow herself to stiffen. He was a good man who served their company well, and she didn't need to take her sleepless night out on him. On the other hand, he couldn't be allowed to treat her as though she was a wayward child.

With a cutting stare and a faint smile, she responded, "Perhaps you could remember to whom you are speaking, Marcus."

He straightened even more and his lips thinned, though he dropped his gaze. "I cannot do this company any good if the information I have to impart is not heard."

Kai interrupted. "Marcus, you have something on your mind. You've been dancing around it for the past half hour. If you got to the point, my sister might be more inclined to listen."

It was a deft rebuke for them both. Sin shot her brother a wry smile, but he was focusing his solemn attention on Marcus Feeney. The older man shifted in obvious discomfort, still looking down.

"All right. As you may have heard"—he shot Sin a cool glance—"I was speaking of the galactic economy and our place in it. While Shay Enterprises is a powerful company, which has thus far rivaled any other such, there is a growing concern in myself, and other members of the board, that we will not be able to maintain our position for much longer."

He paused and shifted again, before lifting his

head, his expression set. "Quasicore continues to grow. Even now it has expanded into several different marketing areas and has infiltrated many powerful aspects of our society. Including the government." He hesitated, taking a quick look around at the other board members. *Don't do it Marcus,* she thought with a sinking feeling in her stomach, but he continued, "Even this board."

Sin kept her gaze on him but noted one member twitching out of the corner of her eye. She hoped the others hadn't seen it. The Core had weaseled two spies onto their board, but the twins found them more useful where they were. She didn't need them exposed.

"Marcus, I didn't know you were prone to paranoia," she said in a light tone.

"It's true. The Core is in this very room."

Kai leaned forward. Marcus fell silent at the dark frown on her brother's face. "It was unfairly said, Marcus. This company has stayed strong by believing in itself. Now your fellow members will be looking at one another with suspicion. Are you trying to sow dissent?"

The other board members stared at the older man with a measure of hostility. A lesser man would have folded, but Marcus had courage and years of experience with their father's trials by fire. He lifted his chin and met Kai's gaze with dignity. "You know it was not my intention. I have always had this company's best interest in mind."

Kai relented with a grim smile. "I do know it, old friend. I also know these are trying times, and the Core is like a shadow over everything we do. It's easy to jump at shadows."

Marcus' brow furrowed; he wasn't going to let it go. When he opened his mouth to speak, she interrupted, "Would it ease your mind if we promised the Core has not subverted our company?"

It wasn't a lie. Spies were only effective if the information they stole was accurate and complete. She and her brother had spoon-fed false information to the two Core spies since they'd arrived, watching their every movement with utmost care.

"It would, if it were true," Marcus answered, his brow still furrowed.

They needed to speak with him later, find out his source of information. He would not have raised the subject in a board meeting if he hadn't been certain, and they needed to make sure no one suspected the spies.

"Trust us, Marcus. We wouldn't lie to you of all people," she said, evoking the memory of her father. Marcus and her father had been good friends and Sin used it without a qualm.

Marcus subsided back into his chair with a nod of acceptance, his expression easing, but Sin knew he'd just postponed his concerns until they could speak in private.

"Wonderful," she declared with a brilliant smile, before turning to the rest of the board. "I believe we should conclude this meeting for today. We've run over. Again." She lifted a sardonic eyebrow.

Several members chuckled in response, both Core spies among them, probably in nervous relief.

"And our accountants are chomping at the bit to beat me over the head with my expense account." She grimaced, eliciting more laughter. "Thank you all for attending. Until next time."

Sin leaned forward and tapped the controls. The holograms blinked out of existence and she heaved a deep sigh.

"Feeling all right?" Kai asked. She gritted her teeth.

On any other day, he would scold her for being inattentive during a meeting. She didn't want his sympathy, though. She preferred to bicker with him; it would take her mind off those Sun-cursed dreams.

"You mean besides the toe-shaped dent in my ankle?" she snapped.

He flashed her an accommodating grin as he pushed back his chair and stood. "No more than you deserved, Sissa. You were wiggling like a closten eel over there."

"Better than snoring in their faces." She rose to her feet, joining him on the way through the glass partition of their office. "How long do you suppose before Marcus calls?"

"I'm betting any second now. Should we take it?"

"I want to know who tipped him off." Then she rubbed a weary hand around the back of her neck. "I don't think I'm sharp enough to dig at him today, though."

"I have time before I have to corner Spec."

A chime interrupted and the toneless voice of systems control announced, "Marcus Feeney is on private connection. Do you wish to receive?"

Sin exchanged a wry glance with her brother. "He's all yours," she told him and headed for the accounting department.

Her meeting with the accountants went well and faster than expected. She did a lot of nodding and agreeing. Placated, they let her go ahead of time, and she was able to spend a few moments in her quarters with a soothing cup of tea. It helped relax her but did little to alleviate her weariness.

"My kingdom for a nap," she sighed, sinking down into the inviting cushions of her sofa.

"You do not have to give the Yakamoro Collective the tour of the station. You can send someone else," Mina suggested.

"We can't woo a merger from them by sending a lackey to herd them around. Are they here yet?"

"Their ship is docking as we speak, or I might have suggested you postpone the meeting."

"Do I look so bad?"

"You look lovely, as usual. But you had a difficult night's sleep."

Sin frowned at one of Mina's hidden sensors. "Privacy. You aren't supposed to be watching me sleep."

"I wasn't. You weren't sleeping."

"You know what I mean."

"Yes I do. But you had a difficult day yesterday and I was concerned for you."

"Thank you, Mina," Sin sighed, setting her cup down. "I appreciate your concern, but it's a breach of protocol. What if I'd had someone in there with me?"

The AI gave an uncharacteristic snort. "How was I to miss someone passing through these quarters to your room?" Her melodious voice took on a sweetly sarcastic tone. "But you do have a point. Perhaps we should go over the precepts of privacy, since it has been so long since you've had someone in there with you."

"Low blow, Mina," Sin protested and stood,

propping fists on hips and frowning at the nearest sensor.

"Does this mean you are awake enough to deal with the Collective?"

"This means you and I are going to have a long talk when I return," she admonished, stalking toward the door.

"I look forward to it."

Sin echoed the AI's earlier snort and left.

The Yakamoro Collective had gathered in the spacious and ornate reception area, attended to with dignified efficiency by several members of the Shay staff. The group of a dozen men and women stood wide-eyed and quiet with provincial awe.

The Shay service and elegance had impressed more powerful people than these, Sin reflected with wry amusement. The acquisition of the Collective's holdings would be more of a take-over than a merger. Most other large companies would have run roughshod over them, but the Shays believed in preserving the dignity of the people they worked with. It made future relations with them more amenable, and the respect they gained only helped with further acquisitions. It had been their father's vision, one neither Sin nor Kai could argue with.

Sin took the opportunity to greet each person. She had memorized the names and faces of the visiting members of the Collective and what each did for the company. Greeting them on a personal level helped decrease any hostility they may be feeling toward the merger and Shay Enterprises.

Sin followed the greetings with a tour of the Shay Station. She was careful to keep them out of more sensitive areas like Research and Development while still giving them the impression of being allowed deep into the workings of the company. She left the courier section to last.

The armada of Last Chance's courier ships impressed the Collective, and many exclaimed at the wide variety of slicers in the docking bay. She consented to their requests of a closer look at the Shadow ships with a smile, directing the floater holding them toward the maintenance bay.

Her crew was hard at work on several slicers, doing the more delicate maintenance themselves rather than let the automated systems handle it. She smiled when several heads popped out from between slicers to grin at her. Knowing better than to interrupt a business tour, they continued their work as she moved along the double row of slicers with the Collective in tow.

A new Shadow stood in the line, both Del and Kai were working on it. Her heart gave an extra thump when Del looked up, his dark eyes vibrant and his expression unreadable.

Sin pulled her gaze away and looked to her brother. Kai lifted his eyebrows in question and she gave him a slight nod in response. One advantage of being a twin, knowing each other so well it was like mind-reading. Kai would now be preparing to take over for her with the Collective, at least for the Shadow demonstration.

She was in the middle of describing the characteristics of their prized Shadow slicers when a member of the Collective interrupted her with one of the questions she'd been expecting.

"Ms. Shay, is it true you are a slicer pilot yourself?"

Sin smiled at the portly gentleman and did him the courtesy of not pointing out the obvious data port behind her ear. "Yes, it's true. Our father wanted Kai and I to be well versed in every aspect of our company. A great excuse for a hobby, don't you think?" She flashed them a mischievous smile and received a smattering of chuckles in return.

A young woman stepped forward, her features set. "We have also heard you fly the off-lanes yourself. Wouldn't slicing be more than a hobby for you?"

"I have an efficient, competent crew of slicer pilots to make the off-lane courier runs, Diana." The young woman flinched at Sin's gentle tone and the use of her first name. "My brother and I travel with them when we head out on business trips to destinations along their path. Flying with experts helps to sharpen our piloting skills."

Someone choked in between the slicers, but Sin kept a serene expression on her face and her eyes locked on the young member. In retrospect, she should have invited these questions somewhere else.

"But isn't it true you haven't lost a slice?"

A subtler question than the last one; Sin had never flown in a legitimate slicing circuit, so this woman was accusing her of illegal racing and implying Sin was a better pilot than she claimed. In other words, the Collective had heard rumors and were fishing for answers.

Sin allowed a hint of a smile to brighten her bland expression. "I'm flattered, but it's not true. We've never flown the professional circuits. When slicing on our training grounds, though, I win more often than not." She raised her voice and finished with, "Right, brother?" without breaking eye contact with the young woman.

"In your dreams, sister," was Kai's mild response as he stepped out from between slicers. He rolled down the sleeves of his shirt and shrugged into his dress jacket, strolling over to stand next to Sin. "Don't let her lead you astray, ladies and gentlemen of the Collective. I let her win."

Sin lifted an eyebrow, meeting her brother's teasing smile while the group chuckled. "Marcus?" she asked low enough not to be overheard.

"Anonymous tip," he answered.

"How convenient."

He gave her a little grimace of acknowledgement before turning his attention to the group. "I'm sure you're all anxious to take a closer look at our most prized slicer, the Shadow. We have one here you may inspect to your hearts' content," Kai said. "Just no drooling please. It shorts the circuits."

They laughed and followed him to the ship at the end of the row. Sin let them pass before heading to the Shadow Del and Kai had been working on. Del was studying her, leaning against the ship. She tried not to watch the muscles in his forearms flex as he wiped his hands on a sani-cloth.

"Del."

"Sin. Your tourists seem awful curious."

"So they do."

"You're a pretty liar."

She let a cool smile appear. "How has your first day been?"

He took the change in subject with only a wry curl at the corner of his mouth. "So far so good."

"You've met the rest of the crew?"

"An interesting bunch," he commented and his smile grew, becoming almost teasing.

Sin had trouble fighting off the effects of his dark gaze and the enticing humor flirting with his features. "I see you have your Shadow. Flown her yet?"

"No, just finishing a refit on her to my specs. I'll have the afternoon to try her out." His tone was casual, but his eyes gleamed with an excitement he couldn't conceal.

She gave him a knowing smirk. "Think it'll be enough time?"

"Probably not," he snorted, turning his head to look at the slicer in admiration. "You do make a flare of a ship."

"We like to think so," she responded, letting her own gaze travel over the Shadow.

They'd done some lightening of the interior and had refitted the inside to accommodate Del's larger frame. She had a sudden urge to ditch the rest of her afternoon responsibilities to be there for his first flight. Her own first moments in a Shadow were a vivid memory, and she wanted to share the experience with him. But shirking responsibility was not in her nature. *My father didn't raise either of his children to abandon duty,* she thought with a hint of bitterness, and not a little sadness.

"Hey," Del rumbled, catching her attention. A faint frown creased his brow, his dark eyes intent. "You okay?" He raised a hand and brushed a strand of hair away from her face.

Her skin tingled at the whisper of his touch against her temple and cheekbone. She had to break eye contact and clear her throat before she could answer. "I'm fine. Why?"

"You look unhappy," he answered, voice dropping to a low intimacy, spreading insidious warmth along her limbs. He raised his hand again, brushing a thumb across the tender skin under her eye. "And a little tired."

The gentle touch brought her startled eyes back to his, captured in his dark gaze. His hand lingered, fingers settling in a fan from her temple to the edge of her jaw. His thumb made another slow pass along her skin while Sin fought with herself. She knew what she should be doing: stepping away, turning cool, and reminding them both of their places in this world. But his touch was warm, his eyes warmer, and she yearned for his warmth like a woman lost on an ice world.

"Didn't sleep well," she managed to whisper. "Bad dreams."

His hand drifted down until it cupped her jaw and his thumb caressed her cheek with mesmerizing leisure. "About what?"

Father. The thought was a dash of ice water on her soul. She took a step backward out of his reach before turning away. "Nothing important," she said with chill calm. "Enjoy your flight."

He said nothing as she walked out from between the Shadows. Laughter came from the Collective and she allowed a grim smile. Kai had them in the palm of his hand and didn't need her yet.

Sin caught sight of Bib waving to her from the opposite row and her smile softened into greeting. She hadn't seen any of the crew after the Pete fiasco. She had a little time to spend with them before she escorted the Collective to their offices for merger finalization. Sin crossed the gap to the other row and the girl waiting for her.

Chapter 6

Touching her had been a mistake. Del knew it before he'd done it, but he couldn't seem to help himself. There'd been a shadow under her eyes and a downward curl to those luscious lips, an irresistible call. She'd stood motionless under his touch, eyes wide with echoes of vulnerability, making him ache to wrap his arms around her. Her skin was cool silk under his fingers and the green pools of her eyes threatened to drown him. The powerful pull of this woman scared him witless. Especially when she could turn to ice and walk away as though he'd ceased to exist.

Del watched Sin hug one of the crew and fought for control. He'd done his best this morning to concentrate on the job at hand and not think about her at all, succeeding with the help of his new Shadow until she'd appeared with her herd of sheep. She was all cool businesswoman today in a sharp gray pantsuit showing a tantalizing hint of cleavage, charm and power wrapped around her like a shield. She'd brushed off her herd's questions like bothersome insects, handing them to her brother with effortless ease, then tortured him with her attention. Unfair, her and her bad dreams.

A sprinkle of laughter came from the Collective, reminding Del of another of his dilemmas. She'd lied to them. Why did she and her brother not want these people to know they did their own off-lane runs? What did they do on these runs? What kind of cargo did they carry? Whatever the cargo, they were well-equipped to protect it. Del ran a thoughtful hand over the weapons array of his Shadow and, for the thousandth time, wondered what he'd gotten himself into.

"Hey, Del," a voice said behind him, making him jump. It was Bibliona Wills, the youngest member of the off-lane crew, draped against the side of the Shadow. She looked like an angel, her golden curls pulled back and enormous blue eyes set in a round face. She eyed him up and down with a jaded appreciation far too old for her age, and far from angelic. She was almost young enough to be his daughter. Del remembered Kai's warning before he'd introduced her, "Bib's friendly. Don't get involved with her or I'll break your legs."

"We didn't get a chance to talk earlier. Manny's such a slave driver," she sighed. Her tone when she talked about Kai held an undercurrent of possessiveness. Del wondered if Kai's warning had been territorial, then remembered the way Kai had treated the girl, with bland affection and gentle detachment.

"Better than no job at all," Del answered.

"Oh sure," she said with an airy wave of one hand. "Best job I ever had. I was just kidding about slave driving. Manny and Sinsi are my favorite people, and not just because they're my bosses." Her little bow of a mouth curled in a cynical way he didn't much like. "From what I saw, Sinsi's one of your favorite people, too."

Del looked away from the uncomfortable knowledge in her eyes. "She and her brother got me out of a bad situation."

"Well, no kidding," she drawled. "You wouldn't be here if they hadn't."

Del frowned at her. "What do you mean?"

"Our bad situations are the reason they picked us. We're all good slicer pilots, but the Shays have enough credit to buy the best there is, as bright and squeaky clean as the newest sun." She cocked her head to one side and studied him. "I'll bet all my next pay receipt your problem was with the Core."

"Good guess."

"No, it wasn't," she snickered, blue eyes twinkling. "All us off-laners had the same problem. So what's your story?"

He blinked at her. "You tellin' me every one of this crew was Core?"

"Well, kind of. I used to be a bed partner for slicer jockeys on the Servo Circuit. The law didn't know about it, a'course. To them, I was part of the cleaning and service staff. But the owner of the place had all us girls and boys running special services. She was Core-owned."

She talked about being a prostitute as matter-of-factly as if she were discussing shoes. Del had the horrifying impression she'd been doing those services for a long time before the Shays came along, which made him wonder how old she'd been when she started.

"So you learned how to slice from pilots you…?" he trailed off, not knowing how to end the sentence in a nice way.

"Serviced?" she finished for him with a hard grin. "Yup. All most of 'em wanted to talk about after was slicing, so I got some to teach me." She shrugged. "It was something to do."

"You couldn't get out of it and join the circuit?"

She snorted and passed a look of contempt over him. "Could you?"

He had to admit she had him there. If the Core had owned the place where she worked, then they'd had claws into everybody, like the ones they'd dug into him. It was just the way Quasicore did business.

"So the Shays got you out?"

"They bought me," she responded with horrifying simplicity.

A shudder ran down his spine. He wished she didn't make it sound so much like slavery. "Why would they get people like us if they can have the best?"

"I don't know," she said and shrugged again. "I guess they're trying to make up for what the Core did to us."

Del frowned. He couldn't picture the twins as benevolent humanitarians, zipping around the galaxy saving lives. "Why? What's in it for them?"

She smirked at him. "Why do you care why? You're clear of the Core, ain't you?"

He shifted to a more comfortable position inside the Shadow, studying her. "You don't know or you don't want to tell me?"

She watched his muscles move with bright appreciation before meeting his gaze, a sultry look in her blue eyes. "Big Del, I'll tell you anything you want."

He gritted his teeth and tried not to squirm. With grim resolve, he kept eye contact. "Then tell me what you know about them."

"Sure," she exclaimed with a bright smile, and

settled against the Shadow with an arm above her head, revealing an expanse of skin at her waist. It also brought her close enough to reach out and run a light hand down his arm. "Jinx used to be a slicer pilot for the Core's courier service, except they always had him running bad stuff. He did it because they kept him hooked on blue. To a junkie, nothing's better than a free fix."

Del shifted out of her reach. "I was talking about the Shays."

"Cassie—you met Cassie, right? The Core framed her for murder. They told her to build some high tech weapon, or something, and she told them no way. They killed her research partner, making it look like she did it. They had all the proof, too, and she didn't have scrap."

"Bib," he tried to stop her, but she continued to talk over him.

"Lynch now, he's been here longer than anybody, since Father Shay's time. Zeke Shay was the one who brought him here. Poor Lynch used to run a slaughter pit—"

"All right, chatterbox," a gruff voice cut her off.

She spun on cat-quick feet, a bright smile on her face. "Big Lynch!"

"Little Bib," the large man rumbled, a frown pulling his heavy brow over deep-set eyes. "You goin' on about things that ain't your business again?"

She set a small, placating hand on his folded arms, and looked at him with guileless blue eyes. "Just telling Del what he wanted to know."

Del grimaced at the blame landing on his shoulders. "What I asked was what the Shays get out of saving us Core rejects."

Lynch turned his heavy-browed glower on Del. "They saved you because Ezekiel Shay raised his kids to know what's right and what's wrong. They're about as different from Quasicore as a star is to a black hole. Just thank whatever star knows your name they chose you, and do your job." The large man grasped Bib by the elbow to lead her away.

She went without protest, still smiling at Lynch as though she'd forgotten Del existed. He shook his head. His relationship with the crew was not starting well.

Kai came around the end of the row of ships, his glance going from the receding pair to Del, wry humor dancing across his features. He stripped off his jacket with impatient movements. "Bib misbehaving again?"

"You could've warned me," Del muttered with a baleful stare at the mercurial twin.

Kai snickered. "I did."

"That's what you call friendly?"

"Think I should have said *very*?" Kai asked, shooting him a grin as he rolled up his sleeves. "She acts the same way with everyone. She has a very needy nature. Fallout from her childhood."

"She doesn't look like she's out of childhood yet."

Kai's expression turned solemn. "She stopped being a child a long time ago."

After the story she'd told, Del wouldn't doubt it.

Without another word, he and Kai went back to work refitting the Shadow. It didn't take much longer to finish. Less than an hour later, Del was running the final diagnostics on the systems while Kai watched over his shoulder.

"Good," Kai said as the results came in. "It could

use a tweak or two, but it's close enough to get you into vacuum. Out you get, Giv."

To Del, the diagnostic results were as close to perfect as he'd ever seen, but he didn't argue. The time he'd spent working with Kai taught him the other man knew more about slicers than anyone he'd ever met. If Kai was willing to show him later what he meant by tweaking, Del was willing to wait, especially if he got to fly her now.

Levering himself out of the Shadow, he followed the other man out from between the slicers.

"Hey, Cass!" Kai hollered down the row, and the little woman poked her head out from under a ship. Kai waved her over. While she wiggled out from under her vessel, he continued in a lower voice to Del, "Cassie's going to be your slicing partner for the next couple of days. She's the best technician we have, and if your new ship is going to have problems, she'd be the first to spot them."

Del nodded, watching the woman approach. She had long, dark brown hair plaited down her back and warm, brown eyes. Her face held a delicate beauty and the rest of her was just as fine-boned. She looked as though he could snap her in half, but a leashed energy in her movements suggested it wouldn't be so easy.

"What do you need, Kai?" she asked in a quiet, reserved tone, a striking contrast to her strident argument with Pete the night before.

"Del's taking the new Shadow out and I need you to partner him. You up for it?"

"Not a problem. It'll give me a break from rerouting circuits." She gave Del a nod and faint smile.

"Cassie's our resident genius," Kai said with a

teasing grin. "If she can't fine-tune your Shadow to match you, no one can."

"Cut it out, Kai." She frowned at him. "You make me sound like a geek."

"You are a geek, Cass," he said with exaggerated patience then gave a low laugh when she curled her lip in a menacing snarl. "You two have fun out there now." He clapped Del on the shoulder and tugged on Cassie's braid before striding away.

Cassie caught Del's gaze and rolled her eyes. "The man's a menace."

"Tell me about it," Del muttered, thinking of Kai's quicksilver changes of mood from dangerous to playful.

At his answer, her lips compressed in a smothered smile and her eyes twinkled, but she didn't comment. "Well, let's get this show on the road." Raising her voice, she said, "Control!"

"Cassiopeia Draegen," a toneless, echoing voice answered.

She winced, darting a glower along the row of slicers when someone guffawed. "I have to get the thing to stop using my full name. Control, lift number ten to the docking bay, please."

"Acknowledged," the mechanical voice responded. A large, crane-like arm swung over their heads, stopping above Del's Shadow.

Cassie moved toward the door leading to the docking bay. Del followed on reluctant feet, watching over his shoulder as the arm unfolded large clamps to grasp his Shadow. Hadn't the twins said something about the conveyors and clamps malfunctioning? He hoped Kai had worked it out with Spec.

"You look as nervous as a new father," Cassie said,

watching him with amusement in her brown eyes.

Del scowled down at her, annoyed he'd been so obvious. "So you're named after a constellation, huh?"

She grimaced. "Touché. I'll be taking you out to the training area. It has sections both in and out of the atmosphere of the gas giant we're circling. The planet provides ideal conditions to test and stress the machines to their maximum."

"Sounds like fun."

"Doesn't it, though?" She grinned up at him. "Excited about your first Shadow flight?"

"Well, I don't think it'll be boring," he said, trying to spot his new ship out of the corner of his eye without giving himself away as they passed into the docking bay.

Cassie chuckled, leading him to an empty docking pad. She pointed out the Shadow ship when it came out of the maintenance bay. The conveyers seemed to be transporting it with effortless ease and he breathed a sigh of relief.

The arm twisted the Shadow into place and lowered it to the pad without a bump. The clamps released and the arm swung away as Cassie said, "Thanks, Control."

Del checked the skin for marks from the clamps before opening the slicer and sliding in. The conveyer had been as gentle as if the ship were a newborn. He couldn't find a scratch on her.

Cassie leaned in while he went through start-up, her expression one of sharp, clinical interest. She tilted her head in a listening posture when the Shadow came to life and then gave him a quick nod of satisfaction. "Sounds good."

He had to agree. The powerful hum of the ship vibrated under his skin like a call to freedom, sweet and wild.

"All right, try the port."

He was reluctant to merge with the Shadow for the first time in front of an audience but understood why she wanted to be there. If something went wrong, he might not be able to remove the connector himself.

When Del slid the connector into his data port, he forgot to breathe at the rush of sensation and information. The ship wrapped herself around him like silk, every powerful drive and vulnerable circuit becoming as familiar to him as his own skin. He explored her with as much reverence as a worshiper entering a goddess' domain, amazed by the sensitivity of the controls and the sheer beauty of her construction.

"Del? How does she feel?"

He opened his eyes. Cassie was frowning at him and dark spots swarmed in his vision. Remembering to breathe, he took a deep inhale. "Like a dream," he rasped, unable to hide his reactions with the Shadow still within him.

Her frown changed to a knowing grin and she patted him on the shoulder. "Just don't let her walk all over you, Del. These Shadows can be capricious."

Nodding and taking another deep breath, he tried to get past his awe and look at the ship's functions with a clinical eye. Cassie helped by asking him technical questions about the different systems and how they responded to him.

After a few minutes, she gave him a sharp nod of approval. "Okay, we're ready. Wait until I'm up, then follow me out."

She ducked out of the slicer and moved down the row of docking pads. Del sealed himself in and commanded the slicer to lift off the pad. The Shadow was moving almost before he'd finished the command and he grinned with delight. This was going to be the ride of his life. His heart rate accelerated with excitement.

Cassie's Shadow lifted off its berth and he turned his slicer to follow her out of the docking bay, exclaiming under his breath at the effortless response from the ship. The difference between this vessel and any other slicer he'd flown was like the difference between a nutrient drink and a seven-course meal.

Cassie led him beyond the station's traffic range, cruising over the swirling fury of the gas giant. "Okay Del, before we put her through maneuvers, I need you to break out her max velocity. So we're going to leave the solar system, turn around, and head back. Clear?"

"Clear," he said, trying to hide his eagerness.

"On three. One, two, three."

The force of acceleration shoved Del into the pilot's seat. Power ran through him in a steady roar, lighting up every nerve ending. It was like being at the center and in control of a nova. Planets and space debris flashed by in brief blips of color. He clenched his teeth to hold in wild laughter.

When he slowed the ship to a stop at the coordinates Cassie had sent, he was panting like a sprinter. "Sun's blood!" he gasped.

Cassie chuckled in his ear. "Yeah I know. Almost better than sex. I don't suppose you noticed how she handled the speed?"

"Uh…" was his creative answer.

"Okay, on the way back, pay attention to nuances, shifts in the drive or hiccups in the circuits. Even subtle glitches like optic fade or sensory slurring are important."

Her dry, clinical tone helped focus his mind. He braced himself to ignore the experience of the return trip and pay attention to the system's functions. It wasn't easy, but when they stopped above the gas giant he could say with confidence the Shadow ran well. If Cassie heard the thrill in his voice, she was polite enough not to mention it.

She led him to an area marked off by locator beacons. The area held an obstacle course, different objects set up to challenge the Shadow's maneuverability. Cassie sent him the specs on the course and he raised his eyebrows.

"Do I get a last request?" he asked.

"What good is a training course if it doesn't test the limits of ship and pilot?"

"I knew this job was too good to be true," he sighed, eyeing the course with an eager grin.

"Oh, give over, Del. You're dying to get in there. Admit it."

"Admit I'm suicidal? I don't think so," he retorted, moving into position next to her at the start of the course.

"We'll go slow the first time," she said, her voice taking on a brisk tone, her way of getting down to business. "Pay close attention to the inertial dampeners and maneuvering thrusters. Keep me informed the whole way."

"Understood," he replied, settling into the cold focus he needed to concentrate on a complicated run.

"On three," she said again and muffled amusement swam under his icy concentration. He suspected Cassie had never been in a real slice.

At her signal, they began the course, moving at a sedate pace. It frustrated him not to unleash the power in the ship, to free the wild delight straining his control. He wasn't sure if the eagerness was his own or the ship's.

Cassie's specific, technical questions helped him contain his energy and focus a detached concentration on the ship's systems, while they went through the different maneuvers of the course. They traversed the difficult course several times, each time at a faster speed, and each time Cassie asked her questions. Finally, she brought them back to the head of the course and gave him his freedom.

"Last time through," she said as they lined up at the starting point. "This time I want you to go at the fastest pace you can. I'll watch from a distance and see if I can pinpoint any problems. We may see more from her than she's shown so far. Keep an eye on the systems I've talked about and let me know if you see anything."

"Will do," he responded, trying to keep the grin out of his voice. At last he could push the ship to her limits.

"Let me get in position," she requested. He sensed her ship leaving his side, maneuvering to a spot with a clear view of the whole course. "All right, any time you're ready."

Del didn't bother answering. He shot into the course, whipping his Shadow through the obstacles with reckless speed. The ship responded to him as sweetly as he could have wished, spinning vibrant threads of pleasure through his body as they dodged, twisted, and roared through the course. He was right, flying a Shadow was as much profound ecstasy as touching a goddess. The end of the run came too soon and he spun the ship back into the course, unwilling to let the moment go.

"Del?" Cassie asked with amusement.

"In a minute," he rasped, letting the power and fantastic suppleness of the ship soak into him. The smooth, effortless response made him feel invincible. Only in his dreams had he found such ecstasy, dreams of green eyes and a luscious mouth.

He gasped and wrenched out of the course. Swearing under his breath, he coasted to a halt, heated foolishness burning under his skin. He hadn't let his concentration break so bad since he'd been a teenager. But when the dream he'd had of Sin snuck up on him, the sensations of the ship took a more lustful turn than he could handle.

"Del, are you all right?" Cassie asked, her ship drawing alongside him. "What happened? I didn't detect any system failures."

"I'm fine," he responded, feeling even more foolish. "Just got distracted."

"Well, stop it," she snapped. "You scared the crap out of me."

"Sorry. Next time I'll warn you when I plan on losing concentration."

"You know, I can recognize sarcasm when I hear it, you big oaf," she grumbled, but relief laced her tone and he grimaced in remorse. "You two did make a nice couple while it lasted. I caught a few minor hesitations, only visible on the sensors, but other than those she was smooth. Did you detect anything?"

Grateful for the change in subject, he went into detail for her, going over each system as he remembered them. She was very thorough, analyzing his every observation with as much clinical interest as a doctor. But he couldn't tell if she was satisfied with his answers or not. At the end of each string of questions, she would make a noncommittal sound before moving on to the next system.

At last, she announced they were ready to stress the ship in the gas giant's atmosphere. They dipped below the course and dove into the swirling mists of the upper atmosphere. Visibility dropped and the sensor readings shrank to the surrounding area only. Invisible forces jerked and smashed at their ships. This was something new for Del. He'd never flown a slicer in such a miserable environment. Out of the dense clouds, the sudden appearance of another training course surprised him.

"You're kidding."

Cassie chuckled. "Nope. This one takes you farther into the atmosphere before bringing you back up. No better way to stress a ship than gravity. I'll send you the specs so you know what you're getting into."

The specs showed a less complicated course, not much comfort when the swirling pockets of gas battered his Shadow. "And me without a will."

Cassie laughed and aligned her ship with his at the start of the course. "Just think of it as a challenge."

"That's what they always say about death."

"You're a tough guy. You can handle it. Just don't get distracted this time."

He snorted. "On three?"

"Don't mock me or I'll keep you out here past

dinner time."

"You're a heartless woman, Cass."

"Don't you forget it. Ready?"

"Let's do it."

Del had no idea how long they ran the cloud course. Time seemed to stop inside the giant's atmosphere, enveloping him in a pocket of never-ending challenges. His eyes burned with useless straining to see through the thick mists, his neck muscles on fire with tension, and his reflexes were on the verge of failing by the time Cassie called a halt.

"We'll have to cut this short. I'm getting a signal from the station. Someone's trying to contact us."

Del shook his head in dismay. How much longer had she planned on keeping him out here? "Not dinner time yet?" he tried to tease, but his voice was hoarse.

"Sun's sake, Del, if you needed a break, all you had to do was ask," she exclaimed. "Come on. The atmosphere blocks most transmissions, so we have to get above it."

Del sighed in relief when he broke out of the swirling mists and into the steady emptiness of space, a sweet and blissful peace after the angry battering of the atmosphere.

"Cassie here," she said in her usual brisk tone. "You rang, station?"

"Hey, Cass," Kai's voice answered. "Get your cute bottom back here and pour me a drink."

"Party's on, then?"

"Already started. Any luck out there?"

"A couple issues. One of the exchangers has a pin leak and the aft injector's baseline is off by a few microns. She's also slushy in a one-eighty twisting roll to starboard."

This was news to Del. As far as he knew, his Shadow had performed above all expectations, but he kept his mouth shut. He wasn't familiar with Shadows and Cassie had shown an incredible amount of technical knowledge during their flights.

"Stabilizer alignment?"

"Probably. I'll run a diagnostic on her to be sure."

"Tomorrow."

"No argument," she replied, heading toward the station.

Del caught up with her, waiting to be sure Kai was through before asking, "Party?"

"When the bosses have been gone for a while, we have a welcome home party for them."

"They've been gone a while?"

"It took them almost a week to find you."

"A week," Del mused, thinking back. They'd been looking for him before he'd started running from the Core. How had they known he would head for the Fringe and Hector's slices? Was it luck or had they followed him out there? If they'd tracked him, then the Core could have done the same, but Trev and Brax would have been on him before the Shays. Unless the Core allowed the Shays to pick him up, but wouldn't this mean they were working together?

Del pressed fingers to aching temples. He was weary, both in mind and body. He needed rest before he could figure out what this news meant, if anything.

"I'm glad they came back when they did, though," Cassie added, reminding Del of the drama the night before.

"Did you know Pete well?"

"Well enough. He put on a good show for the Shays, but I think he was a plant. Not a very bright one, though. You'd think the Core would pick a spy with more brains." Her voice was acid enough to burn, and Del wondered what she thought of him. As far as he knew, the crew didn't know his background. Even if she was right about Pete being a spy, her paranoia might turn toward him.

Remembering what Bib had said about Cassie's past, about how the Core had framed her for murder, Del kept silent. If the story was true, she had plenty of reasons to hate and suspect them. His own experiences hadn't taught him any different.

They entered the docking bay and landed without further conversation. Del wouldn't have believed it possible, but he was relieved to disconnect from the Shadow. He couldn't remember ever feeling this tired after slicing.

Cassie studied him after she exited her own slicer. "I need a san. How 'bout you?"

At least she wasn't telling him outright he was sweaty and stunk. With a wry curl of his mouth, he answered, "Could use one."

She gave him a little grin before glancing past him and grabbing his arm, tugging him away from the landing pads. He looked over his shoulder then ducked when the conveyor arm swung past his head to clamp onto his Shadow.

"Sorry, I forgot to tell you I'd asked Control to take her in," she winced as he hustled out of the way.

"Just don't drop her, Control," he said for Cassie's benefit then jumped when a voice answered.

"Acknowledged, Adelmo Givliani."

Cassie snickered and tugged on his arm again. "Come on, let's get cleaned up. They'll be way ahead of us by now."

He always seemed to be a source of amusement for her. Irritated, he muttered, "And you've got a drink to pour?" as they moved toward the maintenance bay.

She narrowed her eyes. "Don't you take that tone with me, Givliani. Kai and I are just friends. Don't get me wrong, he's gorgeous, but he's also a pain in the rear. Besides, he's my boss." She sent him a pointed look and he wondered if she'd seen him with Sin earlier.

"Pain in the rear, huh?" he asked to lead the conversation away.

"If you don't know it by now, you'll find out soon enough." Her eyes brightened, a teasing smile bringing out a dimple in her right cheek. "Has he given you the stay-away-from-my-sister speech yet?"

The woman was smarter than was healthy. Or she could read minds. He scowled at her. "It was more like broken birds and Shays don't mix."

Her smile faded and she nodded. "Another reason Kai and I will stay friends and nothing more. I think it's his way of protecting himself."

"Protecting himself? From what?"

She gave him a cool, searching look as they crossed the maintenance bay to the door leading to the lift. "You're the same way. Connecting with people leaves you vulnerable to hurt."

Del glowered down at her. "Do you psychoanalyze everybody you meet?"

She made a face and brushed a hand across her forehead, looking away while they stepped aboard the lift. "Sorry. Reflex."

Reflex? Del studied the little woman with sudden wariness, but she kept her face turned away. The lift doors opened on the pilot's level and she stepped out at once.

"See you back here in fifteen? They're up in the Gold Rooms in case we miss each other."

"Gold Rooms?"

"The suites outside Sin's place. Do you know which level it is?"

He nodded. She strode at a brisk pace up the corridor, pausing at a door several down from his and disappearing inside. He entered his own place, amazed again at the size. Shaking his head, he moved through the suite to the lavatory. Its size was ridiculous and Del grumbled to himself about wasted space while he undressed and stepped into the body sanitizer.

Moments later he stepped back out, feeling energized, his skin tingling. Moving into the bedroom, he found a clean shirt and slacks, pulling them on with swift efficiency. He was striding to the front door when he realized he'd been rushing. Coming to an abrupt stop, he clenched his hands into fists and swore. He must be a glutton for punishment, charging up there to see her.

Chapter 7

Del turned away from the exit with a grim flex of his jaw and sat in the living room, activating the large viewer covering most of the wall. It flickered to life with a settings menu. He clicked one titled *Voice Response Activation* then twitched when a toneless voice said, "Welcome and thank you for activating the Voice Response System. Would you prefer your VRS to be male or female?"

"Uh, female," he answered. He'd thought the setting meant activating the viewer by voice command. He hadn't expected the walls to start talking to him.

"Your choice has been recorded," a woman said, in a voice similar to Mina's. "Would you care to change the default settings on your living quarters?"

"Um, such as?"

"You may change the temperature, the light settings, the humidity levels—"

"No, it's all fine," he cut her off, rubbing the back of his neck.

"Do you require a massage?"

"What?"

"Humans often massage their muscles, as you have done, when they are tense or sore. You are unable to administer a proper massage to yourself. Do you require a massage?"

"You can see me," he realized, an ominous feeling

in the pit of his stomach. They were watching him.

"I have sensors monitoring these quarters."

Only an AI would use the pronoun *I*. Paranoia crept over him. The only people he knew who had AI units in their homes were way above his class level, with very good connections.

"Why are you here?" he asked.

"To provide you with comfort and convenience. I am also programmed to assist you with your schedule and finances, and can provide you with—"

"No, I mean why do I get an AI?"

"Because you are a pilot in the employment of Shay Enterprises."

"The other pilots have AIs?"

"That is correct."

"So they watch us all?"

"No other AIs have access to your quarters."

"I mean the Shays. You're recording my every move for them, aren't you?"

"No information has yet been recorded, except your choice of VRS voice and your decision not to change the default settings on your quarters."

He blinked at the viewer. "Can they see in here or not?"

"These have been designated private quarters. You have not yet authorized any transfer of information from my systems. As a default setting, I am allowed to notify those requesting entrance to your quarters of your presence or absence. Would you like to change this setting?"

He rubbed his forehead. "So if the Shay's try to get info on me from you, you can't give it?"

"Not without your authorization."

"Oh." They hadn't set a babysitter on him after all. He ran a hand over his short dark hair and wished for a strong drink.

"Would you like me to change the setting for those requesting entrance?"

"No, just leave it." He sat for a minute, wondering if he should shut the thing off. He'd never lived with an AI before and the idea was intimidating. He'd chosen a female voice, too. Undressing was going to get a little uncomfortable. "So what's your name?"

"You have not yet given me a name."

"Well, what names have other people given you?"

"There have been no other people."

Del stared at the viewer. "You're that new?"

"I am newly installed, yes." Before he could think of a response, she continued, "You have a visitor."

A gentle chime at the door sounded and Del rose to answer it. Cassie smiled at him when he opened the door. She'd unplaited her hair. It was an astonishing wavy length of a variety of browns, with hints of gold and red. She'd changed out of her coveralls into casual slacks and a sleeveless top, looking much more relaxed.

"Ready to go?" she asked with a tilt of her head.

Del glanced over his shoulder, thinking of the brand new AI system he'd activated by accident. "Oh, yeah," he snorted and stepped out into the corridor.

She lifted her eyebrows. "Sick of your quarters already?"

"Somebody installed a new AI in there and didn't warn me," he explained, matching his stride to hers down the corridor.

She grinned, brown eyes sparkling. "Let me guess. You picked female, right?" Del shot her a disgruntled look and Cassie chuckled. "It'll take some getting used to, but if you decide it's not for you, we can always uninstall her. Don't deactivate her, though. We'll find her a new place."

"How did the Shays get so many AIs?"

Cassie's expression turned shrewd. "You asked some questions, didn't you? Not as many as you should have asked, though, judging by your suspicious face. Shay Enterprises also has an AI Research and Development business. Aside from the usual uses for artificial intelligence, we've been playing with the idea of putting them in slicers."

"In slicers?" Del was so stunned by the idea of AI slicers, it took him a second to register what else she'd said. "Wait, did you say we?"

She looked away with a strained expression as they stepped into the lift. "I, uh…I help sometimes with AI research. I've had some education in the area." She keyed the lift to go up several levels, avoiding his gaze. "Who knows, maybe you'll be one of the first people alive to fly a Shadow AI."

As a diversion, it was a pretty good one. "Don't tease me."

She snickered. "It's not so farfetched, you know, but it's still in the testing phases. The disparity between human minds and mechanical systems might be lessened by an AI mind, or the merging might overload the human consciousness." She paused, her unfocused gaze sliding past him. Then she continued as though speaking to herself, "We still have research to do."

Del blinked at her. This little woman was more than a simple pilot and mechanic. He wondered what else these people were hiding. "Didn't Kai call you a geek?"

She shot him a narrow-eyed glare. "Like I said, he's a pain in the rear. Not a trait you should emulate."

He grinned but said nothing further, waiting for the lift doors to open on the Gold Rooms. The suite was as luxurious as he remembered, but the people in it didn't seem to notice.

Sin was curled on a divan with the burly pilot Lynch, engrossed in a discussion while they played with a deck of floating cards. Bib and Jinx dodged in and out of the expensive furniture, playing some kind of holographic game, their laughter echoing around the room. Kai held court with the other three pilots around the bar, telling a story with lots of pantomime and exuberant gestures.

Del and Cassie stepped out of the lift then jumped back in as the two holo-game players careened by.

"No cheating!"

"Don't be a tool, Jinx! How else am I supposed to win?"

Neither acknowledged the newest arrivals, but Sin caught sight of them and smiled, waving them in. Del clenched his jaw against the effects of her smile and moved with Cassie toward the divan.

"Hey, you two," Sin called, but Lynch flicked a card at her, catching her gaze.

"High card, Sinsi," he rumbled.

"Suns curse it. How many times in a row do you plan on winning, Lynch?"

"When you remember how to play, little girl, maybe you'll win, too."

She made a face at him and shoved the cards in a floating jumble before looking up at Del and Cassie.

"He's fleecing me, I know it."

Cassie perched next to Lynch and flung an arm over one enormous shoulder. "So cheat."

Lynch sent her a glower from under his bushy brows while he shuffled the cards. "Don't go teachin' her your tricks, Constellation."

Cassie gave him a cuff on the ear. He didn't seem to notice. "I told you not to call me that."

"Call you what, Connie?"

Sin grinned at the two of them then sent a quick glance at Del. "How was the training flight?"

"Good." Del lowered into a chair next to the divan with a muffled sigh of relief. His whole body weighed him down like lead.

"Better than good," Cassie interjected, her face sobering to steady-eyed sincerity. "He's an amazing pilot, Sin. Fantastic reflexes and the kind of refined control I've rarely seen outside of the ascetic orders. As a matter of fact, he rivals you and Kai for talent. You were lucky to find him."

Del stared at the little woman in dumb surprise. She hadn't said a word of praise on the training courses.

"Don't I know it," Sin murmured and he turned his baffled gaze on her. She was smiling in a secretive way, both tantalizing and nerve-wracking. The smile altered when she caught his eye, and she leaned toward him. "Del, I hate to cut this party short for you, but I have someone I'd like you to meet."

Off balance, Del cleared his throat and agreed in a mumble.

"Don't keep him too long, Sinsi," Cassie said as the two of them rose to their feet. "Del's worked hard today and deserves a break." But she didn't look at them when she said it, busy stealing cards from under Lynch's big hands.

"Understood," Sin answered, leading the way back to the lift.

Del's first thought when the doors closed wasn't a comfortable one. *Alone,* his mind whispered. He took a deep breath to counteract a sudden increase in his heart rate as her scent filled the air. Caught in a sudden lascivious fantasy, it took him a second to register her faint frown when she keyed their destination into the lift controls.

"I hope you won't think I overstepped my bounds," she said, turning to look at him.

"What do you mean?"

"Well, I didn't consult you. You may not appreciate my inviting him."

"Who?" He frowned down at her, feeling muzzy and dull. The lift stopped and the doors opened on the Shay offices. Sin stepped out ahead of him and walked across the room toward the overstuffed chairs flanking the fireplace. Del followed, watching a man rise from one of the seats. There was something familiar about him.

Del slowed to a stop, his heart taking a tremendous knock in his chest when his eyes met a pair as dark as his own. Sin paused to look over her shoulder at him, but for once someone else captured his attention.

"Del, I'd like you to meet Nicholo Givliani," Sin said with a thread of amusement in her voice.

He barely heard her, a ringing in his ears. He stared at the man who used to be a boy once as inseparable from him as his own limbs. "Nick?" His brother had changed so much.

"I'll leave you two alone," Sin said, heading toward the glass partition. "I'll be in the next room, if you need me."

Nick watched her leave then took a step toward Del. His face, filled out and hardened from the youthful one Del remembered, seemed uncertain. "So, are you mad at me?"

Del stared at him for a long moment. "What? Nick, is it really you?"

Amusement softened his brother's face and he took a step closer. "I don't look that different, do I?"

"You…" But Del couldn't speak past a sudden thickening in his throat. With two quick strides, he reached his brother and hauled him into an embrace. Tears pricked the backs of his eyelids when his brother returned his hold with equal intensity.

"It's been too long, brother." Nick's voice was hoarse with emotion.

"I know." Del tightened his hold for a second before pulling back to study his brother's face. Dark brown hair brushed over his forehead, eyes night dark, skin a deep gold, and strong jaw shadowed with stubble; it was like looking in a mirror. Clearing his throat, Del said, "You grew up while I wasn't looking."

"Ain't it a kick?" Nick grinned despite the bright, liquid gleam in his eyes.

Del couldn't answer his grin just yet. Guilt gnawed at him. "I missed you, little brother. I'm sorry I never…"

Nick gave a fierce shake of his head and clapped Del on the shoulder before stepping back. Del discovered they were now the same height and the same muscular build.

"Don't start, Del. You did what you had to do. I'm just sorry I didn't do anything earlier. So, are you mad at me?" His brow furrowed in uncertainty again.

Del made an exasperated noise in the back of his throat. "Mad at you about what? I'm the one who dropped you in the middle of nowhere to get along on your own."

"You left me with good people. I was lucky to have them." Nick narrowed his eyes on Del's face. "You really don't know what I'm talking about?"

"Well, if it helps any, if you don't spit it out, I'm bound to get cranked," he drawled.

Nick flashed a grin and inclined his head toward the seats. Del sat across from his brother, still having trouble believing he was there. He had the sudden urge to poke him, to check the reality of what his eyes said was true.

"I don't know why they wouldn't tell you, but I'm the reason the Shays went after you."

Del frowned. "How are you the reason?"

"I knew what a bind you'd been in for so many years. I've always known but couldn't do anything about it until now," Nick started. "I'm an FPA investigator, in case you didn't know. Just made the rank a few months back. I've been saving up to help you, and the promotion was a powerful boost to my salary. I saved enough to come to the Shays for help."

Del stared at his brother, a rollercoaster zooming around in his head. "The Shays," he said in vague response.

"Yeah, I knew the Core would just brush me aside if I went to them. I learned some things about the Shays from my partner. He likes to call their courier service an 'interesting outreach program,'" Nick said with sardonic amusement. His voice was heavy with implications Del was too tired and distracted to sort through. "So I asked the Shays to get you out, and gave them the credit to pay off your debt."

"Wait…you put up the hundred grand?"

Something in his voice must have tipped his brother off. Nick's expression turned wary. "I saved it up over the years."

Del rose to his feet and turned to the glass partition. "Shay!" he roared, his booming voice echoing in the large office.

Sin stood on the other side of the glass, talking with someone over a viewer. He didn't think sound penetrated the partition, but either she'd been listening in on their conversation or the office's control system had relayed his shout. She glanced over her shoulder at him then turned off the viewer and strode to the partition.

The glass melted away from her and she moved toward them, the corners of her mouth turned up in faint amusement. "You bellowed?"

"You took my brother's credit?" he asked, fury based on a sense of betrayal building in his chest.

"Yes I did," she answered with cool calm. Her eyes flickered to Nick as he rose to his feet then returned to Del with a subtle tensing in her form.

"You paid off my debt with my brother's credit, and didn't tell me?"

"I took his credit but didn't use it to pay off anything. I did buy something with it. Your brother now holds stock in Shay Enterprises, more specifically in our slicer development department."

"What?" Del and his brother said in unison. Nick stared at her, a storm gathering on his brow. "Lady, I gave you credit to free my brother."

"And so I did. Just not with your credit. Feel free to remove your stock any time you like. They've only gained a fraction since I've invested them for you, but it's your credit. Do with it as you please."

Del glowered down at her to hide his relief. She'd deceived them both, but at least his debt was still his to pay off. He wasn't sure he could have handled his brother saving him, after all those years thinking it was the other way around.

Nick didn't look relieved. "Suns curse it, all you did was make him yours instead of the Core's!"

Sin gave him a bland smile then turned toward the lift. "You gentleman have a lot to catch up on. The party will go on for a while, but don't feel you have to make an appearance. Goodnight."

They watched her go in thwarted silence. "The woman is dangerous," Nick said.

Del couldn't argue. "She's right about catching up, though. Come on, let's get out of here. This place is about as comfortable as a bed of nails."

"No kidding. What's with that, anyway?" Nick complained as he followed Del to the lift.

"Intimidation."

"It works."

Del snorted, closing them in the lift and keying the pilot's quarters. "At least I'm not the only one."

"Tell me you didn't make a permanent arrangement with these people."

"Can't. Signed a contract," Del replied, ignoring the disgusted expression on Nick's face.

"Sun's sake, Del," his brother started, but Del cut him off by stepping out of the lift. Moving down the corridor to his quarters, he thumbed open the door and waved Nick in.

"Welcome," a female voice greeted them.

It took Del several long seconds to remember his new AI. He cursed under his breath. "Ah, AI, do you have some kind of privacy mode or something?"

"Of course. When you require my assistance again, request the VRS to resume. Privacy mode is now on."

Nick stared at him with raised eyebrows. "You have an AI?"

"Guess so," Del said with weary amusement as he moved into his new home.

"How did you rate one of those?"

"Don't ask me. The Shays develop those, too, and all their pilots have 'em." He paused at the entrance to the kitchen. "Drink or something? I'm still getting used to the place, so I'm not sure what I have."

"Anything wet would be good," Nick answered, looking around with curious eyes.

Del explored and discovered a stocked bar. With an evil grin, he pulled out two glasses and made supernovas. May as well get this reunion started with a bang.

"It's a huge place, Del. How are you going to fill it?"

"No clue," Del answered, reentering the living room. "I'm just getting used to having a place again. Here, try this on for size," he said with a grin, handing the colorful drink to Nick. "Start slow, though. It's got a kick."

Nick gave the glass a dubious look then took a

cautious sip. But caution meant nothing with a supernova. Del chuckled, watching his brother gasp and blink to clear tear-blurred vision. "Sun and Stars," Nick rasped.

Del gave him a clap on the shoulder. "I know, but it grows on you." He sat on the couch and with a fortifying breath, sipped his own drink. When he blinked his eyes clear, his brother was sitting next to him with a grin on his face.

"Masochist," Nick accused.

Del laughed. "You get used to it." To prove his point, he took a second sip, which was a little less vicious. "So tell me about your life, little brother," he managed to say without croaking. "How did you get to be a FPAI?"

"Nope, you first. I need to know how deep you are into the Shays, starting with your contract."

"You can read it for yourself." Del gave a defensive shrug and turned on the viewer. He pulled up his own file and found the contract. "I made her add the part about the debt she paid off to the Core."

Nick shot him a look he couldn't interpret; his little brother really had changed. Then he leaned forward to read the contract with sharp intensity. Del watched him and knew when he reached the part about his debt. A quick frown pulled his brows together and he shot Del another look, this one easier to read. "What's with the extra credit?"

"Griffin made sure letting me go was worth the effort," Del answered with a grimace.

"Griffin? The Griffin, the CEO of Quasicore?"

"Sin cut a deal with him direct."

Nick shook his head, glancing over the rest of the

contract before turning a worried frown on Del. "Listen, brother, be careful with the Shays. This contract sounds like a friggin' dream come true. I don't trust it and I don't trust them. I won't pretend to know everything about them or what they're up to, but I know enough to be nervous. The Shays aren't Core, but they deal with them all the time and it's not legal. The weird thing is, the FPA knows about it but doesn't do anything, and I don't know why. As an investigator I can find out, but it'll take time."

Deep down Del had been expecting this. He'd had enough hints. What surprised him was how defeated and depressed it made him feel. How alone.

"Don't worry about me, Nick. Compared to the Core, these guys are pussycats." He smiled for his brother and took a large swallow of his supernova, the burn a welcome distraction.

Nick took a drink from his own glass then stared down at it with a frown. "I suppose if you have to be an indentured servant, this ain't such a bad setup. I just don't want you to get in so far you can't get out again." He raised his head and looked at Del with his familiar dark eyes, conflicting emotions vibrant in their depths. "Like you did with the Core, for me. I can't let you do it again."

"Won't happen, bro. Count on it."

"I'll keep working from my end. So far the Shays don't have a problem with me getting in touch with you." He stared into the distance with a confused frown. "She insisted I come see you. I wasn't gonna say no, but you're bound to tell me things. Why would she want an FPAI to have so much access to her company?"

"You're working your brain too hard, Nick. Let it

go. I haven't seen you for ten years and I wanna know what you've been up to."

Nick gave him a half-smile and shrugged a shoulder. "My story's easy. Aunt Sal and Uncle Bo were great, but I'm no farmer. I had to help you, do my part to pay off the debt, so as soon as I was old enough, I joined the FPA service. Worked my way up to investigator. Like I said before, my orienting partner knows some things about the Shays and he likes to talk. Probably why he's a newbie orienter instead of a field investigator. He gave me the idea to approach the Shays about you. He told me they like to snag people out from under the Core and put them to work in their courier service. I was hoping they'd get you out with no strings attached if I paid for it. Guess I was wrong." He grimaced and ran a hand through his wavy dark hair.

"Well, I'm out from under the Core, so it ain't all bad."

"Let's just hope it's not frying pan to fire."

They toasted the thought and downed the rest of their drinks. Del shuddered at the wildfire spread of heat through his body and watched his brother grimace.

"Eh, it's acid," Nick rasped. "Got more?"

Del chuckled and took his brother's empty glass. "You'll have to stay here tonight. Another one of these and we'll both be flat out."

"The Shays set me up in guest quarters. Told me I could stay as long as I wanted. I don't have much leave time yet, but if I put this down as an investigation, I'd be in the clear to stay."

Del got to his feet, remaining where he was for a long moment while he made sure his legs would hold. The last time he'd drunk a supernova, he'd had a full stomach. "Sounds good to me. Come help me find food. I'm starving and I'm pretty sure another nova will kill me on an empty stomach."

Nick chuckled and followed him into the kitchen, swearing under his breath when he bumped into a counter. Del smirked at him and he glowered back. "Don't start. You're not too steady on your feet either, brother."

"Dinner for two, then. Let's see what we got."

They rummaged through the stocked kitchen, finding reconstructed steak dinners and another round of supernovas. They sat down to eat at the kitchen table and Del told part of his own story, from when he fled the Core to the present. They'd finished dinner and were working on an apple pie while Del described his first flight in a Shadow.

His brother stopped eating and stared with a rapt expression, gratifying him. "I thought Shadows were just a pretty rumor. Think they'd let me take a look at one tomorrow?"

"Don't see why not," Del answered with a grin. This at least was familiar territory. Seeing the eagerness in his brother's eyes was like taking a trip back through time. Their father had gotten them started with slicing, but he hadn't known how hard his sons would fall in love with it.

"I haven't sliced in years," Nick said, looking down at his pie. "It didn't seem right to enjoy something so much when it's why we're in this mess. But hearing you talk makes me want to get back into it."

"I don't think they'll let you fly a Shadow, but I got an X780 I'm not using. We're about the same build now, so it wouldn't need much adjusting."

Nick flashed him a grin both familiar and strange. His brother's features had matured and gained a new confidence. "Brother, you got yourself a deal."

As they cleaned up the kitchen, Nick asked a few casual questions about Del's recent life. At first, Del answered without thinking, but after a few minutes he looked at his brother with new eyes. The questions weren't as casual as they seemed. Nick had already started his investigation. Del didn't object, answering what he could while they moved into the living room. When Nick paused to lean back against the sofa, taking a thoughtful sip of his drink, Del tried a few questions of his own.

"So how do you know the Shays do illegal deals with the Core?"

"My partner saw classified files on it."

"FPA files?"

"Yeah."

"So it's not just some FPA agent looking the other way for a bribe. They documented it?"

"Right again."

"Why would they let it go on?"

"Don't know."

Del mused on this. "Sounds like somebody a lot higher up the FPA food chain was bought."

"Yeah, sounds like."

"Maybe you should leave it alone, then. Work it from this side of space instead. No telling what kind of trouble you'd find if you start sniffing around the big fish."

"I'll be careful, but I can't just drop it."

Del shook his head but couldn't fault his brother

for trying to do what was right. "Any clue why the Shays would want Core rejects?"

"None."

"Any idea how they found me in the Fringe?"

"From what I hear, they have some strange contacts in strange places. I'm guessing they put the word out and waited for somebody to roll on you."

It made sense to Del. He could even guess who it had been. But why did Hector act so freaked on seeing the Shays, if he was their contact?

"They sure do have a hold on those people," he mused, thinking of Hector with his hands tucked in his armpits.

"What makes you say that?"

Del described in detail his first encounter with the Shays. He avoided things like his and Sin's amazing flight and their devastating kiss, putting more emphasis on the reactions of everyone else. Nick listened without interrupting, but his expression became more concerned as time went on.

When Del finished, his brother commented in a quiet voice, "You admire them."

Del shifted in his seat. "They're unique." The assessing look in his brother's eyes made him feel like a bug under a scope.

"And Sinsudee Shay is a beautiful woman."

The skin over Del's cheekbones heated. With a wry half-smile, he inclined his head. "Noticed that, too, huh?"

"She's an unhealthy choice, brother. There are lots of other women on this station. At least one of 'em has to be dumb enough to put up with you."

Del responded to his brother's teasing with a

menacing frown. "Watch your lip, young'un," he growled. "You ain't grown so big I can't still paddle your behind."

His brother's laughter was a deeper version of what it used to be, but it still had the same contagious quality. Chuckling along with him, Del described the other women he'd met so far. Nick bent over with laughter at Del's woeful attempt to fend off Bib and his rendition of Cassie's slave driving.

"You make her sound like a little dragon."

"Just don't call her a geek," Del snorted, giving an exaggerated shudder.

To take the focus off himself, he asked Nick how his love life was doing and discovered Nick wasn't Sun-bonded or interested in anyone. In fact, his romantic endeavors had been as sporadic as Del's own. He cited lack of time and Del nodded. It wasn't just time, he knew. Close attachments left a person vulnerable and neither one of them had been able to afford it, considering the circumstances.

This subject led to others, which led to a third and fourth round of supernovas. The night became a blur for Del. He remembered laughing a lot and talking about old times, but the specifics were lost in a hazy cloud of alcohol. When he found himself listening to his brother with his eyes closed, he decided to call it a night.

"Fallin' 'sleep sittin' up," he complained and made a face when Nick snickered over his slurred words. "Won't think i'so funny t'morrow."

Standing was a triumph of human will. Del weaved across the room to the bedroom to retrieve bedding for his brother. He managed to make it back to the sofa, but Nick had already fallen asleep and was snoring like a slicer with a converter problem, head tilted at an awkward angle.

Alternating between snickers and curses, Del took several long minutes to maneuver Nick to a horizontal position with his head on a pillow. He wasted a full minute wrestling with the blanket before he managed to cover at least part of his brother. Calling it good enough, he staggered back to his room and tumbled into bed. With a sigh of relief, he closed his eyes and passed out.

Chapter 8

"Sun's mercy," Del muttered between clenched teeth, clutching his head with desperate hands.

"Shh, you loud jackass," Nick whispered next to him, not bothering to raise his head from the cradle of his arms.

"Today," Del said with care, lowering his voice to an accommodating whisper, "I'll kill Manakai Shay."

"Good," Nick mumbled, reaching out to wrap a trembling hand around his coffee mug without lifting his head. A pause while the two of them suffered in silence, then Nick asked, "Why?"

"He showed me how to make those Sun-cursed 'novas."

"Then I want a turn killing him."

"Perhaps I may be of assistance," a feminine voice interrupted their murder plans. A very loud feminine voice.

Both men groaned in agony.

"Make it stop," Nick moaned into the tabletop, letting go of his coffee mug to cover his head.

"AI, if you don't shut up, I'm disconnecting you," Del hissed through gritted teeth.

"Samantha," she answered in a much reduced volume.

"What?"

"Samantha is what the two of you named me last

night."

"We did?"

"Yes. The layman's term for what you are suffering now is a hangover, correct?"

Nick raised his head and squinted at Del. "Does she have to rub it in?" he whispered.

"I have several remedies for hangovers in my database. All are quite effective, and from your conditions, necessary."

"She's laughing at us," Del ground out, massaging his temples.

"If you would place yourselves in the treatment tube, I will give you injections for the pain and nausea. Then I have liquid substances you should consume. These will reduce your symptoms, as well as your dehydration."

"Yup, she's makin' fun," Nick concurred and lowered his head back to the cradle of his arms. Neither man moved for several minutes.

"When do you plan to enter the treatment tube?" Samantha asked, her smooth AI voice taking on a note of impatience.

"Leave us alone, Sam," Del grumped, taking a careful sip of coffee.

"The treatment is for your own good, and you will feel much improved afterward."

Neither answered.

"I am programmed to do my best to assist you in all matters; including your health. I must insist you comply with this treatment."

"Did she talk this much last night?" Nick's muffled voice rose from the table.

"If you do not comply, I will be forced to increase

the volume on my speech centers."

"Threats now," Del observed darkly. "I think I'll kill whoever installed the AI, too."

"Good thinkin'," his brother responded.

They moved toward the living room, assisting each other like a couple of invalids. Feeling noble, Del tucked his brother in the treatment tube first then leaned his throbbing head against the cool wall with a long-suffering sigh. What seemed like hours later, Nick emerged and helped Del into the tube. A cool, soothing aerosol blew in his face and a pinprick of pain entered his arm. The throbbing in his head ebbed away like a tide, his stomach stopped lurching with every movement of his eyeballs, and he started to feel human again.

Stepping out of the treatment tube, he grinned in relief at his brother, who handed him a tall glass of liquid. He downed it in several long swallows. "I guess she's not so bad."

"I am pleased to hear you say so," Samantha said in an uninflected tone. "Cassiopeia Draegen has inquired as to your status and time of arrival in the maintenance bay."

"Told you Cass is a slave driver," Del said with a smirk at his brother. Then a thought struck and he glanced up at a sensor with suspicion. "What did you tell her?"

"I explained your condition and recommended she allow time for you to recover."

Del cursed then glowered at Nick when his brother chuckled. "Don't know what you're laughing at. You were worse off than I was."

Nick looked offended. "In your dreams, bro."

They had a heated debate over who was better able to handle his liquor while they cleaned up and wolfed down a fast meal. Afterward, they hurried out the door with a simultaneous, "Bye, Sam."

"How fast did you say she'd go?" Nick asked, his eyes bright as they entered the lift.

"Faster than anything I've flown before, but it ain't the speed. It's how she flies," Del responded, infected by his brother's enthusiasm. He'd been relieved to leave the Shadow yesterday, but now he couldn't wait to get back into space with her.

"Have you named her yet?" his brother asked with a sly grin.

Without thinking, Del answered, "Lady Shadow." Shocked by his own reply, he shuffled his feet and turned his face away from Nick. "Didn't much think about it." Naming his slicer after the boss he was lusting after was a terrible idea.

"What's the look for? You used to name all your slicers and Lady Shadow's okay. Better than the name you had for your blue X610. What was it again?"

"Beulah," Del said with a sudden grin of remembrance. "She wasn't pretty, but she sure was reliable."

"Right, Beulah," Nick snorted.

The lift opened and they made their way down the short service corridor to the maintenance bay. The place was bustling with activity. Del caught sight of most of his fellow pilots, with the exception of Sin and a quiet fellow named Quan. Manakai wasn't wearing the overalls everyone else had on. He'd rolled his dress shirt up at the sleeves, a cream jacket flung over a nearby tool tray.

"Sun's blood, look at them all," Nick rasped at his side. His brother's covetous gaze danced over the neat double row of Shadows.

"They get better the closer you get," Del teased and led the way toward his own slicer. With a pleased grin, he watched Nick run worshipful hands over the dark, gleaming skin.

"So beautiful." Nick glanced at Del with hope on his face. Del nodded permission for him to open the ship then leaned in, watching his brother settle into the pilot's seat and inspect the controls. "Del, you lucky devil," he breathed.

Del chuckled. "You think looking at her is fine, try powering her up."

Nick didn't hesitate, awed delight blooming on his face when the Shadow purred to life. "Holy Heart of the Sun. I think I'm in love," he sighed.

Del laughed. "Brother, you don't even know what love is yet. Try the port."

With eager anticipation, Nick reached for the connector and brought it to his data port. Before he could slide it in, a voice barked, "Stop!"

Del glanced over his shoulder. Cassie stood, frowning at the two of them, one fist propped on a hip and the other hand tapping a small viewer against her thigh in an aggravated rhythm. "You have an outdated data port. You connect with a Shadow and, in all likelihood, the ship's systems will overwhelm your wetware. So unless you want your brains to turn to mush, I suggest you put the connector back where you found it."

"Yes, ma'am." Nick replaced the connector. "Let me guess," he continued as he levered himself out of the slicer. "You must be Cassie Dragon."

"Draegen," she corrected with a cool look.

"Cass, this is my brother, Nick," Del introduced.

"Pleasure." Nick stuck out his hand. She un-fisted the one from her hip and gave his a brief shake before letting go again. "Good eyes, to date my port from where you were standing."

Cassie straightened her back, her cool expression turning even icier. "Of course I didn't see the model, but I could tell it was the E-series, which puts it back at least ten years. Much too simple for our Shadows."

A dry smile played at the corners of Nick's mouth. "I stand corrected. Or at least put in my place. Anyone ever tell you you'd make a great schoolteacher?"

Her lips compressed and she turned away from him, resting her icy brown gaze on Del. "We've lost good training time this morning and we need to get you familiar with the weapon systems today. Let me know when you're ready to get started." She turned on her heel and marched off, small form ramrod straight and long, plaited hair bouncing against her back.

Del snorted in amusement and looked at his brother. "Did you have to call her a dragon?"

Nick watched her go with an odd expression. "You just said don't call her a geek."

"Well thank the Suns for small favors," Del said and grinned when his brother lifted his eyebrows at him. "She said we're training on weapons today. If you'd called her a geek, I don't think you'd still have a brother tomorrow."

Nick flashed a quick smile before craning his neck to stare down the row after Cassie again. "What weapons?"

Del nudged him then pointed out the bulge in the Shadow's underbelly. "Those weapons."

Nick's expression sobered and his eyes met Del's with dark intensity. "Those are illegal."

"Not according to Sin. She says they've got sanction from the FPA."

"What? How?"

"Another question goes unanswered." Del shrugged and gave him a wry look. "Let me show you where the X780 is before the little dragon turns us to ash. There's a training course over the gas giant with a good bite to it. You'll like it," he said with studied nonchalance, anticipating his brother's reaction to the blistering course.

"You sure my port's up to it?"

Del led the way toward the docking bay. "For Red, no problem. She's a much simpler girl."

"Lucky for me," his brother said with biting sarcasm and Del chuckled.

When they entered the docking bay, Nick looked impressed by the large and varied armada of docked ships. Del pointed out the ships used for the regular courier service and the larger vessels able to withstand the forces of a star-way, before he turned his attention to a row of docked slicers.

"This must be Red," Nick said, his face lighting with anticipation as they approached the crimson X780.

Familiar pride and affection suffused Del on looking at his old slicer. She was no Shadow, but she was still a beautiful ship who had served him well. "Got it in one," he answered and opened her for his brother.

Nick slid inside and made the same inspection of Red as he had with Del's Shadow. His reverence was gone, but the eagerness and admiration stayed the same. "She's a flare and a half, Del. When can I take her out?"

Del leaned in to turn her on. "No time like the present."

With a delighted grin, Nick snagged the connector and slid it into his port. Del watched him, mindful of Cassie's warnings about an aging port. Though Nick's eyes unfocused for a long moment while he adjusted to the rush of information, he seemed okay otherwise. He let out a long sigh and his expression of bliss made Del laugh. "How did I stay away for so long?"

"Beats me. I couldn't do it. Will you be okay without a flying partner?"

Nick shot him a contemptuous look. "I can handle it."

With a grin and a light punch on his brother's shoulder, Del stepped back from the slicer. "Have fun with her."

"Oh, I plan on it," Nick drawled with a wicked grin, adding before he closed the slicer, "I promise to bring her back in one piece."

Del snorted, brushing off his momentary alarm. Stepping away from the landing pad, he gave a short salute as the slicer lifted and spun around with a flirt of her ruby tail. "Bring her back in one piece," he scoffed, heading for the maintenance bay and calling his brother names under his breath.

Manakai greeted him on his return, eyeing Del's baleful expression. "Something bothering you?"

"My brother thinks he's a comedian," Del answered, heading toward his slicer.

Manakai followed with a sound of disapproval.

"Inconsiderate. He should have more care for your delicate condition."

"My what?" Del exclaimed, stopping short to stare at the other man. Kai had an alarming twinkle in his green eyes and a suspicious innocence on his face.

"We heard you weren't feeling well this morning. Dog sick with a hangover. You sure you don't need to sit down?" Sin's brother asked with mock sympathy and an evil expression.

Del groaned. "Did Cassie tell you or did the friggin' AI tell the whole station?"

"Got it from the genius herself. She wanted to know if we should give you the day off."

After Cassie's attitude earlier, Del was surprised she'd thought of it. "Thanks, but I'm fine," he retorted and continued toward his Shadow. "Remind me to kill you later, though."

"Will do," Kai answered, following Del to his slicer. "Got a reason?"

"Got four of 'em," Del said as he opened the Shadow and levered himself inside. "At least I think it was four. Hard to remember now."

"Care to share?" Kai asked, leaning in to inspect the controls.

Del paused long enough to catch the other man's eye. "Supernovas." Then he sat back with a sigh and waited for Kai to stop laughing.

Cassie appeared before Kai was finished and elbowed him out of the way. "What's wrong with him?"

"If I had to guess, I'd say he's wacko."

"Well sure, but what's wrong with him today?" Cassie responded without missing a beat, and Kai paused long enough in his chortling to protest.

"Hey! I resemble that remark." He followed this with a tug on Cassie's plait.

With a long-suffering sigh, she turned a level gaze on her employer. "Kai, we're behind as it is today. Would you please go harass someone else for a while?"

He clapped a hand to his chest, his expression one of exaggerated hurt and betrayal. "Cass, I'm crushed. How can I not be near—?"

"Manakai Ezekiel Shay!"

Kai flinched at Sin's distant shout resounding through the maintenance bay. His green eyes went wide with horror and he clutched at Cassie, whispering, "Save me!"

She snickered and brushed off his hands without mercy. "You're on your own, pal."

Before he could continue his theatrics, Sin came into view, her strides impatient and face set in lines of dark discontent. She caught sight of her brother and stopped with a scowl, hands on hips. "Suns curse it, Kai. We're late."

Kai answered, but Del didn't hear it. He levered out of the Shadow, feeling sucker punched. The black silk of her hair was pulled back from her face, leaving a profusion of curls to fall in dark kisses around her bare neck and shoulders. She wore a creamy sleeveless dress, falling in demure folds from the points of her shoulders across her chest and accentuating her curves with subtle sophistication, ending in an elegant flare around her knees. Narrow panels ran down the sides of the dress, appearing sheer except for a lacy pattern. Only skin gleamed below these panels. She wasn't wearing anything under the dress. Del's heart stumbled to a halt in his chest.

Sin berated her brother while Kai found his jacket and shrugged into it. "I don't want to go to this luncheon either, but we can't back out. You know how important it is for us to make an appearance. It doesn't look good for us to be late."

The luncheon with Webster Griffin. The man would see her, talk to her, and maybe even put his hands on her. Del gritted his teeth against a swell of bitter jealousy. Did she wear the Sun-cursed dress to seduce the old goat? Del gripped the hatch of the Shadow with white-knuckled intensity.

"All right, Sissa," Kai sighed. "You made your point. Let's get this over with." He sent Cass and Del a look of resignation and a dejected salute, before spinning on his heel and starting for the door.

With a shake of her head, Sin watched him go before facing the two by the Shadow. "Have a—" She stopped short when her gaze met Del's. She blinked at him, her brows pulling together in a faint frown. "Have a good day," she finished, spinning on her heels and following her brother.

Del continued to watch, unable to look away from the tantalizing flare in her dress.

A sharp elbow gouged into his ribs. "Del, get that look off your face," Cassie said, her tone a mix of exasperation and amusement.

He frowned at her, both annoyed and relieved by the distraction. He had a picture in his head of Griffin dancing with Sin, putting his murdering hands where her skin glowed through those panels. "What look?"

She wore a half-smile, but her eyes were pitying. "It says you've fallen and you can't get up."

Chapter 9

Kai groused next to Sin as they headed toward the docking bay, but she didn't hear a word, trying to think of a reason for the furious heat in Del's eyes. Was he so angry she'd invited his brother and taken Nick's credit? Or was it because she hadn't told either of them the whole truth?

Considering the immediacy of his fury, the clenched jaw, the darkened skin, the fire in his eyes, those reasons didn't seem to fit. It upset her to a surprising degree. His opinion of her had become too important. A burning sensation settled in the pit of her stomach and her chest tightened as if the bay didn't have enough air.

Not a good sign.

Sin boarded their personal transport and settled into a plush seat, barely noticing the respectful greetings from the pilots. Kai lowered into a seat next to her, still grumping, but she paid no attention until he made a disgusted sound and snapped his fingers in front of her face. "Sinsi, what's wrong with you? I gave you at least three good insults and you didn't blink."

She cast him a frown and pushed his hand away. "Nothing."

"You can't be angry at me for making us late."

"I'm not," she sighed, resting her head against the seat and closing her eyes. With a slight vibration under her, the transport lifted from its pad and headed out of the station.

"I was rechecking slicers for the next run. It's an important one, you know."

"I'm aware." She turned her head to flash him a dry look.

"Funny, you haven't acted like it."

She straightened and narrowed her eyes. "Excuse me?"

"For starters, Del's an unknown quantity. Why would you want him on this run of all runs? He could be a stumbling block when we can't afford one."

"You don't—"

He held up a hand to stop her, tilting his head in an eerie echo of their father when he gave them a lesson. "Plus you invited an FPA investigator here."

"You know why," Sin retorted, her muscles tightening with dismay. Most of the time, they agreed on actions furthering their goals. His dissent left her bereft.

"I know one of the reasons," he commented with a pointed lift of his eyebrows. She turned her face away. "But your timing could have been better. Why not ask him here after the run is over?"

She sent him a cool glance. "You know why. Inspector Givliani knows more than he should, more than is healthy for him. The lure of investigating while we are gone will keep him here and away from FPA headquarters. Do I need to explain why it's important?"

The stern mask dropped from his face and he grinned. "Good to have you back, Sissa. I didn't want to walk into that pack of krells by myself." His expression sobered as he continued, "And I didn't want

139

Griffin near you when you're not your sharpest."

Sin sneered at him. "I'm disappointed in you, brother. Do you think I would go anywhere near the man without being exquisitely on guard? Your lack of trust and faith pains me."

He winced and held up a hand in surrender, eyes dancing with humor. "All right, I get it, nice and sharp. Save it for Griff, would you?"

It was as close to an apology as she would get and he did have a point; she'd been distracted. On the other hand, feigning disagreement just to get a rise out of her was a low blow and deserved a little sibling payback. With a malicious smile, she announced, "Griff's not the only one who's going to be there. Did you know his daughter would be attending?"

"The Ice Queen? I'm surprised she's coming out of hiding," he responded with a dismissive shrug, but his eyes glinted with an antagonism he couldn't hide from her.

Sin bit her cheek to keep from grinning. Liaena Griffin was the only woman who seemed immune to her brother's charms, starting when they were children; she'd kicked Kai in the shin when they first met. Her brother took it personally, reacting to the woman with hostile challenge ever since. Their clash of wills would be the only entertainment Sin would find at this luncheon.

"Her father chooses her appearances with care," she pointed out, watching him sidelong in amusement.

Kai settled back in his seat, a twitch in his jaw. "Sure, a luncheon is a great place to display his little ice statue. A perfect distraction for the unsuspecting masses."

Sin sobered, moderating her tone to soft warning. "And unwary Shays. Griffin isn't blind, brother mine."

He met her gaze and held stubborn for a moment, before giving a slight shrug of one shoulder. "So he uses his daughter to lure me away while he corners you. Divide and conquer?"

"He is fond of the tried and true tactics. Such a traditionalist," she drawled.

He grinned like a wolf. "So we let him believe it."

"Why else did I dress the part?" She returned his predatory grin and relished his laugh.

"Not subtle, but it'll work. Might even stop the old goat's heart."

"We wouldn't be so lucky," she snorted.

Kai started to reply, a teasing light in his eyes, when the intercom interrupted. "Sir, ma'am, we're approaching the star-way. Please secure yourselves."

"Thanks Brie," Sin answered.

She and Kai reached for the seat controls and activated the cushioning fields which were more comfortable than straps, and a luxury most cruise liners couldn't afford. The field closed over her with gentle security and she settled back against the cushions.

While they waited for the jolt of entry to the star-way, Kai asked in a casual tone, "So how long have you known she was going to be there?"

Sin gave a low laugh and didn't answer.

They passed the rest of the trip by discussing the upcoming off-lane run. It was familiar territory; they'd discussed the details so many times they could recite them in their sleep, but Kai deviated from the usual litany by mentioning Del again.

"You sure about adding him?" he asked without

looking at her, pretending an interest in the cuffs of his jacket.

"Yes, Kai," she said with a sigh. "Don't worry, he'll be on my team and I'll take full responsibility for him."

"Sure you will," he said with a sly grin. "What happens if he catches on to what we're doing?"

"I'll make sure he won't. Cassie doesn't think he'll be a problem."

"Cassie's blinded by his biceps," he replied in a dry tone.

"Don't, Kai. Cass isn't so easy to manipulate. She didn't drop at your feet, did she?"

"I didn't want her to," he claimed with insufferable arrogance.

Sin curled her lip in disgust. "Watch it, brother, your ego's galloping away from you again." Then she made a show of checking their location. "Not to worry, we're almost there. Liaena will rein it in for you." She shot him a callous grin and snickered at his sour expression.

"Sir, ma'am," the pilot's voice interrupted again. "We're about to land."

"Thank you, Brie."

They were quiet as the ship maneuvered to settle on the landing pad with a faint shiver. Sin tried not to dwell on what he'd said, but it kept niggling at her. "Do you really think Cass is attracted to him?"

It was Kai's turn to chuckle without answering.

The luncheon was held on a garden planet, famous for its hosting and catering services. When the transport doors opened, they were treated to a view of a walkway flanked by a profusion of flowering plants and trees, leading to a breathtaking building made of a clear, glass-like material. Greenery graced its columns and archways, and its turreted roof flashed with the sun's light.

A greeter in white livery met them, bowing low and welcoming them in a smooth voice. With a gracious sweep of his arm, he led them toward the sparkling building.

Sin tilted her head to get a better look at the structure as they approached. "Nice."

"I like the white marble one more," Kai responded.

Their greeter cast them a furtive glance over his shoulder, faint resentment on his face. When they reached the arching entrance, he bowed again, waving them inside. "Please enter and be welcome. If you want for anything, do not hesitate to ask."

"Thank you, we've experienced your excellent service before. I'm sure we'll want for nothing," Sin replied and the greeter's resentment melted into a pleased smile. It always paid to be gracious to one's host, especially if they were hosting your enemy at the same time.

Passing through the archway, they reached a short flight of stairs. Kai placed a hand under her elbow and they paused in a calculated pose, sweeping the people below with their twin green gaze. It had the desired effect, the rumble of conversation dimming and heads turning to mark their entrance. With their dark hair and light clothes, the prismed light and sparkling glass background, they made a dramatic pair. With many of the people below, image was as much a weapon as credit.

While gliding down the stairs, Sin caught sight of

the Griffins and smothered an ironic smile. They also knew how to display themselves for effect. Despite the midday luncheon, Webster had attired himself in unrelenting black, his dignified gray head a striking contrast to the midnight cloth. His daughter, on the other hand, was a smoldering flame. A sweep of mahogany elegance, her hair turned to fire in the sunlight. Her dress suit was a matching red-brown, made of a rich, soft fabric with a conservative neckline and short hem, leaving most of her slim legs on display. She wore a sparkling gold pin in the shape of the Quasicore insignia on her breast like a badge of courage, or a brand.

Sin glanced at Kai out of the corner of her eye and caught the humorless curl of his mouth. "Let the games begin," she murmured and his fingers flexed on her elbow. They stepped together into the gathering.

The luncheon was a charity function for the sufferers of Mastikie Syndrome, a difficult to treat genetic mutation causing intermittent tissue breakdown. The Order of the Golden Sun had organized the function. Not above using this charity to further their own complicated politics, they'd invited a wide variety of people to attend; heads of state, members of the FPA, leaders of the medical community, plus major credit holders like Quasicore and Shay Enterprises.

Sin and Kai spent almost an hour interacting with other guests before they came face to face with the Griffins.

"There you are, my dear," Webster said in his cultured voice, taking Sin's hand and bending over it in a formal bow. She gave him a gracious smile, hiding how much her skin crawled at his touch. "And

Manakai, as well. It's good to see you both."

"Griff," they said in unison. Sin managed to slip her hand from his.

Kai turned to Griffin's daughter with a charming smile. "Hey, Lie, it's been a long time," he greeted her with casual malice, but she seemed unmoved by the pointed shortening of her name.

Sin added, "Aena, it's good to see you again."

In contrast to the captured flame of her hair, Liaena's lovely face was as serene as a glacial pool. Her gray eyes traveled over them both with no hint of emotion, mouth curled in a distant smile. "Manakai, Sinsudee, always a pleasure," she said in a smooth voice, a feminine version of her father's cultured tones.

"Have you enjoyed yourselves thus far?" Griffin asked, calling a wine server over with a subtle motion. "Try the white. It's quite lovely. Much like yourself, my dear," he said to Sin with an admiring tilt of his head.

Griffin was acting the host, playing his usual game of territorial domination. Sin countered with a dimpled smile and lowered lashes, flashing the paneling on her dress as she reached for a glass. "You flatter me." She took a sip then lifted her glass to him with a slow smile. "As you said, delicious." He smiled back with a hint of irony.

Her brother claimed two glasses of red wine and offered one to Liaena with a little flourish. "You look like you could use some warmth."

Sin bit the inside of her lip to keep from grinning, but Liaena did not appear affected by his snide remark. Mouth still curved in a cool smile, she took the glass from him with courteous thanks but didn't drink from it, gray eyes measuring them both.

At that moment, a trill of chimes sounded, signaling the meal. Griffin gave Sin a slight bow, offering his arm. "Shall we?" With a tilt of her head, she accepted his arm.

The dining hall was a vast open area with casual seating in the tradition of the ascetics. Instead of formal tables, guests sat in small groups of comfortable chairs and lounges while the food rotated around the room on anti-gravity serving trays. The casual atmosphere relaxed guests and fostered familiarity, dangerous when dealing with Webster Griffin. He chose a small divan built for two, excluding his daughter and her brother. Liaena and Manakai sat with a small group a short distance away.

The luncheon began with a speech by the lead Golden Sun ascetic. The guests listened with polite interest and rang the approval chimes when he concluded. While the food circulated, the room echoed with a river of conversation, a fluid network of social politics and transactions.

Sin played her game with Griffin with the ease of long practice. They performed a verbal dance, Griffin's courtship the chessboard on which they sparred. If his goal was to control Shay Enterprises through her, he was playing a long game; they'd been doing this dance for years. Though his advances were a study in refined flattery, she knew the monster beneath his genteel exterior and always stayed just out of reach.

After a while, they arrived at the subject of her courier service. Handing her a delicate little pastry, Griffin watched her nibble it with a hunter's light in his eye and commented, "I hear you've contracted with the

146

Cortecians for an off-lane run. They seem beneath you."

Sin sent him a sidelong glance. "You know only illegal runs are beneath me, Web."

"Hmm. Abantium, wasn't it?"

"Yes."

"Such a poor load. Surely your time would be better spent on richer cargo."

"Corteca has met the fee. The type of cargo hardly matters," she replied in an indifferent voice, amused by his dissembling. Abantium was an inert mineral on its own, but valuable when mixed. Combined with certain substances, it became explosive, useful for the Cortecian miners, or a weapon in the wrong hands.

"The type of cargo always matters, my dear," he demurred, and she smiled at him without comment, waiting. Silence was as useful a tool as words. "I hope you set your fee at a sizable amount."

"Profit often comes from unusual quarters," she said with a pointed lift of her eyebrows.

"So it does," he responded and lifted his glass to her with an ironic tilt of his distinguished head.

She gave him a shrewd smile and clicked her glass against his, satisfied the groundwork had been laid. And she hadn't even been the one to introduce the subject.

"Speaking of your couriers, is the new pilot working out for you?"

Careful, she thought to herself, inclining her head in assent. "I'm told he's coming along nicely."

"Splendid. I'm glad he seems to be answering your needs."

The cynical glint in his eye did not escape her, but Sin ignored the innuendo. "He's untried yet, but we won't be disappointed to have acquired him."

"I'm sure. He looked quite capable."

She ignored this gibe, too, glancing around the room. She caught sight of Kai and Liaena and smothered a grin. Her brother was wearing his wolf's smile. He was sitting close to the red-head, his arm lying along the back of the couch behind her. Nothing in her movements spoke of tension, but she never met his gaze.

"It seems my brother and your daughter are getting along for once," she said in a musing tone, casting Griffin a sidelong glance to catch his reaction.

His gray eyes narrowed a bit when he caught sight of the pair, his only sign of disapproval. He made a noncommittal sound in the back of his throat. "At least this time there has been no bloodshed."

Sin chuckled, wondering if he disapproved of Kai's hunt or his daughter's reticence. Maybe both. "Not yet, but why tempt fate?" She rose before he could protest and began making her way toward the pair, taking a malicious delight in forcing Griffin to trail her.

Kai caught sight of them as they approached and flashed a smug smile, which Sin knew was just to irk Griffin. The calm serenity on Liaena's face said he'd gotten nowhere with her.

"Brother, shall we mingle once more before we go? The Vreen chancellor asked to speak with us."

With a nod of his dark head, Kai set his glass down on a hovering tray and rose to his feet. "Good, the chancellor owes me twenty credits. We bet how many times I could get Lie to say 'no thank you.'"

Sin covered a smirk with one hand then blinked in surprise at Liaena's reaction. Her gray eyes turned into daggers on Kai's back before she lowered her lashes and her lovely features smoothed back into serenity. So, the hot-tempered girl who'd bruised Kai's shin still lay under all those glacial layers. In a perverse way, Sin was glad to see it, but decided not to tell Kai.

"Aena, it was a pleasure to see you again," she said, surprised to find she meant it. Of course, she hadn't had to deal with the younger Griffin for the past two hours. "Please don't be a stranger. You're welcome at Shay Enterprises anytime."

Liaena's gaze lifted to meet Sin's with a pleasant smile, her composure restored. "What a generous offer," she responded. "Thank you."

Sin pressed her lips together to hide her amusement at the other woman's evasion of the invitation.

"It's been interesting as always, Lie," her brother said with a twinkle in his green eyes and a sly curl of his mouth.

"Manakai." She tilted her gilded head, her cool reserve not betraying even a fraction of the fire Sin had seen in her eyes.

The twins turned to face Griffin together. He offered his hand to Kai, regal features tolerant and amused. "Shay, you haven't changed."

Kai shook his hand with a charming smile. "That makes two of us, Griff."

Griffin's look turned dry, but he didn't comment as he turned to Sin. Taking her hand, he bowed over it. "Delightful to see you again, my dear." This time his mouth brushed her skin.

She clenched her jaw to keep from grimacing. "Charming to the end, Web. Until next time," she replied, fixing a winning smile on her face.

With a nod, Kai cupped her elbow and the two of them moved away, much to Sin's relief. She heaved a silent sigh, but Kai was her twin. He glanced down at her with a frown. "Was it bad?"

"It's been worse."

"Get anywhere?"

"He took the bait."

"Good."

They circulated through the crowd, but with their main reason for coming accomplished, they didn't linger after the Griffins departed. The twins curved their path of circulation toward the door and managed their own graceful exit.

Chapter 10

As they walked the pathway back to their transport, Sin glanced around. "We need a vacation. It would be nice to come back here just for the pleasure of it someday."

"We will," Kai answered in an absent tone.

Sin snorted, giving him a disgusted look. "Sure we will."

He caught her eye and tipped his head in acknowledgement. Their chances for a vacation were slim to none in the near future. Even if they did have the time, neither one of them would take a respite. It wasn't how their father had raised them.

Their return trip to Shay Enterprise's main station was subdued after Sin gave her brother an account of her time with Griffin. He had a few questions on specific topics, but when she finished, he grimaced, and wrapped a commiserating arm around her without a word. Grateful for the comfort, she leaned into him and put her head on his shoulder.

After a moment he said, "If I could take your place, I would."

A sweet comment, but it also woke her sense of the ridiculous, and she grinned. "Thanks, but you wouldn't do this dress justice."

He plucked at the cloth over her hip. "Wouldn't be so bad if we let it out some."

She snickered at the image of her brawny brother in soft and revealing femininity. "Dad wouldn't have approved."

Kai went still and Sin winced, calling herself an idiot. Their father was always a touchy topic, the one subject her lighthearted brother could not find humor in.

"Maybe not," he said in a low tone, "but he would have been proud of you just the same."

Tears pricked the backs of her eyes. She kept her head on his shoulder so he wouldn't see how he'd moved her, giving him a silent hug. He kissed the top of her head and they leaned together, giving and receiving wordless comfort, for the rest of the return journey.

As they approached the station, Sin sat up with a sigh, rolling her head to work a kink out of her neck muscles. Kai stretched like a big cat, yawning so wide his jaw popped.

"So did you find Marcus' anonymous tip?" she asked, giving him a mischievous poke in the side to sour his stretch.

He flinched, sagging into his seat with an offended glare and a warning growl. "Becker, from Information Systems, caught the two Core members sending cryptic messages out-of-company."

She made a derisive sound in the back of her throat. "Those two make better krell dung than spies."

"Well, Marcus promised to watch out for them, so maybe he can keep them from screwing up and giving themselves away."

"What are we doing about Becker?"

"He's being transferred to this location. Marcus thinks he's a good man, but I'd like to find out for myself."

"Works for me," Sin responded. "You'll handle him, then?"

He grunted an affirmative, stretching again while keeping a jaundiced eye on her.

She grinned but refrained from poking him a second time. "Need to loosen up? How about the Circle? I have some hostility to release."

He gave her a sour look as they rose to their feet and exited the transport, nodding thanks to the pilots. "Why do you always want to beat the snot out of me after we see Griffin? I don't look anything like him."

"Transference of aggression," she answered with a sage nod, heading toward the maintenance bay.

He snorted, matching her stride. "So transfer your aggression on someone else for a change."

"When you make such a good punching bag?" she asked with a razor-edged grin. "Why would I?"

He bared his teeth at her in a mock snarl. "All right, Sissa, time for another lesson in humility." She burst into laughter, but he ignored her, rolling his shoulders and flexing his arms. "And I could use the exercise."

"Yes, you could," she retorted and skittered away with another laugh when he swiped at her. "Meet you there?"

"You're on." He veered away from the maintenance bay to head in a different direction.

Sin continued with an eager spring to her step, looking forward to the release of tension the Circle of Fire would afford her. Entering the maintenance bay, she took a quick inventory of the Shadows. Cassie and Del's Shadows were missing, they must still be out training. Maybe. A momentary doubt darkened her thoughts before she pushed it away. No matter how Cassie felt about Del, she would never jeopardize the upcoming run by allowing an unprepared pilot to accompany them. Still, an acid bitterness burned in her stomach at the thought of them spending so much time together.

"Just the person I wanted to see."

The deep voice startled Sin out of her thoughts. Del's brother stepped from the shadows, and she smiled in cool greeting. "Nick," she responded, taking in his disheveled appearance, wondering what he'd been up to all day. "Have you been enjoying our station?" she added, looking him up and down with raised eyebrows.

He grimaced, glancing down and straightening his clothes. Even with his face averted, a flush was visible darkening his skin. "Had a run-in with one of your pilots. The blond kid…ah, woman."

She chuckled but didn't comment, turning toward the back door to the bay and inclining her head in tacit invitation. He joined her with an uncomfortable smile, shortening his stride to match hers.

"You wanted to see me?" she asked with polite interest.

"I have a few questions."

"I'll be happy to answer them, but I do have an appointment to attend soon," she said in smooth qualification, unwilling to forgo her time in the Circle with Kai. "I have a few minutes, if you don't mind accompanying me to my suite?"

"Ah…" he temporized as they stepped into the service hallway, looking her over. "Sure," he answered in a dubious tone.

She let her mouth curve in faint amusement, leading him into the lift. "You'll be perfectly safe, you know."

He made a sound in the back of his throat like a choked off laugh. "Sure I will. Nice outfit, by the way."

"Thank you," she replied, not hiding the laughter in her tone. "Not for your benefit, I assure you."

"Good to know." He met her teasing gaze with a wry smile. Then his expression sobered. "Did my brother see you in it?"

The implications in the question and in his dark eyes sobered her as well. She studied him, recognizing the resolve to protect his brother. With a rueful shake of her head, she said, "It wasn't for his benefit, either."

His expression hardened as the lift doors opened into the Gold Rooms. Sin sighed and stepped out ahead of him. He didn't believe her and she wouldn't be able to convince him otherwise, though she had to admit there was a small grain of truth to it. The dress had been worn as one more weapon against Griffin, but she hadn't avoided being seen by Del. She wondered if he'd liked what he'd seen, then pushed the thought away with an impatient shake of her head.

Leading Nick toward her quarters through the luxurious room, she ignored his muffled exclamations and curses at the extravagance on display. Walking down the short hall to her quarters, she keyed open the door and smiled over her shoulder. "Please come in. Mina, this is Nicholo Givliani. Nick, this is my house companion, Mina."

"Welcome, Mr. Givliani," Mina's smooth voice resonated through the rooms.

Nick's eyebrows rose. "Thank you. It's nice to

meet you, Mina."

"The pleasure is mine," the AI answered with warmth. "And I thank you for being a part of my sister companion's naming. Samantha is a lovely choice."

Sin hid a smile when Nick's jaw dropped. "Mina loves to mother the other AIs on the station. She was the first here and considers herself the matriarch."

"They, ah…" He cleared his throat and shifted in place. "They talk a lot to each other?"

"How boring would their lives be if they could only speak to us? Besides, we're gone more than we're home."

"Speaking of which," Mina interrupted, "you received a package while you were gone. It arrived by personal courier from Webster Griffin."

The hair on the back of Sin's neck rose, but she kept her voice even as she ushered Nick into the living room. "Has it been scanned?"

"Yes. There are no dangerous components or substances. The object is made of data crystal matrix but has not been formatted or imprinted with information."

"It's completely clean?"

"Yes."

Nick was watching her with intent eyes; dark, vibrant, and so like his brother's. The package sat on the low table in front of the sofa, but she ignored it, waving him to a seat. "May I get you something to drink?"

He shook his head. "I'm good, thanks. Will you open it?"

She almost laughed, admiring his directness. She could refuse, but it wouldn't ease any of his suspicions.

"Why not?" she said and sat next to him, amused when he shifted away from her. Pulling the package toward her, she passed a nail over the seal to break it and lifted the lid. Staring inside, she sucked in a sharp breath and went still. Nick made a wordless sound of amazement or dismay, but she ignored him, eyeing the object lying with such insidious innocence on blood-red velvet.

Made from purest crystal, the object sparkled flawless and clear as spring water. Some artist with great skill had sculpted a flower of such delicate beauty it hurt to look at it. A thorny vine wrapped around the stem and looped around the petals, surrounding the flower with every thorn pointing inward, threatening the blossom.

"You're certain nothing was imprinted in the crystal?" Sin asked through numb lips but knew the answer already. The gift was message enough.

"I am certain," Mina answered, her voice soft with sympathy.

Sin fought the urge to fling the thing across the room, to smash it into unrecognizable bits. No doubt Nick could see the flow of her emotions, but at the moment she couldn't care less. If Griffin stood in front of her just then, she would have killed him without hesitation.

"It's the Signalan flower of mercy," she clipped. "The Enua."

Nick growled low in the back of his throat. He'd deciphered at least part of the message, *no mercy*, but not all of it.

"The Enua flower is the symbol of my mother's house, Preterat House. She was from Signala originally." She turned her head, watching him absorb the information.

The muscles of his face seemed to wince at the sight of the thing, but he didn't look away from the beleaguered flower.

"My mother killed herself." She said it with a stark lack of emotion.

His head jerked back, the pupils of his eyes dilating until his dark eyes were as black as space. "Sun's blood."

Sin smiled without humor, fury stiffening her features. "You see what kind of gift he gives me. The flower caught among thorns is a declaration of domination." Bitter anger shadowed her voice, but she couldn't stop. Opening this package in front of Nick had been a mistake. "The use of the Enua is a nasty jab at our family history, but even worse it's a threat against our mother's bloodline, against us. He didn't use the insignia for Shay Enterprises, the sphinx. He used our house symbol. He's making this personal, telling us we'll suffer the same fate as our mother. You know what this says to me, Inspector?"

Nick watched her with a stillness, like the eye of a storm, coiled emotion in his dark gaze. He made no reply, but she didn't need one. The vitriol burning in her throat demanded release.

"This gift tells me Griffin has no mercy, no pity, no compassion. What he does have is fear. If we didn't make him nervous, he wouldn't be using this pretty little bludgeon. So, by all the galactic Suns, I'll thank him for his gift."

Unable to remain so near the thing, Sin lunged to her feet and began pacing the room. Her hands clenched into fists while she tried to regain her composure.

At first, Nick continued to watch her, but after a minute he turned away to study the flower, his expression thoughtful. "Will you destroy it?"

Sin paused at the end of the sofa, studying him with as much care as he studied the flower. He was a younger version of Del, with his strong features, dark eyes, and surprising intuition. She waited, blood cooling in the silence, until he turned his head and met her gaze.

With a faint smile he could interpret any way he wanted, she responded, "Why do you ask when you already know the answer, Inspector?"

"If it means everything you say, why keep it?"

"Destroying it gains me nothing, Nick. Accepting it may gain me everything."

A flicker of unease moved in his eyes before he looked away toward the threatened, defenseless flower. "You play a deep game, Shay. A dangerous one." His gaze returned to hers, vibrant with dark demand. "Let my brother go."

She wanted to allay his fears for his brother, to explain the deep and dangerous game he sensed but didn't understand. It was too soon, though, there wasn't enough time, and trust was a factor. Instead, she smiled with a hint of sadness. "I'll leave it up to him."

It was the least she could do.

"I apologize for interrupting, Sin," Mina's melodious voice intruded. "But Manakai has informed me you are late." A slight questioning note ended her statement. According to Sin's schedule, she had no official appointments.

"Thank you, Mina," Sin responded, altering her expression to polite regret. Spending time in the Circle with Kai was now more important than ever. After she told her brother about the gift, they'd be at it for a long while. "I'm sorry, Nick. I realize we didn't address any of your questions. Another time?"

He nodded, rising to his feet and giving the gift a final long look as he rounded the end of the sofa. "When?"

"I'm afraid it might not be for a few days. We leave on business tomorrow," Sin replied, escorting him toward the door. "Please stay as long as you like. I will make sure the station's every hospitality is open to you."

"Thanks." His tone was dubious and a little questioning.

Sin pretended not to notice and gave him a polite smile. "It's no trouble at all." Opening the door, she stepped to one side and held her smile as he passed through. "I'll contact you when we're available to answer your questions."

"Hope not too long," he rumbled with a pointed dark glance, pausing outside her door.

Her smile widened. "Goodbye, Inspector," she said and let the door close between them. With a sigh of both relief and regret, Sin moved away from the door and headed with long strides toward her bedroom. "Mina, make sure that thing isn't here when I get back."

"What do you want me to do with it?"

"Have it put on display in the Reception Hall. Prominent display."

Mina's voice took on a dubious note, not unlike Nick's. "Are you certain?"

"Oh, yes," Sin muttered through clenched teeth. "Quite certain."

Chapter 11

Webster Griffin found his daughter in the Aqualyr, or the Water Room, as she had so crassly named it as a girl. As usual, she sat at the fountain in the center, ignoring the numerous extravagant sculptures, paintings, and other liquid art gracing the room. *Always the fountain,* he thought with a small grimace of distaste, but he hadn't come to revive the old argument. She had done well today, and though he wouldn't go so far as to praise her, he'd give her the reward of his attention.

"Daughter," he began in an even tone.

She interrupted without turning her gaze away from the tumble of water. "The gift was a mistake."

His lips tightened as a flare of anger burned through him. He controlled it with the steely discipline branding his every waking moment. He hadn't made Quasicore what it was today by giving in to his emotions, but he was hard-pressed not to react. She dared disapprove of his decisions?

"Mind your tongue, daughter," he said without changing his even tone, but she glanced over her shoulder at him with a cool, knowing look in her gray eyes.

Only those eyes marked her as his daughter. She was like her mother in every other aspect, from her appearance to her attitude. As a general rule, she stayed malleable and obedient, but every once in a while she became intractable. Today she seemed in the mood to test him. For some reason, she had those moods most often in this room.

She smiled at him with aggravating patience. "Father, what use would I be if I didn't tell you the truth of what I see? You have enough people under you who mind their tongues. A whole galaxy, in fact."

Flattery and insult in one. She'd at least paid attention when he instructed her, though turning her training on him was unacceptable. He returned her smile with a gentle one of his own. "I judge the measure of your usefulness, Liaena. I have no use for a disrespectful daughter who contradicts my decisions."

She lowered her eyes in submission, but her smile remained to taunt him. "I mean no disrespect, Father. My choice of words may have been poor, but I feel it's my duty to warn you the gift will anger the Shays. And angering them is—"

"A mistake?" he interrupted in silky animosity.

But she seemed immune to his lash. "Dangerous," she finished, her expression sobering as she met his gaze again.

He curled his lip, eyeing her with disgust. "They are no danger to Quasicore. You overestimate their abilities." The arrogance in his voice gave him a certain measure of satisfaction. He'd been wary of Shay Enterprises at one time, but no longer. The passing of his opponent, Ezekiel, had sealed their fate. Having them at his mercy was only a matter of time. At the thought of his old nemesis, a pang went through him he refused to acknowledge as sorrow.

He turned away in dismissal.

She stopped him in his tracks. "You underestimate them," she said in a voice as cold as the silver ice in her eyes. Then she turned her back on him as if he'd become insignificant.

He punished her, of course. She had forced him into it. But she took her punishment with the same remote stoicism as when she sat at the fountain, as if he couldn't touch her even with pain.

Chapter 12

Del rolled his head from side to side, trying to release the knot of tension in his neck and shoulders while he waited for the lift to stop on his level. Training with Cassie had been as grueling today as it had been the previous day, maybe worse. She'd been more critical and a harder taskmaster. He had no experience with the kind of weapons installed in his Shadow, so his performance had been abysmal.

Cassie, it seemed, was a Sun-cursed perfectionist. She'd kept him out on the ranges flying evasive maneuvers and practicing his targeting until his whole body burned with tension. Finally, she'd let him return to the station with an uninspiring, "It'll have to do."

She was evil incarnate.

The lift doors opened and he moved down the hall to his quarters, grimacing at the protesting stretch of his muscles. Grumbling under his breath about domineering little women, he entered his quarters then jumped when a feminine voice greeted him.

"Welcome home, Adelmo. You have a visitor."

Del remembered the AI and made a face. She was going to take some getting used to. "Hey, Sam," he said in a listless tone. His brother rose from the couch, catching his eye. "Hey, Nick. How'd you get in here?"

His brother grinned, but it was Samantha who answered. "My apologies, Adelmo. Nicholo assured me you would allow him to wait within for your return."

"He's right, but he's the only one, got it? And stop calling me Adelmo. I'm Del. He's Nick."

"I understand."

Nick's grin turned conspiratorial as Del flopped onto the couch with a sigh of relief. "I sweet-talked her, but she wouldn't have done it if it wasn't me. Since I was part of her naming and all." He lifted his eyebrows, sitting down next to Del.

Del snorted, eyeing his brother with weary amusement. "Think it gives you special privileges?"

"No more than bein' your brother," Nick answered, his tone light but his expression sobering. "Naming a house companion is a big deal, though."

Del studied his brother's face for a second. "Been busy today?"

"Yes, I have." There was no mistaking the somber note in his voice.

With a quick frown, Del cleared his throat and said, "Hey, Sam, could you do privacy mode for a little bit?"

"Certainly. When you wish to end it—"

"Request VRS to resume. Got it," Del finished for her.

"Privacy mode is now on."

A small silence hung in the air while the brothers looked at one another. Then Nick opened his mouth, but Del held up a hand to forestall him. "Wait, let me take a quick san and grab a bite to eat. Think you can remember how to make a supernova?"

Nick's expression lightened. "You sure you wanna go down that road again?"

"Not all the way down, but I could use a muscle relaxer. The little slave-driver was at it again."

Nick chuckled, clapping Del on the shoulder before getting to his feet. "Go get cleaned up. It'll be ready when you come out."

"Thanks." Del levered himself to his feet with difficulty and cursed Cassie under his breath. Who knew flying a slicer could make a body so sore?

Nick had more than a drink ready when Del finished. Delicious smells filled the place and pulled Del to the kitchen and the plates of food on the table.

"You're awful handy to have around," Del commented as he sat, eyeing the food with anticipation.

"Handy, that's me," Nick answered with a smirk, setting the supernova in front of Del and joining him at the table.

Del dove into the meal with relish, wolfing down the food like a starved animal. His brother watched him with tempered amusement, but he ignored Nick in favor of his demanding stomach. When he finished, he sat back with a satisfied sigh and downed the rest of his nova.

"Better?" Nick asked.

"Much. Thanks, bro."

"No problem. Did the little dragon starve you, too?"

"Yes she did," Del answered in an aggrieved tone. "She enjoyed every second, too. The woman is pure evil." Nick chuckled, but his eyes had a somber gleam. Del pushed his plate aside then gave the younger man a grim stare. "So spit it out, Nick. What'd you find?"

Nick sighed, pushing his own half-eaten plate away. "You won't like it."

"What a surprise," Del drawled.

Nick gave a wry tip of his head, but his eyes met

Del's with alarming seriousness. "You have to get away from these people. Whatever they're up to, it's big and it involves Quasicore. It's not just business either. It's personal." He sat forward, his expression earnest and the lines around his mouth tight with dismay. "It's a blood feud, Del, with Webster Griffin. You stay and you'll get crushed between them."

Alarm sank through Del's skin and leeched into his bones, turning to cold dread. "How do you know?"

"I was with Sin when she opened a package from Griffin. I don't think she was expecting the kind of gift she got or she wouldn't have opened it in front of me. It was a warning and a threat."

"What was it?" Del asked, dread still chilling his core.

Nick's expression hardened. "A crystal flower surrounded by thorns."

Del looked away to hide the flare of bitter anger surging through him. A declaration of possession. Why didn't Griffin just brand her with the Core insignia and be done with it? "How'd she take it?"

"Not well," his brother answered, dry amusement not hiding an undertone of strain. "I gotta say, she's even more beautiful when she's ticked off." Then his face sobered again, eyes alive with warning. "She uses it like a weapon. And her brother's just like her. You get between them and Griffin, and you'll be just a smear on the floor."

"I don't plan on getting between them," Del said, his whole body tightening with dismay.

Nick leaned closer, taking Del's wrist in a hard clasp, eyes sharp. "You stay here and you won't have a choice. It's bad enough to stand between titans, brother.

Anybody'd get crushed. Even worse to be in the palm of her hand."

Del pulled away from his brother's grip, standing to clear off the table. "I got a year's contract to carry out and a debt to pay."

"She'll let you go," Nick said in an insistent tone.

Del paused to look at him. "How do you know?"

Nick shrugged, his expression reluctant. "I asked her to, and she said it was up to you."

Del dropped the plates back on the table with a crash and glared down at his brother. "You did what?"

"I told you I'd do everything I could to help you."

"You call trying to get me fired help?"

"Yes," his brother answered with calm resolve, sitting back and hooking one arm over the back of his seat.

Del stared at him for a long moment before snorting in disgust. "Well, cut it out. She might just decide to make my life miserable instead."

"She isn't already?" Nick shot back with a sardonic look. "Did you see what she was wearing today?"

The question caught Del by surprise. So did the memory of Sin draped in delicious cream and temptation. Nick's mocking half-smile said his brother knew what was going through his head. Clenching his jaw, Del folded his arms and refused to answer, staring back at Nick with resentment.

"Get out now, while you still can, Del."

But he couldn't. The Core had held him hostage with his father's honor and his brother's safety. The Shays had more insidious bonds, but they were just as strong, the lure of the Shadows not the least of them.

Grabbing the plates, Del turned away so Nick

couldn't read his face. "I didn't ask for your help, little brother."

"I know. You're too Sun-cursed stubborn to ask." When Del didn't comment, Nick continued, "Just don't be stubborn about this. Tell me you'll leave."

With a calm he didn't feel, Del glanced over, eyebrows raised in polite question. "Dessert?"

Nick snarled a curse, pushing away from the table and lurching to his feet. "Of all the stupid, mule-headed, krell-brained…" His voice trailed off into unintelligible mutterings as he stalked out of the kitchen.

Del finished cleaning then went to the entrance into the living room. Nick paced around it like a caged tiger. Del folded his arms, leaning against the entry. "How'd your flight with Red go?"

Nick shot him a black look and continued to pace.

"Did you bring her back in one piece?" Del asked with casual humor.

Nick stopped in his tracks and glared at him. "Yeah, no thanks to you."

Del put on a wounded expression. "What'd I do?"

"You could've warned me about the training course. A Core gang high on blue would've been less dangerous."

Del grinned. "Had a good time, did you?"

Nick's expression eased, one corner of his mouth curling. "After I got over my near death experience, sure."

With a chuckle, Del straightened and walked over to clap his brother on the shoulder. "Thought you would. So, since you've been busy today, take me on a tour of the station. I haven't seen it myself."

Nick gave him a reluctant grin. "Didn't see enough to play tour guide. I did find this little place on the common strip, looks like fun. Don't know if they make supernovas, though."

"Let's find out," Del said, slinging a companionable arm across his brother's shoulders and heading for the door.

"Don't forget Sam."

"Oh, yeah." Del paused at the door. "Reactivate VRS."

"Privacy mode has been terminated," Samantha declared in her smooth voice.

"We're going out, Sam. Watch the fort."

"Fort?" she asked in a perplexed tone. "I was not aware we had a—" The closing door cut off her words.

The little place on the strip did, in fact, make supernovas. They returned to Del's quarters with a great deal more cheer and less grace than when they'd left it.

"This cannot be healthy," Samantha commented when they staggered through the door.

The alcohol turned her comment into the funniest joke ever. Helping each other to the couch, they collapsed onto it, laughing. Their laughter wound down into the occasional chuckle after several minutes.

"Hey, didn't the Shays give you quarters?"

Nick cursed in a conversational tone. They stared bleary-eyed at one another. "I ain't gonna make it back there. Barely made it here."

"Couch again?"

Nick gave a solemn, wobbling nod. "Couch."

"I insist you take fluids and allow me to medicate you before you retire," Samantha said in a severe tone.

They were in no shape to fight her. Afterward, Del couldn't remember ever sleeping so well, though it didn't last long enough.

Chapter 13

Del woke to Samantha's persistent voice. "You have a visitor. Cassiopeia Draegen requests entrance to your quarters. You must wake now. You have a visitor. Cassiopeia—"

"Yeah, yeah, I'm awake already," he mumbled, rolling to a sitting position and rubbing his face. "What's she want, Sam?"

"She said it is time for you to wake."

Mouthing obscenities, Del yanked on pants and grabbed a shirt, heading for the living room. He was in time to catch Nick opening the door. On the other side, Cassie stood with an impatient frown and folded arms. "Well, it's about t-time…" she stuttered, voice trailing off and eyes widening at Nick's bare chest.

Nick turned with a smirk and gestured her into the room. "If it isn't the little dragon. Here to crack the whip?"

Cassie recovered, giving Del's brother a chilly stare as she sidled over the threshold.

Shrugging on his shirt, Del grumbled, "Sun's sake, Cass."

"We're getting an early start this morning."

"No kidding." Del folded his arms and looked down at her in disgust.

Mimicking his stance with a pinched expression, Cassie raised her eyebrows. "Well? The day's not

172

getting any younger."

Nick snorted and passed between them, catching Cassie's glance as he padded toward the kitchen. "I'll get coffee," he said with a tinge of irony.

Del sighed and headed for his bedroom. "Give me five to san and change."

When he returned, Cassie bounced to her feet from her perch on the edge of the couch, the look in her eyes a little wild. Slouched into the cushions, Nick watched her with a lazy grin, steaming cup of coffee in hand, still shirtless. Del wondered what kind of mischief his brother had unleashed on the little woman, and how much she'd make Del pay for it.

"Ready to go?" Cassie asked and headed for the exit like she was escaping.

"I don't even get coffee?" Del complained, not moving after her.

Cassie paused by the door, looking back with a twitch of impatience. "Coffee's down there with breakfast. We're practicing with the courier ships today and everyone's participating. We might be back for lunch, but just in case we run out of time, you'd better say goodbye to your brother now. We leave for the run late afternoon and we won't be back for days."

"What, no goodbye from you, little dragon?" Nick called after her as she stepped over the threshold.

Cassie's back stiffened, but she didn't pause, walking away without another word.

With a rueful grimace, Del looked from the closed door to his brother's unrepentant grin.

"Prickly little thing, ain't she?"

"Around you, anybody would be," Del retorted with a wry shake of his head, approaching the couch.

"Try not to get into trouble while I'm gone, little brother."

Nick sobered, staring up at Del with a frown pulling at his brows. "So you're gonna go."

"It's what they pay me for," Del said then ruffled his brother's hair, grinning at the disgruntled cuff he got in return. "Will you be here when I get back?"

"Yeah," Nick answered, his eyes dark wells of concern. "Be careful, Del."

"As careful as I can," he answered with a jaunty grin and headed for the door. "Sam, take care of him."

"I will," the AI responded.

He gave his brother a quick salute as he stepped out the door and got one in return, but Nick's expression was somber.

To his surprise, Cassie was waiting for him by the lift. She gave him a cool smile, but made no comment as she stepped into the lift with him.

Trying to gage her mood, he cleared his throat. "Good morning, by the way."

"It should be one," she answered, her smile warming a bit. "Test flights are fun."

"You said the whole crew, right?"

She shot him a knowing look. "That's right, including the bosses."

His heart sped up at the news. He took a deep breath and tried to keep in mind what his brother had told him last night. *Just do your job and don't get involved,* he thought but his heart didn't slow. "Is it normal to take everybody on a run?"

"No," she answered as the lift doors opened. "But this one's a little different."

He glanced down at her while they made their way

to the maintenance bay. She gave a small shrug and gestured at the scene before them.

The bay was almost empty, a few ships off to one side. The double row of Shadows had disappeared. The entire crew was present and boisterous, clustering around a hovering table of beverages and food. Sin and Manakai stood out like ominous dark beacons. Dressed entirely in black, they moved through the group with the smooth, predatory grace Del remembered from his first encounter with them. The Shadow twins were back. His heart lurched and he took a despairing breath, watching Sin with a hunger he couldn't deny. *In the palm of her hand.* Nick had been more right than he knew.

"Down boy," Cassie murmured next to him as they approached the crew.

He shot her a scowl, but she didn't seem to notice, waving to someone from the group with a smile. Bib bounded toward them, a welcoming smile lighting her angelic face. "Big Del!" she cried and flung herself at him.

Unprepared, he staggered a little when she collided with him, his arms catching her about the waist.

"Good morning," she whispered in his ear, her voice a throaty invitation, her soft body pressing against his in seductive welcome.

With a grimace, he unwound her arms from his neck and set her away with firm hands. "Morning, Bib."

Unphased by his rejection, she beamed up at him. "I met your brother yesterday. I like him," she added with a gleam in her sky blue eyes.

"You like everybody," he countered and shook his head when she laughed.

Insinuating herself between them, she gave Cassie a kiss on the cheek, and slipped an arm through each of theirs. Tugging them toward the group, she exclaimed, "I love practice flights! Do we know what teams we're on?"

"Not yet," Cassie said in a tolerant tone, amused brown eyes meeting Del's.

"'Bout time you showed," Kai said when he caught sight of Del.

"My fault. I forgot to tell him what time we were meeting this morning," Cassie responded, extracting herself from Bib and heading for the table.

Kai's jaw dropped in feigned shock. "You forgot? You?" Cassie rolled her eyes and he turned to sweep the group with a stern frown. "Did the universe end and someone forgot to let me know?"

"You didn't get the memo?" Sin answered, flashing a teasing grin at her brother before glancing at Del. The amused twinkle in her bright eyes and the curve of her luscious lips was enough to make him hot all over. "Morning, Del."

He didn't get a chance to respond. Bib dropped him like yesterday's news and slipped in between the twins, wrapping an arm around each of them. "So whose team am I on? You're not sticking me in the hauler again, are you? I get to slice this time, right?" With wide-eyed pleading, she looked from one to the other.

Jinx's young, grinning face appeared over Bib's shoulder. "Hey, what's wrong with flying the haulers?" He must have pinched her; she jumped and squealed, spinning on quick feet to lunge after him when he darted away.

Sin exchanged a tolerant glance with her brother before looking at Del again. "We'll give you time to eat before we get started."

He nodded, pulling his gaze from hers with an effort and shifting around the twins to the table.

Quan, a small, soft-spoken man with a quick smile, made room for him. "You in the mood for sweet or meat?" he asked, gesturing to the pastries. "Me, I like sugar in the morning, but not everybody does. I think these are egg and cheese, and those on the right are sausage."

"Thanks." Del reached for coffee first before he grabbed a pastry. Whatever it was, it went down fast. While he ate, he watched the loud debate going on across the table.

A young man named Owen Risk, who liked to be called Sundog, was telling a wild tale. Lynch and the other pilot Fern, a handsome middle-aged woman, had heard it before and scorned his version. Sundog retaliated with bawdier renditions.

Cassie appeared at Del's elbow, eating a sugar-coated pastry with dainty precision. She glanced across the table and snickered. "Sunny's been taking lessons from Kai again."

Del snorted. "At least he has imagination."

"Bets on which boss breaks it up," Quan commented on Del's other side, a wide grin on his face.

"Too late," Cassie answered.

Kai rounded the table toward them. "Save it for the trip, kids," Kai told the debaters, his voice carrying in spite of their volume. He was grinning in lazy amusement, but his tone brooked no argument. "You'll have plenty of time for Sunny's fantasies on this run."

"What is this run?"

"Yeah, don't keep us in suspense, man."

Kai glanced around at the rest of the group with raised eyebrows. "Everybody ready? Let's get to it, then." Pulling out a holodisc from his jacket, he tossed it into the air with a careless flick. The disc flipped then paused, spinning a holographic image into the air, a stretch of space with several points blinking throughout. The crew ranged themselves around the disc and Kai in a loose semi-circle, and Del joined them.

"We've been contracted by the Cortecian Mining Guild to courier a shipment of abantium to their two biggest mining operations," Kai began, his tone and demeanor hardening to a businesslike polish. Usually a reckless and carefree menace, now he was in cool control.

"We'll accept the shipment at the supplier, here," Kai continued, pointing to one blinking spot in the hologram. "Just off a high traffic lane, so security won't be an issue. From there we take this lane"—he traced a line across the hologram—"until it angles away from our destination. At this point, we go off-lane. A day's off-lane travel will get us to the Corteca system. Then we split up. The two mining facilities are in systems flanking Corteca. This means two teams and we bring both the Rock and the Tank."

Del frowned and looked down at Cassie in question.

"The cargo haulers," she whispered.

"Corteca's close to Fringe space, so the baddies will be out in force, looking for just this kind of cargo. It's been a while since we teamed it and we have a new crew member, so we're going to drill before we set off this afternoon. Questions?"

Lynch made a rumbling noise to catch Kai's attention. "Does the cargo need any special handling?"

"No, abantium's stable unmixed, so we don't have to worry about it blowing up. The supplier says it'll be sealed in protective containers and ready to throw on the haulers."

"Manny, what teams are we on?" Bib cut in breathlessly, blue eyes bright.

He sent her a wry grin. "You, Lynch, Fern, and Sunny are with me. Cass, Del, Quan and Jinx are with Sinsi."

Bib grabbed Jinx's arm and shook it but didn't take her eyes off Kai. "So I'll be slicing this time?"

"Yes, Bib. Lynch will pilot the Rock, and Jinx will take the Tank."

She gave a whoop, throwing her arms up in the air and doing a little wiggling dance with her hips. The crew laughed at her antics until Sin set a hand in the middle of her back and guided her forward. "All right, Biblet, celebrate on the move. We have work to do."

Kai snagged the disc out of the air and waved for the crew to follow him, but he headed away from the door to the docking bay. With a frown, Del hesitated and Cassie paused with him. Sin touched her shoulder and the two women exchanged a glance. Cassie nodded and followed the crew.

Giving Del a slight smile, Sin inclined her head after the group. "Shall we?"

"Where are we going?" he asked, moving after the others.

"Another bay sits on the other side of this one. We call it the storage bay, but it's just an excuse to come and go without the regular couriers taking note. They fuss when Kai and I give this group special attention."

Del gave her a dubious look, doubting they'd have a whole separate bay just to keep peace between the off-laners and the normals.

Sin's smile widened and she changed the subject. "How's your brother?"

"Good," he answered with caution, studying her features. He could think of a few reasons she'd ask, none of them harmless.

"You had a good reunion, then? I didn't get a chance to ask yesterday."

They approached a door hidden from view by the massive conveyors.

"It's great to see him again."

"I'm glad," she murmured, then flashed him a glance so enigmatic his stomach muscles tightened. "I'm also glad you're still here this morning."

A flush of confused emotion climbed his neck. He had no safe answer, so he went on the offensive as they stepped into a smaller bay. "Nick's gonna dig while we're gone."

"I would be disappointed if he didn't," she responded with unruffled calm.

He stared down at her, brows pulling together.

She met his gaze with a hint of amusement and gestured ahead of them. "The left one's the Tank and the other is the Rock," she said, pointing to two large ships in turn. They were the ugliest things Del had ever seen. A dull charcoal gray, they squatted on their pads with the grace of toads, massive and clunky. They didn't have a smooth curve on them, their sullen bulk pitted with strange indents.

His expression must have shown his revulsion. Sin chuckled. "What they lack in beauty, they make up for in function. No ship is more reliable, and they have their own special qualities."

Del followed her toward the two vessels then paused, realizing none of the slicers were in view. "Ah, where are the—?"

"Inside. The haulers can dock slicers."

Eyeing the long divots in the haulers' sides as they mounted a ramp leading to the ship's hatch, he asked, "Did you make 'em this ugly on purpose?"

Sin chuckled again, ducking into the hauler ahead of him. Following her down a short corridor, he blinked when they entered a large control room. It seemed more elaborate than necessary for a ship of this size and function.

Jinx sat in the main pilot's seat, his hands moving with swift precision over the controls encircling the chair. When he caught sight of Del, his face lit with a wide, boyish grin. "Welcome to the Tank. What d'you think of her?"

"She's a brute."

"She sure is," Jinx said with a look of pride.

Quan clapped the young man on the shoulder. "Think you can put her in space before Lynch gets the Rock off her big ol' behind?"

Jinx flashed the pilot a wicked grin. "Watch me."

Cassie groaned. "You bust this ship and I'll bust your rear."

Jinx either didn't hear or ignored the threat, his face glowing with excitement.

Sin glanced at Del, an amused crinkle at the corners of her eyes. "You'll want to grab hold of something. This isn't going to be pretty."

Cassie strapped into the second's seat. Del gripped the back of it as the engines snarled under his heels. No matter how the ships looked, the sound of those engines said they had well-toned muscle to spare. The deck lurched, the ship launching off the pad and spinning with clumsy speed toward the exit. The Rock launched right after them and angled to get ahead.

Del swore as both ships pounded toward an opening not large enough for both of them. Jinx laughed with reckless delight, his fingers flying over the controls. A moment later, the Tank rolled like a whale in shallow water and the Rock mimicked the move, both squeezing through the atmospheric shield on a diagonal.

"Age before beauty, brat," Lynch's voice rumbled over the com.

"So I gotta follow your slow ass, gramps? Don't think so," Jinx chortled in return.

Del gritted his teeth as the two ships jockeyed for lead position, appreciating more than ever the smooth, effortless grace of his Shadow.

"Getting space sick yet?" Sin asked at his side, grinning at his disgruntled look. "Come on, let me show you the rest of the ship before we get space born."

He followed her out of the control room, glad to take his eyes off the lurching viewer. "Where are we going?"

"Somewhere we can drill in relative privacy." They headed down a long corridor. Halfway down, a pair of doors faced each other. Sin gestured to each in turn as they passed them. "The common room and the communal crew quarters. Private quarters take up too much space," she added when he lifted his eyebrows. "This is a hauler, not a cruiser." She gave him a teasing grin and keyed open the door at the very end of the corridor.

The vast space beyond distracted him from the thought of sleeping in the same room as Sin. "Whoa," he breathed. The four docked Shadows looked small and forlorn sitting in so much space. Two large cargo loaders stood secured at the far end.

"This is the cargo bay, which doubles as a docking bay, as you can see."

"Got a lot of room here."

"This ship is a baby compared to our regular couriers. Sitting in one of those cargo holds, the Tank and Rock would look like these Shadows do here."

"So is this your company's main business?"

She hesitated, tilting her head. "One of them."

"What other—?" he started but didn't get to finish. Quan and Cassie came through the door behind them. His brother would have done a better job questioning her.

"Almost there," Cassie said with a quick smile.

"All right, let's go," Sin responded and headed toward the slicers.

Del headed for his own Shadow with long strides, giving the ship a welcoming caress as he rounded her nose, a thrill of anticipation dancing across his skin. He started her up and grinned when she purred in response. Connecting with the Shadow was a homecoming, contentment and excitement in one.

"You guys ready?" Jinx's young voice intruded.

"Clear the way, Jinx," Sin answered.

The bulkhead above slid away and Del lifted

without prompting toward the dark freedom of space. The others joined him, Sin's Shadow moving with thoughtless enticement at his side. He took a deep breath to fight the lure of her.

Outside the Tank, empty space surrounded them on all sides, no solar system in sight. The other hauler flew close by, its Shadows making a mockery of its homely bulk. Del had no trouble figuring out which Shadow was Bib's. She danced around the others like a moth around a flame. When Sin's team appeared, she broke away from her team to weave in between them in enthusiastic greeting.

The reaction of the others surprised a laugh out of Del. Bib's teammates sped after her while Cassie and Quan dodged around and arrowed toward the other team. The five Shadows met between the haulers in a breathtaking, intricate dance. Del could no longer tell which Shadow belonged to which pilot, until one broke away and blazed toward them with reckless speed. Kai declared, "You're it, Sinsi."

With a throaty laugh, Sin's Shadow rolled away from Del's side. The others sped after her in a whirl of silky blackness. Catching Sin was too much temptation. Del joined the race, blood beating an urgent, primitive rhythm.

In a close cluster, they chased Sin around the two haulers in elaborate twists and rushing spins. It was not only the most profound experience of his life, but the most fun he'd had since childhood. He couldn't remember the last time he'd laughed with such careless freedom, so attuned and powerful in the shaft of Shadows, like a dark god frolicking with his brethren. Shouts of encouragement and wild laughter accompanied their reckless flight.

Sin must have played this game before. She stayed just out of reach, taunting them with flirts of her ebony tail. They almost had her trapped between the haulers once, half the group splitting off to box her in, but she made what looked like an impossible, wrenching turn and fled away from the haulers with effortless ease. Growling half with frustration and half with admiration, Del followed with the rest.

They gained on her, Kai and Del jockeying to be first in the hunting pack. Anticipating victory, Del swore when she flipped around, striking at them like a vengeful arrow. The group scattered with exclamations and startled laughter when she blew through the middle of their Shadow cluster.

"All right, I'm caught," she announced, spinning once again to face them.

"Ah, no fair!"

"We almost had you this time."

"Coward," Kai drawled amidst the protesting voices from the rest of the crew.

"Insults stopped working when I was twelve, brother mine. Come on, children. We have work to do."

"My sister's greatest talent," Kai sighed, passing her on the way back toward the haulers. "Sucking the fun out of everything."

"When you grow up, you'll understand," she said with patronizing tolerance. "All right, first thing's first. Let's show Del why our haulers are so ugly."

The group returned to the haulers with whispers of anticipation. Del followed, bemused.

"Del, the color of our Shadows is no accident. Their skins have a function beyond beauty, something I don't think Cassie explained to you yet."

"No, I didn't," Cassie chimed in, a grin in her voice.

"What function?" Del asked as they drew closer to the bigger ships.

"We'll show you. Get a good view of both haulers and watch."

He did as commanded, watching with a perplexed half-smile while the rest arrayed themselves over their respective ships.

"Everyone, secure Shadows."

The slicers settled into the long divots in the surface of the haulers, their shapes fitting with seamless perfection, their colors blending into the skin of the larger ships. Del gaped in astonishment. They'd gone invisible. If he hadn't seen it happen right before his eyes, he would now think the haulers were the only ships in this region of space. Even the sensors didn't detect them. Any approaching ship would be unaware of the seven lethal Shadows lying in wait to protect the haulers.

"Holy Heart of the Sun," he breathed. Delighted laughter drifted over the com.

"We have yet to lose any cargo to hijackers, one of the reasons our off-lane service has such a good reputation."

"And we have kickass pilots," Kai added. Whistles and whoops of proud agreement followed his comment. Del grinned in spite of his unease at how far the Shays were willing to go.

"Too true, brother. So securing and scattering are the first maneuvers we'll practice today," Sin continued. "Shadows scatter."

As one, the slicers burst from their hiding places, spinning like dervishes away from the haulers. Any ship coming upon the haulers would be caught completely off-guard.

"You see?"

"Yes," Del answered, seeing more than just the maneuver. Military discipline underlined their actions and unnerved him. The earlier chase had been both a warm up and an affirmation of their group bond; a kind of nonverbal pep talk. These Shays were more subtle and dangerous than he'd given them credit for.

"Good. Take position, then."

Del had never attended a military flight school, but as the day wore on, he suspected it would be a lot like these drills. He learned flight formations, defense patterns, offensive tactics, and disabling maneuvers with both the slicers and the haulers. They even ran several attack simulations, but with dry targeting only, no live weapons fire allowed. In these situations, Del's weapons proficiency improved, which pleased him. An aggressive Shadow bearing down on him was better motivation than a sterile targeting field.

The drills were gratifying, even if they had repercussions he didn't want to think about. He'd never flown in a team before and it satisfied some deep part of him he hadn't known existed. The challenge of racing against other pilots in a slice had its own primitive excitement, but to be in tandem with a flight of slicers seemed as natural and comfortable as his own skin.

Chapter 14

When Kai called a halt to the drilling, Del was surprised to find it was afternoon. Disappointment flared in him when Kai told everyone to dock. Whatever else the Shays might turn out to be, he'd at least thank them for this experience.

"First call on the bathroom," Cassie announced when they settled into the Tank.

Del gave a rueful snort, wondering who'd fight him for second call. They'd been out a long while.

As they levered themselves out of the slicers, Sin called, "Hey, Jinx."

"Yeah, boss?"

"Will you get on the com with the station and have lunch sent down for us? We have time to eat before we roll."

"On it."

"Thanks," she said, catching Del's eye with wry humor. "I assume I'm not the only one who could use food."

He nodded, pacing her as they followed a quick-moving Cassie toward the door. "I'm starving."

"You should be. You worked hard today." She slanted him a warm look, spearing him down to his toes. A smile played around her mouth. "You looked great out there, Del. I'm glad you're with us."

He wanted to kiss her so much it was a pain in the

back of his throat. Good sense took a back seat to the sudden need rushing through him. He reached out to draw her close, but he got no farther than brushing his fingertips against her arm.

Quan startled him, clapping a hand to his shoulder. "She's right, you were great. Now I see why Cassie raves about you." Sin sent the other pilot a sharp glance, a quick frown passing over her features, but Quan didn't seem to notice, sidling by them. "And I call second on the bathroom."

Sin rolled her eyes, following Quan through the door. Del entered behind her, wondering why she'd frowned at Quan's compliment while trying not to watch her smooth stride and the sway of her hips. Quan disappeared into the crew's quarters and Sin continued on toward the control room. Del hesitated then followed Sin, reasoning the bathroom would be busy for a while.

"Hey, boss," Jinx greeted her, grinning at Del. "Hey, man, smokin' moves out there."

"Thanks," Del responded, uncomfortable. He wasn't used to praise. The Core's idea of a reward for a job well done was to not kill him.

Sin ruffled the boy's hair. "So what's for lunch?"

"It's a surprise," Jinx answered with a mischievous wink.

She narrowed her eyes. "It had better not be beer and chips again."

"It ain't."

"Or fish," she added. "You know I hate fish."

"Ain't fish neither. Relax, boss. I was good this time."

Del smothered a grin at the disbelieving eyebrow she arched at the youngster.

Jinx turned a disgruntled look on Del. "Don't know what's wrong with chips and beer."

"Or fish," Del responded, grinning when Sin folded her arms and gave them both a stern frown.

"Fish stink," she said with crisp emphasis. "Beer and chips are not a healthy meal."

"But so good goin' down," Del responded with a slow smile.

Jinx snickered. "Got that right."

Quan stepped in the control room. "Bathroom's open."

Del looked at Sin, but she waved him away. "I'm all right, you go ahead."

Del entered the corridor just as Cassie stepped out of the commons room. She hoisted a bottle and lifted her eyebrows. "Water? It's nice and cold."

"Sure."

She tossed it to him, passing him on her way to the control room. "What's for lunch?" she asked over her shoulder.

"It's a surprise," he answered with a grin, pausing at the door to the crew's quarters.

"Uh-oh."

He chuckled and stepped through the door. Opening the bottle, he took a long swallow, looking around. Six wall beds hung to his left and an arrangement of furniture and exercise equipment sat on his right. The beds looked comfortable, long enough to accommodate his length at least. Each end of the long room held a door. He guessed the one opened on a lift to the engineering section below and the other was the bathroom.

He made use of the bathroom, and on his way out,

the ship shuddered under his feet. Stepping into the corridor, he caught sight of Cassie at one end.

"We're home," she stated with a pleased smile.

The words had a strange effect on him, a warm rush of pleasure followed by a pang of dismay. Getting in the middle of a blood feud wasn't the only danger here. He liked these people, but could he afford to form ties with them? Were their actions any better than the Core's, just because they used more subtle means? Then again, it might already be too late; ties were forming, whether he wanted them or not.

"Are you all right?" Cassie asked with a crease of concern on her brow.

"Yeah." He cleared his throat and moved toward her. "Figure out the surprise yet?"

She grinned. "Not yet."

The surprise turned out to be that Jinx had been very good, for once. Lunch was sandwiches and salads, both green and fruit, soups and light desserts. What it lacked in sophistication it made up for in quantity. Enough food for half the station rested on tables hovering in the middle of the maintenance bay.

Jinx took some ribbing on this point with a good-natured grin. "Least we ain't goin' hungry."

Del didn't complain. His stomach cramped at the delicious smells and he grabbed a plate, making a beeline for the mountain of sandwiches. Sin was already there, studying the assortment with a critical eye.

"Thought you were hungry," he commented, reaching past her to snag two sandwiches.

"Just making sure he didn't sneak fish in there somewhere," she answered with a hint of a smile and a twinkle in her eye. "Or worse," she added, giving his plate a pointed glance.

Del peeked inside his sandwiches. "Looks like roast beef and smoked bird."

"Oh, I'm sure it is," she said with wide-eyed blandness, a smile still playing around her mouth.

Answering her tacit challenge, he took a huge bite. If it wasn't roast beef, it was a fine imitation. He lifted the sandwich in smug salute.

She chuckled, slipping one onto her own plate. "Have you said goodbye to your brother yet? We have about an hour before we leave."

"Saw him this morning," he mumbled around a mouthful, swallowing before he added, "don't think I'd find him in time, anyway."

"Finding him is the easy part," she said then raised her voice. "Control, please locate Nick Givliani."

"Nicholo Givliani is in the vestibule of the Red Sun temple," the toneless voice answered without hesitation.

Del blinked at her in astonishment. "The Order of the Red Sun has a temple here?" The reclusive and militant order was very selective about the locations of their temples. Del had never heard of one on a busy commerce station. The gregarious Golden Sun Order was far more likely to settle in such a populated place.

"They believe they have a calling here," she said with studied care, her expression hard to interpret. "Your brother hasn't wasted any time. Are you sure you don't want to track him down?"

He couldn't resist the challenging gleam in her green eyes. He shrugged and said, with as much disinterest as he could, "He'll tell me all about it when I get back."

She suppressed a smile and tilted her head in acknowledgement. "I'm sure he will," she responded and moved toward the garden of salads.

Lunch passed much like breakfast. The group hadn't lost energy in spite of the intense drilling. Jinx started Sunny off on another story. Cassie and Bib had a mini vegetable flinging war across a table, until Kai and Quan chased them with vegetable skewers. Squealing, the women hid behind Lynch who scowled the two stalkers down, arms folded in a forbidding stance. In the face of such grim opposition, the two men gave up, opting for drinks instead.

Del watched with baffled humor. They reminded him again of an extended family, triggering a faint ache of loss and longing deep inside him. He refused to explore what it meant.

Soon it was time to go and they all piled back into the haulers. Their exit from the station was a stomach-lurching repeat of the morning's performance, but their journey to the star-way proved uneventful. Their solar destination was a popular one, so they had to wait in a long line of ships to go through the ring. After the ring, their journey to the abantium supplier's system was just as uneventful and the crew found themselves at loose ends. Quan opted to take a nap, asking them to wake him when they arrived. Sin stayed with Jinx in the control room while Del and Cassie played a series of card games in the common room.

The common room served many purposes, part kitchen, part entertainment, part medical facility. Cassie and Del sat across from each other at a long table in the dining area, a deck of hover-cards between them.

Del stared at the cards in his hand in disgust. "Hit

me."

"Again? You're a glutton for punishment, big guy," she responded, grinning when he made a face at her.

"Joke's gettin' mighty old, Cass."

"Cranky? I suppose you thought this trip would be more exciting. Don't worry, it'll get plenty exciting later on." She flipped a card over and tsked at it. "High card. You suck at this game."

"You cheat."

She gasped with wounded innocence. "I do not. Play again?"

He eyed her, smirking in cynical humor. "Only if I deal."

"Oh, fine." She pushed the deck across to him, mumbling something derogatory under her breath.

With the deck in his hands, his luck took a dramatic turn for the better. They were having a debate on the merits of cheating when Jinx's voice interrupted them. "Heads up. We're on approach to the refinery's docking bay."

"Time to make a good impression," Cassie announced, shoving the pile of cards into a compartment and standing. "Come on, let's get changed."

"Changed?" He followed her to the crew's quarters.

"It makes a better impression if the crew wears the company insignia."

In the crew's quarters, Sin stood over Quan with a thoughtful frown, dressed in a crisp pants suit with a sphinx on her breast. She raised her head when they entered and waved them over. "Water this time?"

"Overused," Cassie answered, staring down at the sleeping man. "He'll get suspicious. Last time was the sound blaster in his ear."

A pang of sympathy went through Del for the unsuspecting pilot, but he couldn't hold in a smirk of mischief. "How 'bout yanking him out?"

The two women glanced over their shoulders at him then gave each other a considering look. Cassie shrugged. "Haven't dumped him in a while."

"Grab a leg."

Quan didn't stop snoring until his body hit the deck in an untidy heap. "Hey! Wha—?" He struggled to a sitting position, staring at them with bleary eyes.

"Oh, dear," Sin said, squatting next to him with an expression of sublime sympathy. "Are you all right? You fell right out of bed."

"Again?" he mumbled, rubbing his face.

She patted his shoulder. "You should be more careful."

Cassie grabbed Del's arm and pulled him away.

"You do that a lot?"

With a quick glance over her shoulder to make sure they wouldn't be overheard, Cassie grinned up at him. "Poor guy thinks he sleepwalks, too. We've moved him all over the ship and he never wakes up."

"He has no idea?" he asked as she opened a receptacle and pulled out some clothing.

"Not a clue," she snickered, handing him a shirt before disappearing into the bathroom.

Sin left with a bland expression on her exquisite features.

Quan meandered over, all sleepy befuddlement. "Hey, man, you wanna hand me one of those?" he asked, running careless fingers through his hair. With a smothered grin, Del pulled out another shirt, tossing it to the smaller man. "Thanks," Quan said through a yawn.

They changed shirts, the new ones a soft gray with the dark silhouette of a sphinx on the shoulders. Jinx entered and threw on a shirt just as Cassie left the bathroom in a neat coverall with the company insignia on her left breast. "Jinx, who's flying the ship?" Cassie asked, tugging with tidy care at her sleeves.

"Sin took over. She told me to go change while she yakked at 'em." A soft shudder vibrated through the ship and Jinx nodded, pulling at his collar with impatient fingers. "And docked."

Cassie clapped her hands then waved at them, her voice turning schoolmarm. "All right, crew, let's go look pretty for our adoring public."

Quan snorted and Jinx rolled his eyes, but they went without protest. Del followed, giving Cassie a wry look she ignored. They met Sin coming out of the control room. After a sweeping glance, she flashed an approving smile, cutting through Del's defenses as if they were tissue.

They met Kai and the rest of the crew between the two haulers. Sin's brother wore a jacket matching the somber gray of his sister's suit, his dress shirt sporting the sphinx in silver at its collar. The twins exchanged a quiet word before heading toward the welcoming party with the crew following.

A small group of people in dark green uniforms stood in a cluster behind a stern looking woman in white. At some unknown signal, the crew stopped several meters away from the party. Del halted with them, watching the twins continue forward. The woman in white greeted them with solemn propriety, but their voices didn't carry back to the crew.

"Who's the one in white?" he asked Cassie.

"The owner of the refinery," she replied, tone curt. Her fine boned face held an odd tension.

He frowned and studied the owner. "Is there a problem?"

Cassie cast him a quick look, her face smoothing into a serene half-smile. "Of course not."

Cassie wasn't very good at lying. Del stared at her, mind working at a furious pace. "Why is the owner greeting couriers?"

"Well, they are the Shays," she answered with a layer of arrogance.

Del grimaced. "Right, the great and powerful Shays." She shot him a quelling glare, but he persisted. "How did the owner know they were on board?"

"I assume they announced themselves on approach." Her expression turned impatient. "Hush, Del. And quit slouching. We're supposed to be professionals."

He straightened even though he wasn't slouching. "Watch it, Cass. Your scales are showing."

She glared at him and clipped him in the ankle, but said nothing. They watched the twins return. Del studied their faces, looking for any indication of trouble, but they both seemed relaxed.

"Time to go to work," Kai said with a grin. "They're bringing the canisters around. Make sure everything's sealed before loading them. Afterward, the refinery has a full spread waiting for us, dinner on the house."

The crew cheered, but Sin raised a cautionary hand with an expression of dry humor. "Just remember—"

"No drunken stupors!" the others finished for her in unison, laughing.

"Exactly," she responded with a quirk of her lips. "We have a big day tomorrow."

A rumbling behind them pulled Del around. A carryall stacked high with canisters rolled at a ponderous pace toward the haulers.

"All right," Kai exclaimed, clapping his hands together. "Let's do this."

Sin glanced at her brother with tolerant contempt, folding her arms and looking him up and down. "Are you going to change first or will you ruin yet another dress shirt and jacket?"

He made a face but headed toward the Rock's hatch, shrugging off his jacket in one smooth motion as he went.

Sin rolled her eyes and faced the crew again. "We'll be right back. Lynch, will you organize the loading, please?"

"Yes, ma'am," the big man rumbled.

Over the next couple of hours, Del learned a new skill. The cargo loaders shortened the work of getting the canisters up the loading ramp and into the haulers, but the machines were disagreeable. The crane used to pluck the canisters from the carryalls was sensitive and finicky. In contrast, the loader drove like a lumbering ox, no finesse at all. When they were finished, Del was just relieved not to have destroyed any of the containers, though several had dents from his inexperienced handling.

The rest of the crew took malicious delight in his

first time loading. They scattered when he approached with feigned expressions of terror, calling out warnings to one another. The other loaders made exaggerated swerves to avoid him and the grounded crew inspected each canister he'd handled with elaborate care.

Del took this ribbing with good humor, ignoring them while getting used to the loader, then chasing them when confident enough in his handling. Far from discouraging them, his chases inspired more antics. Only Lynch didn't join in, regarding the whole scene as a breach of protocol. He glowered and shouted orders, treating all of them like unruly children, even his bosses.

The Shays pitched in and surprised Del, loading as if they were regular crew, taking orders from Lynch without protest, and working just as hard as the rest. Kai took over one of the loaders while Sin inspected and settled canisters with the grounded crew. Del tried to picture Griffin doing the same thing and couldn't even come close. Whatever else they were, the Shay twins were unique.

The refinery workers watched the lot of them with both curiosity and puzzled humor. The loading drew a small crowd, which dispersed only after the crew disappeared into the haulers to clean up.

While standing in the sanitary, Del wondered if the antics of the crew had drawn their attention or something else. The others had done a good job of distracting him, keeping him from asking questions or noticing things by putting him into a loader for the first time. They'd stowed a huge amount of abantium on both ships, consuming almost all the space within the cargo bays and leaving only enough room for the

Shadows and loaders. He had no experience with couriers; he didn't know if the amount was normal. But he meant to find out.

When he left the Tank, he found most of the crew idling between the haulers. Chairs lined the sides of the ships and music played somewhere. Cassie supervised the loading of the refinery's food onto a long table hovering between the ships. The crew waited with quiet patience, chatting in a more subdued way than he'd seen so far. They must finally be getting tired. He sure was.

Sin and Kai sat a little apart from the rest, dressed again in disquieting black. Kai stretched out like a lazy lion, chair tipped back to rest against the side of the Rock and hands linked behind his head. Sin sat next to him, leaning forward with her elbows on the chair arms and rolling a bottle between her hands. They regarded the rest of the crew with faint, aloof amusement, like cats watching mice play within reach. Unnerving and irritating, how the two of them could look so dangerous and so attractive at the same time.

Approaching the table, he muttered to Cassie, "Do they have to look like they just swallowed a canary?"

She hummed and handed him a plate. "They're pleased everything's gone so well today. Including you, by the way." She gave him a brilliant smile when he glowered at her. "You're fitting in so nicely," she simpered, batting her eyelashes at him.

"Cut it out, Cass. You'll kill my appetite."

"Be nice or I won't let you help me carry their plates over." She slanted a look at him through her lashes. "We might just overhear something."

He gave her a level stare. "You're a devious little

thing."

"Thank you," she said with a smug expression.

"And," he continued, filling his plate, "You know a lot more than you let on."

The serene half-smile reappeared on her face and Del snorted. He kept his peace, though, and helped her fill plates for their bosses. Each carrying a pair of plates, they headed toward the Shays. As they approached, Kai's lazy demeanor disappeared and he surged forward with a look of hungry anticipation on his handsome face. When Cassie handed him food, he purred, "My angel."

She scoffed and handed the other plate to Sin. "Only when I bring him food."

Sin chuckled and thanked them. They sat in chairs nearby, Del claiming the one closest to Sin. Del gave Cassie her plate and she murmured thanks as they began to eat. In spite of what Cassie had implied, the Shays didn't seem inclined to talk at all.

"I'm surprised they didn't mind bringing the food here instead of their cafeteria," Cassie commented at the start of the meal. The siblings only shrugged, but Del stared at Cass, considering her words.

He had the good sense to hold his questions until they all finished eating, though. While Cassie gathered their plates and returned them to the table, he asked, "Why so much abantium?"

The twins exchanged a look of secretive amusement. Del ground his teeth. Kai leaned back into his relaxed pose, and Sin turned her gaze on Del. "It was the amount required," she said, eyes assessing as they traveled over his face. He wondered just how much she could see when she looked at him.

"Is it normal to load the haulers so heavy?"

"It's common. If we'd taken larger ships, the trip would just take longer."

"Are we expecting trouble here?"

Sin tilted her head. "Why do you ask?"

Cassie returned in time to hear his question and kicked him in the ankle, but he ignored her. "The owner made a point to talk to you. The refinery workers are real curious, and you got us eating here instead of leaving the haulers alone."

A slow smile curled her mouth and touched off fire inside him, but she said nothing.

With a lazy roll of his head, Kai gave Del a heavy-lidded look of amusement and flashed him a white grin. "This is why I like you, Giv. You're such a suspicious devil."

Sin gave a slight shake of her head. "There's no trouble here." She was more convincing than Cassie had been. In fact, she looked like she was telling the truth.

With a crease between his brows, he subsided in his chair.

Without comment, Cassie handed him a drink, nodding when he thanked her. The other crew members had been quiet during the meal, but Bib convinced Sunny to dance with her. Jinx and Fern teased him about his performance. Sunny scoffed at them to do better, so they rose to the challenge.

"Where do they get the energy?" Cassie sighed and Sin chuckled.

Sinking lower in his chair, Del watched the dancers with mild amusement and an insidious feeling of contentment. Some of it was the good meal and a job well done, but another part worried him; the gratification of being with this group, being part of this group. And sitting next to this woman.

Del studied Sin out of the corner of his eye, taking covert pleasure in the fine curve of her cheek and the dark sweep of her lashes. He should be wary of her and he was, but it only added to her attraction, her dangerous beauty a fraction of what called to him. The way she could change from teasing imp to cool commander, from bloodthirsty predator to touching vulnerability fascinated him endlessly. He wanted to know her inside and out.

"Uh-oh," Cassie said, breaking into his thoughts. He gave a guilty start, but she wasn't looking at him. "You know where this is going," she whispered to the Shays, eyes flicking to them before settling back on the crew.

Sin and Kai both smiled as they watched the crew. Something in those smiles made the hair stand up on the back of Del's neck and he focused his attention on the group. They'd gotten much louder and more energetic in the time he'd been mooning over Sin. They weren't arguing, their expressions still light, but they all spoke over one another. He couldn't tell what they were saying until Fern stepped toward the Shays. "Come on, show us how it's done."

The others babbled encouragement, waving for the twins to rise.

"Just this once."

"Please?"

"Yeah, show us!"

They fell silent while the twins looked at one another. Then Kai shrugged. "Why not? A little demonstration wouldn't hurt."

A quick, eager murmur ran through the group before they fell silent again, waiting for Sin's response. "All right," she said in a tone as bland as oatmeal. The group erupted into cheers and whistles.

When the two of them stood, Cassie declared, "Not a good idea." She cast a nervous glance around the docking bay. Neither Shay acknowledged Cassie's warning and she subsided with a pinched look.

"What's going on?" Del asked her, but she just shook her head.

The crew fell into a breathless silence as the twins moved to the center and faced one another, their features solemn. Tension built to a palpable level, crackling through the group, and Del eyed the two siblings with growing concern.

Then Kai stepped forward and caught his sister around the waist. Without hesitation she lifted her arms, placing one hand on his shoulder and one on his palm. They spun into a grand waltz, dancing together with mesmerizing liquid grace, their movements blending in perfect accord. It didn't matter the music wasn't a waltz.

The crew groaned and yelled insults at the dancing pair until Kai swept Sin into a deep dip, her back bowing in a graceful arc, hair cascading toward the floor in a ripple of black. They paused, both sets of green eyes blinking at the crew with baffled innocence. "What?" they asked in perfect harmony.

"Dirty rotten trick, you guys!" Jinx yelled.

Cassie was snickering behind one hand, her nervousness gone.

Del leaned closer and asked, "What just

happened?"

The crew was still haranguing their bosses, who straightened and dusted themselves off with expressions of offended injury. "Everyone's a critic," Kai said, and Sin sniffed in autocratic agreement.

"Ever heard of the Circle of Fire?" Cassie asked Del in a low voice.

"No," Del responded. "Wait, is it part of the Red Sun Order?"

"Yes. You know their order is a little, ah—"

"Violent? Militant? Crazy?"

"Right." She slanted him a look of dry amusement. "They have a series of challenges for their ascetics, often performed in the Circle of Fire. Hand to hand combat, with or without weapons, in an arena neither can leave until there's a victor." She paused, watching him with cool brown eyes.

"So? What's the Circle got to do with this?" He paused, blinking at her. "They wanted a demonstration. Are you telling me the Shays are Red Sun ascetics?"

She shook her head, a smile finding its way across her mouth. "They never accepted the calling. But they've both been in the Circle. A great many times."

Del sat back in his chair, trying to absorb the implications, watching the Shays pretend to be insulted. Now he understood why they moved with such dangerous, sleek precision, and why Sin had reacted to Nick being at the Temple. She'd said the Order believed they had a calling at the Shay station. Would the Order subject itself to a busy station just to influence or convert the twins? The Shays did have power, but enough for a religious sect? The Golden Order followed political and commercial lines of power, not Reds. What was the Red Sun's motivation for influencing the Shays? Or was it the other way around?

Del shook his head, thoughts swirling in ever more complicated twists through his mind. Looking up, he met the sharp clarity in Cassie's brown eyes as she studied him. How much of his musing was written on his face? "What are you thinking?" he asked on impulse.

She turned away with a wry smile curling one corner of her mouth. "I'm thinking it's time for us to catch some shut-eye." She nodded toward the group.

The Shays had stopped dissembling and were herding the protesting crew toward the hatches while refinery workers cleared the table.

"I need you all rested for tomorrow," Sin said with implacable calm.

Kai nodded. "And I could use some peace and quiet." When they gave him disagreeable grumbles, he continued in a mocking tone, "Don't forget to brush your teeth, san behind your ears, and go potty. There's a good crew."

He got some chuckles and insults, but they went without further protest. Sending a furtive glance at the refinery workers, Cassie rose to her feet and Del followed suit. Cassie smiled for the twins, saying nothing as she and Del headed for the Tank's hatch. Del nodded to Kai, but as he passed Sin, she said, "Goodnight."

Del paused with a faint frown. "Aren't you coming?" he asked then could have kicked himself for how it sounded.

"In a bit," she said with an evasive smile, eyes

sliding away.

He couldn't pursue it without looking even more like an idiot, so he gave her a curt nod and followed Cass through the hatch. Cassie shot him a knowing grin over her shoulder but didn't stick around for his scowl. Calling first on the bathroom, she disappeared into the crew quarters. The sound of Jinx babbling away filtered out of the common room, so Del ducked in there.

Quan and Jinx didn't look like they were getting ready for bed. Quan was fiddling with some virtual reality gear while Jinx fidgeted next to him and rambled, "To level three, but I got scragged midway. There's some trankin' scorbs I could use a wingman on. With your help, we could blast 'em to picons! Ain't never seen level four…hey, Del." Jinx gave him a quick grin.

"What's this?" Del flicked a finger at the VR gear.

"The Tenth Hell of Karse," Jinx answered in a reverent tone, eyes flashing with anticipation. "Best VR game in the galaxy! Wanna play?"

"No, thanks. Wouldn't sleep after. Doesn't it hype you guys up?"

Quan flashed Del a heedless grin, making him look as young as Jinx. "This here's warm milk to guys like us. Right, Jinx?"

"Got that right!" Jinx exclaimed, reaching for one of the thin headsets.

With an amused shake of his head, Del said, "Have fun," before backing out of the room and heading for the crew's quarters. He paused to let his eyes adjust to the near darkness of the quarters.

Cassie's voice floated through the darkness to him. "Don't turn on the light."

"I won't," he answered and headed for the bathroom. When he returned, he had to let his eyes adjust again. Cassie was a small lump in one of the bottom beds. Shuffling over to the sleeping area, Del pulled up and rolled into one of the top beds.

Not too shabby for a ship bed. He stretched and scrunched the pillow under his head, linking his hands beneath it, and staring at the dark bulkhead above him. His muscles grew heavy with a pleasant lassitude, but his mind wouldn't stop. He reviewed the day's experiences and revelations with obstinate repetition, keeping him from falling asleep for a long while. He was still awake when Jinx and Quan scuffled in and flopped into their respective beds. Time ticked by and Del's eyes began to droop.

When he struggled to open them, he realized he'd been fighting off sleep. He was waiting for Sin. He fell asleep waiting.

Chapter 15

"You should tell him," Cassie said, handing a cup of coffee to Sin and sitting down next to her at the commons table. "He's too smart and curious. He's going to figure it out. If you don't tell him, he might find out just enough to make him dangerous."

"I'm aware," Sin answered with patient calm, sipping her coffee. She hadn't slept well in the pilot's chair, but sleeping within a few feet of Del would have been impossible. Spending so much time with him yesterday hadn't dulled his effect on her. Made it worse in fact, honing it to a fine edge, whittling away at her defenses. She'd been grateful for the buffer of her brother and the crew. If she'd been alone with Del when he'd asked in his deep voice if she was coming to bed, his dark eyes sending shivers of heat and cold over her skin, her answer would have been very different.

"But are you awake?" Cassie asked with dry amusement, studying Sin.

"I look tired."

"You look tired," Cassie confirmed with a nod. "Did you keep watch all night? I could have taken a turn."

"I slept a bit," Sin evaded, not willing to admit the real reason she hadn't slept. Cassie didn't suspect her growing attraction to Del, and Sin wasn't about to enlighten her.

Cassie made a noncommittal sound and took a sip of coffee, lowering her gaze. She was quiet for a moment, and Sin waited. The tension around her friend's mouth suggested Cass had more to say. "I told him about the Circle," Cassie blurted, not meeting Sin's gaze.

Sin had suspected as much. She remembered the look on Del's face after she and Kai had danced a waltz instead of the deadlier dance the crew had wanted to see. "Bad Cassie. Bad," she drawled.

Cassie slanted a quick, amused look at her. "You're not mad?"

"Oh, terribly. You're grounded." Sin narrowed her eyes before a smile spread across her face. "He was going to find out soon enough. His brother was at the temple when we left."

For some reason, Cassie's humor faltered and she looked away, sipping her coffee. "Well, no harm done, then."

Sin tilted her head in keen curiosity, but before she could ask her friend what was wrong, the subject of their conversation entered. Her heart kicked in her chest at the shock of Del's intense dark gaze. The inevitable flood of heat spread through her as she watched him move into the room, his muscles tensing and sliding with smooth strength. She gave a polite response when he greeted them, but she knew she'd give herself away somehow if she stayed.

Making an excuse, she stood, far too aware of her clothes whispering over sensitized skin. At least she had enough presence of mind to take the coffee with her, but his gaze burned into her the entire way out. When the door closed between them, she breathed a sigh of relief and went to find the steadying presence of her brother.

She found Kai reclining in the hatchway of the Rock, one foot propped to keep the door open. He was studying a viewer with a bored expression she didn't buy for a second.

"Something wrong with the air recyclers?" she asked, flicking a finger at the open hatch.

"Just waiting for you to get your lazy rear out of bed," he answered, still staring at his viewer.

Crouching next to him, she snatched the viewer from his hands with cat-quickness. Ignoring his warning growl, she took a look. He'd been studying the schematics for the Cortecian mining facilities. Giving him a sardonic smile, she handed the viewer back. "Good morning to you, too. Nervous, brother?"

He gave her a shriveling look and snagged her cup, ignoring her wordless exclamation of protest and draining it in one swallow. Handing the cup back, he announced, "I'm about as nervous as you are. Ready to go?"

She raised an eyebrow. "My coffee's gone, I must be."

Kai grinned and rose to his feet, pulling her with him. Then he lost his playfulness, eyes meeting hers. Sin knew what he was thinking. This was the last time they'd be face to face until it was over.

She pulled him to her for a hug. "Be careful."

"You, too, Sissa." He squeezed her until her ribs creaked.

Letting go, she turned and walked away.

"Good hunting," he called after her.

She glanced over her shoulder. His wolf's grin

made its inevitable appearance. She couldn't help but respond with her own grin of predatory anticipation. Dangerous as this game was, it also held an attraction hard to resist.

Entering the Tank, she made her way to the empty control room. Settling in the pilot's seat, she went through start up procedures and notified the refinery of their departure. When she received the all clear from the refinery, she clicked on the ship-wide com. "Good morning, crew. We're heading out. Brace for launch."

Heavy with cargo, the Tank and Rock were sluggish and less maneuverable than usual. Neither Sin nor Kai risked the cargo in a dash for open space, their departures smooth and sedate.

Not long after they'd left the refinery, Jinx entered the control room with a jaw-splitting yawn. "Sorry, overslept," he mumbled, shuffling over.

She gave him a lenient grin. "The Ninth Hell again?"

"Tenth," he corrected, sending her a look of youthful contempt.

"Had breakfast yet?"

"Uh, no."

"Go eat. Take your time. I have the first part of the run."

"'Kay. Thanks, boss."

Sin settled back against the pilot's chair with a sigh. The rest of the day would be one long stretch of balancing on a razor wire of alertness when they went off-lane, so she should enjoy this quiet time. But the tedium of waiting grated and the inactivity didn't help her weariness.

She was considering another cup of coffee when

the door opened behind her. She knew who it was without looking. His powerful presence filled the room and raised the temperature around her by degrees. "Del."

"Sin." His deep tones turning her name into a sensual weapon.

She breathed deep, hiding the shiver sliding down her spine.

He was dangerous, this slicer pilot of hers, for more reasons than the possible exposure of their plans. Duty and her father's demanding shade had driven her to pull Del out from under the Core's brutal claw. Duty also required her to treat him with impersonal respect and not take advantage of the interest in his eyes when he looked at her. It was harder to ignore his attraction than she'd imagined and even harder to hide her own response.

But she hadn't spent all those years under her father's tutelage for nothing. "Did you sleep well?" she asked with cool politeness and a faint smile, glancing over her shoulder.

He leaned against the wall next to the door, arms folded and eyes shrewd. He hadn't come just for the pleasure of her company. She could almost smell the challenge on his golden skin and had to bite the inside of her lip to quell a hungry grin.

"No. Too much to think about."

Turning away from the dark invitation in his eyes, Sin made a pretense of checking the control panels. "Such as?"

"Circles and Red Suns."

Sin let her amusement show, swiveling her chair to face him. "Cassie confessed she'd told you."

He looked down, a wry quirk at one corner of his mouth. "Figures. But the Red Order, Sin? Do you know what they say about them?"

"I know plenty of Red jokes."

His smile widened and he slanted a glance at her, devastating in its unintended sensuality, the corners of his eyes crinkling with mischief. "What's the S stand for in sun?"

In self-defense, she turned the chair again, breaking eye contact and propping her feet on a panel with a cynical grin. "I've heard this one. For the orders, White, Gold, Blue, and Red, the S stands for sober, social, sensual, and savage."

He grunted. "I heard different."

"Sullen? Sinister?" she asked with raised eyebrows.

"Screwy," he responded, meeting her gaze with a smirk. "Suicidal."

She chuckled. "Some are both. Religion can make fanatics out of the most ordinary people."

"You're not ordinary," he said in a low voice, dark eyes vibrant.

Retaining a cool smile by sheer force of will, Sin tore her gaze away. She could still feel the heat of his gaze on her skin, though, and battled the urge to stretch like a cat in languorous delight. "I'm also not part of the Order."

"Does it make you less a fanatic, or more?"

His quick wit pleased her more than it should. With a low laugh, she answered, "Only the Suns know for sure. Our father wanted us to be able to protect ourselves, so he sent us to the Red Order for training." She spread her hands with a slight shrug. "Simple as that."

"With you, nothing is as simple as that." His tone dry, he stepped over to the second's seat and lowered into it. He studied her with obsidian sharpness. "I didn't know the Reds would train somebody who wasn't an initiate. Why'd they train you two?"

"I've often asked them the same thing. Have you ever noticed religious sects have a knack for avoiding questions they don't want to answer?"

"Kinda like my bosses," he said with a pointed look.

She smothered a grin and lowered her gaze. "It's a learned skill," she conceded, brushing nonexistent lint from the fabric over her knee.

He made a rude noise in his throat. "Who taught you it?"

"Who do you think?" she retorted.

His gaze softened. "What was he like?"

She blinked at him. She'd meant Griffin had taught her to be evasive, but she didn't think he was asking about the head of the Core. "Who?"

"Your father."

Sin looked away, slow tension seeping down to her bones. Speaking of her father was never easy. With anyone else she would have changed the subject, but Del snuck under her guard. More proof he was dangerous for her to be around.

"My father was a great man. He loved us very much, as we did him. He did his best to protect us."

"But?" Del asked in a gentle tone, cutting through her like a cold wind, bringing her to her senses.

She reinforced her defenses, meeting his gaze with a chilly smile. "But nothing. He was a wonderful father and a shrewd businessman, clever, capable, and compassionate. My brother and I were lucky to have such a strong foundation." Tilting her head to one side, she went on the offensive. "And your father? What was he like?"

It was his turn to look away. "Dad was flawed," Del said in a low voice.

Sin winced. "I'm sorry, I didn't mean to—"

"Yeah, you did." His expression filled with resentment and hard resolve. "Doesn't matter. He didn't pass it on."

Guilt heated her face as he rose and headed for the door. She straightened and swiveled the chair toward him. "Del, I'm sorry."

He didn't look at her. "Me, too. Touchy subject all around."

Then he was gone. Sin settled back in her seat with a sigh of regret. When threatened, she couldn't set aside the training she'd received for most of her life, the lessons she'd learned to become a capable businesswoman and formidable opponent for Griffin. Del was a threat, not so much to their company, but to her peace of mind. Without even trying, he reached parts of her she'd thought safely enclosed in layers of protection.

Suns have mercy if he did start trying.

With another deep sigh, she fixed her attention on piloting the hauler, doing her best to ignore the ache in her chest.

Chapter 16

"I can't believe they're payin' me for this," Del repeated for the hundredth time, scanning the surrounding space again. The sensors still showed no other vessels besides the two haulers with Shadows hiding on their surface. It had been the same for hours.

At regular intervals, Sin ordered one of them back into the Tank for a break, the only thing keeping Del from going crazy. He couldn't ease his boredom by talking with the others. They had to stay off the com so they wouldn't give the Shadows away. The enforced solitude and inactivity gave him too much time to think about Sin.

He'd struck a nerve when he'd asked about her father. He was too curious, though, and pressed her on it. He should have known better. She'd turned and attacked with the smooth ease of long practice. Avoiding questions wasn't the only skill she'd learned. She'd painted a heroic picture of her father then dared him to do the same, reminding him of his place in her world. She'd said she didn't think of him as broken, but he didn't believe her now.

"Picking up a krell pack on long range scanners," Jinx said, breaking into Del's reverie. "Heading this way fast."

"Type and count?" Sin asked.

"Vega class, looks like plasma cloud skippers.

Count, ah…"

Lynch's voice picked up where Jinx trailed off. "Seven, wedge attack formation. Pirates."

"Play dead," Kai said in a casual tone, as though he were sitting with his feet up and drink in hand. Del wondered how many times he'd done this to be so calm about it.

"Aye, playing dead," Lynch rumbled. The haulers slowed, powering down.

"Be easy, everyone," Sin soothed. "Skippers are no match for Shadows."

"Silence is golden," Kai added. "Watch and wait."

They watched and waited, Del listening to the pounding of his heart while the pirates bore down on them. Fear was a small part of the energy rushing through his veins. After the long boredom, he was eager for action, though his eagerness held a worrisome, predatory thread. The Shays were starting to rub off on him.

"Stand to and prepare to be boarded," a rough voice announced over the com. "Your cargo's forfeit."

"What, no introduction?" Kai said in a lazy, amused drawl. "Rude pirates. How does kiss my ass sound to you?"

Del grinned, watching the skippers come on without slowing. They were about to do a flyby in a show of strength.

"You best be civil," the rough voice snarled, "or we'll leave nothin' behind. Catch me?"

"Catch you?" Kai mused as they began their flyby. "Don't mind if I do. Shadows scatter."

As one, Del and the others launched away from the hauler, bursting through the pirate's formation like black cyclones. The sudden appearance of the Shadows disorganized the pirates into mass confusion. Del chased skippers with dogged intent, chaffing under the Shays' orders not to fire on the pirates until fired upon.

Then someone cried out, sounding like Bib; one of the pirates had taken a shot. Del sank into a cold rage, bearing down on a skipper with reckless vengeance. His first burst of weapon's fire went wide when the pirate twisted out of the way.

Intent on his target, Del didn't notice a pirate approaching from the side until someone yelled a warning. Cursing, he spun away, dodging the slower skippers with a Shadow's ease. Their crossfire was harder to dodge. One unlucky shot caught his Shadow down her right side. No pain translated to his nerve endings, though he felt the wound like a mental stab. He turned on the pirate, firing in a blaze of red fury, forgetting his orders to disable only.

The skipper exploded with a soundless burst of light, the shock wave buffeting Del's Shadow until he turned into it. The stunning flare of light snuffed his anger. Breathing hard, he ran a quick diagnostic, keeping an eye on the fighting. He watched the other Shadows dance with cool precision and realized he'd lost control in the battle. A dull flush of shame climbed his neck.

They were working in tandem, as he should have been doing. One Shadow culled a skipper from the pack with ruthless delicacy, chasing it toward another slicer. The second Shadow scored the skipper with a precise burst of fire, destroying its weapons array, and the skipper fled. The fleeing pirate was followed by the rest of the pack.

The diagnostic showed the hit on his slicer was superficial and Del headed for the haulers with humiliated reluctance. He'd never lost control in a slice before. He forgot his humiliation at the sight of a Shadow speeding after the fleeing pirates like a black arrow. Sin's Shadow.

"Sin, what are you doing?"

"Stay with the group," she answered in a cold, distant voice. "I'll be back soon."

He turned his Shadow to follow her. "Are you nuts? You can't take on—" He bit off the rest with a curse when another Shadow cut in front of him.

"Let her go," Kai said, his voice a diamond-hard command. "Give me a damage report."

"Minimal damage on a simple diagnostic. No main functions affected." Del watched Sin disappear with an agonized tightening in his chest. "You can't let her go alone."

"Can't catch her now."

"Watch me," Del growled, dodging Kai to speed after her, but a flare of weapon's fire flashed close. Del sucked in a breath and wrenched his Shadow to a halt.

"I'd rather not disable you and drag you back, so get in the Tank and run a full diagnostic. I won't say it again." Grim authority coated Kai's voice.

With a snarled curse, Del spun and headed to the Tank. Another slicer joined him in the docking bay. Cassie popped out of the slicer like she was on a spring, brow furrowed with concern, bending to the scoring on his Shadow's skin. With a snort, he opened the slicer and leaned out.

"Are you okay?" she asked, running gentle fingers along the charred groove.

"You askin' me or the ship?"

"Don't get snippy. Sin will be all right."

"Sure she will. One Shadow against a whole pirate pack. Great odds."

She stood and frowned at him, hands planted on her hips. "We disabled them before they ran. Kai wouldn't let her go alone otherwise."

"There might be more. Why is she chasing them anyway?" he snarled. He was taking his frustration out on her but couldn't help it. He'd rather take a swing at Kai, but the man hadn't docked yet.

"I'm sure she has her reasons. Start the diagnostic, Del."

Muttering under his breath, he settled back in the slicer and ran the diagnostic.

Cassie leaned in, hissing her own string of curses at the results. "All our work, and you go and get hit," she said in disgust.

"Thanks for your concern." Humiliation crawled back over his skin.

Cassie sighed. "I didn't mean it. I saw what happened, and I'm glad you're such a good pilot or you'd probably be dead. It scares me to see my friends in harm's way. I'm sorry I'm taking it out on you."

"Pretty sure nobody else got hit. Your friends are fine."

She stared at him for a second. "Del, you big idiot, I was talking about you."

"Oh." He ran a distracted hand through his hair. "Thanks. Uh, glad you're okay, too."

She rolled her eyes. "Bib did get scored. She's all right, but she had to dock in a hurry."

"Hope she didn't take it too hard."

Cassie grinned. "She was swearing like a dockhand when she went in, so I wouldn't stress. You only have to worry when she cries."

Del grunted, distracted by the final results of the diagnostic. He cursed and disconnected, levering out of the slicer. "Stabilizer's compromised," he told her, inspecting the damage.

"Lucky the skin held." Cassie knelt next to him. "The pressure and heat made the conduits rupture. The stabilizer itself isn't damaged, so we can fix it for the return trip."

"Good, where are the parts and tools?"

She shook her head. "Later. I need to get back out there, and Jinx could use your company. Runs like this work his nerves. He can't slice and hates watching from inside the hauler."

Del frowned, following her back to her Shadow. "What do you mean, he can't slice? He has a data port."

"Blue destroyed too many of his synapses," Cassie explained, a solemn look in her brown eyes. "I don't know how he held on as long as he did before the Shays pulled him out. He was close to a meltdown. He might slice again, given time, but he hates being grounded."

"I don't blame him." Del wondered what he'd do if he was told he might never slice again.

"The good news is the Tank has more sensitive long range scanners than the slicers, so you'll be first to know when Sin's back."

"How do you know she'll make it back?"

Her smile was both knowing and secretive. "Faith. You should try it." She patted his arm and slid into the slicer.

With a grimace, Del watched her leave then headed

for the control room. One of these days, he was going to corner the little woman and find out what she knew about the Shays.

Jinx looked around with a welcoming smile, his face paler than usual. "Hey, Del. Close call out there, huh?"

"Yeah," Del sighed, slumping into the second's seat. "My own stupid fault, though."

"Don't sweat it, man. How's the Shadow?"

"Fixable," he answered, running aggravated fingers through his hair.

"'Kay, good." Jinx's expression became wary.

Del straightened, reminding himself not to take his irritation out on the boy. "Yeah, it is. Any idea why Sin flew off?"

"Naw, but I ain't worried. They do it all the time and always come back."

"So what happens now?" Del asked, watching Jinx's fingers dance over the panels.

Jinx shrugged. "We keep going. Don't know what we'll do when we reach the separation point. I s'pose Manny'll have Cass take this team 'till Sin catches up."

If she catches up, Del thought with an acid clench in his stomach. "You handled the Tank great through the attack, Jinx."

"Thanks." The youngster grinned at Del with a hint of hero worship.

"Do you always fly the haulers?"

"Yeah. I can't slice no more 'cause my nerves is shot from blue." He made a face and shrugged with sullen defiance. "Don't matter. I like hauler duty."

"You're young yet. The damage might not be permanent."

"Sure," Jinx responded, but his tone was glum.

Del wracked his brain for something to make the kid feel better. "So, how far did you get with the Tenth Hell of Arse?"

"Karse," Jinx corrected with a snicker. "Quan's a trankin' wingman, we got all the way to the end of level five…"

He rambled on about the game, going over highlights in some sort of gaming language Del didn't understand. He nodded and made an occasional appreciative noise to keep Jinx going, all the while trying to hide his own anxiety. Where in the Sun's name was Sin?

This went on for some time until one of the control panels beeped. Jinx jumped a little and checked it, then grinned over his shoulder at Del. "Toldja she'd be back."

Del sat forward. "How's she look?"

"Gorgeous like always," Jinx said with a wink, and activated the com. "Manny, Sin's comin'."

"About time. Thanks, Jinx," was Kai's indolent response.

"Nothing wrong with her Shadow?" Del persisted.

"Nope, looks good as new."

Del sagged back in his seat on a wave of relief, followed by anger. He chewed on his fury as he watched her approach, grinding his teeth together when she said, "Hey, Jinx," over the com with cool calm.

"Welcome back, Boss."

"Thanks. Open her up. I'm coming in."

"Already done."

She sped over them like a flash of black lightning. Her casual tone pounded in Del's head and he shoved to his feet, stalking out of the control room. He was going to get answers out of her if he had to shake them out. Marching down the long corridor, he entered the docking bay. She was striding toward him without a scratch on her, which enraged him even more.

He opened his mouth to vent his temper, but she beat him to it.

"Don't you ever scare me like that again!"

It was almost word for word what had been on the tip of his tongue. He blinked at her in mute astonishment.

She slowed to a stop in front of him, lips pressed together, a frown between her brows. Then she made an abrupt gesture with one hand. "Forget I said it," she said in a clipped tone. "It was my fault. I shouldn't have pushed you into this run with so little training." She brushed by him and headed toward the exit.

"Wait just a Sun-damned minute," he protested, spinning on his heel after her.

"We'll talk later," she snapped as she left the bay.

He hesitated before righteous anger won out over confusion, then stalked after her. "Talk now, Sin," he snarled at her retreating back as he stepped into the corridor. "Tell me why you'd fly off after pirates."

She didn't pause, her voice tight and cold. "I'm not answerable to you, Del."

"Get back here!" he shouted, following her, "Or I'll—"

She whirled, eyes blazing green fire as she whispered, "Or you'll what?"

Danger gleamed in every line of her sleek form, her face tightening with predatory sharpness. A belated, cautionary light blinked in a distant corner of his mind, but it was too late. The look in her eyes touched off wildfire in his blood, turning his aggression to a raging need heedless of any warnings. He stalked toward her, a primal growl rising in his chest. He was a step away from grabbing her when the door to the control room opened.

Jinx eased out into the corridor, eyes wide and expression wary. "Hey, Sin. Manny's on the com for you."

Del jerked to a stop, clenching his hands into fists and breathing hard. The rational part of his mind filled with grim relief despite the need thundering through him. He ached to put his hands on her, press his body into all those sleek curves and taste her again, but touching her right now held more than one danger.

Sin gave Jinx a sharp nod, lashes sweeping down over the fevered battle-light in her eyes. Her lips formed a thin, furious line, a faint flush over her cheekbones, but her tone was smooth and controlled. "I'll need to speak with Kai alone." Her lashes lifted, and the icy flick of reproach in her eyes struck Del like a lash. Then she strode past Jinx, the door to the control room sliding closed between them with chilly finality.

Chapter 17

Sin sank into the pilot's chair, and touched the com with trembling fingers. She shivered to think how close she'd come to losing total control. *Del, why do you have to be so…* Too many disconcerting ways to finish the thought. She said her brother's name instead.

"I'm here," he answered.

She drew in a shaky breath, grateful as always for the steadying influence of her twin. "We were right. They were Griffin's dogs."

"Why am I not surprised?" he retorted then softened his tone. "Any trouble?"

"No, they were whipped."

"You sure?"

"Yes, why?"

"Because you sound like there was trouble."

She grimaced. Their closeness allowed him to be her rock in difficult times, but also made it impossible to hide things from him. "Not with them," she said in a clipped tone.

"Let me guess. Del?"

"Spot on, brother," she sighed, rubbing weary hands over her face.

"And here's the part where I say I told you so. Did you leave him in one piece?"

Irritated at the gloating hilarity in his voice, Sin snapped, "Do you want to hear the details of the drop or

227

not?"

"Hmm, tough choice. I do like rubbing it in."

"Kai," she growled.

He relented with a chuckle. "All right, lay it on me."

She described the fleeing pirates and their reaction to her chase, then explained the details of the agreement she'd reached with them. She concluded just as the haulers entered the Corteca system. It was time to separate.

"Good work, Sinsi. I'll see you on the other side."

"Hunt well, brother mine."

"Don't I always?"

She chuckled and severed the connection. Setting the hauler onto its new course, Sin swiveled out of the pilot's seat and left the control room, heading for the docking bay.

Del and Jinx looked up from where they knelt next to Del's wounded Shadow. Sin almost flinched at the midnight intensity in Del's gaze, a wave of heat flushing through her and tingling on her skin.

She turned away and seized the ragged strands of her control. "The Tank's all yours again, Jinx," she said with fabricated calm. "We've split and I've changed course."

"'Kay, Boss." Jinx bounced to his feet and scampered off.

Sin headed for her Shadow, ignoring Del as best she could.

He didn't let her escape, though. "Sin."

She paused, turning her head, but not enough to meet his gaze. His deep voice added chills to the heat rippling over her skin. She was sure he'd see it in her eyes.

"I was out of line earlier. I apologize."

Not trusting her voice, she only nodded and climbed into her Shadow, heading out into the dark of space, trying to ignore how much it felt like running away.

****

The journey to the Cortecian mining facility passed without incident. As they drew close, Sin contacted the facility and received instructions on where to dock from a deferential official. Thanking him, Sin ordered all Shadows back to the Tank.

Climbing out of her slicer, she waited for the Tank to go through docking maneuvers and land. Then she exited the hauler by the side hatch and met the Cortecian official waiting for her. He stared at her dark attire with an uneasy flicker, but greeted her with gracious professionalism. The Cortecian unloading crew stood ready nearby.

"Are you aware of the special circumstances regarding this cargo?" she asked him as her own crew appeared, Cassie herding them with her usual brisk bossiness to the loaders.

"Yes, ma'am," he answered with a respectful nod, but his eyes flickered again.

She gave him a reassuring smile. "There's no need for concern as long as my instructions are followed to the letter."

"Of course."

"Good. Let's get on with it then."

The unloading of the abantium was more subdued than the loading. The furtive glances Sin received suggested the crew knew of her confrontation with Del.

229

Jinx wasn't good at keeping secrets. Sin couldn't complain about their efficiency, though, the cargo removed and deposited in the appropriate holds.

The Cortecian official invited Sin and her people to a late meal, and Sin drew Cassie aside. "Will you make sure the men come right back here after they've eaten?"

"No problem," Cassie answered.

"You know what precautions to take."

"Of course." Cass waved a dismissive hand. "Stop worrying. We'll do the polite thing then be back and tucked in bed before you know it."

"Good enough." Sin smiled and turned away before Cassie could ask the question lurking in her warm brown eyes.

Heading back into the Tank, she fixed herself a solitary meal and ate in the control room while she calibrated the proximity alarm to maximum sensitivity. Nothing would get close to the hauler without her knowing it. She also kept an eye on the facility's traffic, incoming and outgoing ships, as well as the local Cortecian vessels.

The ship she'd been expecting approached the sprawling mining community and docked without fanfare. Sin scanned but couldn't pick up its companions in the system close by. She hummed in approval and set the hauler to run periodic scans of the newcomer, just in case they decided not to play by her rules.

Then she waited. It wasn't easy. She tried to meditate as her Red Sun Mendani had taught her, but her traitorous body wanted to fall asleep instead. So she paced around the control room, reciting what she could remember of the Red Order's forms of war and amusing herself by fabricating what she couldn't remember. She was making a mental note to retain some of her more entertaining creations for Kai when the proximity alarm blared.

Adrenaline sharpening her focus, she swung back into the pilot's seat then relaxed with a sigh. The crew had returned. Resetting the alarm, she tried meditating again, knowing she still had plenty of time. Breathing deep, she concentrated on finding her center and dispelling emotion, clearing her mind of distractions. She was asleep within minutes.

"Sin," someone whispered, a hand settling on her shoulder.

Sin grabbed the hand and jackknifed to her feet. Seeing Cassie, she let go and slumped back into the seat, measuring her breath to get her thumping heart back under control. "Suns, Cass, I almost broke your wrist."

"Glad you didn't," Cassie answered, a smile lurking around her mouth. "I did call your name. You were out."

Sin rubbed a hand over her face, shaking her head. "I was trying to meditate. Mendani T'Zai would send me back to first lessons if he knew I fell asleep."

Cassie grinned and patted Sin's shoulder. "You needed the rest and there's no harm done. The scans all look clean and the alarm is still active."

"Then why did you wake me?" Sin snorted.

Cassie chuckled. "I thought I'd spell you ahead of time so you could get there early and check the place out."

Sin rose to her feet. "Thanks, I will. It shouldn't take long, but keep an eye on the troller," she said with a nod toward the ship she'd been scanning.

"Will do." Cassie caught Sin's wrist when she shifted past her, brown eyes solemn. "Please be careful, Sinsi."

Sin smiled, clasping her friend's hand with gentle reassurance. "Don't worry, that's one lesson I won't be falling asleep on."

Sin left her to the watch, heading to the commons room. At this late hour, it was empty. Finding a little-used storage compartment, Sin keyed in the sequence to unlock it and retrieved a hidden weapon. Double-checking its power level, she tucked it into the pocket of her jacket and strode from the room, heading for the cargo bay.

For some reason, the lights were on in the bay. Sin paused then tensed at a clink and rustle among the Shadows. The alarm should've sounded if someone had snuck aboard, but none of the crew would be up. Sin slipped the weapon from her pocket and sidled to the closest slicer, slinking around it with predatory intent. Her target seemed oblivious to her presence, working without stealth on one of the Shadows. Recognition dawned, followed by dim dismay.

"Del?" She meant to ask what he was doing, but the words faded from her mind. He was shirtless, his bare back to her. The expanse of golden skin and smooth ripple of muscles beneath stole her breath.

He threw a quick look over his shoulder and said something about fixing the stabilizer, but she wasn't listening. Hot blood rushed in her ears, covering his words. She sagged against a nearby Shadow, unable to take her eyes off his muscular form. A faint sheen of perspiration gleamed on his skin and she licked her lips, swallowing at the wet curl of hair against the nape of his neck.

Through the heat and pounding of her heart, she noticed his sudden stillness and silence. Raising her eyes with a flash of alarm, she met the stunned knowledge in his gaze. With a silent curse, she turned her face away.

When Sin called his name in a puzzled tone, Del had rushed to explain, gathering his tools with hasty chagrin, embarrassed by his sleepless obsession with his Shadow. He was in the middle of telling her about rerouting conduits when he looked over his shoulder and caught her expression.

She devoured him with her eyes, her lips parted and cheekbones kissed with color. Shock and stunning desire chained him in place. She wanted him. All this time he'd thought she was indifferent, tolerant of his attraction but untouched by similar feelings. The hungry slant in her green eyes set off concussions of blinding lust, frightening in their intensity.

Then she met his gaze and turned away in denial. It was enough to drive a man insane.

Dropping the tools with a clatter, Del rose and turned toward her. "What do you want?" Desire coated his voice in rough velvet.

"What do you mean?" she asked, gaze darting to his then away.

Anger licked at him, fanning the heat pulsing in his blood. "You know what I mean," he gritted through clenched teeth, taking a slow step toward her. "What do you want?"

She shook her head, a light frown creasing her brow. "Nothing."

"Don't run me a line, Lady Shadow." He took another step closer. "You stared at me like I was your next meal. Now...what do you want?"

Her green eyes lifted, clashing with his. "Del," she warned, raising a hand to hold him off.

He ignored the warning and took a final step, planting his hands on either side of her against the sleek surface of the Shadow. Her cool fingers met the heated flesh of his chest, and he sucked in a breath. "You know what you want," he said in a low growl, her scent clouding his senses with maddening seduction. "So take it."

"Del," she whispered, looking down at her hand. He tensed, waiting for her to push him away, but her fingers stirred then flexed against him. Nails scraped his skin and sent gooseflesh rippling across his torso. Her eyes rose, smoky with desire.

With a groan of relief and need, he captured her mouth with a hunger driven by the memory of her taste and long nights of tormenting, empty dreams. A low, luscious sound in the back of her throat, she teased him with the hot, silky slide of her tongue as she ran her fingers around the nape of his neck to tangle in his dark hair. He pressed against her, delirious at her yielding softness, shuddering when her fingers slid under his waistband at the small of his back, her fingernails a sharp demand in his flesh.

Shaking with need, he clasped her hips and lifted, pressing her back against the curve of the Shadow and growling when she captured him between her thighs. The heat and friction against his arousal was a sweet agony. He couldn't resist a slow thrust against her core. She gasped and writhed with a sensual flex of her smooth muscles, sinking her teeth in his lower lip. On the verge of exploding, he tugged at her clothes, hands clumsy with titanic lust.

A booming crash echoed in the cargo hold, as shocking as a club to the side of his head. He jerked up with dazed alarm then almost toppled to the ground when Sin heaved and twisted like an angry cat. Launching out from under him, she landed beside the Shadow and pulled a stinger from the pocket of her jacket, a weapon illegal in anyone's hands but the FPA. With sinuous and lethal grace, she rounded the end of the slicer then stopped, hissing a curse.

Del straightened, shaking from both unabated desire and shock. Moving to the end of the slicer, he stared from Sin's disgusted expression to Jinx, collapsed in a tangle of tubing at the threshold of the lift to the engine room. The young man cursed and struggled to get free of the tubing.

"Jinx, what in the Sun's name are you doing?"

Del couldn't argue with the frustrated anger in her voice. A whole galaxy of frustration roiled inside him and he leaned against the Shadow, trying to even out his breathing. Sin tucked the weapon into the waistband at the small of her back and tugged the jacket over it with swift and furtive efficiency just as Jinx looked up. She was hiding it from the boy.

"Oh, hey, boss. I was just, ah…well, I had this dream about the converter system and I wanted to check it. I found a bunch of stuff and was just gonna stow it." He scrambled to his feet. Sheepish humor colored his young face. "Tubing tripped me up a little bit there."

"You need sleep, Jinx. Just leave it and get to bed."

He wilted like a scolded puppy. "Yes, ma'am," he mumbled and scurried for the exit.

When he was gone, Del asked, "What are you doing with a stinger?"

Sin's features hardened with flinty resolve, raising warning signals in his over-stimulated brain. "It's none of your concern. Clean up and get some rest. We have a long way to go before we're home." She turned and headed for the hatch as if there were no more to say. As if nothing had happened.

Del started after her, snarling a curse under his breath. "Wait, where are you going?"

"Out," she snapped over her shoulder, her swift glance full of narrow-eyed warning.

"With a concealed weapon? You're asking for trouble, Sin."

"As I said, it's none of your concern—"

"Screw that," he exclaimed and caught her arm, pulling her to a stop. But he let her go at once. Touching her again when his body hadn't even started to cool off was much too enticing. "You signed me up, remember? I'm in your business up to my eyeballs. Everything you do affects me and everybody else working for you."

"I don't have time for this," she hissed and turned away.

He stepped in her path. "Make time. Why are you acting like this? Are you just gonna ignore what happened back there?"

She lifted her head and he almost winced at the hard glint in her eyes, her face a cold mask. "Yes, I am. It was a mistake and it won't happen again. You're my employee, Del. We had no business touching each other. I have to go."

This time when she stalked toward the exit, he didn't try to stop her. He turned on stiff legs, jaw clenched against a bitter ache in his chest. "You can't go out there alone."

"I'll be fine," she said in a distant voice, not looking at him as she stepped out of the hatch. "Stay here. I won't be gone long."

He stood still with hands fisted for a moment, her cold rejection stinging across raw nerves. He didn't believe her. Where was she going with a stinger?

Pushing what happened between them to a distant corner of his mind, he spun on his heel and went back to the Shadow for his shirt, jerking it on and heading through the hatch. He meant to find out what she was doing this time.

He caught a glimpse of Sin disappearing through an exit and jogged after her. When he reached the corridor, he was just in time to see her take a left turn down a different passage. He followed Sin past the public nightlife of the facility, a series of bars becoming more listless the farther they went, before she disappeared through an entryway. He approached with caution and looked around. The corridors were empty, so he slipped through the entrance and into the darkness beyond.

"Nobody said you could bring a weapon," a rough voice snarled from a dim area ahead of him. Inching forward, his eyes adjusted enough to recognize a storage room.

"Calm down, Tracer. I didn't hide it from you and I even gave it to Stan for safekeeping," Sin answered in a light tone. "Are you still so afraid?"

"Search her," the rough voice responded.

Sin's mocking laughter echoed around him as Del made his careful way through stacked canisters. He eased toward light between stacks, keeping concealed by peering around the canisters.

Sin faced away from him, her stance casual and relaxed. In contrast, the three men before her bristled with attitude and aggression. One of them held her stinger, not quite pointed at her.

"Rule number one, boys: no one touches me. Besides, does it look like I'm carrying more weapons?" She ran a hand over one sleek hip with a playful tilt of her head. "Can we get down to business?"

"Abantium," one of them barked.

"Name of the game," Sin replied, her voice still holding a light tone. Del suspected her expression would be very different, though.

"We could just take it. The Cortecians got it now."

"We've been through this," Sin said with exaggerated patience. "Your skippers are no match for me and mine. Shall we try it without bloodshed this time?"

With a thrill of alarm, Del realized these men were the hijackers they'd fought off earlier.

"You'd fight for it still? But you delivered, and the Cortecians paid you."

"Why not get paid twice?"

Her answer seemed to put the men at ease, though they exchanged sour glances. The one with Sin's weapon let his arm relax to his side. "Core don't give us enough cut for this," one of them complained.

The ground dropped out from under Del. His brother had been right. She was dealing dirty with the

Core. She and her brother might treat him better than the Core, but they were still playing the same nasty games, and using him to do it. Bitter, disillusioned anger filled him and made him reckless. He straightened and stepped out into the open. "Suns curse you, Shay."

He became the center of attention, the three pirates eyeing him with dangerous animosity.

Sin frowned over her shoulder. "Del, you shouldn't have come."

"Who's this piece of krell dung?" the center pirate growled.

"Stop foaming at the mouth, Tracer. He's with me," Sin answered with careless ease, as if she couldn't see the hostility building in them.

"We said come alone!" Tracer shouted and backhanded her, rocking her with the blow.

Instant, blinding fury flooded through Del, his vision vanishing in a sea of red. He lunged forward with a snarl, but Stan yelled in warning and aimed the stinger at him. Halting with an effort, Del stood panting and clenched his hands into fists.

Sin raised a slow hand, wiping at her mouth then looking at the blood on her fingers. "Well, this is disappointing," she said, studying the red stain. "Forgot rule number one already, did you?"

Tracer's eyes widened in sudden alarm. Then Sin moved in a sinuous twist, driving a fist into his solar plexus. She lashed out with a foot at the same time, sending the stinger skittering out of Stan's hand.

It was enough for Del. Sin was still moving, but all his focus centered on the man who'd dared lay a hand on her. Tracer clutched his stomach, trying to straighten. Baring down on the pirate, Del drove a fist into his face with enough force to knock him off his feet. He gave the bandit's ribs a hard kick, but the man was out cold. Del turned to pick another target.

There were none to pick. Sin paced back and forth, shaking a hand idly as if it stung. At her feet, one man sprawled in an untidy heap, blood on his unconscious face. Next to him, the last hijacker crouched on hands and knees with his head lowered, breath rattling in wrenching coughs.

"Deep breaths, Stan. In and out," Sin instructed in a distant voice.

"Sin," Del gritted.

She held up a hand, still staring at Stan. "Give him a minute. He's sore."

Wheezing, the man looked up at her. Del tensed at the hate twisting the man's face. The pirate said something too garbled for Del to understand.

"Now, that's not very nice," Sin responded, voice reverting to its former gaiety, her eyes shining with a predatory light. "Does this mean you want to play some more?"

He shook his head and hunched away from her.

"So I thought." She crouched next to the laboring man. "I'm sure you'd love to see the last of me, so let's get this business over with. I'm willing to let you take the abantium from the Cortecians, but there's a price. Are you paying attention, Stan?"

The man gave a ragged cough and nodded, looking at her through his straggling hair. At the rabid gleam in his eyes, Del shifted closer.

"Good, because this is a little tricky. My price is information and silence, though I'll be paying for your silence. How, you ask?" The man stared at her and she grinned like a shark. "Excellent question. You take the abantium, like a good little thief, and turn it over to the Core. The Core gives you my asking price for the abantium and…are you listening, Stan? If you give me the information I want, and tell no one you gave it to me, then you keep the entire amount. Sounds good, doesn't it?"

Stan shifted a little, rocking back on his heels and clutching his arms around his chest in a pained gesture. The greed on his face spoke volumes. "They find out we turned a deal on 'em, and we're fried," he croaked.

"Which is why your silence is so important. It protects us both, you see?"

The pirate mulled it over. Del's mind raced over the possibilities. What was she up to?

"What's the info?" the man rasped.

"Glad you asked," she said with a brilliant smile. "The Core has a secret facility in this area of space. Do you know of it?"

The man shook his head too fast, his eyes darting away from her. "Don't know nuthin'."

"Too bad," she sighed and rose to her feet. "Deal's off, then."

"Wait! Guess I've heard of a place. Don't know it's Core. The big blue factory what you after?"

"Yes."

Del stared at her.

"I tell you where to find it and we get full price, that the deal?"

"That's the deal." Sin's face was expressionless.

The pirate chewed on the inside of his cheek then nodded with a gurgling cough. "Done," he rasped and rattled off a set of coordinates.

"Thank you." Sin crouched in front of him again. "One more thing, thief. The abantium cargo I brought to this facility. You will take only half." A thunderous frown formed on the man's face, but Sin held up a warning hand, her tone hardening. "Half, or I hunt down every one of your skippers skulking around this system and destroy them all. I won't have my courier reputation trashed just because you got greedy. The other half can be found at the second Cortecian mining facility. I brought more than enough to satisfy your buyers, so don't disappoint me, Stan."

He subsided with a sullen expression and nodded.

"Good boy." She rose to her feet, sending Del an inquiring glance. "I'm all done here. How about you?"

Del clenched his jaw, suppressing the urge to shake her. He needed answers, but showing weakness in front of these men would be dangerous. He gave her a stiff nod, ignoring the measuring look in her eyes. When she headed for the exit, he matched her stride.

On the way, she scooped up the stinger. Catching his accusing stare, she shrugged. "They expected me to be carrying. If I hadn't brought it, they'd have been much more nervous. Giving it to them was supposed to calm them down and give them something to focus on. It would have worked, too, if you hadn't interfered."

He snarled at the faint accusation in her tone but said nothing. He bided his time, waiting until they were in a quiet passage with no witnesses. Then he grabbed her arm, his fingers digging into her smooth flesh. "I want answers and I want 'em now." His low voice shook with the effort not to shout.

She frowned at his brutal grip but didn't try to

remove it. "I'll tell you what you need to know when we get to the hauler."

"Now," he growled, shaking her once. "What are you up to and why did you have to drag me into it?"

"It's not safe to talk here."

"Too bad. I'm not goin' back there without a damn good reason."

She lifted her chin, eyes meeting his with steady directness, sending a shiver of longing down his spine even through his bitter anger. "Del, you're hurting me," she said, her tone calm and patient.

Even though she was no better than the Core and used people with the same ruthlessness, even though he meant as little to her as a pawn, he still couldn't stop a flush of shame. He let her go, clenching his hands into fists. Controlling his tone with an effort, he said, "You're in bed with the Core, Sin. I can't be part of it."

"So they believe." Her gaze didn't falter. She tipped her dark head back toward the pirates. "So they all believe. Didn't your brother tell you about the gift?"

"Twisted version of love thy enemy."

She smiled and shook her head. "Your brother saw less than I thought. Come back to the hauler and I'll tell you everything. I'll answer every question, Del."

Her calm green eyes filled with intimate sincerity, with Sun-cursed honesty, but he was too hurt and wary to buy it. He gave her a stiff nod of assent, not because he believed her, but because those eyes touched him in places he couldn't defend. She could lead him down the throat of a black hole with just this look in her eyes.

And Suns save him, he would go.

Chapter 18

Del rationalized his decision as they made their way back to the Tank in silence. He shouldn't just abandon the rest of the crew. He didn't know about the others, but he was sure Jinx had no idea what the Shays were doing.

They reached the Tank and Sin touched the outer com. "Cass."

"It's open," was Cassie's immediate response. "Everything all right?"

"Right as rain," Sin answered.

If Cassie heard the faint sarcasm in her voice, she didn't let on. "Good. All's well here, too."

Under Sin's touch, the hatch slid open. Del followed her slim form inside the hauler with a mild sense of claustrophobia. Here he was, dragged back into the special hell the Core had found for him. How long would it be before the Shays asked him to do the same things? How long before he was stealing and brutalizing those who couldn't defend themselves? How long before they asked him to kill?

Sin shot him a quick glance over her shoulder, her eyes grave, but she said nothing, leading the way to the commons room. Once inside, she moved to the kitchen area and pulled out two mugs, filling them with a stimulant. "It's been a long night and it's only getting longer," she explained under his stare.

He took his mug without comment and eased onto a seat at the dining table. When she sat opposite him and sipped her drink, he said, "All right, we're here. So tell me. Tell me about the abantium. Tell me what you want with the blue factory. Getting Jinx back into his old business?"

She flashed him a burning look. "I need to start at the beginning. It'll be easier for you to understand."

He waited. When she did nothing but stare down into her mug, he made a rude noise in the back of his throat. "So start already."

With a sigh, she met his gaze, and he winced at the weary pain in her eyes. "Beginnings are hard, especially this one." Looking down again, she took another sip then touched tentative fingers to her wounded lip. The flesh was starting to swell and bruise.

Del's gut clenched.

"My grandfather started our company. I never met him, but I'm told he was a formidable man, much like my father. No surprise there. He raised my father in his image, strong, fearless, and ruthless."

She paused, turning the mug in her hands, her fingers trembling a little. "Shay Enterprises was still a rising company when my father took control of it. He had to fight for every advance and concession. But Grandpa Shay had taught him well. He dealt with the competition without mercy, no holds barred."

Bitterness crept into her tone and Del shifted in his seat, a frown forming between his eyes. What did this have to do with the abantium deal?

Sin rubbed her eyes and continued, "One company rivaled ours, mirroring many of our products. It stood out from other competitors, strong enough to cause my father real trouble. They thwarted his every effort to cause their downfall and push them out of his road to success. His every legal effort. But Grandpa Shay had taught him failure was not an option. All is fair in war. To my father, business was war."

She lurched to her feet and began pacing the room, shrugging off her jacket and tossing it over a couch. Even in his bitter wariness, Del couldn't take his eyes off her sleek limbs as she prowled the room. The bare skin of her shoulders and chest gleamed like soft alabaster against the black of her sleeveless shirt.

"Many different crime syndicates existed in those days, gangs, mafias, cartels. They warred with each other, keeping each other in check with their endless feuding. The FPA didn't have much trouble with them, then. And the Core wasn't born, yet."

"Sin," Del tried to interrupt, confused and impatient.

She shook her head without looking at him. "Let me tell it. From the beginning, I said."

He subsided, but for a minute she didn't continue. Pausing with her profile to him, she stared down at the ground with a grim expression. Then she reached up and started to undo her braid with slow, preoccupied fingers.

"Griffin was in control of one of those syndicates, just one more rat in the garbage heap. His group had more discipline and less mercy than most, but he was still just one among many. My father went to see him."

Her fingers untangled the dark strands with dexterous ease, but her face became pinched with emotion. Del's chest tightened in foreboding.

"He offered his worst rival to Griffin on a silver

platter. He gave Griffin information allowing him complete access to their systems and their products. He expected Griffin to destroy them, to be greedy and suck the life out of his rival."

The braid undone, Sin raked her fingers through the long strands of blue-black hair in punishing strokes, mouth twisting.

"He didn't know Griffin then. He had no idea the depth of cold ambition lying at the man's heart. Griffin took the access information, but instead of consuming the company, he made it his. Quasicore was born."

Del stopped breathing as a spasm of shock went through him, freezing him from head to toe, though a molten lump in his chest beat with misery. Sin returned to the table, her eyes downcast. "You…" he tried, but his voice faltered. *That's insane,* he wanted to deny, *impossible.*

"My father, Ezekiel Shay, was responsible for the birth of the most terrible force of our age. The Core grew and devoured. All the other crime syndicates either merged with Griffin's, or died under him, until the only underground was Core. The only black deeds and atrocities were Core." Truth lay in the tautness of her lovely features, in the black sweep of lashes against too-pale skin. "My father caused this."

She met his horrified gaze, her eyes tortured. "Sins of our fathers, Del. You've been trapped and tormented by your father's mistakes for ten long years. But my father's sin started it. We're responsible for every horrible thing done to you, and for every horrible thing you've done in the Core's name."

In a distant corner of his mind, Del raged at her dead father, but the pain on Sin's face was too immediate and the responsibility she claimed too large. He denied it with a slow shake of his head. "You aren't responsible for what your father did," he rasped.

She barked a humorless laugh. "This from the man who allowed the Core to swallow him whole on the basis of his father's tattered honor."

"They didn't give me a choice." He shot to his feet, taking his turn to pace around the room.

The silence vibrated with tension, spinning between them for a long moment. Then Sin spoke again as Del paced.

"My father discovered his mistake too late to stop the takeover and the consumption of the other syndicates. If he'd known what the Core would become, he would have fought harder to kill it, but he still expected Griffin to revert to form and devour himself along with everything else. By the time he understood Webster Griffin, it was much too late to stop it."

She paused, and Del contained his bitterness behind gritted teeth. "It was Dad's wake-up call," she continued in a flat tone.

Del glanced at her. She followed his movements with dark sorrow and he looked away in a spasm of misery. *Those eyes,* he despaired.

"He was determined to make it right. Grandpa Shay may have lacked humanity, but my father couldn't discard his lessons. Shays don't quit. Failure is not an option. He didn't stop trying to fix his mistake until the day he died. Along the way, he met my mother and had two precocious children."

Del slowed to a stop next to the couch, eyes finding her again. She wore a pained smile, her hands clasped in a white-knuckled grip.

"My mother discovered what he'd done and despaired at the responsibility. She dwindled, as if the Core were wearing her away, until she killed herself when I was fourteen. After our mother's funeral, my father sat us down and explained why. It was our wake-up call."

"Sin," he rasped, unable to stand the terrible emptiness on her face.

But she blinked and waved a hand, as if dismissing old ghosts. Rising to her feet, she rounded the table and moved to stand before him, hands on her hips. "Old news. The new stuff's more interesting."

He shook his head, misery welling in his chest like a gray cloud of poisonous smoke.

A brief, humorless smile touched the corners of her mouth. She tilted her head to one side. "Didn't you demand answers?" Brushing by him, she sank with grace onto the couch, patting the cushion next to her. "Make yourself comfortable, Del. This was only half the story."

Sin watched Del's grim features and listened to the slow thump of dread between her temples, waiting for his response. He might leave. He might hate her. Telling Cassie hadn't been this hard, though Cass had figured out some of it on her own.

Without looking at her, Del ran a hand through his hair and gripped the back of his neck with enough force to whiten his fingertips. He let out an explosive sigh and dropped his hand, his dark eyes finding hers. "My brother said it was a blood feud," he said in a rough voice, tension pulling his skin taut across his cheekbones.

"Your brother is a bright man without all the facts," she responded carefully. "He is both right and wrong. Please, sit."

Mouth compressing in a grim line, he sat, facing her with one arm along the back of the couch. If he lifted his hand, he would brush the nape of her neck. Sin suppressed a quiver but couldn't shift away. He would read it wrong.

"Thank you," she murmured and cleared her throat. "It's only a true blood feud if there's animosity on both sides. Griffin has never suspected how much we despise him. After all, my father opened the door for him to become what he is today. He can't grasp concepts like duty, honor, and compassion. If anything, he sees them as weakness instead of strength."

Del's expression turned impatient, uninterested in the inner workings of Webster Griffin's mind. She wished she could afford not to be.

"My father tried to fix things the way he'd been taught by my grandfather, all out, no holds barred, no quarter given. It didn't work. Griffin had too great a hold on a world out of my father's reach, the dark underbelly of our societies. Desperate, my father solicited help from other sources, even asking the Orders for advice."

Del tensed and Sin curled the unbruised side of her mouth. "The Red Sun Order took an interest in him and our company. Reds don't often care who wins the battle as long as there is battle, but they don't like the idea of Griffin controlling them any more than we do. Even back then, they could see the threat of Quasicore. My father asked for advice and they gave it. His strategies became much more long term."

Del narrowed his eyes. "This doesn't explain tonight. What your father did was—"

"What my father did was raise his children to understand responsibility, duty, honor, and compassion, quite a bit different from how he was raised. We still have the Shay stubbornness, though, and inability to fail. My actions have, and always will, reflect these things."

Del shifted and frowned, his dark eyes blurred with confusion. Her words didn't match what he saw tonight, but she had to tell this her way. If she skipped ahead, he wouldn't understand and might not believe what she told him.

"Griffin is a megalomaniac, but he didn't allow his ego to stand in the way of his creation. He built the Core to stand even if he should fall. We could kill Griffin, but someone would take his place and the Core would go on devouring everything in its path.

"So my father went to the Orders and received advice from the Red Sun. Then he approached the FPA for their cooperation, and began playing Griffin's game against him. It wasn't easy making contacts under the Core's shadow. My brother and I joined him when we were old enough, but it was still an uphill battle for all of us. As he was bound to do, Griffin discovered what we were doing and offered to help."

"What? Why?" Del shook his head.

"Ezekiel Shay gave Griffin a new life, through an act of moral, ethical, and legal corruption. In his mind, it placed my father in his circle, and he always believed Shay Enterprises to be his friendly rival. He welcomed the competition between our companies for how it honed his own skills, but he viewed my father's clean business practices as a weakness. He rejoiced when we began delving into the dark corners of his world. My father was becoming the adversary he needed."

"Sin," Del interrupted, rubbing his temple with impatient fingers. "You don't make sense. Are you enemies or not?"

"In Griffin's eyes, we're official business rivals and unofficial cohorts in corruption. But we only play his game hoping someday we'll bring the Core crashing down around his ears, and put right what my father made wrong so many years ago."

Del made a rude noise. "All this talk of fighting him and fixing what's wrong, but you act just like him. You made a deal with a bunch of pirates tonight, Sin. How is that right?"

She smiled despite the pain it gave her tender lip. "My father would've liked you, Del," she commented. His expression darkened. "Fine, let's talk about what happened. Do you remember asking why we were carrying so much abantium?"

He nodded, eyes narrowing again as if he expected her to evade him.

"We bought extra, twice the contracted cargo, paid for by Shay Enterprises. We'd already made it clear to Griffin we'd be carrying the cargo and we knew he'd want it. Left to his own devices, Griffin would have ordered the pirates take it all from the Cortecians after we delivered it. So we controlled the deal, for our half of the cargo."

"Wait," Del cut in, holding up a hand and shaking his head. "That's not what happened. They attacked us."

"Yes, well, bad boys don't always play nice. They

tried to cut out the middleman by stealing the cargo from us and doing the deal with the Core themselves."

"I still don't buy it was just a good deed for the Cortecians. You said you let Griffin know you were carrying abantium. You made sure he would come after it."

"We needed some way to flush out someone in this sector of space who would know the location of Griffin's hidden facility."

He scowled at her. "What do you want with a blue factory?"

Sin leaned closer and locked her gaze with his. "I want to destroy it. But I can't just now. Griffin knows we're in the area, he'd know it was us. We'll come back later and scout it."

With a thoughtful frown, he studied her. "How big a factory is it?"

"Our intel shows it's the Core's largest producer of blue."

"So if you destroy it, it'd be a big blow to him."

"Yes, it would hurt Griffin, but it wouldn't stop blue production."

"So what good does it do to destroy it?"

She gave him a lopsided smile in deference to her throbbing lip. "Now you're catching on. We've run countless attacks on his holdings with no effect to the strength of the Core. We have to think bigger, which is where the FPA comes in."

He tilted his head, puzzled. "You'll tell them where it is?"

"Yes, but not until we've had our crack at it."

"What d'you mean?" he asked, suspicion tightening the skin around his eyes.

"We need to find out who is running Griffin's entire blue production and cut off the operation at its base. This factory is the key. It's big enough they'll know who is in control. We turn the person, or persons, in to the FPA, along with the location of the factory as proof."

"Wild plan. If it works, though, the FPA would take the Core apart."

"We hope," Sin responded with a dispirited half-shrug.

His head lifted like a prelude to challenge. "You don't think the FPA'll do it?"

She sighed, closing her eyes and rolling her neck in an attempt to ease the aching muscles at the base of her skull. "Like I said, Griffin made sure the Core would stand. He's corrupted so many areas of our society, including the FPA."

He swore in a low voice. "If they're in his pocket, what's the point?"

"They aren't all on his payroll, and someone has to stop him before they are. The point is; failure is not an option." Sin met his gaze with grim determination. "The Core continues to grow, Del. If we don't stop him now…" she let her voice trail off and shook her head.

His mouth compressed in a bitter line, eyes searching hers with breath-stealing intensity. "And the factory?"

"It's the beginning of the Endgame." Unwilling to explain too much and strain his fragile acceptance, she angled for distraction, giving him a faint, challenging smile. "Want to come with us when we go after it?"

The tightness around his mouth eased into a cynical half-smile. "Why does it feel like you're asking me to shoot the rim again?"

"Because you're the suspicious sort," she retorted. "We'll slip in, get the info we need, and slip back out. Nothing to it."

He snorted, giving a lock of her hair a gentle tug. "Little liar. The factory won't leave the front door open and the landing lights on for you. They're gonna have security."

Sin lowered her gaze, curling her legs under her and trying not to lean into his heat like a frozen comet pulled into a sun. "We're good at improvising," she said. His touch returned and she lifted her lashes.

Del studied her, his fingers caressing the silk of her hair. "You're really one of the good guys, aren't you?" he asked in a low voice.

She gave a soft laugh to cover a wave of relief and longing, her muscles weakening and a flush heating her skin. "We do our best. You didn't believe it until now, did you?"

He grimaced a little, gaze drifting to her mouth and speeding up her heart. "What'd you expect?" he answered in an absent way, face darkening and brows drawing together. He lifted his hand, still entwined in her hair, and touched a thumb to the bruising at the corner of her mouth. "Should've hit him a few more times," he muttered with a spark of grim violence in his eyes, but his touch was infinitely gentle, his thumb brushing over the abused flesh.

"Well, I would have, but you knocked him out," she said, trying for a light tone, but a shiver of yearning ruffled the sound.

His expression lightened, a fleeting smile passing over his mouth, but he didn't lift his gaze. His thumb made soothing, mesmerizing passes over her skin. "How bad does it hurt?"

"Not bad," she whispered as his thumb skimmed her lip, leaving behind a tingling line.

He hummed, leaning toward her with a faint, absorbed frown. "Maybe we should put ice on it."

The words barely registered. She watched with her breath caught in her throat as he bent his head to hers. He moved slow, giving her time to pull away, but Sin went still with the effort not to lean into his touch and turn her mouth to his like a supplicant.

The first touch of his lips on her bruised flesh sent a shiver of longing down her spine. She couldn't stop a faint whimper from escaping. Del whispered wordless contrition against her skin, cupping his hand against her cheek. With slow gentleness, he covered her bruised skin with kisses, his other hand caressing her arm with soothing strokes, as if erasing his earlier brutal grip.

His tenderness brought the sting of tears to her eyes. She closed them in dismay, trembling on the brink of restraint. In slow motion, she raised her hands, resting them against his chest and trying to find the strength to push him away. But with each sweet and seductive brush of his lips against her skin, it became harder and harder for her to remember why she should.

He moved his attention from the corner of her mouth to her lower lip, the brush of his mouth soothing, gentle, and maddening. She quivered, hands closing around fistfuls of his shirt. At the silky slide of his tongue against her sensitive flesh, she sighed in surrender and turned her mouth to his. He went still moment then whispered something broken against her mouth before sliding his hand into her hair and deepening the kiss with slow care.

It stung her split lip, but she didn't care. It added poignancy to the sweetness of his mouth moving over hers with tender, thorough deliberation. The aching promise in his caress stripped her defenses away as if they were meaningless, exposing every vulnerability. In that instant, if he asked, she would whisper her heart's desire.

"Oh! Um, s-sorry." Cassie's voice was a hard slap of reality, shocking and painful.

Sin pulled away with a gasp and shudder of dismay, hiding her face and lifting a trembling hand to her temple. Del said her name in low protest, his rough murmur overlaid by Cassie rattling on about activity on the troller.

Sin ignored them, pushing to her feet and spinning around for the exit. She should stay and smooth it over, but she couldn't. Bad enough to lose control with Del twice in one night. But in the cradle of his hands and under the spell of his kiss, she'd made a discovery too shocking for her to remain. Despite the sheer folly of doing so, she'd fallen ridiculously in love with him.

"I'm really sorry," Cassie whispered when Sin passed, but she left the room without a word.

Chapter 19

Del didn't watch Sin go. He spanned his forehead with one hand, gripping his temples hard enough to make his head ache. It didn't stop the ache in his chest. Rejected again. This time, he couldn't tell himself it was for the best, she was bad news, and he should just leave. She and her brother were doing what he'd always dreamed, taking on the Core, fighting back against the corruption in all their lives. How could he walk away from that? How could he walk away from her?

"Del, I apologize for interrupting."

He grunted.

Cassie rounded the end of the couch and eased down next to him. "I wouldn't have come in if I… Do you want to talk about it?"

"No."

"All right, what do you want to talk about?"

He dropped his hand. Cassie was watching him with an anxious expression and compassion in her soft brown eyes. "Nothing. Just leave me alone, Cass."

She looked away but didn't leave. "You came back with her. Does this mean she told you?"

He paused, wondering if he could just ignore her. Then he heaved a weary sigh. "Yeah, she told me. Why didn't you say anything, Cass?"

She shrugged, looking down. "It wasn't my place. So you know why we're here in Cortecian space."

"The factory."

"And they told her the location?"

"Yeah."

"So it's started." With a twitch of her hand, she pulled her braid over her shoulder and ran it through her fingers as if the silky twists held the power to reveal the future.

He narrowed his eyes. "How deep in this are you, Cass?"

Blinking, she glanced at him then turned her face away. "As deep as I need to be, Del. The real question is, how deep are you willing to go?"

Del let out an impatient snort, dismissing her question. She knew the answer already or she wouldn't be asking. The real question was, just how involved was she? "What's your part in this, little dragon?"

Cassie faced him, chin lifting and eyes determined. "I'm just their employee. No more, no less. What did you say when she told you about Zeke Shay?"

He frowned at her obvious lie, running rough fingers through his hair. "Nothing."

"Nothing? What a relief for her," Cassie commented with a bland smile.

He glowered at her. "What do you want me to say? The man didn't do his own dirty work and it came back on him? He was a greedy, immoral bastard?"

"Yes, but in case Sin didn't make it clear, Ezekiel Shay became a new man when he realized what he'd done. He put his single-minded purpose to a better cause than personal gain. Though, what he did to his children wasn't good. They both believe they have a duty to heal the wound their father created with the Core." She tipped her head to one side and studied him.

"Our previous associations with the Core makes us their responsibility. They feel obligated to put right the wrongs done to us. Do you understand?"

He grimaced, lunging to his feet and pacing the room in aimless aggression. "We're broken and they wanna fix us."

Cassie frowned, flipping her braid back over her shoulder and folding her arms. "Kai," she said with a shake of her head. "The man needs to reacquaint himself with the definition of tact. We're no more broken than they are, Del. I was trying to make a different point. Let me put it another way. If you had someone you were responsible for, would you take advantage of them?"

He halted across the room and looked over his shoulder, hands clenching into fists. "What's that supposed to mean?"

She bent her head, avoiding his gaze. "I'm trying to help you see the difficulties of your situation," she answered, tightening the arms across her chest like a woman wrestling with doubt. "If you had someone in your care depending on you, would you take advantage of a weakness of theirs? For example, if they were attracted to you, would you—"

"Suns curse it, Cass, I said I didn't want to talk about it," he snarled and stalked out of the room.

The trip back to Shay headquarters seemed eternal. Sin avoided him, or brushed him off when she did see him. Cassie, Quan, and Jinx watched the two of them with worried eyes, whispering among themselves whenever Del entered or exited a room. He took to camping out in his Shadow, just to have some peace. They left him alone, for which he was grateful.

Kai wasn't so tactful or discreet. Once the haulers rejoined one another for the return trip, Kai stopped in to visit Sin. Afterward, he stalked through the cargo bay to Del and slammed him against the side of the Shadow, green eyes blazing. "What did you do to my sister?"

"You think I hit her? Get off me," Del snarled, shoving him away.

Cassie scurried over, face pale and eyes dark with dismay. "Kai, stop! What are you doing?"

"I was about to rearrange his body parts. Something's wrong with my sister. What do you know about it, Cassiopeia? You told me she was fine."

"Did you ask Sin?"

"I'm asking you."

"If you're asking me, then she wouldn't tell you. If she didn't tell you, then she didn't want you to know. Some people value privacy," Cassie added with a lift of her eyebrows.

"Move, Cass," he ordered with icy calm.

"Yeah, let him pass," Del growled, more than ready to let off steam and beat on Sin's obnoxious twin.

Cassie cast a white-lipped glare over her shoulder at Del. "So you two can indulge in a moment of senseless violence? I don't think so. It's none of our business, Kai."

"She's my sister. She is my business."

"What do you think she'll do to you if you hurt him?"

Kai frowned at her then lifted a cold stare to Del. "Might still be worth it," he mused.

Del stared right back in challenge. "Don't let her stop you, Shay."

For some reason, instead of jumping him like any normal guy, Kai smirked and relaxed. "Some other time, Giv." He turned and sauntered away as if the whole incident hadn't happened.

Del scowled down at Cassie.

"Don't give me that look," she snapped, expression as severe as a schoolmarm's. "He would have flattened you."

He snorted. "Give me a little credit, Cass. I've been in a fight or two."

"Bar brawls and street fights? They're nothing compared to what he could do to you, trust me. The man's had more militant training than FPA soldiers." Her face softened a little. "I know you're looking for an emotional outlet, but violence isn't the way. Have you tried—?"

"Stop head-shrinking me, Cassiopeia," he growled and walked away.

They took a more direct route home and reached HQ late in the evening. Del left the Tank with a subdued Cassie at his side, though she brightened when they met the rest of the crew between the haulers and headed for the maintenance bay. The twins came into view, their raised voices echoing. He and Cass exchanged a tense glance then moved in tandem toward the arguing siblings.

"What is the matter with you, Kai? You didn't have a problem with this before we left."

"Until you started acting like a Lana bird at hunting season."

"You're the one being an idiot. If we wait too long, those pirates are going to crack and you know it."

"It wouldn't do any good to go now and have you

crisp out on me."

The twins didn't seem to notice their approach, and Cassie cleared her throat. "Um, Shays…"

They ignored her.

"That's ridiculous!" Sin snapped, folding her arms and glaring at her brother. "There's nothing wrong with me, and you know we need to go before the factory gets word we're coming."

"Bosses, this is kind of a public place to—" Cassie tried again, with the same result.

"We're not going."

"You might not be, but I'll go alone if I have to. It needs to be done now."

"You are not going alone!" Kai shouted. "I forbid it."

Del raised his eyebrows. Slapping an ultimatum on Sin seemed kind of suicidal.

"You—" Sin started, eyes flaring with fury, but Del interrupted.

"I'll go with her." Del moved to stand at Sin's elbow. They both stared at him. He faced Kai, meeting his boss's gaze with cool directness while trying to ignore Sin's light, captivating scent. No matter what either Shay wanted, he couldn't let Sin go into that rat's nest alone.

"What a fine idea," Kai responded, his hot anger transforming into chilling animosity. "My sister alone with a man who's had one day's worth experience off-lane, crippling his ship. A man who can't keep his hands to himself." Del drew a sharp breath, but Kai wasn't done. "What do you expect to do? Besides the obvious," he added, shooting his sister a searing look. "Just ask them to open up?"

Del clenched his jaw, answering with as much restraint as he could muster through his teeth, "You didn't take me on just because I can pilot. You know what I did for the Core."

Kai's eyes narrowed and his voice took on a silky menace. "You're not going either. Do I make myself clear?"

Del stared hard at the man, refusing to back down. Tension built between them like electricity.

"Fine, we'll wait," Sin broke the standoff in a clipped tone. "We won't go until you're up to it. Satisfied?"

Her brother studied her, his expression smoothing despite the acid in her tone. When he nodded, Sin spun on her heel and stalked away. Kai watched her go with a faint frown. "I don't like being at odds with my sister."

Stinging from yet another rejection from Sin, Del retorted, "Then maybe you shouldn't pick fights with her."

Icy green eyes fixed on him, and Kai's face emptied of all emotion. He took a step toward Del, but Cassie slipped between them again, facing Del with wide eyes and pale face. "So Del," she squeaked, holding her hands up and bracing her back against Kai. "H-how are you doing with Samantha?"

He frowned at her. Had she lost her mind all of a sudden? "What?"

"Samantha. You know, the AI who lives in and maintains your quarters. How are the two of you getting along?"

"Fine, I guess."

"You guess? Haven't you spent time with her?"

Her hands went to her hips, exasperation threading through her tone.

Kai started to smirk, an added irritant to this strange conversation.

"Uh, no Cass, I haven't been here."

"I mean before we left. Didn't you talk with her?"

He shrugged. "A little, sure."

She shook her head and pointed toward the exit. "Let's go."

"What?" he asked again, both annoyed and baffled.

"I assumed you'd be curious, ask her questions, and talk to her. My fault for thinking you'd do anything so normal. So let's go. I have to assess how much damage you've caused."

Kai chuckled and she glanced back, elbowing him in the stomach. "What are you laughing at?"

"Just thinking better him than me," he said with a merciless grin at Del before moving away.

Del watched him go, scowling. "What's wrong with him?"

"Don't ask. It would take days to explain and we don't have time." Grabbing his arm, she tugged him toward the exit. "Come on, Del. Let's go survey the wreckage."

Chapter 20

Del didn't know which was worse; dealing with Kai's quicksilver moods from menacing fury to mocking humor, or putting up with Cassie's disgusted tyranny. His mind shied from thoughts of Sin's blunt dismissal as if it were an open wound. He didn't want to remember how she'd brushed him away with so little respect or trust, how she'd confirmed her brother's contempt. Broken.

He glowered down at Cassie the whole way to his quarters as if she were responsible for the ache in his chest and the pounding in his head.

Without meeting his eyes, she rebuked, "It's not my fault you don't have sense enough not to get between the Shays." As they reached his quarters, she continued, "AIs aren't just programs you can use and throw away. They're people, too, Del." After delivering her one-two punch, she waited with pursed lips for him to open the door.

Several brutal replies came to mind, but he bit them back with an effort. She'd stepped between him and Kai, after all, though he'd been happy to oblige the violence in the other man's eyes at the time. And she was his friend, though she had an odd way of showing it sometimes. Grinding his teeth as if he could chew out some patience, he let her in his quarters.

Sending him a quick glance out of the corner of her

eye, she stepped inside.

"Greetings, Cassiopeia Draegen. Welcome home, Del." Samantha's disembodied voice sounded just as smooth and calm as ever, no trace of wreckage as far as Del could tell.

"Hey, Sam," he responded, giving Cass a pointed look.

She ignored him. "Samantha, it's good to speak with you again. Do you know me?" she asked, moving to sit on the couch.

With a grimace, he joined her.

"Yes, Cassiopeia. You are my creator."

Del's jaw dropped, and he stared at the small woman next to him.

She met his gaze for a fraction of a second with a faint, pained smile. "Well, one of them. Please call me Cassie."

"I will do so. My living mate Del appears to enjoy calling me Sam."

"Do you enjoy being called Sam?"

During the ensuing pause, Cassie sent him an accusing look. He returned it with a baffled, questioning shake of his head, but she only pulled her braid over her shoulder and plucked at the ends with restless fingers.

"I am not certain. I do not have parameters for this contingency. Should I enjoy this?"

"There are no parameters for what you can and can't enjoy. It's for you to decide. Were you satisfied with your naming?"

The answer was immediate. "Yes."

"So you enjoy the name Samantha?"

"Yes," the AI replied, but in a less confident tone.

"But I do not understand it."

"How so?"

"If my living mate has chosen this name, why does he use another?"

Cassie shot him another black glance. Del opened his mouth to defend himself, but she beat him to it, taking on the brisk, dry tone he recognized from their training sessions. "Often humans will shorten one another's names as a sign of affection, friendship, or familiarity. It's a verbal way to forge an intimate connection. In this case, by shortening your name, Del is showing his trust in you and his appreciation for your companionship."

I am? He stared at Cassie as if she'd grown a third eye. She didn't seem to notice.

"I see. So, in asking me to call him Del, he is asking for my trust and appreciation?"

"In a way, yes. He is asking you to participate in forging a connection, forming an intimacy with you without outright discussing it."

This was getting weirder and weirder. Del cleared his throat, but Cassie sent him a narrow-eyed glare of warning and he subsided in confusion.

"Is this your motivation also, when you ask me to call you Cassie?"

"Yes, Samantha. I wish to be your friend. Is this acceptable to you?"

"Yes, it is. I would enjoy it very much. Would you please call me Sam?"

Cassie smiled and relaxed against the couch as though she'd won a victory. "Thank you, Sam. I'd be honored."

"May I ask you a question, Cassie?"

"Please do."

"Shortening of names is an inefficient method for creating intimacy. You have asked for my friendship. Why does my living mate not do so?"

Embarrassed panic went through Del, but Cassie answered without hesitation, sweeping past his discomfort.

"Humans are uncomfortable expressing their emotions, because of the possibility of rejection. If you had told me no when I asked for your friendship, I would have been hurt. Rejection is painful. Also, reiterating one's emotional intimacy over and over gets monotonous. Therefore, we find other ways to connect; such as body language, endearments, physical contact, and social rituals or customs like the shortening of names."

Uh-oh, Del thought at the words 'physical contact.' He lunged out of his seat and headed into the kitchen before the two of them reached the subject of sex. As he left, Sam asked, "Why would someone reject an offer of intimacy?" He winced, wiping at his forehead. He had no idea why Cassie thought he'd have conversations like this with the AI, but he thanked the Suns she didn't ask him to participate.

Making himself a stiff drink, he nursed it in the kitchen and tried not to think. His head swam with weariness, but he wasn't sure he should go to bed. Sam's predicament, whatever it was, triggered a vague sense of responsibility. Speaking of responsibilities…

Del asked the systems control to connect him with Nick. His brother's gravelly voice answered after a few moments.

"Sorry, did I get you out of bed?"

"Naw, I don't sleep much these days anyway. How'd it go?"

Del frowned. He'd learned a lot since he'd last seen his brother. How much should he tell Nick? The Shays and FPA were after Core-corrupted FPA agents. If he explained this to Nick, would he back off or start his own investigation and give up the game somehow? How much danger would he put himself in, stepping in the middle of this mess? Del ground the heel of his hand to one eye, too tired to work it out. For now, he'd just give Nick the bare facts.

"The run was good, most of the way. A pack of thugs tried to hijack the cargo, but we chased them off."

"Hijackers? Did you report it?"

Del snorted. "Ain't my job, Inspector. Ask the Shays."

"I would, but getting them to hold still for an interview is like trying to hold air. Anybody get hurt?"

Del thought of the pirate he blew up and grimaced. He'd run from the Core because they'd wanted him to commit murder. Even though the battle with the pirates had been self-defense, he'd turned into a killer anyway. "The crew's all fine," he answered in a dull tone. "I'm pretty wiped, though."

"You sound like it. Get some sleep, I'll catch up with you tomorrow."

Del ended the connection with a sigh and rubbed the back of his neck. He didn't want his brother involved in this business any more than he'd wanted him involved with the Core. But how was he going to avoid it?

Cassie called his name and Del winced. His escape had been too good to be true. He slunk back into the living room, but she only wanted him to be an example of sorts as she and the AI worked through a series of cryptic questions.

At one point, Cassie lost him in a discussion of algorithms and neural paradigms. He let their voices fade into a droning background, dropping his head to the back of the couch and dozing.

"Del, you have a visitor," Sam's voice broke in on a dim dream of being lost in a maze of shattered glass.

"Wha—?" He straightened and rubbed the heels of his hands into his bleary eyes.

"Somebody's at the door," Cassie told him before continuing her discussion with the AI.

Del blinked at her, eyeing the focused intensity of her delicate features with exasperation. "No, don't get up. I'll get it," he muttered as he rose to his feet, but Cassie didn't pause.

Sighing and rubbing the back of his neck, he strode to the door and hit the release, wondering who would be here at this late hour.

Sin was the last person he expected to see.

She rested a shoulder against the door jam, arms folded in a casual stance, expression rueful as she met his gaze. "Del..." she started, but her voice trailed away.

He braced a hand on the wall, his heart pounding. Conflict darkened her eyes, sending spears of hope and need through him. His breath stuttered in his chest. She had come to him, late at night, her mouth in a vulnerable curve and a suggestion of passion in her voice.

"Sin?" he whispered, reaching out with slow care as if she were a mirage.

Before he touched her, Cassie laughed in the distance behind him.

Sin's eyes widened, her transformation acute and painful. Dropping her gaze, she straightened, features smoothing into a cool mask of indifference. "I didn't realize you had company. I'll speak with you in the morning," she said in a precise, toneless voice, then spun and headed down the corridor at a brisk pace.

"Sin, wait," he called and started after her retreating form. "Cassie's not company, she's just here to talk—"

"What you do with your private time is none of my concern, Del. I'm sorry to have disturbed you," she said over her shoulder, each word frosted with ice.

"Sin, stop a second." He caught her elbow, keeping hold of her even when she raised her eyebrows and looked at him with devastating, chilly politeness. Trying to find his way past the glacial barrier in her eyes, he asked, "Why did you come here?"

"To discuss our mission to the factory. But I was inconsiderate to disturb your..." she paused, eyes flickering a bit. "Your rest. Please, don't let me keep you." She brushed his hand from her arm with stinging gentleness and continued down the corridor.

With a long stride, he caught up and matched her pace. "What mission? You told your brother you weren't going."

"I lied. He's being intractable. We'll have to go without him." She slanted him a measuring look and added, "If you're still willing to go."

"Of course I am." He wanted to shake her.

"Good," she responded as they reached the lift and she stepped within. "We'll go over the details in the

272

morning."

She touched the door release, but Del braced an arm in the opening and kept the door from closing. When she glanced at him with cool enquiry, he clenched his jaw and fists, and braved the ice again. "Was it the only reason you came to see me, Sin?"

"Yes, Del. Why else would I?" Her distant gaze never faltered from his, her ruthless beauty unrelenting from its arctic stillness.

With the slow caution of a man who fears his limbs have become untrustworthy, Del lowered his arm and stepped back. As the door closed between them, she looked away as if he'd ceased to exist.

For a long moment, he stared at the blank metal and fought a losing battle with the pressure building inside him. Eyes as blank as the metal, he drove both fists into the barrier between them, feeling the flash of pain in his knuckles with grim satisfaction. Any pain was better than the one lodged in his chest.

Sin covered her face with trembling hands and let the tremor overtake the rest of her body in one long quiver of emotion. Her brother was right. She was in no condition to go to the factory. She'd lost her focus and strength of purpose in Del's kiss, not to mention her integrity. She was his employer. She had no business showing up at his door in the middle of the night with an excuse as tissue-thin as her willpower.

It served her right to find Cassie there, though the thought of them together burned like acid. She had no right to him, and Cassie did. Another long quiver passed through her, but the lift stopped and she forced her hands to her sides. With a bitter sickness in her stomach, she crossed the Gold Rooms and entered her suite, barely pausing for the door to open.

"Sin? Are you all right?"

"Privacy, Mina," she rasped.

"Of course," the AI answered as Sin reached her bedroom. The faint hurt in Mina's tone twisted her guts.

But her control had frayed beyond retrieval in the darkness of her room, and she wouldn't subject her friend to the tears burning down her face. Crawling into bed, she curled around the illness in her stomach and wept without sound into her pillow. After a while, the effort and exhaustion overtook her, and she fell into a void of sleep as black as oblivion.

The morning brought a welcome return of her control. She deflected Mina's concern with gentle reassurance and faced her brother's scrutiny in their offices with cool discipline. Kai studied the shadows under her eyes but didn't ask, greeting her with the careful politeness he always used after one of their rare fights.

At any other time, she would brush off the tension and reestablish their closeness. Though she needed the comfort of his steady support, she continued to be cool. She had to keep the distance between them or he'd discover what she meant to do.

"Weren't we going to contact Griffin this morning?" she asked him in a detached tone while leaning over the desk and calling up their schedule on the viewer.

He hesitated. "Do you feel up to it?"

Straightening, she crossed her arms over her chest, stared at him, and said nothing.

In the face of her bitter silence, he grimaced and ran a distracted hand through his dark hair. "Sorry," he said and touched the controls. Rounding the desk, he stood at her side with a wary light in his green eyes. "I hate it when we fight."

She couldn't afford to relent. "Then perhaps you shouldn't instigate them."

"Your man said the same thing," he responded in a low, rueful voice as the viewer flickered and Griffin appeared before them.

Thrown by his oblique approval of Del, Sin remained quiet and allowed Kai to greet their nemesis.

"Griff, good to see you again."

"Manakai, Sinsudee, what a delightful surprise," their enemy said with warmth in his rich voice and smile, though it didn't reach his eyes. "To what do I owe this pleasure?"

With a smile matching his for sincerity, Sin lowered her arms and sat on the corner of the desk. "I didn't get a chance to thank you for the gift, Web." Kai's tension rose behind her. If she'd left this to her brother, he couldn't have concealed his protective rage over Griffin's cruel arrogance. "Business took us away for a few days and I was unable to contact you."

"I understand. Was it to your liking, then?" His gray eyes gleamed with malicious delight.

She wouldn't give him any satisfaction. "It was quite lovely, a true creative masterpiece. Too beautiful to waste. I placed it on display in our Reception Hall, so everyone may enjoy it." *So everyone may see how you've insulted and maligned us,* she thought.

Comprehension tightened the skin around his eyes. "It could never match your beauty, Sinsudee. I am delighted you are so pleased with it." His smile was small, but genuine this time, gloating.

Sin dropped her gaze, mouth in a flirtatious curve. "Such a shame I had to leave and not give the gift its proper due. My people tell me it was received very well."

He took the opening. "You work too hard, my dear. Was your business at least concluded to your satisfaction?"

Sin looked up and let real humor touch her face. "Very well, thank you for asking. All of our runs should be so profitable."

He inclined his head, an answering amusement on his features. Let him think the abantium deal had blunted their anger over the gift and their display of the beleaguered Enua was the limit of their retaliation.

Now comes the misdirection, Sin thought as Kai moved to the desk, attracting Griffin's attention. They needed to keep Griffin's focus away from the factory, to give them time to do what needed to be done. But they had to be careful. If he grew suspicious, he might backtrack to find out what it was they'd led him from.

"Your courtship of my sister aside," Kai began in a wry tone. Griffin chuckled in response, watching her twin with masculine amusement. "We did have another reason for contacting you. We've been working on a merger with the Yakamoro Collective. They have some fine, creative minds in the area of cybernetics. We came down to a final deal when they balked, and we suspect someone made a competitive offer. Wouldn't be you, would it, Griff?" He used just the right tone of amused irony, as if the answer were a foregone conclusion. Flattery implying Griffin was the only competitor worth considering.

"Perhaps," their nemesis temporized with an

enigmatic smile, watching them both with his cold, hunter's eyes. As it happened, the Collective had all but thrown themselves at the Shays. Sin and Kai were the ones delaying the cementing of their compact, but Griffin didn't know this.

Kai's expression hardened, the lines of his body radiating ruthless aggression. "That's what I thought," he said in a firm tone, as if Griffin had confirmed his suspicions. "So what'll it take for you to back off?"

As rehearsed, Sin made a small, abortive gesture as if to call her brother's words back and snapped in a low voice, "Kai!" Then she smiled at Griffin. "I apologize for my brother's tactlessness. He's still weary from our trip."

"There's nothing to apologize for," Griffin said smoothly, but they'd caught his interest. With luck, he would wonder why the Collective was so important to them. The trick was not to overdo it.

"What he was trying to say," she continued with a cool look toward her brother, "was we would be willing to negotiate if you happen to be the competitive offer."

Kai rubbed the back of his neck and shot her a sullen glare. *Gently,* she thought at him while she smiled at their enemy. But his instincts were always true when it came to Griffin. The man saw her twin as a nuisance, an obstacle to his courtship of her, but not a real threat. He was playing to Griffin's belief now, producing just the right amount of petulance when she took over the conversation.

"An interesting proposition. You will give me time to consider it, I hope?"

"Of course." Sin let her smile falter just a bit and watched with grim satisfaction as he absorbed her subtle dismay.

"Very good," Griffin responded. "Is there anything else I may do for you today?"

Sin extended the conversation with some small talk, flirting a bit more than usual with him.

Kai withdrew out of Griffin's view, a grim smile on his face as he watched her play with their enemy. When she ended the call, he grunted in satisfaction. "It'll keep him occupied."

"But for how long?" she asked without looking at him. When Griffin found nothing interesting about the Collective, he would catch on to the misdirection and turn a laser eye back on them.

"Long enough," he answered in a clipped tone. He wasn't going to change his mind about waiting to go after the factory.

Stubborn idiot, she thought, but pressed her lips together and turned away. "I'm going down to check on the crew, then I'll be back in my office for the rest of the day taking calls."

"All right. I'll be here."

She walked out without checking to see if his forlorn undertone was reflected in his expression.

The bustle of activity in the maintenance bay was less enthusiastic than it should have been after their success on such a dangerous run. The crew watched her with wary eyes, and a pang of guilt shot through her for her public fight with Kai.

Sin started at Bib's station, engaging her in easy chatter, relaxing the girl until she stopped giving her boss wide-eyed, worried looks. Then Sin proceeded down the rows, treating the rest of the crew the same way and taking pains to mention the hazard pay and bonus they'd received for the hard run. She avoided Del until she could speak with Cassie.

With speculation in her brown eyes, Cass watched her until Sin stopped at her station. Sin hoped she wouldn't mention the previous night.

"Hey, Cass," she said in as casual a tone as she could manage. "How are things?"

"As well as can be expected," her friend answered. "Are you and Kai okay?"

Leave it to Cassie to ask the hard questions. Sin gave her a faint smile and broke eye contact. "We will be. How are the repairs coming on Del's ship?"

True to form, Cassie said in a careful voice, "As far as I know, they're good. But why don't you ask him yourself?"

With calculated hesitation, Sin gave her a reluctant nod and turned away, feeling another pang of guilt as she did so. Manipulating her friend into providing the excuse she needed to speak with Del did not feel good. But Kai might ask the crew about her actions. Her speaking with Del needed to look natural, so her brother wouldn't suspect what she was up to before they left.

Del was waiting. She wasn't prepared for the impact of his dark eyes or the restrained power in his muscled form as he leaned against his Shadow. She also wasn't prepared for the wary, haggard expression on his face or the grim set to his mouth. It reminded her of the look in his eyes when she'd said, "Why else would I?"

Heart thumping out a painful rhythm in her chest, she slowed to a stop before him. It took all her willpower not to ignore pride and duty and fling herself at him. Training her eyes on the steady pulse beating in his throat, she asked, "Is your Shadow space ready?"

"Repairs are done. Just a series of diagnostics and test flights left," he answered in a low voice.

"Good. Will you make sure our Shadows are transferred to the storage bay? I don't want to attract attention when we leave."

"When?"

She named a time in late evening.

"I'll make sure everybody's gone before I move them."

"Thank you." She paused. "We'll go over the plan when we leave. Kai might get suspicious if I spend too much time talking with you."

He made a rumbling noise, which could have meant any number of things. Keeping her eyes lowered, she turned on her heel and walked away. Every step tore at her deep inside.

****

Griffin strolled through the vast garden, allowing a smile for its symmetry and perfection. Nature could never have created such a place, without flaws or blemishes. This was holographic programming at its best. Deep satisfaction flowed through him, not for the garden's beauty and grace but for the level of control in evidence. Life was managed and structured, not a leaf out of place, every blossom where he'd ordered it to be. Even the Enua, the symbol of the Shays' family house, grew and flowered according to his whim. He paused by the flowering shrub and let his smile widen. He had conceived of Sinsudee's gift while standing in this spot, studying the obedient growth and bloom of the Enua flowers.

Soon, he thought with a tingle of anticipation along his spine. Soon all the worlds would resemble this room.

"Sir," a low, breathless voice addressed him.

Griffin turned without haste, regarding the man standing with one leg inside a potted tree. "Hoyt. You're late. And you're disrupting my garden."

The man looked down and skittered to one side, his holographic image blurring with the movement. His system was not as well programmed. "S-sorry, sir. I had difficulty getting away unnoticed."

"And your cohort?"

The skinny man blinked several times, a nervous tick Griffin found repulsive, reminding him of a lizard for some reason. "She sends her apologies and regrets, but is unable to communicate at this time. She expressed concern we are both being watched."

Griffin stared at him, letting his cold, steady regard convey his disapproval. "Spies are not useful if they do not report their findings in a timely fashion."

"Sir, Marcus Feeney suspects us, or at least suspects someone on the board of Shay Enterprises. He almost called us out in a board meeting not long ago."

Griffin raised his eyebrows. "Why am I hearing this only now?"

"W-we've had to be more cautious, we didn't want to draw attention."

"Hm." Griffin swept his gaze over the rows of neat, regimented plantings. "And how did the Shays react?"

"They chastised him for causing dissent and potential distrust between board members. He seems to have fallen out of favor with them. Perhaps he would be a good candidate to approach for infiltration?"

Griffin scoffed, leveling an icy stare on the quivering spy. "Marcus Feeney is loyal to his bones. He would never betray the twins or their company. I pay you to think, not blunder about and cower like a mouse."

"Y-yes, sir, I apologize for the suggestion."

"Let's move past your whining cowardice, shall we? Perhaps you can still redeem yourself and prove you have not outlived your usefulness. I need information on the Yakamoro Collective and their dealings with the Shays."

"Anything you need, sir."

"Well? Out with it, man. On the surface, the Collective does not appear to be a company of great interest, yet the Shays seem quite keen to acquire them."

Hoyt linked his hands at his waist like a child about to recite his lessons. "My understanding is the Collective has a cybernetics focus, of interest to the AI research and development division of Shay Enterprises. Their inclusion in the company should have been a routine merger, yet the Shays gave them undo attention in the process. They were invited to Shay headquarters for a tour of the facilities, given by the Shays themselves. I have also heard through discreet channels they have lavished gifts upon key members of the Collective. This does suggest, sir, there is more to the company than meets the eye."

Griffin studied the man with a distaste he didn't bother to hide. "Look into it further, but be discreet. If the Shays catch you asking about a company they so recently brought to my attention, they may give more credence to Feeney's claims of spies on the board."

"Yes, sir."

"And Hoyt, tell your associate one of her family

members is about to suffer a terrible accident. If she does not respond to my summons in the future, such accidents will turn fatal. Do I make myself clear?"

Hoyt blanched, eyes fluttering with his spasmodic tick, mouth opening and closing without sound. He gave a jerky nod and disappeared from Griffin's sight.

Griffin shook his head. He could have wished for spies with greater backbone, but his pool of board members had been limited. Marcus Feeney would have made an excellent spy, if he hadn't been so devoted to Ezekiel and Shay Enterprises.

A flicker of movement at the corner of his eye caught his attention. He looked down at the Enua bush and frowned. Had the hologram failed momentarily? If so, it would be the first he'd seen in this garden. Staring at the now perfect blossoms, his lips thinned, vague unease moving through him. Then he banished the unusual feeling with a lift of his chin, spine rigid with discipline. He would have words with the programmer. Imperfections were unacceptable.

Spinning on his heel, he headed for the exit, the rebellious Enua and garden already dismissed from his thoughts.

Chapter 21

For the rest of the day, Sin stayed in her private office, burying herself in the build-up of messages, calls, and issues. She ignored the careful approaches of her staff and the not-so-subtle passes Kai made by her office. The time dragged by, the monotony threatening to drive her insane. By late afternoon, she'd had enough and left, heading to her suite for a quick bite to eat and a nap.

When the time came, Sin made sure the way was clear of witnesses and headed down to the bay with brittle determination. No one was in the maintenance bay, and two slicer stations stood empty as she passed between the rows. Someone would notice, but not for a while. By then, she and Del would be long gone.

In the storage bay, two slicers reclined in the shadows between the Tank and Rock. Leaning on his Shadow, Del watched her approach, his arms folded across his chest. He'd dressed in unrelenting black, his golden skin gleaming in sensual contrast. Wariness tightened the lines of his face and sharpened the darkness in his eyes, digging needles of regret into her heart. Pressing her lips together and avoiding his gaze, she tossed him a bulging carrysack on the way to her Shadow.

"What's this?"

Opening her Shadow, she unshouldered her own

sack and stowed it behind the seat. "Provisions and equipment for the trip. Some of it we might not need, but better safe than sorry." She paused and glanced over her shoulder at him. "Ready?"

He nodded and tossed the carrysack into his slicer. "I suppose you have a plan for leaving here without being noticed."

"Not possible," Sin said, meeting his gaze with a faint smile before sliding into her slicer. "But courier traffic is minimal at this time, and the station's record of our departure won't be noticed until it's too late."

"Your brother?"

"He'll follow," was all she said, sealing her slicer. Kai would not appreciate being forced to trail after her, but it couldn't be helped. He might be right about her, but he was wrong to wait. Greed had blinded the pirates into accepting her terms, but when they'd spent their credit, they were bound to remember self-preservation. If anything happened to the factory, it might end up on their heads. Their best course of action would be to warn the factory.

Sin brought her Shadow to life and joined with it, taking a deep breath as power and certainty suffused her form. For the first time in a long while, she felt ready for what they were about to do. With a grim smile, she lifted off the pad and headed toward space, flashing out of the bay and over the gas giant like a streak of black lightning. Del was a solid presence at her side, not faltering for a moment, as if he'd read her mind and anticipated her movements. It filled her with such pride and longing, she clenched her teeth and shivered.

When he asked, "What about the star-way?" it took

her a second to unlock her jaw and speak in a normal tone.

"We're taking the long way around, coming at it from the other side. We need to use the ring to get where we're going as fast as possible, but we don't want anyone to track us."

"How do we stop them? They register every ring use. These slicers are too small to make it through a wormhole and any ship we dock with will have a record of it."

With a hard grin, she told him how, waiting for his reaction. It wasn't long in coming.

"Are you nuts? What kind of Sun-baked plan is that?"

She chuckled. "Having second thoughts, Del?"

"Hell, yes," he declared. "I should drag you back to headquarters for a full psych eval."

"How sweet," she said with sardonic humor, "but unnecessary. I'm not having a mental aberration. We've done it before."

"Like shooting the rim? Did you do this at twelve, too?"

She sobered, tone settling into quiet seriousness. "No, this kind of thing came much later, after we understood what was at stake."

He was silent for a few minutes, and Sin waited, tense. If he turned back, she would continue on alone, but it wouldn't be easy. She both wanted and needed him at her side. Then he sighed and she sagged into her seat in relief.

"All right, Lady Shadow, tell me what to do," he said in his calm, deep voice, sending delight dancing across her skin.

It didn't take long; the maneuver wasn't difficult to understand, but it wasn't going to be easy to do. Until she'd met Del, the only other person she knew who had the skill to pull it off was her brother.

"Well, this should be interesting," he predicted in a dry tone when she finished.

She grinned and pushed her Shadow to maximum speed, her smile widening in satisfaction when he matched her without effort. At this velocity, they reached the ring in little time.

When they entered the solar system, Sin cautioned Del to silence, since Ring Control would be monitoring all communications. Approaching the sun from the anchor ring side, they waited until the rings were activated to slip around the sun to the launch ring, trusting the interference of an active wormhole to hide their approach. It was a rough ride, the solar winds and gravity wells of both the sun and wormhole wrenching at their Shadows, but the ships were designed for endurance as well as speed.

Del remained at her side as they fought the elemental pull of the wormhole to reach the outer, stable loop of the launch ring. In contrast to its spinning center, this immobile loop provided necessary resistance against inertia, keeping the ring from wobbling out of control and falling into the sun. The two Shadows slipped around to settle against its surface as the inner ring slowed and the vortex dissipated.

The Shadow skins provided camouflage, blending with the surface of the rings and hiding the ships from detection by Ring Control. Now they had to wait for a ship going their way.

Sin took advantage of the respite to stretch and roll

the tension out of her neck and shoulders. Reaching the rings undetected had been the easy part. She needed to be at her best for the next maneuver.

The ring started again. Sin checked the launch schedule, but the destination wasn't near the place she and Del needed to go. She continued stretching while her Shadow shivered with the ring's vibrations, wincing when the vortex opened in a flash of brilliance and sensory disruption. Watching the debarking ships instead of the disturbing, compelling entrance to the wormhole, she waited as five ships disappeared through the ring. They would have to endure this sequence one more time before they hit on their destination.

Sighing, she wondered how Del was holding up. She'd done this before, so she knew it was possible, but Del was new to it. The slightest slip and either one of them would be just a memory of molecules shattered by the wormhole.

The wait seemed interminable, but when the time came, it rushed toward them with relentless speed. Sin pressed her lips together and readied her Shadow as the wormhole opened on their destination and the line of ships began moving forward. She'd told Del to wait for the last ship and the last possible second so they wouldn't be seen. The ship's sensors would be blinded by wormhole distortion.

Taking several deep breaths to steady herself, she watched the last ship lumber toward them, her muscles thrumming with anticipation. Cool calm descended over her as the last seconds ticked away and the ship began to slip into the vortex.

Both Shadows sprang away from the ring, launching toward the massive ship disappearing into the wormhole. Fighting the hungry pull of the vortex and the roaring force of the vessel's engines, they struggled to get behind the shielding flaps protecting the ship's fragile engine venting. A bare moment before the rear of the ship vanished into the wormhole, they settled into the protective crevice between the flaps and the venting, carried safe and undetected through the ring.

Sin wiped a film of sweat from her forehead with a trembling hand, wishing she could contact Del and make sure he was all right. He'd been beside her the whole way, so she hoped he'd been able to attach in time, but the wormhole denied communication or sensors of any kind. She would have to wait until they exited on the other side to find out if he'd survived.

It was a long wait. By the time they burst out of the wormhole into a different solar system, her stomach had formed a hard knot of nausea and the muscles at the back of her neck had clenched into bands of pain. The instant her systems came back on line, she kicked her Shadow away from the surface of the ship and hunted for Del. When she found the dark form tumbling beside her, she had to bite down on her lower lip hard to keep from crying out in relief.

But they weren't safe yet. In a reversal of their previous maneuver, they battled the expelling force of the vortex and the fierce barrage of the ship's engines to reach the anchor ring quickly enough not to be detected. Fighting for control, Sin concentrated with grim determination. Distracting herself with thoughts of Del could kill her.

After what seemed like hours, they settled side by side on the surface of the ring as the spinning slowed and the hole flickered out of existence. Breathing deep to calm the racing of her heart, Sin clenched her jaw against the almost irresistible urge to contact Del. They had to wait until the way was clear before detaching from the ring and leaving this system.

When their piggyback ship was out of range and the ring had begun to spin again, they launched from its surface and raced away from detection. As soon as she was able, she contacted him.

"Del? Are you all right?" His Shadow flew steady, but she chewed her lip until she heard his voice.

"Still in one piece, anyway," he rasped.

She gasped in silent relief before she could respond, trying for a light tone. "Every time we do it, I say never again. Want to take our chances with a courier ship on the way back?"

"Best idea you've had all day," he answered, his deep voice still rough with strain.

Frowning, she sighed. "I could use a drink."

"You and me both."

"Too bad I forgot to pack one."

"You're fired," he shot back.

She chuckled. "Don't write me off yet. I did remember to pack restoratives, which should take the edge off." Reaching behind her, she pulled the pack onto her lap and opened it, digging through the provisions and equipment to the medicines. Debating whether she should use an oral or injectable, she settled on tearing open a packet with her teeth and swallowing the cool, stinging fluid. Her muscles loosened and a surge of energy went through her body as she absorbed the restorative.

"Better," Del said.

She nodded. He did sound better. "I packed drinks

and munchies, if you're in the mood."

"Uh, how long are you expecting us to be out here, anyway?" he asked with a dubious note.

Sin smirked, wondering if he was eyeing the large amount of provisions, or the waste disposal and sanitizer units. "Shay rule number one, prepare for all contingencies."

"I thought your rule number one was nobody touches you."

Sin frowned before she remembered she'd said the phrase to the pirates. "I have my own set of rules."

"I noticed."

Not knowing how to answer his bland tone, she stayed silent. Increasing her Shadow's speed, she sent the coordinates of the factory to Del, along with the course she meant to take to get there. It wasn't a straight line, staying away from any populated area to avoid detection, but if they maintained a high speed, they should arrive in short order.

He made no comment on the course and the silence stretched between them for a distance. The monotony of the unchanging black of space wore away her relief and elation at their survival of the trip through the rings, allowing other things to surface; such as the pain and humiliation of her late-night visit to Del's quarters. Stirring in restless defense, she searched for something to keep her mind on the business at hand.

She was about to describe her communication with Griffin when Del broke the silence instead.

"Did you know," he said in a too-casual voice, "AIs aren't just programs you can use and throw away?"

She lifted her eyebrows in bemusement. "You

don't say."

"Never had one before. Must not be real good at it from the way Cassie lit into me yesterday."

Sin tensed at the mention of her friend, but Del wasn't finished.

"She spent half the night grilling me and the AI, fixing whatever I screwed up with Sam. I told her if she was gonna give AIs to idiots like me, she should hand out instruction books at the same time."

A smile tugging at her mouth, Sin cleared her throat. "Cass thought something was wrong with Samantha?" Was it the only reason Cassie had been in his quarters?

"Sam's a new install. My brother and I named her, but I guess it's the only thing we did right. Cassie tore me up one side and down the other when she found out I hadn't been paying attention to Sam. How was I to know I had to bond with her?" he said with baffled disgust. Sin muffled a snicker.

His description sounded much more like Cassie than a late night liaison with a fellow pilot. From the first day they'd brought Cass home, she'd been almost as single-minded and dedicated to their purpose as the Shays.

His voice reverted to careful casualness again. "She sure does know how to make a guy feel stupid. I understood about one word in ten coming out of her mouth. At least, what I heard of it. I was out cold when you showed up."

A slow warmth spread through her and a smile curled the corners of her mouth. Thank the Suns they were in different ships so she couldn't reach him. Containing her longing with an effort, she held her tongue.

After a moment, he sighed and said in a voice like rough velvet, "She's not the woman I want, Sin. You know that."

Her eyes slid closed and she sank down into her seat as the warmth became a throbbing, molten heat at her center. The Shadow responded to her weakness, a surge of power roaring through her, urging her toward complete abandon. Biting the inside of her cheek hard, she clutched the armrests with desperate fingers and wrestled herself and the ship back under control.

She couldn't acknowledge his last comment without starting a conversation that would get them both into big trouble. Taking a shaky breath, she said in a light tone, "Cass makes everyone feel stupid. She can't help it. She has more brains than all of us put together."

He was quiet, and Sin worried he wouldn't follow her lead. "I believe it. Does she make all your AIs?" His tone was bland, but his voice still held a faint huskiness, sending a shiver over her skin.

"No, we had AI development long before Cassie arrived, but she gave it a big boost. AIs were her specialty before she came to us."

"And slicers, I'm guessin'," he said with dry humor.

"No, she didn't know anything about slicers until she joined us."

"What? She knows these Shadows inside and out."

"She learned," Sin drawled then chuckled when he made a disgusted sound. "Makes you sick, doesn't it?"

"My IQ just dropped like a stone."

She gave a soft laugh and an easier silence settled

around them. Sin checked their progress. They still had time before reaching the Fringe, so they didn't need to cut communication just yet.

"What was your plan for getting in when we get to the factory?" Del asked.

"I don't know. I haven't seen the place yet."

"I shoulda known," he sighed.

Sin grinned. "Losing confidence in me, Del?"

"Of course not. Failure's not an option, right? Just looking forward to the challenge."

She snickered at his heavy sarcasm. "Way to be positive, pilot. I brought you to help me get in."

"Guess we got nothin' to worry about, then."

She laughed, realizing how much she was enjoying herself. The chance to be with him without having to govern her every expression or impulse was irresistible and enervating. As long as they didn't stray onto a topic leading to disaster, she could enjoy being with him without guilt.

"Hey, what are these round, brown things?"

She assumed he'd gotten into the provisions. "Those are chewy nut clusters. Kai can't get enough of them. He says they're a food group all their own. I suspect he might even kill for them."

"Thank you," Del breathed with exaggerated gratitude.

With a quirk of her lips, Sin played along. "For what?"

"For the ammo. Dealing with your brother ain't easy. A nut cluster addiction will help."

She snickered, picturing Del leading Kai around with a handful of clusters. "He's not usually susceptible to bribery, but you might have him there."

"I was thinking verbal ammo, but bribery's good, too."

"Battle of wits?"

"Wouldn't wanna go unarmed."

With a hum of humor, Sin pulled a bottle of water out of her pack and took a swallow. "In that case, let me tell you all of Kai's weaknesses."

"You're a goddess," he intoned and she couldn't help but smile in delight. "A crafty, sneaky goddess."

She laughed again, reveling in the freedom of it. It wasn't often she had the chance to just be herself, not the corporate predator, the conscientious employer, or her Shadow persona. Just Sin.

"Kai's greatest weakness is women."

"Not a newsflash, Sin. He's a guy."

"Wait, the ammo's coming. I have a little story about Kai's greatest weakness."

Sin proceeded to tell him about a riot on the Shay station a few years ago. It was started by three women who owned different businesses in the commons, the station's marketplace. They'd discovered, to their immense dissatisfaction, they all had one thing in common. Kai. "The cleanup cost was enormous. To decrease the odds of a repeat performance, I forced Kai to make a solemn oath to never have a relationship with any woman on the station again."

"No hardship for him. The galaxy has other women."

"Sure, but we rarely leave the station for pleasure. Most often, it's on runs like this, out in the middle of nowhere."

Del started to chuckle. "You're an evil woman, Sin Shay."

"My brother thinks so," she responded with a smirk. "But you've seen how women react to him. If I didn't curb it, there'd be a riot every other day."

"I hate to break this to you, Sin," he said in a low voice, sending chills dancing from her head to her toes, "but men react to you the same way. You're a riot waiting to happen yourself."

Gritting her teeth against the surge of heat flooding her body, she schooled her voice to dry humor. "No wonder Kai made me take the same oath. But there's more ammo. I know of at least one woman who is immune to my brother's charm."

"No kidding. Who?"

"Liaena Griffin."

"Griffin? As in…"

"The daughter of, yes. She kicked Kai in the shin when they first met and it's been war between the two of them ever since. She wants nothing to do with him and it drives Kai crazy."

"Poor guy," he drawled without a hint of compassion in his tone. "I'll have to tell him how bad I feel next time I see him."

"That's the spirit. Don't forget to mention how sorry you are about his banned dating on the station, too."

"First chance I get," he said with such relish, she laughed again. Then his tone sobered. "Looks like we're in the Fringe."

"Already?" she murmured with a pang of regret. "We'll have to keep communications to a minimum from here. Run as silent as we can."

"Will do," he responded.

Sin thought he sounded disappointed, but it might

have been wishful thinking.

Keeping a careful eye on the long range sensors, they traversed the meandering course toward their goal. Sin had chosen their path well. They saw no one until they zeroed in on the location of the factory, which turned out to be a bit of a surprise.

Chapter 22

"Holy Suns," Del whispered.

Sin had to agree.

A roiling, turbulent nebula stretched before them, so large it could swallow whole star systems without a hiccup. The coordinates placed the factory somewhere in the outer border of this monster, still dangerous but not as fatal as the flaring, violent center of this sun nursery. The perfect hiding place. Who would be crazy enough to go in there?

Sin sighed. "Feeling crazy today?"

"Every day since I met you," he answered with cutting humor.

She grinned. "Let's do it, then."

She didn't worry about being overheard by the factory. It would be just as blind and deaf to their presence as they were to it. Without the exact coordinates, they'd never have found the place, even if they had thought to search the nebula. With slow caution, she headed toward the leading edge, scanning the chaotic currents of dust and gases for a non-pulverizing path.

"There," Del noted and slipped past her toward a darker area, a still pool between conflicting currents.

With a hum of approval, she followed. Riptides of force, the distant ripples of protest from newborn stars at the violence of their birth, buffeted their Shadows.

Concentrating on keeping her ship steady, the sudden appearance of the factory took Sin by surprise. With a wrench, she spun her slicer away from the dome of force covering the facility and dove into a boiling mass of dust and gas.

Fighting for control, she wrestled her ship to a thinner area so she could scan the factory. Del's Shadow appeared at her side, almost colliding with her, and he cursed.

"Well, this is fun," she said in bland tone and he grumbled something in reply. "The good news is we weren't seen. The bad news is I have no idea how to get in there."

The factory was a sprawling station, lumped together in an ugly assortment of additions, as if the place had been put together piecemeal over time. An energy force field surrounded it in a glowing bubble, protecting the place from the wrath of the nebula. It pulsed in time with the flare of lights reflecting through the gas currents, a reddish beat like a pumping heart. It looked about as penetrable as the nebula's center.

"We could find one of their couriers to hijack and trick our way in there, but it would take a long time. We could wait just outside the nebula, catching a ship as it entered, but I don't know when—"

"I've seen this before," Del interrupted in a thoughtful tone.

"Do tell," she responded, fighting a strong gust sweeping her Shadow away.

"One of Trevani's lessons for me," he answered, his voice bitter. "He and Brax were assigned to handle me, keep me in line. They dragged me along after some rich tech trying to get out from under the Core. When we ran him to ground, he was holed up in a place with a shield just like this one. Took us a couple of days to hack out its frequency, but we managed to make a hole."

A frown pulled at her brows. "What did they make you do?"

He said nothing for a moment then answered in a harsh voice, "I didn't kill him."

"But they made you hurt him."

"Yeah," he rasped, "and for nothing. He wouldn't or couldn't give Trev what he wanted, so Brax killed the guy. Anyway, I think I remember the frequency."

With a grimace, Sin followed his lead away from his painful past. "Can you test it without alerting them?"

"I think so."

"But if we do make a hole, they'll know, won't they?"

"Oh, yeah. It'll be like busting down the front door."

"All right, you work on making a hole and I'll work on a distraction."

"What kind of distraction?"

She grinned at the aggressive suspicion in his tone. "Trust me."

"Sun's blood," he swore.

She chuckled and allowed the current to snatch her away. Studying the chaotic forces of the surrounding area, she chose a swirling pocket of gases with just the right volatile elements and dropped a capsule into it. Setting the capsule's timer, she fought her way back to where she'd left Del. "Any luck?" she asked in a casual tone.

"Almost there."

"Good, because in about sixty seconds we either get inside the shield or die out here."

"You sure know how to show a guy a good time."

"No pressure," she said idly, checking the countdown. "Just a chain reaction setting off this whole region in a series of spectacular explosions. They won't even notice the front door opening."

He muttered an insult about her upbringing, which she chose to ignore. "Tell me when."

"When you see a blinding light off to your starboard side."

"Won't they wonder what started the reaction?"

"I imagine this kind of thing happens when someone sneezes hard around here. This place is a bomb waiting to ha—"

The first explosion almost blinded all her sensors. Wincing, she burst out of their hiding spot and fled toward the factory. The murky depths of the nebula lit up all around them and the force of the detonations was a brutal kick, sending her spinning. She fought for control, Del tumbling next to her. The solid shield rushed toward them.

"Del!" she cried out in alarm, but there was no time to break away. Bracing for a shattering impact, she caught her breath, then let it out in a rush when the field flickered a microsecond before she reached it.

"No faith," he rasped as they plummeted past the field into a stunning calm.

She'd complain later. They had to get into the factory before the explosions faded and the facility's sensors recovered enough to spot them. Not an easy task, considering her own sensors were working at less than thirty percent of normal. Going by both her memory of what the place had looked like from the outside and the sporadic readings from her Shadow, Sin arrowed in on the facility.

But the area she chose had no visible docking bay. They searched like the blind feeling their way to salvation, until Del said, "There, looks like storage dock."

They plunged into the opening, gambling no one would be there to see their entrance. Away from the radiation and fitful energy waves of the nebula's fury, their sensors recovered enough to prove Del right. They were in a storage dock, cargo pods stacked in neat formations, waiting for a hauler to tow them away.

As they landed between two rows away from prying eyes, Sin grimaced at the number of cargo pods in the cavernous bay. Blue traffic must be doing very well for Griffin. Powering down her Shadow, she disconnected and opened the seal, grateful for the chance to stretch her muscles.

Del levered out of his own Shadow with a grim glance at the canisters towering over them. "Business is good," he commented with a sour curl of his lip before cocking his head in a listening posture. "Do they know we're here?"

A siren wailed away in the interior of the facility. Sin listened then crept to the side of the pods to scan the bay. "No, they'd be all over us by now. My guess is it's a warning system for the firecrackers outside."

He snorted and gave her a wry look, dark eyes pulling at her like gravity. "Some firecracker."

She lifted her eyebrows with a smirk, heading back to her Shadow. "Well, it worked, didn't it?"

"We need to get you a new self-preservation instinct, Lady Shadow. You lost yours someplace."

She chuckled, reaching inside her slicer and retrieving the carrysack. Rummaging inside, she pulled out a smaller bag and slung it over her shoulder. "Goodies," she said when Del looked at her in question. "Grab yours. We'll need it."

"What kind of goodies?" he asked as he leaned into his own slicer to copy her actions.

She took a second to eye his well-formed posterior with an appreciative smile. "Weapons, explosives, tech toys, and a snack for the road. All the necessities for a rousing Fringe adventure."

He backed out of his Shadow and shot her a disgusted glance, slinging his own bag over his shoulder. "We also need to get you a new sense of humor."

"Everyone's a critic," she sighed, pulling out a hand weapon and tucking it into her waistband. "Ready?"

He nodded, expression turning somber. "Sin…" He reached out and brushed a strand of hair away from her face.

She wanted to close her eyes and lean into his touch, to fall into him and never come back out, but they had a job to do. And he was still her employee, her responsibility. With a faint smile, quivering despite her efforts, she clasped his hand. "Come on, let's get this over with."

His warm fingers closed around hers with gentle strength before he let her go.

Breathing deep to regain her focus, she led him around the pods toward the entrance to the factory.

"First order of business," she said when they approached the solid vacu-seal doors, "is to find an access terminal and figure out where we are."

"This place looked like a rat maze from outside."

She nodded, taking a cautious peek through a small, porthole-like window in the doors, checking the corridor beyond for company. "Wandering around won't get us anywhere but dead in a hurry. The info we're looking for won't be lying around, either. We need to find their main terminals."

"What about security?"

"Man or machine?" she asked, pulling a small device out of her bag.

"Both."

She nodded. "Not as much as you'd think. The nebula cuts down on the need for heavy security."

With a precise flick, she opened the control panel to the doors and settled the device over the door's systems.

"Whatcha doin'?"

She grinned at the impatient undertone in his casual drawl. "I don't think there's much security, but we shouldn't just waltz in without checking first."

He tilted his head in acknowledgement before leaning over her shoulder to inspect the device, which was vibrating with an almost audible hum. He was close enough for her to feel the heat from his body, and it took a vast amount of willpower not to fold into him.

"How's it work?"

"Ask Cassie," she answered, and smirked at his rumble of disgust.

"This, too?"

"Jill of all trades, our Cassie-girl. The quick and

dirty version is it'll detect the presence of heat, motion, auditory, and visual sensors in the immediate area. In other words, any kind of security systems."

"Handy."

She hummed agreement, watching as the display on the device scrolled an assessment of the area. "Good, just one visual sensor over the door. Let's go." She detached her detector and hit the door release, striding through without pause.

Del growled a wordless warning, catching her elbow as he followed. "Didn't you just say there's a sensor?" he snapped, jerking his head toward the door.

With a smile, she flipped the detector in the air and caught it again. "It also deactivates what it finds."

"Now she tells me." He gave her a dark look then brushed by her and headed down the corridor.

She followed, admiring the powerful bunch and slide of his muscles as he moved. *Focus,* she admonished herself as they approached a split in the corridor. Placing a cautionary hand on Del's arm, she flattened against the wall and slid up to the split, snatching quick looks down the three, odd-angled corridors forking away from them.

"Clear," she whispered and chose a corridor heading more toward the center of the structure. They moved into it, Sin watching for more visual sensors like the one over the bay door, while Del kept an eye on their retreat. But a short way down the corridor, it folded back on itself and split again, the appearance and structure of the walls changing. Sin guessed either they were leaving an addition to the factory or entering one.

Slipping a knife out of her bag, she dug a small scratch into the wall to mark their passage, and chose a corridor. Two more of these choices later, they found another vacu-sealed door. A visual sensor guarded above this one as well.

"We can go a different way," Del suggested, but she shook her head, snatching a glance around the corner.

"If they're concerned about security for what's beyond this door, it's worth checking out. At least we should find an access terminal there."

"So, does Cassie's toy work long distance? Or maybe turn us invisible?"

"You're so cute when you're being sarcastic," she whispered, lifting an eyebrow at him and pulling a metal ball, about the size of her thumb, from her bag. "Watch your eyes. This might be little, but it packs a punch."

Depressing the end, she flicked the ball around the corner toward the door. It made clinking sounds as it bounced, but was too small to catch the eye of anyone monitoring the approach.

"Be ready to run," she said and buried her face into the crook of her elbow. A small, undramatic popping sound was followed by a flash of punishing, white light. Before it diminished, she reached out and caught a fistful of Del's shirt, tugging them both around the corner. The whiteout should have fried the sensor, but better safe than sorry.

They fetched up against the wall next to the door, squinting at each other like moles in the bright light of day.

"Suns curse it, woman, warn me next time."

She opened the control panel and put Cassie's toy to work again. "What, and ruin the surprise?" she asked then gave him a wink when he growled at her. "Now, Del, where's your sense of fun?"

He scowled and gestured the way they'd come. "Back at your station with my common sense." His tone was sour, but his dark eyes snapped with life.

She laughed low in her throat and detached the detector, flattening herself next to the door as it opened. A quick glance showed the corridor empty. It was also much better lit than the ones they'd traversed so far. Sin exchanged a tense look with Del at the antiseptic flavor to the air with an ugly, underlying odor both familiar and abhorrent. Not the smell of a blue lab. This area had the look and stench of a medical ward. Numbered doors lined the corridor and monitors sprouted at intervals from the walls.

With new caution, they moved down the corridor, alert for signs of movement or security. It didn't take long for them to find both. Voices bounced around the corner of the branched corridor to warn them.

Del made a sharp gesture at the nearest door and Sin opened it, slipping inside with Del on her heels. The door slid shut behind them, cutting off her view of two men in uniform striding around the corner. They'd been deep in conversation, though, and hadn't seen the intruders.

In the next breath, Sin lost interest in the two security personnel when a vile odor assaulted her senses. Del swore, low and harsh, and they turned as one to view the interior of the room.

Four gel-beds bisected the room, forms floating in the gel, recognizable as human only by their general shape. Twisted and grotesque, they lay naked and on merciless display under hot exam lights. Their limbs were shriveled, cracked, and oozing, bruises and sores violating large areas of their flesh while tubes and wires trapped them in a heartless web. What skin wasn't ravished by marks or invading technology had a familiar, sick blue undertone. In the nearest bed, indigo tears slipping out of the corner of the victim's closed eyes.

"Test subjects," Sin breathed, gagging on the stench and the sight.

With a groan, both nauseated and incensed, Del strode to the nearest bed and reached for a sinuous tube diving into the patient's heart. Within it flowed a liquid the color of the twilight sky.

"No," Sin whispered, lunging after him and catching his wrist as his hand closed on the tube. "You can't save her. She's too far gone. But there are hundreds of thousands of people out there who look forward to this as their future, if we don't stop it. Remember how many cargo pods they'd stacked in their storage bay."

He met her gaze. The flat grimness of his dark eyes and the white tension around his mouth made her throat close with empathy.

"This is the face of the Core, Del," she squeezed past the constriction in her throat. "Help me kill it."

He glanced down at the ruined body in the bed, before closing his eyes and turning his head away. Releasing the tube, he slid his arm through her clasp until his fingers closed around hers. "Let's get out of here," he rasped.

"Sun's mercy on you," she whispered under her breath for the tormented souls she couldn't save and turned her back on them. Swallowing nausea as much from guilt and anger as the stench, she moved to the exit, listening at the door before she opened it.

They left the room in grim silence, making their swift way along the corridors until they came to what looked like a monitoring station. It was unmanned. Sin grimaced, revolted at this lack of concern for their patients. Their test subjects weren't even afforded the dignity of human contact, watched over by cold and indifferent machines.

On the other hand, it made her job easier. Signaling Del to keep watch for personnel, she slipped into the booth. Surrounded by the steady hum of monitors detailing the vital statistics of people who were effectively dead, she searched for and found an access terminal. She touched the screen, pleased when it responded without requesting clearance. In no time at all, she was looking at schematics of the factory. She passed over the engineering, production, and lodging areas, but her attention was caught by the word *Administrative* and she traced possible pathways to it.

Del gave a warning hiss. She ducked out of sight as a worker came into view. Crouching on the balls of her feet, she pulled the hand weapon out of her waistband and listened to the footsteps approaching. They paused once, just outside the booth, before moving on. A long moment passed before Del whispered, "Clear."

Rising to her feet, she confirmed their path to Administrative then shut down the terminal and returned to Del's side. His eyes flickered to the weapon in her hand, his mouth twisting in what could have been grim amusement or disgust, but he said nothing.

"This way." She led him from the monitoring station.

They made steady progress at first, the corridors almost empty, but their path grew more populated the closer they came to Administrative. Slowed by caution and unexpected detours, they crept toward their goal with frustrating slowness. Sin finally gambled on a shortcut, an area under construction.

Easing along the wall struts of a half-finished, dim corridor with Del on her heels, Sin froze at the shadows dancing around the corner up ahead. Even worse, footsteps and a raucous laugh threatened them from behind. Del swore in her ear, wrapping an arm around her waist and lifting her through the struts into a darkened room-in-progress. Ducking behind a stack of wall sections, he set her on her feet, bracing his hands on either side of her shoulders.

He surrounded her.

People passed in the corridor beyond, the laugh ringing out again, but it was fast becoming a distant concern. Every breath she took held his scent, a spicy, mouthwatering male smell. The air warmed against her skin, as if he were wrapping her in an envelope of his heat. At every inhalation, his chest brushed against her sensitized breasts, and when he exhaled, his breath feathered across her cheek and neck like teasing kisses. His pulse throbbed under the golden skin of his throat. The sudden urge to lean forward and taste him, to fill her mouth with his flesh, turned her entire body to molten liquid.

Caught between burning desire and a barely remembered reason why she shouldn't go farther, she swayed in the circle of his arms, bracing hands on his waist. Her body brushed against his, sending tingling fire through her breasts, hips, and thighs.

He made a deep sound in his throat, a heavy rumble rubbing over her nerves like rough velvet. She glanced up. He looked as dazed and staggered as she. His dark gaze tangled with hers, and his lips formed her name with a slow sweep of his lashes. Her knees came unhinged and she began to sag into him.

A distant shout seeped through the fog in her brain and coaxed some disjointed thought from her. They couldn't do this, not here. Too dangerous.

She sagged against the wall sections instead of him. Closing her eyes, she swallowed hard. "Are they gone?" she breathed, listening to the slow thunder of her heart. Losing control in the middle of a mission might prove suicidal.

The air changed around her as Del shifted back a little, his deep inhalation a soft sound in the darkness. "Looks clear," he answered, the bemused huskiness in his voice weakening her limbs even more.

Concentrate, she admonished herself with clenched teeth. They were getting nowhere with their current approach. They needed to change tactics. "We'll never get into their main systems this way," she whispered. "Even if we could get there unnoticed, they'll have them protected. We need a different plan before they figure out we're here."

"Like what? I don't see how, unless you wanna blow it up." He sounded testy.

"I am partial to explosives, but leaving would be tricky." She chewed on her lip. "Besides a bomb, what do you need to open a lock?"

"A key," was his immediate response.

"Let's go find a key," she whispered. When she tried to shift around the stack, he kept his hands planted on either side of her.

"I'm gonna need a little more, Sin."

She had a quick fantasy about giving him much more, before taking a deep breath and shooting him a grim smile. "If we can't get in, we need to find someone who can."

Comprehension tightened the lines of his face, and an intense spear of satisfaction shot through her. If she'd been with anyone else, they would have needed a full explanation, but Del understood what she meant to do. The only other person with whom she'd ever had such accord was her brother.

"Let's go hunting," was his simple response, and she bit her tongue hard to keep from pouncing on him.

Without another word, they slipped like shadows through the darkened room and into the corridor beyond. Moving with caution, they passed from the construction area into a better lit section. It appeared to be rows of offices. Sin chose a door at random, lifting her eyebrows at Del and getting a nod of agreement in return.

She opened the door and they rushed inside. It was empty.

With a disgusted sound, Sin exchanged a frustrated look with Del. "Just once I'd like an op to be simple and easy."

He grimaced and went to the door, prying the seal open a crack so he could watch the corridor beyond.

Sin made a quick exploration of the room. "This'll do as a safe hole for us."

"Got a group coming," Del announced, his body tensing with predatory intent.

"How do they look?" she asked, moving to stand

next to him.

He was silent for a moment, then he grunted and shifted away from the door, letting it slip closed. "No good. Small fish."

She nodded without comment, prying open the door control and slipping the detector inside. "Just in case," she whispered, the rustle and voices of a small group moving past.

Del pulled his goodie bag forward and rummaged around inside, drawing a riot rod out with a wry glance at her. Both ends electrified when extended and powered up. "Also illegal."

She gave him a coy smile and pulled out her own rod, letting the bag drop to the floor. "Also sanctioned by the FPA," she responded, depressing the activator. The rod extended in sections until it was three feet long before locking in place, its ends shimmering with force.

He shrugged one muscular shoulder and activated his own. "Not as noisy as your stinger."

"Exactly." She pulled the hand weapon from her waistband and dropped it on the discarded bag. If they went after their key with audible firepower, more company would arrive in a hurry. "Just watch where you point it."

His dark eyes crinkled at the corners with humor. "Same goes for you, Lady Shadow," he rumbled, before prying open the door seal again. He tensed, his voice turning clipped. "Got another group. Bigger fish."

Sin moved in as he shifted out of the way. The group consisted of three suits and two bodyguards. "It's the one in the middle," she hissed, pulling out another flash popper and showing it to Del.

He nodded, hefting the riot rod in his hand and

bracing his back against the wall. Sin moved to the other side of the door, put her fist on the door release, and waited. The heavy-booted guards announced their approach. When they were right outside, Sin triggered the door and flicked the little metal ball into their midst.

She shielded her eyes, the flare of light outlining the world beyond her eyelids in stark black and white. When it faded, she whirled out into the corridor, Del at her side.

It was over in seconds. All five were blinded and disoriented. Sin went for the bodyguards first while Del reached for the suit in the middle, yanking the man out from his entourage and slamming him face-first into the wall. Sin missed how he handled the other two, her focus on the guards. Ignoring their cries of alarm, she backhanded one with her rod and buried her foot in the other's abdomen. The man she'd touched with her rod fell to the floor in convulsions, gurgling past the bloody mess she'd made of his nose. The other staggered back, bending double and wheezing his pain. A clip to the back of his head with the rod dropped him into a mass of clenched, seizing muscles on the floor.

Del had the others well in hand. Their target slumped against the wall, holding a hand over his bleeding mouth. The other two suits joined the guards in a convulsive dance, Del standing over them.

"Let's get them out of sight," she ordered.

He nodded, grabbing the target first and yanking him to his feet. Sin caught the nearest flopping body by the collar and wrestled him into the room.

Del followed her with their hostage, shoving the man toward her. "I got the rest. Watch him," he bit out.

She didn't argue. He had the muscle to get the job

done fast and their target was the only one still capable of giving them trouble. She looked the disheveled man in the eye and smiled. "Please, have a seat."

The man blanched, flinching away from her as if she'd snarled like a rabid animal. "What d'you want?" he cried, beady eyes flicking from side to side.

She advanced on him, still smiling. "For starters, I want you to sit," she said in a gentle voice. The sounds behind her indicated Del was dragging bodies into the room.

The man stumbled back, eyes widening in horror as he looked past her. "Oh, Suns," he moaned. "What did you do to them?"

Sin lifted the rod and spun it in front of his eyes. "Electric shock therapy. They'll wake up in a while with a whole new outlook on life. Now, sit."

He sat.

Watching his trembling form with sharp eyes, she moved until she stood next to him. Then she spared Del a glance.

He dragged the last one into the room, the limp form still twitching. Dropping the guard, Del lunged for the door control and it slid shut. "Clear," he panted, meeting her eyes. "Door's locked."

"Good. If you'll watch our guest, I'll make our new friends less comfortable."

He flashed his teeth in a white grin, prowling toward her. "They won't need it."

"Better safe than sorry," she murmured with a smirk as she passed him. Deactivating her rod, she tucked it in her waistband before straddling the first limp form and yanking at his belt.

"Who are you people?" their hostage cried in a

hoarse voice.

Del made a derisive sound. "Mayhem and Chaos. Nice to meet you."

Sin snickered, pulling the unconscious man's arms forward so she could tie them together with his belt. "No, I'm Chaos. You're Mayhem."

Del sent her a mock frown while the man gaped at them both. "How come you get to be Chaos?"

She started on the next body, throwing him a cheeky grin over her shoulder. "Because I'm the woman."

He pondered this with a thoughtful rumble as she tied the next two people together. "Got me there."

"More to the point, who is our new friend?" she asked with a sharp look at their hostage, moving on to the last still form.

"Nobody!" the man exclaimed. "I'm nobody."

"Oh, yeah, that was convincing," Del snorted.

"Name and position, if you please," Sin requested, tightening the restraints with a jerk and rising to her feet.

"I'm just a minor supervisor, nobody important. My manager's at your feet. She's who you want."

Sin rolled her eyes, stepping over the person in question. "I don't believe in fairytales, mister." She moved to stand in front of him and crossed her arms over her chest, studying him with a faint smile. "Friendly tip. You're a terrible liar. One would have thought a man like you would be better at it."

"Name and position," Del growled, clenching his fist around the riot rod. It quivered with suppressed violence.

"All right!" the man squeaked, hunching away

from Del, the whites of his eyes flashing. "All right. My name's Vislovski. I'm an operations manager. Not the whole facility, just the experimentals."

"An operations manager," Sin repeated, exchanging a glance with Del. His dark eyes reflected her own skepticism. "What do you mean by experimentals?"

"We test concentrations and variations of our product on human subjects." Vislovski wasn't looking her in the eye.

"So you manage the Medical ward," she concluded, her tone hardening.

"Just the experimentals. Not all of Medical. I'm really not important."

"Protesting a little hard, aren't we?" she gritted, leaning down to brace her hands on the armrests, pinning him in place with her gaze. Del shifted closer with a faint shimmer of his riot rod. "Why the guards, Vislovski?"

His mouth compressed into a thin, white line, his face turning bitter. "I'm not well liked. They don't trust me."

"Who are they?"

"My bosses. My colleagues."

"I'll need names. Who is in control on site?"

He seemed happy to direct her attention elsewhere. "Brickston, Matiel Brickston."

"And who controls Matiel Brickston?"

He blinked, a puzzled frown forming between his brows. "What?"

"If Brickston runs this place, if he's responsible for the factory's production, who does he report to?"

He blinked again, eyes skidding away from hers.

Sweat beaded on his forehead. A drop slipped down his temple and over his cheekbone. "I'm—I'm not sure."

"Another fairytale, Vis?"

He met her eyes, desperation written in their muddy depths. "No! I told you, I'm just an unimportant operations manager. I just always figured Brickston dealt with the buyers…"

His voice trailed off when she laughed low in her throat. "Who owns this facility, Vis?"

He looked away, voice dropping to a near whisper. "The Core."

"Do you honestly believe the Core would let Brickston sit out here and distribute their product? Who does he report to, Vislovski?"

"I don't know," he said then flinched when she made a sound of disgust. "I don't know, I swear!" His eyes flickered to Del, more sweat tracing down his temples. "I'd tell you if I knew."

"Can you get into the main systems of this place?"

A frown creased his brow at her swift change of subject. "Of course."

Giving him a brilliant smile, she straightened. "Just what I wanted to hear." Turning, she moved toward the door and the discarded bags.

"Are you people FPA?"

Del snorted as Sin searched her bag. "Do we look like FPA?"

"Who the hell are you?"

"Let's not ask questions we really don't want the answers to," Sin admonished, finding what she was looking for and returning to the men.

"What do you want?" Vislovski asked in a strained voice when she smiled down at him.

"We want information. You're going into the main systems to get it for us."

He was shaking his head before she finished speaking. "I can't access it from here. If you try to take me to the access core, they'll be on you in minutes."

"We don't need to go with you, Vis," she said in a soft, persuasive voice. "You'll be a good boy and fetch it for us."

Hope lit his eyes before he shuttered them, his expression morphing from fear to cunning. "You'd trust me to go alone?"

She exchanged a quick grin with Del before leaning over him again, trailing her fingers over the front of his shirt. "Love will open every door," she breathed, holding his gaze as she tugged his shirt open. She smirked at the flicker of confused speculation in his muddy orbs. Holding up one of the objects she'd retrieved from her bag, she continued, "Love, and the appropriate application of high explosives."

Clicking the center of the round object, she slapped it on his bare skin. He cried out in surprise and pain when it attached to him. A bead of blood appeared at each entry point.

"Trust isn't a factor, Vis," she said in a hard tone as she backed up a step. "I just put a bomb on your chest and I'm holding the detonator. If you want to live, you'll behave yourself."

He gaped at her then reached for the thing.

She slapped his hand away. "Don't touch! You'll set it off," she snapped.

He froze, darting panicked looks from her to the object on his sunken chest.

Sin lifted her gaze to Del, giving him a crooked

smile. "Behold, our key."

"Works for me." His expression was bland, but his eyes sparkled with life.

Turning her attention back to their hostage, she pulled up a second chair and sat, propping her crossed ankles on the man's knee in a relaxed stance. "So, here's how it'll to go. You trot down to the access core and retrieve all information on who runs this place, their stats, who they have contact with in the Core, everything. You will place it on this data crystal." She held it up before his eyes. "Then you will return to us and place the crystal in my hand. Just to make sure you don't get any suicidal impulses and decide to squeal, I will place this on you as well."

She rolled her fingers and the crystal disappeared into her palm, a button appearing between her fingers. "With this, I'll be able to see and hear all you do. If you mess up, I'll detonate the bomb. If you refuse to go, I'll trigger an explosion which will rip your chest apart and you'll die." Pausing, she smiled into his eyes. "Any questions?"

He was panting, gaze darting down to the device on his chest every few seconds. "You—you wouldn't set it off when you're so close to me. You'd die, too."

"To tell you the truth, it's not meant to be used like this." She said in a confidential tone, flipping the button over her knuckles. "It's supposed to be used on locking mechanisms and such, destroying whatever it's attached to. It's a very controlled, directed explosion. At the moment, it's directed at your heart. I might get blood on me, but luckily I'm wearing black and the stains won't show."

Showing him her teeth in a humorless grin for

emphasis, she leaned forward and attached the audiovisual button to his collar. He strained away from her with a strangled sound but didn't bolt.

"Ready?" she asked with a polite lift of her eyebrows. When he stared at her without speaking, she gave him a sharp nod and held out the crystal. "Good. Go fetch, Vis."

Chapter 23

Vislovski didn't move for a long minute, staring from her to Del with wide eyes. Then he lifted a shaking hand and grasped the crystal. Closing his shirt with white-faced care, he rose to his feet and stumbled toward the door.

Sin dogged his heels. Reaching into her bag, she pulled out a headset and settled it in place, flicking the holo-display over her left eye. "Vislovski," she said when he reached for the door.

He froze, staring at her out of the corner of his eye.

She held up the detonator without expression. "I'll be watching. Be swift."

His throat convulsed with a gulp. He armed sweat off his face before opening the door and stepping out of the room.

Closing the door, she turned to find Del sitting in her chair backward, his muscular arms resting on the back. His dark eyes gleamed with speculation. "Would you blow him up?" he asked in a low voice.

"If I had to."

"Do you want to?"

She looked away but didn't hesitate. "Part of me does. He's responsible for those poor people down in the Medical ward. Monsters like him shouldn't be allowed to live."

"And the other part?"

"The other part has control over this," she said, holding up the detonator and meeting his eyes again. "I won't use it unless he forces me."

His dark gaze was calm and undisturbed. "I did things I'm not proud of, too."

"I know," she whispered, the sting of tears burning the backs of her eyes. "But we take the chance to fix what we've done when we can."

"What if we run out of chances?"

She nodded as if he'd made a statement, not a question. "I know," she whispered again, blinking away tears and trying to focus on their target. Leaning against the wall, she adjusted the headset and cleared her throat. Concentrating on the display overlying the vision in her left eye, she listened to Vislovski's harsh breathing with a grimace. "He's moving quickly, but he's going to give himself away with all his nervous energy."

"You did tell him to be swift."

She hummed in acknowledgement but said nothing, focusing on their gofer. He was getting some curious looks, but no one stopped him or spoke to him. He entered a lift, fidgeting while it moved. When it opened, he proceeded at a more sedate pace, receiving fewer glances. He must have realized how dangerous it was to show his fear and anxiety.

Approaching a clear, guarded door, he had his first conversation since leaving Sin and Del. "Forgot something, Strobe," he said in a strained voice.

The other man didn't seem to notice his strain. "Yes, sir. Go on through."

Everything beyond the door was bright white or glass. Vislovski passed people who nodded to him, but none looked at him twice except a small woman with a pinched face and bitter eyes.

"You look terrible, Jan," she announced with a satisfied undertone.

"Cafeteria food," he mumbled, brushing past her. "Try the meatloaf, Betty. You'll love it."

He moved down a couple of corridors and through a double set of heavy, clear doors, entering an oval room with monitors crowding the walls. He moved to one and a seat folded out of the wall in invitation to sit.

"Identify," a mechanical voice said and he spoke his name. His first name was Janice. No wonder the man had issues. The system accepted him without protest. He inserted the data crystal, searching through the system for the information Sin had demanded.

"He's accessing now," she said for Del's benefit, keeping a close watch on Janice's monitor. He might have lied about being able to access all the information she wanted, but he seemed to be hunting in the right places. He searched through Administration, downloading personnel files to her crystal. Brickston's file flashed past along with a file with the Core's insignia on it.

He searched for a few seconds longer, but when he found nothing else, he shut down the system and yanked the crystal free. His hands shook wildly.

"He has it, but he's panicking about something."

"Besides the bomb on his chest, you mean?"

"He wasn't shaking this much when he went into main access. Come on, Vis, don't crisp out on me now."

"Maybe they tagged him and he knows it."

Sin pressed her lips together and said nothing. She

watched Vislovski retrace his steps, this time without any conversations. The guard had nothing to say, but Sin clenched her jaw at the wary speculation in the man's eyes.

"You might be right, Del. Get your gear. We need to be ready to roll." Following her own advice, she crouched to gather her bag and weapon, watching as Vislovski stepped onto the lift to return to their level. Then she cursed. He wasn't alone.

"Trouble?" Del asked in her ear.

She nodded. "He has two guards with him. They're telling him they need to escort him to Brickston's office. The boss needs a word."

"Sun's blood," he said with weary emphasis.

"Agreed. Let's go get our pigeon." She was about to open the door when Vislovski improvised. "Wait," she said, putting a hand on Del's arm. Then she grinned. "Oh, good boy. He says he's forgotten some important documents in his office Brickston just has to see. He's inviting the guards with him, will only take a second, and so on. They're stopping on this level."

Del's boyish grin made her heart flip over. "Nice. Wait here or go to them?"

"If they're suspicious, every second counts."

"So, grab the crystal and run like rabbits."

"Pretty much," she agreed with a nod.

"Sounds like a plan to me." He opened the door.

They rushed down the corridor, hoping to meet the lift when it stopped. They only surprised one person on the way, but Del didn't pause as they rounded the corner and passed her. He tapped her with his riot rod on the way by, and she dropped with a strangled shriek to the ground.

325

They weren't quite in time. The guards and Vislovski had left the lift and were coming toward them. Sin cursed but didn't stop, and neither did Del. Surprised, the guards' aim was off when they fired their weapons, but one did manage a garbled warning on his communicator before Sin and Del hit them both like sledgehammers.

Sin swore again, turning away from the convulsing guards. "Cover's blown. Let's get out of here." She turned to the man huddled against the wall. "Crystal, please."

He plucked it out of his pocket and dropped it onto her palm with alacrity.

"Thank you." She tossed him the detonator. "You'll have to have it surgically removed. Sorry."

Turning on her heel, she sprinted down the corridor with Del at her side.

"You're not sorry," he accused as they charged around a corner.

She sent him a mischievous grin. "True."

Sin's marks on the walls helped to find their way and they no longer worried about being seen, so their return through the facility was swift. They moved too fast for security to muster any kind of response except an all-out chase, but a few shots from Sin's stinger discouraged close pursuit.

When they burst into the cargo bay, Sin had a moment of optimism until a mechanical churning sounded above them. She glanced up in alarm. "Artillery!" was all she managed before the world exploded around them.

The floor buckled and flung them off their feet, large craters appearing in the metal, as if by magic, stinging bits raining down on them. Scrambling to their feet, they grasped each other for balance and staggered toward the slicers.

The world exploded again. Sin cried out in fear and fury when her Shadow tumbled away from them in flames. She lunged for it, but Del caught her with an arm around her middle.

"No time, we gotta go!" he bellowed in her ear as cargo pods began to topple around them. His arm an iron band around her waist, he staggered to his Shadow. Falling into the pilot's seat, he pulled her in on top of him, closing the hatch and reaching for the controls at the same time.

"Suns curse it, my Shadow," she snarled, straining against his hold, fingers flying over the control panel. Del's slicer started with a roar and lurched forward in rough acceleration.

Not a second too soon. The space they'd occupied exploded in a violent outrush, kicking their ship with brutal force.

Del cursed, but Sin couldn't spare him any attention. "We need to get out of here. This part of the factory is going to explode," she gritted through clenched teeth, fingers still flying over the controls.

Del grabbed her wrists, yanking her back against him and holding her in a steely grip. "Let me drive."

The urge to take control, to do something, ate at her, but Del was right. It was his ship, calibrated to his specifications; he had to fly her. She kept still, but couldn't relax. Without being connected to the Shadow, she was blind and clueless to what was happening around them.

He seemed to sense her frustration. "The last blast

did us some damage, but not enough to stop us. We're away, reaching the shield." The Shadow lurched and Del cursed. "We got company."

"Don't worry, they're about to change their minds."

"What'd you do?"

"Set my Shadow to self-destruct. It won't blow the entire factory, but it'll take a good chunk."

The ride grew rough in a hurry. Sin was glad Del had such a strong hold on her, her teeth rattling in her head.

"It worked," Del panted in her ear. "Company's gone."

But their ride wasn't any more comfortable. "What's going on?" Sin gasped.

"What happens when you set off a bomb in a bomb?" Del asked in between jolts.

Sin's heart sank. "The nebula?"

"Lit up like a nova," was his disheartening response.

"Not good."

"Nope," he gritted, his hold tightening until she could barely breathe.

The next few minutes were some of the worst of Sin's life, not knowing how bad things were for them. How far were they from the edge of the nebula? Were they moving fast enough, or was the damage to the ship too extensive? Would they live?

She didn't bother asking Del, he had enough to handle. She concentrated on being the least of his concerns instead, not fighting the bruising force of his hold or the jolts their bodies received. Closing her eyes, she thought *please* in a silent prayer.

When the slicer stopped bucking under them like an angry beast, it took her a second to realize it. She was still bracing for the next slam of force, the next sickening roll.

"Sun and Stars," Del breathed in her ear. "I thought we'd had it."

"We're out?"

"We're out," he acknowledged, a suspicious reserve in his tone.

"What's the bad news?"

"She's busted. We're not gonna make it back to HQ. We won't get far before they catch us."

She didn't argue the Core might not come after them. They hadn't been tidy guests and they'd taken some major information. "We need to find a place to hide, then."

"Won't work. They'll find us, unless our air runs out first."

"The air recyclers are busted, too?" she asked in a dismal tone.

"No, but they were made for one body, not two."

"Kai will have to hurry, then."

"How will he find us?"

"We'll drop a distress beacon," she answered.

He was silent for a moment, before saying in a careful tone, "Did you hit your head? The bad guys will jump on a beacon."

"It sends out a frequency like star noise. They won't think anything of it, but it's coded as a distress. Kai will pick it up."

"You sure?"

"Positive."

"If you say so. I found a system with a ringed

planet. Asteroids would be better, but no belt is close enough. We can hide out in the rings."

"Good enough," she responded then waited a full minute. "Del?"

"Yeah?"

"I can't feel my hands."

"Oh, sorry." He released her wrists with alacrity and withdrew his arms from around her, then didn't seem to know where to put his hands. He finally settled them on the outer part of the armrests, away from her body.

Massaging her wrists, Sin took careful breaths and tried not to think about anything at all.

"Dropping the beacon," Del said, his voice a little husky. "Entering the rings. I'm putting us down on one of the bigger rocks, dark side. Maybe this Shadow skin'll blend."

"It will," she confirmed.

The ship shivered then went still.

"Powering down everything but life support," he said.

"I'm sure Kai won't be too long." She continued to massage her wrists for something to do. Something to take her mind off her current impossible position.

The silence hummed between them before he spoke close enough to her ear for his breath to tickle. "Did I hurt you?"

"No, I'm fine," she forced out and clasped her hands in her lap.

The silence stretched on, and the tension in Sin's muscles began to hurt. The heat from his hard body baked through her, coaxing her to relax into him, a disaster waiting to happen. They'd been forced to share a slicer, but it didn't give her free rein to take advantage of him. She tried to cling to good intentions while his scent surrounded her, his heat soaked into her, and his heart beat a deep, steady vibration, an irresistible call.

He made a small noise then choked, "Elbow."

She realized she was digging it into his ribs in an effort to put some space between them. "Sorry," she breathed, pulling her arm across her body. It put her off balance and she shifted on his lap to accommodate the change. It was a mistake.

His swift, indrawn breath, increased heart rate, and the hardening of his body against her tailbone set her on fire. "Just…be still," he managed in a ragged voice, his breath puffing against her burning cheek.

She couldn't say a word. She was too busy swallowing a moan. Waves of heat rolled through her, her skin sensitive to the least brush of clothing. She gritted her teeth against sharp stabs of pleasure as her nipples hardened, trying to breathe in a slow, steadying rhythm. Heat pooled and throbbed between her legs in time with the pulse of flesh at her tailbone.

Del's heart pounded out an urgent beat against her back, his knuckles whitening as he gripped the armrests. "I'm trying," he gritted, his breath hot against her ear. "But you've been driving me crazy since we met. I'm not sure I can… Suns, Sin, I need to touch you," he groaned, hands clenching so hard the armrests creaked.

Seduced beyond all reason, she whispered, "I need you, too." Then she braced her limbs against the sides of the Shadow and executed a flip, kicking the armrests away to straddle him.

Del had never seen anyone move with such fluid,

ruthless grace. The vision of her settling over him, green eyes flaring with primitive heat, pushed him beyond any hope of control. He grasped her hips and tugged her into tight, tormenting contact with his arousal, his groan melding with her whimper as their lips met. Her arms wrapped around his shoulders and her thighs tightened on his waist, mouth teasing his in a series of wild, steamy kisses tasting like fire and promising paradise.

It was too intense. Her lithe body burned into him. Her touch, her taste, her fiery-sweet scent soaked through him; an invasion of the senses so profound he started slipping away, his will and essence overwhelmed by her, pushing him toward insanity or oblivion. It took him a second to figure out why. They weren't one seductress, but two, the Shadow stroking his nerves from the inside.

Without hesitation, he yanked the connector free from his port and dropped it. He'd once thought piloting a Shadow would be like making love with a goddess, but it didn't compare to the real thing. Without the Shadow's inner distraction, the physical sensation of Sin in his arms and her taste on his tongue magnified, spinning him into a different kind of delirium. She rotated her hips in a slow undulation against him and the spike of pleasure chasing up his spine nearly sent him over the edge.

With a growl, he wrenched his mouth free of hers and began pulling at their clothing, desperate to feel her skin. She cooperated, shifting back to shrug her jacket off her shoulders and yank at his shirt, the sweet friction of her movement against his hardness dimming his vision. Panting, he ripped his shirt over his head then did the same with hers.

"Oh, Suns, thank you," he breathed at the sight of her bare torso, his hands shaking as he ran them over her cool, smooth skin. Cupping her full breasts, he lifted them to his mouth, tongue rolling over first one hard nipple and then the other. He could have stroked and tasted her forever, but Sin interfered.

With a luscious sound deep in her throat, she dug her fingers into his hair and lifted his head, her mouth meeting his in a deep, heated kiss. Her hands swept down his neck and over his chest and abdomen in swift fire, before she began working on the clasp to his pants.

Removing the rest of their clothing was awkward in the pilot's seat, but they managed, Sin's sinuous wriggling both a visual and tactile pleasure. He didn't help much. Her writhing was too tempting and he couldn't keep his hands from exploring what she revealed.

When he found the heat and wetness between her thighs, she stilled before arching against his touch with a soft cry. Groaning with agonized pleasure, he sank his teeth into her shoulder as he slid his fingers inside her, more than willing to watch her come apart in his arms.

With a gasping moan, she pulled his hand away and wriggled around until she straddled him again. Bracing her hands on his shoulders, she locked her green gaze on his and slowly sank onto his length.

Breath caught in his throat, he watched her lashes sweep down and gritted his teeth at the throbbing pleasure of her warmth clenching around him. Her nails dug into his shoulders as she seated herself upon him all the way, and he growled in response. But when she moved, he caught her hips and held her still. His whole body hummed with pleasure, and he was afraid the least little movement would expand the hum to a roar, shattering his world.

Bending his head, he captured her nipple between his lips, softly nibbling. She whimpered in his ear, undulating against him again. He gasped, pleasure shooting up his spine like lightning then rolled out to his extremities and back like thunder.

"Be still, sweetheart. I can't—"

"Please," she moaned, capturing his face between her hands and licking his bottom lip. "Oh, please." Little tremors shivered through her and around his length. He realized with a groan of primitive delight she was as close to the brink as he.

With a shudder, he captured her mouth with his and cupped her bottom, rocking against her. With a soft cry vibrating into him, she clenched her thighs around his waist and began a rhythm guaranteed to render him mindless. The pleasure built with ruthless intensity, too swift and all-encompassing for him to control, and his fingers dug into her soft flesh as he thrust into her.

She tensed against him with a keening cry, her body bowing as his world splintered. With her cries following him, he tumbled into a pounding pleasure so vast, it consumed his entire being, reshaping his universe.

When it released him enough to become aware of his surroundings, he realized his arms were wrapped around her in too tight a hold. He loosened his grip but couldn't find the will to let her go. She clutched him just as tightly, her breath bursting against his ear in fast, hot gusts. He panted for air, his heart thundering in an almost audible rhythm.

In all his life, he'd never felt so wildly out of control and at the same time, so much at peace. It seemed as though all the crumbled pieces of his life had just clicked into place and the restraints around his soul had fallen away. The soft body pressing against him and around him felt like freedom, like hope, like home. He'd been trying for some time to deny he was crazy in love with her, but he couldn't do it anymore. His need for her, a need which now beat at the back of his throat and throbbed in his groin, made denial impossible.

He moved against her and she groaned in unison with him at the sweet torment on their sensitive flesh. She shivered in his arms and he murmured against the cool skin of her shoulder, "Slicing will never be the same."

Her breathless laughter filled him with delight, and he turned his head to place an open-mouthed kiss on her throat. He wanted this woman, not just her flesh, but every part of her, for the rest of his life. But would she want any more than this moment from him, from a Core reject? She was a Shay and he was just…broken.

Her throat vibrated against his mouth when she spoke. "Neither will I. They didn't make these seats with this activity in mind."

He raised his head. She lifted one leg with a faint tightening of her fine brow and a rueful smile. Red marks marred the soft skin of her lower thigh and the inside of her knee from the rough sides of the seat.

"Suns, I'm sorry." He lifted her and helped her twist around until she reclined on top of him.

"I'm not," she sighed, relaxing into his arms, her soft smile sending a bolt of primitive satisfaction through him.

With a low rumble of pleasure, he nuzzled her ear, breathing in her scent like an addict. Her silky, sleek form was too much temptation and he began to explore her curves with long, slow strokes. "How long did you say it'd take Kai to find us?"

She chuckled, arching under his touch like a contented cat. "Got something on your mind, Del?"

"Not a thing," he rumbled, nipping at her ear. "Had a meltdown a little while back and it ain't workin' yet."

"Everything else is working just fine." Her voice was husky as his fingers teased the silky skin just under her breasts. When he cupped one delicious mound and ran his thumb over its taut peak, she gasped.

He grinned and suckled at her neck. "Glad you noticed. And since I got you right where I want you…" Slipping his other hand between her thighs, he cupped her.

She groaned, arching against his hands and reaching back to spear tense fingers into his dark hair. "Keep it up and I'll get more marks on my thighs."

"No, you won't," he whispered in her ear, amazed to discover he was already hard, throbbing, and as desperate for her as the first time. But this time he meant to go slow, to discover every curve, every mystery, and every sweet torment of her.

Arching up and reaching between their bodies, she caressed his length with too-talented fingers, turning her head to whisper against his mouth, "How?"

"I'll show you," he groaned between clenched teeth.

And he did, with as much fervent passion as the first time. It disturbed him, when he became capable of rational thought again, how she could shatter his control with such ease. She had such a strong hold over him. What else would she shatter?

He did his best to ignore the question, concentrating instead on the quivering lassitude of his muscles and the lingering simmer of pleasure through his body as they lay halfway on their sides. He was still trying to catch his breath, and he wondered whether the recyclers were having trouble. Sin was also breathing in a swift rhythm, her body trembling with aftershocks against him.

He swept a hand down her side in a soothing motion, pressing his face into her hair and curving closer around her. "Not complaining, but next time, let's try a bed." She didn't respond and he lifted his head with a pang of alarm. Pulling up onto an elbow, he leaned over her. "Sin? Honey, are you okay?"

Her eyes opened, the green intensity of their depths catching at his breath. "Oh, Del," she murmured, reaching up to stroke the side of his face with trembling fingers. A desperate darkness shadowed her eyes, a depth of feeling sparking both fear and fragile hope in him.

But she said nothing else and he couldn't resist the pull of those eyes. Lowering his head, he brushed gentle kisses over her full lips, a tender answer to the ache in her gaze.

She answered him in kind, before pulling back a little to smile at him. The darkness was gone, or at least hidden, from her eyes. "I'm very okay," she purred. "Is it my imagination, or is it stuffy in here?"

"I think it's the recyclers. If I can find my connector, I'll check," he answered, twisting to grope next to the seat.

She braced on an elbow and frowned at him. "You're not connected?"

A flush warmed his neck. "Yeah, well, the two of you were too much for me. I had to yank her." His fingers brushed the connector and he lifted it, shifting upright in the seat and meeting her gaze.

"Good." She moved until she was sitting across his lap, eyes narrowed on him. "I don't like to share."

He grinned in masculine satisfaction, slipping the connector into his port. Then he swore, tightening his arms around her in shock.

She tensed. "What?"

His mouth in a grim line, he made the necessary connections and powered up the ship.

Chapter 24

Kai's voice boomed into the interior of the Shadow. "Answer me! Where are you?" His fury wore an undertone of desperate fear, giving Del a lurch of guilt.

"Shay, we're here," he answered, signaling their location.

"Givliani, you had better have my sister."

"I'm right here, Kai. Stop crisping out," Sin replied, her voice calm but expression concerned.

"Why haven't you answered me?"

Del cleared his throat in embarrassment. "Sorry, my fault. I powered down to life support, no coms, then disconnected."

"Why in Sun's name—" A brief pause, then Kai released an explosive sigh. "Never mind, I can guess," he continued in a grim growl. "Next time, if you don't want to be rescued, don't drop a distress."

Sin stirred on his lap, shooting Del a wince of dismay. "He did say he was sorry, brother. How does it look out there?"

"It's clear, for now. They searched this system not too long ago but missed us both. Hold on, I'm hooking you now." Kai's voice was clipped.

Del wondered how long Kai had been searching for them. How long he'd gone without knowing if they were dead or alive. Guilt gnawed his insides, and the tension in Sin's face and form suggested guilt needled her, too. He wondered if she was regretting their time together. His only regret was causing her brother unnecessary anguish.

A muffled thump and lurch in the ship signaled Kai's Shadow attaching to them. The sensors told Del the grapples were secure and the other ship should have no trouble moving them.

"All right, we're off," Kai announced. "Del, keep her powered but let me do the flying. If you move her, you'll break loose."

"Got it," Del rasped, keeping a close watch as they lifted away from the rock. The grapples held and the other Shadow didn't strain with the extra mass at the speed Kai was going. He nodded when Sin gave him a questioning look, reassuring her all was well.

She gave him a somber nod in return, reaching behind the seat to tug at the provisions pack. He helped her pull it forward and watched her rummage through it until she brought out the sanitizer. He was a little unnerved by her silence and by the pensive curve of her mouth. With hesitant fingers, he brushed the hair from her face.

She glanced up at his touch, a smile forming, but it had a sad curve to it and the reserve in her eyes sent a dull ache of alarm spreading through his chest. The sweet kiss she brushed against his mouth helped ease the ache but didn't dissipate it all the way. They cleaned up and redressed in silence.

They shared some water and had a few bites to eat, before Sin curled against his chest with a sigh, head on his shoulder and supple body sweet and heavy against him. An expanding warmth overshadowed his unease.

He wrapped his arms around her, holding her close. With a rumble of contentment, he nuzzled his face in her hair, breathing in her scent and wishing the moment would go on forever.

Sin lifted a hand to curl around the nape of his neck and snuggled closer to him with another sigh. Then she whispered against his throat, "How are the recyclers doing?"

"Hanging in there," he answered, his eyes sliding closed at the feel of her mouth on his skin. "They do okay when we're not, uh, active."

She laughed low in her throat and a startling hunger rippled through him. *Again?* He thought with a mix of humor and dismay. Addicts could go longer than this, but her hold on him was stronger than any drug.

In Kai's disapproving presence, though, he figured Sin wouldn't welcome his touch this time. With a sigh of regret, he searched for something to take his mind off the sleek form pressed against him. He thought about asking where they would go from here with the information they'd acquired, but he shied away from discussing the future with a quiver of unease. He didn't want to bring up a time when she would be leaving his arms.

He had been wondering about Ezekiel Shay. It wasn't a subject she seemed comfortable with, but neither of them was going anywhere for a while. "Sin."

"Mm?"

"What happened to your father?" he asked then held his breath. The last time they'd talked about the man she'd shut Del down hard. He wasn't looking forward to a repeat.

Sin tilted her head, meeting his gaze with her own

solemn regard. No anger or rejection shadowed her eyes, but she studied him with a clinical appraisal. She was deciding what he should and shouldn't know. This suggestion of distrust hurt.

After a minute, she sighed and took her hand away from his neck to rub her eyes. "He was killed," she said, voice soft and matter-of-fact.

Del winced. Running a soothing hand over her hip and thigh, he vowed not to ask how.

She seemed to hear the question anyway. "He'd gone to confirm some information about a group of weapons dealers with Core backing. He should have let my brother and I go. He and Kai fought about it, the last words they ever exchanged. But our father always was stubborn."

She stretched a little then curled into him again, tucking her face against his throat. He couldn't see her expression. "They didn't appreciate him snooping. My best guess is they thought he was stinging them for the FPA. So they killed him."

"I'm sorry, Sin." The words seemed lame when facing the muffled pain in her voice.

"They were sorrier," she said, her tone hardening.

It wasn't prudent, but the question slipped out anyway. "What did you do?"

She rubbed her forehead against his throat. "Nothing. It was done for us by the time we reached their hideout. All dead, except for the informer."

"Who was the informer?"

She gave a mirthless chuckle. "Hector."

"Oh," Del responded, now understanding the black fear and hate he'd seen in the grimy man's eyes. "He'd stuck his hand where it didn't belong."

"True enough."

"He's lucky to be alive."

"We thought so, too." She laid her hand over his.

He twinned his fingers with hers and brought her hand to his lips, savoring the silky feel of her skin. "So who killed your father's murderers?"

"Griffin," she answered in a mild tone, as though it wasn't important.

His fingers tightened, surprise drawing a strangled exclamation from him. "Griffin? Why?"

"Griffin admired and liked my father. He wouldn't have ordered his death. He would've enjoyed destroying my father's life, but he would never have killed him. Zeke Shay was, after all, the progenitor of the Core," she said in a voice carved in bitterness. "I think Griffin was shocked by his death, enraged. His sparring partner was gone, snatched from him by a bunch of senseless animals. So he slaughtered them."

Del shuddered, a chill racing up his spine at both Griffin's diseased outlook on life and Sin's cold description of it.

"He did us a favor," Sin continued. "We were devastated, Kai and I. We wanted to tear those butchers apart with our bare hands and would've paid a terrible price for it. The FPA lets us bend the law but frowns on mass murder. They would've had to bring us to justice, which would leave Griffin with no opposition. No one would have been safe from him and the Core."

He tightened his hold on her, dismayed by her idea of a terrible price, not their lives or prosecution by the FPA, but an unopposed Core. How could these Shays shrug off their own welfare as if it meant nothing? "Did Griffin know? Did he know what you meant to do?"

"No, I think he reacted on impulse and I don't think he lets his emotions rule his actions very often. Even if he'd known, though, he wouldn't have taken advantage of the situation to get rid of us."

"Why not?"

"He likes the challenge. He wants to dominate us on his own merit. If anyone is to destroy us, he means to be the one."

"The man's sick in the head," Del ground out. He couldn't grasp the kind of calculating arrogance it would take to be the person Sin described.

"No argument here," Sin said with a hint of humor in her low voice. She shifted a little then asked, "Everything still clear out there?"

Del had been monitoring their progress with a portion of his attention while they talked. "Still good. We're going slow, but making progress. No nasties in sight."

"Good," she responded, twisting her fingers with his in a gentle caress. Then she cleared her throat. "Del, you shouldn't tell your brother anything when we get back."

He frowned. "Why not?" He didn't want to keep secrets from his brother. Nick deserved better from him.

"It'll put him in danger. His questions have already made him a target, which is why we suggested he come to Shay headquarters. It's safer for him. But if he learns all you know, what do you suppose he'll do?"

Del thought about it. If his brother was the kind of man he thought he was, he wouldn't back down from the truth. He'd meet it head on. "He'll go back to the FPA and try to find the rotten apples."

"Exactly. What will they do to him if he does?"

Del grimaced. "Well, they sure won't wine and dine him."

"Right again. He's safer thinking we're the ones who need to be investigated, at least for now."

Del fought the logic, picturing his brother's face, the disappointment and anger when he'd said he wouldn't break the contract. "He'll find out at some point."

"I know, but letting him find out on his own gives us more time."

"Time for what?"

"To decrease the danger," she answered in an evasive tone.

More secrets, Sin? He thought with an inner grimace but didn't pursue it. He didn't want her to confirm she was keeping things from him and still didn't trust him. "I've spent my whole life trying to keep Nick out of trouble. Hasn't worked yet, but I can't give up the habit now," he conceded without much grace.

"Brothers do tend to have minds of their own," she responded with wry amusement. "Speaking of brothers, will you connect me with mine?"

He did so almost before she'd finished speaking. "Go ahead."

Sin sat up, her form stiffening with subtle tension. "Kai?"

"What?"

Her mouth thinned at his surly tone. "Just wanted to let you know we got what we came for."

Kai didn't speak for a moment. When he answered, his voice was less sharp, though still abrupt. "Not a total loss, then. I can't haul you all the way back to

HQ."

"I know. Are you heading for Jake's place?"

"Yes. We'll be there soon."

Sin flashed Del a quick look before dropping her gaze. His stomach clenched at the hint of dismay in her expression. "Is the way still clear?"

"For now, until someone catches all the chatter. Cutting communication. We'll talk later." Kai severed the connection.

Sin gave a small shake of her head. "He'll get over it," she said without meeting Del's gaze.

"Sure he will."

"He's not the type to hold onto anger. He'll be making jokes about it by dinner time."

Del was less concerned with Kai's attitude than with Sin's down-turned eyes. She reclined against him again, but her body held an alarming tension. "What's wrong?" he whispered into her hair, trying to keep his hold from tightening like a man reaching for an impossible dream.

She shook her head and didn't reply.

Clenching his jaw and feeling like a coward, he didn't press her for an answer. The possibilities made his heart thump with dread.

The rest of the trip passed in heavy silence. When Kai announced their approach to the way station, Del's stomach dropped. Sin's only response was a small sigh. Kai dropped the grapples and let Del limp his slicer into the docking bay on his own.

As he landed and powered down his Shadow, he tried to catch Sin's eye, but she sat with her face turned away and opened the hatch without word. A bitter taste in the back of his throat, Del helped her out of the slicer before leaving the ship himself.

Kai strode toward them with a grim twist of his mouth. "Well, I hope you two enjoyed yourselves."

"Kai, would you give us a minute?" Sin interrupted her brother in a low voice.

Standing behind her, Del couldn't see her expression, but Kai paused and studied his sister with an arrested air. His cool green eyes flicked up to meet Del's for a brief second. Then he nodded, handsome face softening. Kai retraced his steps to lean on his Shadow, arms folded across his chest, watching them with sharp interest.

Sin turned to Del. The cool, guarded expression in her eyes sent a spurt of anger to join the dread tightening his chest.

"I suppose you're gonna give me crap about being my employer again," he rasped, propping casual hands on hips, trying to look impatient and not alarmed.

She confirmed his fears in a gentle voice, no trace of regret on her face. "It's not crap, Del. I am your employer and as such, I have a responsibility to you. What happened between us was a—"

"I've been responsible for myself for a while now," he interrupted with a snap of sarcasm. He couldn't let her call what they'd done a mistake. "I don't need some employer to run my life. I make my own decisions."

She dropped her gaze, staring at his chest. "I know, but we can't continue as we are. It's impossible."

"Nothing's impossible, Sin," he protested in a lower voice, battling a desperate need to pull her back into his arms.

She shook her head, not meeting his gaze. "This is. I can't have a relationship with you and be your employer at the same time." Her arms came up in slow motion until she clasped her elbows, shoulders hunching as if she felt a chill. "I was wrong to take advantage of the situation, and of you," she continued in a tight voice. "It can't be undone, but I will make sure it doesn't happen again."

Hurt stopped his breath, spreading a burn through his chest like fingers of acid. So she did regret their time together. Or maybe she'd gotten what she wanted and was through with him now. Unattached and unimpressed with a broken Core reject.

"How are you gonna make sure, Sin?" he gritted through clenched teeth.

She was silent and still, eyes downcast and lovely face as expressionless as glass. Then she took a deep breath. "You could quit."

He didn't hear the hesitant, hopeful strain in her words, only sensing another rejection. "I'm not quitting," he snarled, folding his arms over his chest to contain the agony lodged under his ribs. "And you have no grounds to fire me. We have a contract, remember?"

You can't get rid of me so easy, Lady Shadow, he thought with a flare of bitter fury, trying to ignore the panic and desperation twisting his insides at the possibility of never seeing her again. Anger was easier to accept than the truth; he couldn't walk away from her.

She stood like a statue in front of him for another long, silent moment, not even appearing to breathe. Then she gave a short nod and spun on her heel, striding away from him.

Del clenched his jaw until it hurt, trying to hold onto his anger as he watched her dismiss him again.

She approached her brother and Kai's expression darkened like an oncoming storm as they spoke. Del couldn't see her face or hear their conversation, though her stiff back relayed her tension. When Kai raised a hand as if to touch her, she flinched away. Her brother moved aside, mouth in a thin line.

She slid into Kai's Shadow without a glance in Del's direction. The slicer growled to life and lifted from the landing pad, heading for the exit. Del watched Sin leave with a sharp pain in his chest like a spike cleaving through his ribcage.

Out of the corner of his eye, he caught Kai's approach and faced him. Sin's brother had cold murder in his eyes, his movements as predatory as a stalking panther. Del clenched his fists and waited for the other man with a surge of relief, welcoming the violent outlet. Anything to avoid the anguish rushing through him like a black storm.

But Kai slowed, his expression clouding over as he studied Del. A few feet away, he stopped and frowned.

"Got somethin' on your mind?" Del taunted, muscles tightening against the desperate emptiness in his chest. "Get on with it, Shay."

Kai heaved a deep sigh, shook his head, and turned away. "Come on, Giv. Let's get a drink and you can tell me what happened." When Del didn't follow, he paused to glance over his shoulder. "Well?" he snapped.

Del glowered at him. "I'd rather hit you."

With his usual mercurial change of mood, Kai's expression lightened with a chuckle. "I know the feeling. Settle for drinking me under the table?"

Del didn't move for a second, still glaring at him. Then he dropped his gaze and ran a hand over his face.

With a sigh of his own, he joined Kai and matched his stride to the exit, muttering in a sour tone, "What's with you and booze, anyway?"

"Everyone needs a hobby."

Del snorted but said nothing further until they were seated at the Sun Way café, drinks in hand. Jake served them, his greeting jovial until he caught their mood. Then he left them alone.

Kai lifted his drink in a sardonic toast. "So, tell me what I missed."

Del told him, watching the light glance off his glass as he turned it in meditative circles on the tabletop. He didn't hear the catch in his voice whenever he said Sin's name, but felt it like a hook dragging through his insides.

When Del reached the part where he'd flown the battered Shadow into hiding, he paused. His eyes slid closed at the bittersweet memory, one white-knuckled hand gripping his drink and the other pinching the bridge of his nose. "Then we waited for you," he rasped.

Kai said something under his breath and Del dropped his hand, glancing across the table. The other man sat with arms folded across his chest, glowering at a holographic seabird as if the creature had wronged him somehow. Del still felt bad for putting the man through hell, but he couldn't regret a single second of the intimacy he'd shared with Sin. And he wouldn't apologize for it again.

"Now what?" Del asked his boss.

Kai took a long swallow of his drink then ran a careless hand through his hair, mussing it even more than usual. "Now we sit tight. I called for a hauler to retrieve us. They'll be here in a few hours. Sin has the info, so she'll put things in motion when she gets back to HQ."

"What kinda things?"

Kai met his gaze and raised an eyebrow. "Don't tell me my sister kept you in the dark about what we were after at the factory."

Del scowled. "You Shays are full of secrets."

Kai acknowledged this with a tilt of his head and a wry smile, setting his drink down and folding his arms across his chest again. "Things, meaning she'll contact the FPA and give them the info you stole."

"And then?"

"And then," Kai repeated with a shrug, "we watch what happens."

Del studied him with a bitter twist of his mouth. "You already know what's gonna happen, don't you?"

"I appreciate your confidence in my abilities, Giv, but I'm no good at clairvoyance. Left my crystal ball at home."

Del snorted and shook his head. "Like pulling teeth, getting anything out of you two."

"Well, you could wait until I'm flat drunk," Kai suggested with a grin.

Del remembered his conversation with Sin about her brother, a pang of loss twisting inside him along with a thread of weary humor. "How about bribery? I hear you got a thing for nut clusters."

"Shouldn't listen to vile rumors," Kai responded with a solemn shake of his head.

"And women," Del added with a smirk.

"Ah," Kai sighed. "Well, that addiction I'll admit to."

"Sorry you're not allowed any on the station."

Kai narrowed his eyes with a mock-scowl. "Sure, be an ass and rub it in."

Del chuckled and downed a swallow of his drink with a small measure of satisfaction. He wasn't sure he'd mended anything with his boss, but at least they were on drinking terms. Now, if he could only harden his heart, he might just survive these devastating Shays.

Chapter 25

The wait for the haulers and the trip back to Shay headquarters passed in a haze for Del, a weary emptiness leeching all the interest and color from the world. Avoiding the crew, he stretched out on one of the hauler's bunks but couldn't rest. His body needed sleep and he yearned for the blissful oblivion of it, but his traitor mind kept cycling over the past few days in an endless, tormenting loop. When the hauler docked, he dragged himself from the bunk, heading for the cargo bay and his wounded slicer.

Kai intercepted him. "Quan is handling your Shadow. Follow me," he said in a clipped tone.

Del would love to tell him to shove it, but that required more energy than he had. They left the hauler and marched across the maintenance bay, riding the lift to the offices. The large main office was empty, though the beach scene behind the desk had changed to many different screens. Some looked like views of different locations, several were news feeds, and many were filled with data, graphs, and scrolling text.

"Wait here," Kai ordered and walked through the clear partition.

Del glanced at the screens but couldn't find enough enthusiasm to investigate. Moving across the room, he slumped into one of the armchairs by the fireplace, rubbing at the stubble on his face with slow, meditative fingers. He should let his brother know he was back and in one piece. "Control."

"Adelmo Givliani."

"Connect me with Nick Givliani."

After a short pause, his brother's voice echoed in the spacious room. "Del, where the hell did you disappear to? Nobody knew where you were."

Del grimaced, hating what he was about to do. "Had something come up, a side job. Rush work, so I had to leave in a hurry."

"What kind of side job?" Nick asked with a darker thread in his tone.

"Not the kind you're thinkin' of, bro. Full sanction by the FPA."

"What did you get yourself into? You don't sound right, Del."

How was he supposed to explain? Vivid images of their journey flashed through his mind: the perilous piggyback ride through the wormhole, their race through the factory, the exploding nebula, and Sin, sultry and seductive in his arms. Pinching the bridge of his nose, he settled for, "I wrecked my Shadow."

"You hurt?" The tension in Nick's tone said he was on full red-alert.

"Take it easy, little brother, I'm fine. Gotta go, tell you what I can later."

Nick muttered a disgruntled agreement and ended the connection. Del slumped farther in the chair and rubbed rough hands over his face. The evasions and lies pricked him like a thousand needles. At least when he'd sent Nick away and went to work for the Core, he hadn't had to do this ugly dance with his brother.

Del was about to say screw it and head down to his

quarters for a much needed san and sleep, when Kai reentered the office with Sin, Cassie trailing behind them. Del's entire body tensed as if from a blow, the emptiness inside him filling with a burning agony he could've done without. Sin didn't meet his gaze when she walked past him to the desk, her face pale with shadows under her eyes.

Bitter anger warred with aching need as he rose from his seat and moved closer. Not too close, though. He didn't trust himself to get within arm's length of her, to come close enough to breathe her scent.

"Hey, Del," Cassie greeted him with a quiet smile while the twins studied the screens. "Nice work with the factory."

"What's going on?"

"Sin alerted the FPA the second she returned. They're at the tail end of a raid on the factory and have detained several Core personnel, including the main guy in charge of production. You missed all the excitement," she added with a wry quirk of her lips.

"I had enough excitement. What else?"

"They discovered more blue factories through data retrieval and when detainees gave up locations. They won't find them all, but since they caught the people in charge, blue production is now crippled. Instead of one massive operation, blue runners have to deal with a bunch of small producers. Most will fall apart without the funds or the protection of the Core." Cassie wore smug satisfaction while she relayed these developments.

Del frowned at her, not sharing her delight. "But did they bring down the Core?"

With a grimace of regret, she shook her head,

pulling her plaited hair over her shoulder and toying with the strands at the end. "Griffin is denying all knowledge, denouncing his own people for besmirching Quasicore's good name by committing such atrocities," she simpered and rolled her eyes. "What a paragon."

"So they don't have a case on him?"

"They're trying to make one, but it doesn't look good. He's too slick. They can't get a good grip on him. He just slithers away like a slimy snake," she said with a curl of her lip.

He stared at her, exhausted beyond comprehension. Was she telling him they'd done all this for nothing? "Then what's the point?" he asked. "Won't he just start blue back up again when the dust settles?"

"Ah," she said with a twinkle in her eyes, lifting a finger. "Here's where phase two comes in." She lifted her eyebrows, tilting her head and stretching her finger across the desk.

With reluctance, Del lifted his gaze to the twins standing in front of the screens. They were studying the different views, every once in a while pointing out something to the other with an abbreviated murmur.

"Look," Sin said, tapping a screen.

"Expected," her brother responded with a careless shrug, before pointing beyond her at another view. "But that's new."

She made a sound of agreement and they watched the viewer together for a minute. Something on it must have disagreed with them, though. They both snorted, Kai shaking his head while they scanned the other screens.

Del had no clue what they were doing. With weary resignation, he looked down at Cassie's teasing grin. He almost lost his patience, but managed to contain it by grinding his teeth. "All right, what's phase two?"

Her grin faded and her expression softened. She didn't make him wait for an answer. "We never expected to bring down the Core with just this attack on blue production. It would have been nice, but we didn't count on it. We hope to flush out some of the FPA's bad seeds, the ones owned by Griffin."

She glanced away from him, eyes running over the screens with a grim tightening of her features. "We can chop at his operation as much as we want, which is what the Shays have been doing for years, but the thing just grows back like a weed, or cancer. All because Griffin bought himself protection from the law." She paused, as if it should all make sense now.

Del sighed and rubbed his eyes. He supposed he ought to try following her reasoning and figure it out, but he was just too tired. "Cut to it, Cass," he growled without lowering his hand.

"We're poking the hive to see what comes out to protect it," she said with a hint of impatience. "It's been a very public attack, on all the news feeds, every step broadcast across the galaxy. Griffin's little FPA rats have to scramble to cover his tracks, erase data, hide documents, and pull strings. They'll make mistakes and some will get caught."

"Some already have," Sin interrupted in a low voice.

Del's head jerked up, his glance meeting hers for a brief, agonizing moment, before she turned away. Heart thudding in time with the headache growing between his temples, Del wondered at the darkness he'd seen in her eyes.

"Three so far," Kai continued, still facing the screens, his dark head swiveling back and forth as he searched for new data. "One tried to free the blue leader, which takes the moron prize. Griffin will have him killed for sheer stupidity. He wouldn't want the detainees freed now. He'd want them dead. I'm guessing it'll be the next catch of the day."

"The other two were nearly as obvious," Sin added, also not facing Del and Cassie. "One tried to destroy evidence and the other offered a bribe to one of our loyals."

Her voice, distant and emotionless, dug at him like claws embedded in his flesh, goading him into lashing out. "So all this was just to help the FPA clean house? I expected more from the great and powerful Shays," he sneered, aiming his attack at Sin's back. She stiffened but didn't turn.

Kai shifted around with a lazy grin over his shoulder. "Your faith warms my heart, Giv," he drawled, lifting an eyebrow in sardonic emphasis.

Cassie was more direct. "Don't be stupid, Del," she snapped. "We need the FPA free of Core, so next time they can act."

"Next time?"

She humphed with an exasperated frown. "Did you think this was the only thing we had planned? Suns preserve us, Del, you don't kill a hydra by cutting off one head, and you can't win at chess unless you think several moves in advance."

Del stared at her for a second, before looking back up at Kai.

Sin's brother had a lopsided grin warming his features. "Need a translation?"

"Please," Del responded with heavy irritation.

Kai chuckled. "This is just the beginning of what we have in store for Griffin and Quasicore."

"The beginning of the Endgame," Sin murmured.

Her brother glanced at her, sobering. "Ready to talk to Griff?"

She nodded without turning her head from the screens.

Instead of a verbal command, Kai turned and touched something on the desk. A graphic flickered to life, floating ghost-like above the desk's surface. It looked like a great tree, with many pale, dense branches and no main trunk. A touch from Kai and the thing seemed to grow, expanding out of sight until only one of the branches was visible. Another touch and the thing flickered out of existence.

Kai turned back to the screens, leaning against the desk and crossing his arms over his chest. When nothing happened, the twins exchanged a knowing glance. "Think he's busy?" Kai asked with a touch of malice.

She didn't get a chance to answer. Griffin's face appeared at the center of the screens, just as calm and collected as the last time Del had seen him.

"Sinsudee, Manakai, what can I do for you?"

It could have been Del's imagination, but he thought he heard an added note of briskness to the man's cultured tones.

"You can die and go to hell," Cassie mumbled at his side.

Del glanced down in surprise. She watched Griffin's image with murder in her eyes, hand yanking with brutal force at her braid. He reached over and unknotted her fingers, clasping them in his to keep her from mutilating herself. She sent him a quick, pained smile then fixed her gaze back on Griffin as the twins greeted him.

"Web, we've heard the distressing news," Sin said, her voice smooth and warm with concern. "Is there anything we can do for you?"

"You are sweet to offer, but it's only a matter of bringing the offending parties to justice. Of course I'm appalled to find these people have been abusing my trust, and I'm grateful the FPA has taken such swift action."

Del would never have guessed he was lying through his teeth. Griffin shook his dignified head with an aggrieved expression, as though saddened by the circumstances but by no means worried about them. Del's stomach took a slow, nauseated roll.

"I'm sure it was a shock, to find yourself so betrayed," Sin replied and Griffin's expression sharpened a little. "And a blow to your company as well. The market isn't looking favorably on you today. If you need any help, financial or otherwise, please call on us."

"You are too kind," Griffin said in a gentle, patronizing tone.

"What are friends for?" Kai interjected. "Our relationship with you has been too lucrative to dismiss. We'll do what we can."

Griffin paused for a brief second, pinning Kai with a silvery, razor-sharp gaze, before he smiled. "I'm gratified by your staunch support. I don't believe I'll need any assistance, but if it comes to it, I will be pleased to turn to you."

"Good to hear," Kai responded, before his tone deepened to steely warning. "But in the future, Griff, you should be more careful."

Griffin lost his smile, staring at Kai with his cold, hunter's eyes. "Careful?" he asked with silky menace.

"About who you hire, of course," Sin answered in a light, teasing voice.

Griffin's expression eased, a faint smile reappearing on his thin lips. "Of course. Whatever would I do without your singularly brilliant advice?"

Sin laughed and Del closed his eyes, breathing slow through the clenching pain in his chest. The last time she'd laughed like that, she'd been in his arms, saturating all his senses with pleasure.

"We know you're busy, so we won't keep you. Thank you for taking our call," Sin said, humor still warming her tone.

"It was my pleasure," Griffin responded, his smile widening in an imitation of affection. "You have been a bright light in an otherwise bleak day."

"Until next time?"

He tilted his head in acknowledgement then his image blinked out of existence.

Both twins sighed, Sin sagging against the desk next to her brother. Del wondered if it was relief or weariness prompting the sound. He didn't want to feel concern, but the dark shadows under Sin's eyes tugged at him.

"Well," Cassie announced, letting go of Del's hand with a quick smile and directing her gaze at the twins, "it went all right, don't you think?"

Kai grunted, watching his sister with a faint frown. "I can handle it from here. Go get some rest, Sissa," he prompted in a low voice.

She nodded, but Del couldn't see her face to read her expression.

"Has it been sent?" Sin asked.

"Yes," Cassie answered with crisp reassurance. "It'll arrive later today."

Del didn't bother asking what this new cryptic exchange was all about. His mind was bleary with apathy, killing any curiosity he had left. He watched Sin straighten and head for the back door. Something twisted in his chest when she slipped from the room without a glance in his direction.

"I have to get back to work," Cassie said in a distracted tone, worrying at her braid again and shifting in place.

Kai nodded, giving her a crooked smile. "I'll send you updates."

"Thanks." With a tight, sympathetic smile for Del, she spun on her heel and marched through the clear partition to the offices beyond.

Leaving sounded like the best idea he'd heard in an eternity. Del muttered, "Need to check my Shadow," and headed for the exit.

"Hold it," Kai commanded, his tone autocratic enough to make Del grind his teeth. "We have some business to address, you and I."

Del turned with slow reluctance to meet the other man's gaze. Kai was still behind the desk, both hands planted on the surface, his green eyes cool and direct. When Del didn't move, Kai gestured him closer with an imperious flick of one hand.

He is your employer, Del reminded himself to keep from snarling at the man like a rabid dog. Taking a deep, fortifying breath, he strode forward until he was across from Kai. "What business?" he asked with an impatient bite.

"Two things," Kai responded with cool briskness. "First, I'm delighted to inform you your debt to us is now paid, due to the bonus and hazard pay you received from the abantium run, plus hazard pay for this last mission to the blue factory."

"What?" Del stared at the man, bewildered.

"We wouldn't garnish your wages and would have accepted payments at your discretion, except you've had a change in circumstances."

Del wasn't thinking straight, but Kai's comment still made him tense. "What change in circumstances?"

Kai straightened, folding his arms across his chest like a judge, expression taking on an alarming air of satisfaction. "You're fired."

"What?"

"You disobeyed a direct order from me not to go to the factory. Grounds for dismissal, per our contract. Since the conditions of your debt have also been met, our contract has therefore been terminated. You're fired, Givliani."

"You can't," Del ground out, shaking with fury and underlying panic.

"I can. It's done." The faint, smug smile curling Kai's mouth almost made Del launch over the desk at him.

They couldn't get rid of him like this. He refused to let them. "Did Sin put you up to this?" he snarled, his voice so thick with emotion he almost didn't recognize it.

"Why don't you ask her yourself?" Kai responded,

his tone silky smooth, humor still tugging at his expression. "I'm sure you remember where her suite is."

"You bastard," Del panted. "Why?"

The humor receded from the other man's face, replaced by something even more humiliating. Compassion. "As I said, you went against a direct order. For any other reason, you'll need to speak with my sister."

"Fine," he choked and spun on his heel, unable to look at the man any longer without giving in to violence. Stalking out of the office, he launched himself into the lift and drove his fingers into the control pad. While the lift was in motion, he splayed his hands on the door's surface and watched his arms tremble, trying to contain the rage rushing through him.

When the doors opened, he crossed the Gold Rooms in long, stiff strides, spinning down the short corridor to Sin's door like a cyclone. Ignoring the discreet door chime, he used his fist on the door with satisfying violence.

"Mr. Givliani, how may I be of service?" Mina's smooth voice responded.

"Open the Sun-damned door," he snarled through his teeth.

To his surprise, she did. Surprise didn't stop him from crossing the threshold, though. Marching into the cool welcome of Sin's quarters, he was struck by her scent, the fiery-sweetness taunting him with agonizing memories. The sight of her almost brought him to his knees.

She came into the room with a look of startled dismay, tightening the belt on her robe. It was full length and covered her neck to ankles, but it was a thin, silvery material clinging to every supple curve. "Del, what are you—?"

Only his anger kept him moving. "You are not getting rid of me!" he shouted, stalking toward her.

Her brows pulled together in confusion. "Getting rid of you? What are you talking about?"

Her eyes pulled at him, the green depths clear and blameless, but he was too angry to be swayed this time. Prudence steered him away to pace her living room before he came within touching distance.

"You know what." He sent her black looks, doing his best not to hold her gaze. Her eyes had always been his downfall. "I ain't leaving. You wanna fire me, fine, but you'll have to drag me out yourself if you want—"

"Fired?" she interrupted.

Something in her tone made him slow. Clenching his hands into fists, he growled, "Your brother just fired me."

His heart plummeted when a delighted smile lit her face.

"He did?"

"Yeah." He turned away before she could see the agony tearing at him. She hadn't known her brother was going to fire him, but she was thrilled just the same. She was happy to see him go.

"But you're angry about it."

He didn't answer, baring his teeth at the emptiness in front of him and leaning his weight on the back of her couch, shoulders tensing with violence.

"You wouldn't quit."

He pushed off the couch hard enough to make it skid, rounding on her. "So you figured you'd force me out, one way or the other?"

"Why would we—?" she started then shook her head, hands coming up to cup her elbows. "Del, you're not making sense. We don't want you to leave."

That rocked him. "What?"

Lowering her eyes to his chest, she added, "I don't want you to leave."

Feeling dense, he stared at her. "Then why the hell am I fired?"

She pressed her lips together and glanced around the room, shifting in place. Then she fixed her gaze on his chest again. "Why do you want to stay?"

Staring at her downcast eyes in mute dismay, he realized he should have anticipated the question before he came charging up here. But he hadn't been thinking straight and still wasn't. Lifting his hands palm up in a helpless gesture, he let them fall back to his sides and sighed, "I can't leave."

Her eyes shot to his, their bright depths holding him hostage. "Because of your debt?"

"No, it's paid," he rasped. "Bonuses and hazard pay."

"Your brother, then?"

"You, Sin," he surrendered quietly. "I can't leave you."

One of her hands rose to her mouth, as if shocked or distressed. "But you wouldn't quit," she whispered behind it.

He ran a hand through his hair with a low, frustrated growl. "What's quitting got to do with it?"

Blinking at him, she lowered her hand, uncovering the beginnings of a soft smile. "Del, I thought it meant you didn't want me anymore. Not being your employer was the only way we could be together. I couldn't fire you, but Kai found a way."

He closed the space between them in two long strides, hauling her up against his chest with more desperation than gentleness. Capturing her mouth with his own, he kissed her with all the anguished passion in his soul.

After an eternity, he lifted his head and stared down into wild green eyes. "Not want you?" he ground out, giving her a little shake. "Suns curse it, Sin, I'm stupid in love with you."

With a low sound in the back of her throat, she slipped her arms around his neck and pulled his head back down, molding her lips to his in hot demand and pressing her luscious curves against him. His frustrated anger and anguish burned away as fire roared through him, obliterating everything except the succulent mouth searing his own and the soft body arching into his in silent command.

He pressed her closer, desperate hands running over the arch of her back and cupping her silk-covered bottom with an aching groan. She whimpered into his mouth, fingers spearing into his hair and nails scraping his skin. Crazy with need, he bore her to the floor, yanking on her robe.

"Oh, yes," she whispered when the cloth slipped away from her skin and his weight pressed her to the floor. "Yes, Del."

The fire in her eyes and the feel of her sleek limbs wrapping around his waist drove him wild. Burying one hand in her hair and running the other over the silky skin of her hip, he tilted his pelvis in a slow press against her core, growling with primitive delight when she gasped and arched into him. Her eyes slid closed and her teeth sank into her bottom lip as she quivered in his grasp. With a luscious sound in her throat, she pulled his shirt up and sank her nails into the small of his back, urging him closer.

Desperate to oblige, he tore at his clothes. She assisted, though she didn't speed things up, pausing to caress and tease the flesh they uncovered. By the time he was naked, he shook with delirious desire. Whispering her name over and over, he twisted his fingers in her hair and settled his weight between her sleek thighs. When he thrust inside her, burying himself all the way, they both cried out.

Del froze, muscles going rigid as he fought the primitive urge to let go, to pound into her with savage passion and possess her utterly. The awkward pilot's seat hadn't let him be this deep inside her and experience every soft curve pressing into him.

"Del," she moaned in his ear, her hands sweeping his back in urgent demand, hips shifting against him.

"I can't," he panted.

She nipped his ear. "Yes," she hissed, "you can."

Her teeth sinking into his shoulder destroyed the last of his control. Tightening his fist in her hair, he drove into her as he brought his mouth to hers, his low, savage cry mingling with her own. His movements had no finesse, just a desperate need she matched, thrust for thrust, kiss for kiss. The pleasure was immense and uncontainable, rolling through his body in wild waves until it broke him apart, destroying him with a sensation too vast to comprehend or resist.

"Suns," Sin sighed in his ear a while later as they lay quivering in each other's arms. "We missed the bed again."

He began with a chuckle. It escalated into full-fledged laughter, a gust of humor born of relief and released tension. Keeping hold of her and still laughing, he rolled until she reclined on him.

She was giggling into his chest. His Lady Shadow, giggling.

"Couldn't crawl that far if I wanted to," he managed through his chuckles. He wasn't exaggerating, his whole body gelid and heavy with satiation, a pleasant exhaustion.

She lifted her head. A wicked grin curled her full lips, the brightness in her eyes warming him down to his toes. With her dark, tousled hair framing her face and a flush coloring her cheekbones, her beauty stole his breath.

"We could start at the couch and work our way to the bedroom, as long as Mina…" She paused on a gasp, her eyes widening. "Oh, no. Mina?" she called in a wincing tone. When no one answered, she sagged into his chest with a sigh, eyes sliding closed. "Thank the Suns. She put herself in privacy mode."

He started laughing again. After a moment she joined him, planting kisses on his skin between her snickers. Sliding a hand in her hair, he pulled her face up to his, tasting her smile with slow relish. When he eased his hold, the smile had changed to something far more sensual. The tender light in her eyes and the gentle brush of her fingers as she traced his face made his heart stumble.

"Sin," he rumbled, "I hate to tell you this and ruin the mood, but I'm gonna have to kill your brother."

Without hesitation, she responded, "No more than

he deserves, I'm sure." Then she tilted her head. "Why?"

"He never said why he was firing me."

"Yes, well, Kai does love his petty revenge. We did give him a bad time out there. Or maybe he was testing you to see if you'd leave." She slipped off to one side, snuggling against him with a sigh. "He does approve of you, you know. He wouldn't have fired you if he didn't."

Del snorted. "That just doesn't sound right." Her low laugh did crazy things to him and he closed his eyes, breathing deep against a wave of heat. Trying to focus, he continued in a casual tone, "So, what will I be doing, since I'm fired?"

She tensed and he stiffened with renewed anxiety. Her only answer to his declaration of love had been a kiss. He would take her any way he could get her, but the idea of a temporary affair made his heart thump with dread.

"There is a position I'd like you to take on," she said with measured care, sending a chill of disappointment down his spine.

"Which is?"

Leaning up on her elbow, she stared into his face with a faint frown, her teeth worrying at her bottom lip. "I was wondering," she hesitated then continued in a lower voice, "Would you be interested in, or have you thought about… What would you think if—?"

"Sin," he growled, more unnerved by her uncertainty than anything he'd experienced over the past few days.

She sat up, her expression firming with resolve, meeting his gaze with terrifying directness. "I'd like us to be Sun-bonded."

"W-what?" he wheezed, his head blanking as though he'd just been blindsided by the Tank.

She dropped her eyes, worrying at her lower lip again. "Well, you did say you loved me. But maybe you're not ready for a commitment."

"You want to be bonded?"

"Yes."

"With me."

"Yes," she said again, flicking him a quick, worried glance.

"But you're a Shay."

Her gaze snapped to his with a burgeoning frown. "So?"

"I'm just a nothing Core reject you're trying to fix."

Her eyes blazed with fire and she planted a hand in the center of his chest, leaning forward with a grim expression. "I don't want to hear you say that again, Del Givliani. You are not nothing and there isn't a single thing I want fixed. If you think for a second—"

He didn't let her finish the rant, yanking her against him and rolling so he was once again weighing her down. With a delighted grin, he linked his fingers with hers, trapping her hands above her head. "I get the point. Just to clarify, you want to be bonded with me because…?"

"Well, obviously because I love you," she answered with a testy huff.

He gave her a fierce, possessive kiss. "Sun's mercy, woman, I thought you were never gonna tell me."

Her eyes blazed with a different heat now, but she

still managed a frown. "I thought I had."

"I would've noticed, believe me. I think our first vow ought to be you say it at least once a day."

"Dictating our bond already, are we?" she asked with silky menace, slipping her legs around his waist while she spoke, pressing him closer.

He groaned as her movements sent a wave of pleasure through him, his hardness throbbing against her with rising need. "Damn right," he growled against her mouth. "You might be a Shay, but you're my Shay now."

Her answer needed no words. His last thought before she drove him mindless was, *who needs a bed?*

Epilogue

Griffin watched the displays flying across his viewers with bland attention, sipping his drink. Alcohol was not a vice he indulged in often, since it tended to loosen his control, but today had been one of those days. It had been a long time since his empire had endured such a blow, and he was savoring the challenge as much as mourning his creation's wounds.

It had been an interesting day, full of curious developments, not the least of which was the call from the Shay twins. What were they offering now, these wily offspring of his late adversary? He had no doubt it had been an offer, one almost too blatant and obvious. The warning had also been unusual, connected with nothing he could see.

Musing on the delightful prospect of a new challenge from the strongest of his rivals, he didn't raise his head when the door opened, though he was aware of his daughter's approach.

With quiet grace, she moved to stand at his elbow, her silence gratifying as she waited for his acknowledgement.

Taking another sip of his drink, he made her wait, pondering the displays in front of him for a few more minutes. When he could see no new developments, he sighed, "Yes?"

Without speaking, she leaned forward and placed a

box on the desk in front of him then straightened again.

A frown creased his brow and he made a conscious effort to smooth it. Her continued silence was unusual and he hated surprises, especially hers. "What's this?" Another glance at the box answered his question. "Ah," he breathed with rising triumph and amusement. "Did she return it after all, then?"

It was the gift box he'd sent to Sinsudee Shay, the message he'd coated in beauty and malice. With a chuckle, he unsealed it and lifted the lid. Then he burst into laughter, rocking back in his seat with delight. Shards of crystal lay on the blood-red velvet, flashing their shattered and flawed message back to him.

"Father, you misunderstand," his daughter's quiet voice cut through his amusement like a sun flare.

Chuckling now more for effect than in real humor, he stared at his irritating offspring and lifted a contemptuous eyebrow. "What's not to understand, dear girl? Out of fear and impotence, they destroyed the gift and blundered enough to send it back to me, so I would see their weakness."

She shook her fire-crowned head and stepped forward, gesturing at the broken pieces and glancing at him with her cool, exasperating eyes. "There isn't enough crystal, Father."

"What?" he snapped, this time unable to control the frown pulling at his brow. Leaning forward, he examined the contents more closely then stiffened.

With soft and fatal reason, his daughter pointed out what he'd already seen. "It's not the whole gift. From the shape of the pieces here, it looks as though they removed the vine and thorns. I assume this means the rose remains intact."

He straightened, a tide of fury climbing over his momentary shock. He now knew what their cryptic warning had meant. Felt slighted, did they? Ill-used and abused? The insolent brats had no idea how gently he'd been treating them. If they were involved in this disruption of his blue production, he would delight in showing them just how painful life could become.

"I told you it was a mistake."

At his daughter's chilly declaration, Griffin's anger surged even higher, demanding retribution. He was happy to oblige, since she'd made such a convenient target of herself.

Rising to his feet, he turned to meet her eyes. Her gray gaze held the knowledge of what was in store for her, but her lack of fear infuriated him. With deceptive gentleness, he reached out and clasped her hand, bringing it toward the box. Resting her unresisting hand flat on the shards of crystal, he bore down with malicious slowness, still gazing into her eyes.

"Do tell, daughter," he whispered. "What wisdom in your vapid brain brings you to this conclusion? What do I have to fear from the Shays?"

She said nothing. The tightening of her features and the tensing of her jaw spoke of her pain, but her silver stare remained fixed, the cool depths un-cowed.

Frustrated but determined not to show it, he gave her a tight, victorious smile and released her.

She took a step back and raised her hand, showing him the shards of vine and thorn embedded in her flesh, trickles of blood staining the crystal crimson and flowing down her wrist.

Then she answered him with calm finality, chilling and thrilling him to his core. "What do you have to fear? You've goaded them to war, Father. It's the rise of the Red Sun."

A word about the author…

Sci-Fi/Fantasy romance author Michelle O'Leary resides in Marquette, Michigan, which graces the shore of pristine Lake Superior. Born and raised in Upper Michigan, Michelle is a child of nature, enjoying all things outdoors.

Originally published through a small e-publisher, Michelle became an independent self-publishing author before being accepted with The Wild Rose Press, Inc. family where she has also published *Vessel of Power*.

Michelle is a mother first, a dedicated chocoholic, a contented Michigander, and a delirious word lover. She loves all feedback and is always happy to hear from readers!

http://molearyauthor.wix.com/michelleoleary